Hometown Girl

BOOK TWO
OF THE
BUTTERFLY BOX
SERIES

OTHER BOOKS AND AUDIO BOOKS
BY MICHELE ASHMAN BELL:

A Candle in the Window

An Enduring Love

An Unexpected Love

Finding Paradise

A Forever Love

Latter-day Spies: Spyhunt

Love Lights the Way

Pathway Home

Perfect Timing

Timeless Moments

Without a Flaw

Yesterday's Love

A Modest Proposal

Hometown Girl

BOOK TWO
OF THE
BUTTERFLY BOX
SERIES

a novel

Michele Ashman Bell

Covenant Communications, Inc.

Covenant

Cover image: *Talking With a Friend* © Heather McGrath, courtesy iStockphoto.

Cover design © 2010 by Covenant Communications, Inc.

Published by Covenant Communications, Inc.
American Fork, Utah

Printed in the United States of America
First Printing: July 2010

16 15 14 13 12 11 10 10 9 8 7 6 5 4 3 2 1

ISBN-13: 978-1-59811-922-0

Contains the winning story of the "Perfect Proposal" contest

To my mother-in-law, Eloise Bell, who has been an incredible example of faith in adversity, courage through affliction, dignity under pressure, and laughter through pain. I am so grateful to have you in my life.

Acknowledgments

My deepest gratitude goes out to my husband and my children for their constant unwavering love and support. I promise I will never make Hamburger Helper again. I also want to acknowledge my wonderful editor, Kirk Shaw, who has been patient, encouraging, and such an amazing strength to me. I really do know what the word *deadline* means, I promise. And last, but certainly not least, I want to thank my fans, who are so incredibly awesome. Thank you for all the great e-mails and messages asking when this book was going to be released. I have the best fans ever, and I want you to know how much I appreciate you.

Chapter One

Jocelyn Rogers slid a pair of black dress pumps into a plastic bag then tucked them into a corner of her suitcase. There was just enough room left inside for her black jersey knit dress and an extra pair of capri pants and sandals. She never knew what exactly she would need when she was at a Butterfly Girls reunion, but she wanted to have plenty of options, just in case.

Closing the lid on the suitcase, she made a mental note to ask her neighbor, Mrs. Grayson, to collect her mail while she was gone. She also needed to contact the landlord and tell him that he still needed to come and fix her bathroom sink. She was getting tired of brushing her teeth in the bathtub.

She'd offered to pick up her friend Lauryn from the St. George airport. Lauryn's plane landed in less than an hour, just enough time for Jocelyn to water her small box garden and fold her last load of laundry.

The back door groaned as she pushed it open. Midday heat greeted her like the blast from an oven, and she looked with concern at the collection of plants on her little patio, struggling to survive in the scorching southern Utah sunshine. The tomato and cucumber plants were thriving nicely, but the leaves on her summer squash were wilted and limp. She wondered if Mrs. Grayson would mind also watering her garden while she was gone for the next few days. Of course, if she needed to, she could slip over from the hotel each day and take care of things at home, but that defeated the purpose of staying at the hotel in the first place—the reunion was a chance to get away and spend time with her best friends. Heaven knew how much she needed this reprieve from her regular life.

She had barely gotten her end-of-year grades submitted, and she welcomed her summer vacation. She sighed. It wasn't that she didn't enjoy teaching art at the middle school near her home, it was just that nothing in her life was ever different. Ever. All the teachers at her school, all the people in her ward and neighborhood, her meals, her bills, the shows on TV, even the sunny St. George weather never seemed to change.

No, that's not quite true, she corrected herself. *There's always a different something or other going wrong with this stupid, overpriced apartment. And we got a new principal at the school this last year. So what if he's pompous and stubborn and insists on arguing with teachers in front of their students on a regular basis—at least he's different, right?*

She glanced at her watch, anxious for the weekend to start. The last time she'd seen Lauryn or Andrea was at Lauryn's wedding, which was months ago. Emma still lived in St. George, but she spent so much time in Vegas with Nicholas she hardly ever saw her. Chloe was in Cedar City, just forty-five minutes away, but they had trouble finding a time that worked for both of them. Thank goodness for e-mail.

Jocelyn finished off her last-minute phone calls and chores with a few minutes to spare. Then, catching a glance of her reflection in the bedroom mirror, she had second thoughts about the denim capris she was wearing. They were out of style, but she had thought they were more flattering than the saggy silhouette she now saw.

She considered her options, looking skeptically at a pair of white jeans hanging in her closet with the tags still on. She'd purchased them even though they were a little snug in the waist and thigh because the salesgirl assured her that after a few hours of wearing them, they would stretch out. Hoping the girl hadn't been lying, she took them off the hanger.

To her surprise, the pants slid on without her having to collapse onto her bed and have a tug-of-war to get them zipped up.

"Hmm," she said, looking at her reflection. She hadn't noticed that she'd lost a few pounds. It was probably all the salad she'd been eating lately; she'd been experimenting by adding things like beans and rice or oranges and apples to her salads and was really enjoying the new combinations. Fitting into her jeans was just a fringe benefit.

She slid her feet into a pair of white ballet flats and straightened the funky print top that Lauryn had sent her from New York for her birthday. She had just switched her little stud earrings for some dangly ones when the telephone rang.

"Hello," she answered.

"I'm trying to reach Jocelyn Rogers."

"This is Jocelyn." She sat down on the edge of her bed, preparing her answer for the sales pitch that she was certain would follow.

"My name is Bernard Duncan. I am the mayor of Milford Falls."

She sat up abruptly, as if she'd been stuck with a cattle prod. "Yes?" she said.

"Ms. Rogers, you're the owner of the dwelling at 174 Powell Street, if I'm not mistaken."

"Yes, it—"

"I understand that your grandmother left you this property at her passing two years ago," he said without acknowledging her attempt to confirm his information. "I don't mean to be rude, but did you realize that the yard is in disarray and the residence in dire need of repair?"

"Well, no—"

"I didn't think so," he said abruptly. "Now, Ms. Rogers, we here in Milford Falls pride ourselves in the beauty of our little town. We're considered the Mayberry of the Pacific Northwest, and we are proud of our picturesque community. All residents take great care to have manicured lawns, freshly painted shutters, sparkling windows—why, even the gutters are swept on a weekly basis. I'm afraid your grandmother's former home, may she rest in peace, has become something of a disgrace to our community."

"I'm sorry, I didn't—"

"Yes, I expected you didn't know the situation." The man wouldn't let her get a word in edgewise. "Still, the fact remains, something has to be done about your house. If something isn't done within thirty days, we will have to take legal action."

"Legal action!" She jumped to her feet.

"Our city ordinance states that all homes will remain in good repair and yards will be maintained within reason. Noncompliance results in some hefty fines and potentially the city's placing a lien on the property. I assure you, my call is not meant to be anything but informative and helpful. We, the city fathers and I, realize that since you don't live in the home, you are likely unaware of its condition."

She didn't even bother trying to respond.

"Ms. Rogers?"

"Oh. Yes. I wasn't aware—"

"I didn't think so."

He got her again!

"If you do not intend to live here in our fair city, I would urge you to sell the property."

"But—"

"I know of several people who would be interested, or I could give you the name of a fine real estate agent. Of course, you'll need a few days to think it over. You can call me back next week. Perhaps Monday?"

"Monday!"

"As much as your grandmother was a treasured part of our community, we just can't sit by and let her home fall to pieces and mar the beauty of our town. I'm sure you understand. I'll wait to hear from you on Monday." He then gave her his office phone number and cell number.

Dazed and angry, Jocelyn hung up the phone as hot tears stung her eyes.

How in the world could she sell her grandmother's home? Her grandmother had been the most important person in the world to her, and the home was all she had left to remember her by.

Naturally Jocelyn had considered selling before—after all, she could use the proceeds to get a nice place for herself here in St. George. But every time she started to make plans in that direction, she'd managed to find excuses to put off the whole thing. She couldn't sell it. She just wasn't ready.

Pulling in a few breaths to calm her racing heart and boiling blood, she glanced at the clock and realized she had to leave right away to pick up Lauryn.

Thank goodness her friends would all be with her this weekend. Maybe they could help her decide what to do.

* * *

"Joss!" a voice called from the crowd of passengers moving toward baggage claim.

Jocelyn looked up to see Lauryn waving at her.

Warm joy washed over her at the sight of her friend, and Jocelyn again expressed quiet thanks that she was going to be with her friends this weekend.

The two friends raced toward each other and collided in an embrace, nearly knocking themselves to the floor. They laughed as they found their balance then stepped out of the way of other passengers.

"You look amazing, Joss!" Lauryn said with admiration. "You look so trim. What have you been doing to get in such good shape?"

"Uh . . . sitting on my couch doing nothing," Jocelyn said, feeling her face turn red at the compliment.

"I don't believe it."

"I go walking occasionally, and I have a little vegetable garden that gets me outside a bit."

"You have a garden?"

"I do. I know it's hard to believe, but I really enjoy watching my little plants grow. I just wish I had a bigger space."

"I can't even keep silk plants alive," Lauryn said.

Jocelyn laughed. "It's not that hard, and it is kinda fun to eat stuff you grow yourself."

"It must be, because you look great!" Lauryn hooked an arm around her friend's waist. "I've put on twelve pounds since Jace and I got married. The man's a Food Network addict and loves to cook."

"You really hit the jackpot when you married him, didn't you," Jocelyn said.

"I totally did. He cooks, he cleans, and he gives the best foot massages. I'm so spoiled! I don't know how I got so lucky."

Jocelyn was so happy for her friend. Out of the five Butterfly Girls, Lauryn was the only one who was happily married. Chloe and her husband were still struggling to keep their marriage together, and Emma was already divorced. Andrea was looking for love but never stayed put long enough to develop a relationship. Jocelyn herself didn't spend a lot of time worrying about getting married. She knew for certain that she'd rather stay single than marry a man she didn't trust completely.

"How is Jace?" Jocelyn asked. "It's too bad he couldn't come. I would love to see him again."

"He wanted to come, but I told him this was girls only. Besides, he had a business trip to Chicago, so it wouldn't have worked this time anyway. You just need to come visit us in New York sometime, maybe before school starts in the fall. Or, if you don't have plans yet for Christmas, you could come then. Or both!"

"I would love that." Jocelyn wanted to get away. But having purchased a new—albeit used—car not too long ago, the only vacation she could afford was the kind she could get from a DVD rental and maybe some ethnic take-out food. She was trying to build up her savings again so she could afford whatever emergency came next—like fixing up her grandmother's house, for example.

"Hey," Lauryn said. "You okay?"

Jocelyn nodded her head to try and clear away the dark cloud that surrounded her.

"Oh yeah," she said with an attempt to be cheerful. "I'm fine."

"No, you're not," Lauryn said. "I know you, girl. Something's wrong. Talk to me."

They stood at the baggage claim waiting for Lauryn's suitcase.

"I got a phone call from the mayor of Milford Falls."

"Milford Falls . . . oh, in Washington? What did he want?"

"He called to tell me that my grandmother's house is falling apart, that the yard is out of control, and that I need to do something about it or the city will take legal action."

"Legal action! What sort of legal action?" Lauryn reached for a bag then checked the ID and let it pass.

"Huge fines, maybe a lien. I guess they have some city ordinance that requires upkeep on homes and yards. I had been paying a guy up there to keep the lawn mowed, at least, but he moved last fall, and I haven't gotten anyone else yet. Otherwise I haven't done anything to the place. I don't have much to put toward paying someone to really take care of her yard or do repairs. I feel like I can barely come up with enough money to pay for taxes and insurance as it is."

"What a hassle. What does the mayor expect you to do?" Lauryn reached out and grabbed a suitcase off the carousel.

"I'm supposed to call him back next week. He told me I should sell it, but I can't sell her house. I just can't."

Lauryn nodded with understanding, remaining in thought for a moment. Then she said, "You're just renting your apartment right now, aren't you?"

"Yeah."

"Have you considered going to live in your grandmother's house? You could use the money you save on rent to fix the place up."

"Move to Milford Falls?" Jocelyn exclaimed. "But I would have to quit my job and everything."

"You told me you've been having issues with your new school principal," Lauryn reminded her. "And, if I recall correctly, you got an interview for a position in Seattle a year ago. You were actually considering this move back then."

"It seems I need to remind you that I got cold feet and canceled that interview last summer. And then I got that summer art class position here . . . As for my job, I admit I haven't been thrilled with the administration lately, but I do love teaching."

They walked across the parking lot to Jocelyn's car.

"Well, maybe it's time to look for a job there again," Lauryn said. "Really, what's keeping you here? You've said yourself that you feel like you're in a rut and not going anywhere."

"Yeah, but that's my comfort zone, as pathetic as it is. And at least I'm close to Emma and Chloe." Except that Emma was always with her Greek boyfriend and Chloe never had time to do anything since Roger moved out and she had to work around the clock to make ends meet. Jocelyn didn't have the most fulfilling life, but things definitely could be worse. "I couldn't leave Chloe."

"Joss," Lauryn said, looking her straight in the eye, "you have a house in Milford Falls, a chance to go somewhere new, to start fresh, to meet new people. Chloe and Emma would want you to do what's best for you. You should think about it. Change is scary but it's also exciting. Maybe this is Heavenly Father's way of putting you where you need to be for some reason.

"When I left my job and went to work designing for Laszlo Molnar it was the scariest thing I'd ever done. But in the end it turned out to be the greatest experience of my life. The risk was great, but so were the rewards. I think it's time you took a leap of faith. That's the thing about comfort zones—you can't improve inside of them. All the fun, all the opportunity for growth, all the new, exciting challenges are outside of them. Don't sell your grandmother's house. Go live in it!"

Lauryn's challenge made Jocelyn's heartbeat race and palms grow sweaty. "That would be so hard for me. To just walk away from everything I know."

Lauryn's expression softened. "I just hate to see you pass by an opportunity like this. You can always come back if it doesn't work out."

"I don't know . . ." It was a huge decision and one she would need time to think about. On her mission she'd learned to embrace change and new beginnings. With each transfer to a new area she left behind people she'd grown to love, areas that were familiar to her, only to become attached to her new area and the people there. But that was a long time ago and there wasn't any risk involved.

Jocelyn thought about Lauryn's challenge and rationale. She supposed she could move to Milford Falls. If she hated it there she could sell her grandmother's house and move back to St. George.

Of course, she'd have to find a new job in Washington. What if she couldn't find a teaching job? What good would the house be if she didn't have work? And then if she sold the place and moved back she'd have a nice nest egg but still no job. And it wasn't as if art teachers were in high demand.

Her head started to ache. She didn't want to deal with this now.

"I'm sorry," Lauryn said, giving her a hug. "I didn't mean to stress you out when you've got so much on your mind."

Jocelyn patted her friend on the back and took a deep breath. "It's okay. I guess I need to think about all my options. I'm just not as brave as you."

"Maybe you should ask the others and see what they think."

With a nod, Jocelyn closed the trunk of her car. Her friends were like sisters to her, and she trusted their advice because she knew they loved her and wanted the best for her.

But go back to Milford Falls after all these years? The thought brought mixed emotions for her. She'd lived there with her grandmother for several months. They had been some of the most wonderful but most difficult months of her life. Could she really go back and live there? Even if she only went for a year it would give her time to fix up the house and decide if she wanted to sell it. Then she could come back and buy a house in St. George.

This was going to take a bit of thought and a lot of prayer. Was she supposed to move? Was Heavenly Father's hand in all of this? There was only one way to find out.

Chapter Two

"I can't believe you brought that stupid game with you," Chloe said, rubbing her eyes.

"I can't believe we stayed up until three in the morning playing it," Lauryn said. "If I had any energy I would hit you with one of those drumsticks, Emma."

"Hey, I just thought it might be fun. I wasn't forcing anyone to play so long," Emma said defensively.

"It was fun," Jocelyn said. "I didn't know you were a drummer, Andrea."

"Me either!" Andrea replied. "I totally missed my calling in life. Are we too old to start our own rock band? Can we play again tonight?"

"Yeah, I want to see if I can get the bass down on that Rolling Stones song," Jocelyn said.

"Oh, my gosh, I had that song in my mind all night!" Chloe exclaimed. "I dreamed Mick Jagger was my neighbor and we invited him to a neighborhood barbecue and he showed up in a suit and tie and had a missionary name tag on. He got up in front of everybody and sang "Book of Mormon Stories" Rolling-Stones style and the audience was doing the actions, but it was more like doing the Macarena. It was insane but very groovy."

The other girls laughed as Chloe got up and tried to reenact the song and movements like in her dream.

"You need to quit taking those sleeping pills," Emma told her. "I think they are messing with your brain."

"I already quit taking them. And all the other prescriptions," Chloe replied.

The other girls exchanged worried looks.

"What?" Chloe said, noticing their concern.

"How many pills were you taking?" Jocelyn asked. She knew Chloe had gotten some help from a therapist, but exactly what kind of help was he giving her? Pills that were potentially addictive made her very nervous. One of her brothers was in jail for drugs, and her mother had battled addictions, still did for all she knew.

"I was taking something to get me up and going in the morning, something to get me through the day, and something to make me fall asleep at night. I felt like a cardboard cutout of myself," Chloe confessed. "I feel so much better. It's hard to cope some days, but at least I can feel emotions now."

"I'm proud of you," Lauryn said. "That's not an easy thing to do."

"Well, I wasn't addicted physically; they were more like a crutch for me," Chloe explained.

"How are things with Roger?" Lauryn said.

Chloe nodded thoughtfully. "Supposedly he's getting help for his addiction. The process has been up and down for months. He wants to move back in, but I'm not ready for that yet. He can't still be doing that . . . porn stuff anymore. He has to have it out of his system. For good." She groaned and shook her head sadly. "Our poor kids. I'm trying so hard to protect them from all of this, but I know it's all going to come back to haunt me."

"You have darling, amazing kids," Emma quickly said. "Give yourself some credit."

"It's true," Jocelyn said. "You're an incredible mother."

Chloe got teary eyed and couldn't respond.

Emma, who was sitting next to her, gave her a hug. "They know how much you love them, and that's the most important thing."

"I just don't know if it will be enough." Chloe swallowed and wiped at her cheeks. "Sorry, I didn't mean to ruin the fun."

"You haven't ruined anything," Lauryn said. "Just tell us, what can we do to help?"

"Nothing, except pray. For him, for me, for our girls. He swears to me that he'll never mess up again, but it's so hard to believe him because he said that so many times before. I love him, and I want our family to be together again, but I'm scared."

"It would be hard for me to trust him again because I don't let go and forget about things like this," Emma said.

"Tell me about it," Andrea said. "You've still never forgiven me for accidentally throwing your retainer away at lunch. That was in eighth grade!"

Emma scrunched up her face then covered it with her hands. "I know. I'm sorry. I mean, I do forgive you. I'm over it, really I am. But big stuff like relationship stuff—" she shook her head "—that's tough."

"I've never prayed for guidance so hard in my life," Chloe said. "If he has truly and honestly repented and is changed, then it would be wrong of me not to give him another chance. But I can't help but worry that he'll slip up. I couldn't go through that again."

Jocelyn knew what it was like to have trust issues, and she admired Chloe for making such an effort. Jocelyn really liked Roger as a person, but he had changed as his addiction grew. He wasn't the thoughtful, sweet, funny guy who had worshipped the ground his wife walked on and treated her like a queen. He'd become withdrawn, secretive, and selfish. She hoped he really could turn his life around.

"Nicholas has helped me feel strong and brave enough to dare to love again," Emma said. "He's really helped me let go of some of my past issues. He's so amazing."

"How serious are you two?" Lauryn asked, flashing a look of concern at Jocelyn.

Emma shrugged her shoulders and smiled. "Very serious, I think."

Andrea's brow furrowed.

"What?" Emma asked, a defensive tone to her voice.

"Nothing," Andrea said quickly. "It's just that, um, well, it's just that . . ."

"We haven't met him," Lauryn quickly filled in the blank.

"That's right, Em," Jocelyn said. "It's so nice you've found someone wonderful. We'd just like to meet him."

"I wish you could. He's out of the country right now. He went to Greece for his parents' fortieth wedding anniversary. But Chloe's met him, haven't you, Chloe?"

Chloe's eyes opened wide and she nodded.

"So," Andrea prodded, "what did you think?"

Jocelyn noticed the slightest of pauses before Chloe responded.

"Well, you guys have seen pictures of him, haven't you?" Chloe said.

"Not really," Lauryn answered. "Just cell phone pictures."

"Hard to make out what he really looks like," Andrea said.

"But he's nice looking, from what I can tell. He looks tall," Jocelyn quickly added.

"Chloe?" Emma nudged, obviously wanting more.

"Oh yes," she stumbled. "He is."

"Is what, Chloe? Tall or nice looking?"

"Both!" Chloe blurted out. "He's very handsome, very Mediterranean. And I'd guess he's six one, or two."

"Six two," Emma said proudly. "He's so classy. He's helped me so much with the way I dress and do my hair and stuff. He even paid for me to have a makeover."

Jocelyn had noticed Emma's makeover—how could she not?—but had decided not to mention it. Emma had always had this fresh, natural beauty about her. Her dark hair was usually styled simply or pulled back in a ponytail. She was thin but had a strong build, very outdoorsy and athletic. Now her long hair was layered, dyed almost black, and perfectly coiffed. Her deep brown eyes were rimmed with dark liner, smoky shadow, and heavy mascara. Her lips, which had never seen anything brighter colored than watermelon-flavored lip gloss, were now blood red. Jocelyn just didn't know what to say about any of it.

"I just love my new look. And get this, some people at work didn't even recognize me after I got my hair and makeup changed," Emma said proudly.

"Does Nicholas play Rock Band with you?" Andrea asked.

"Are you kidding? He's much more sophisticated than that. No," Emma said, "he's the *Wall Street Journal,* manicured fingernails, cuff link kind of guy."

"Do you two have a lot in common?" Lauryn asked with concern.

"Yeah, of course we do," she said with a laugh. "He's really helped me define who I am."

"I didn't know you needed defining," Lauryn said.

"Are you kidding? I was a mess before, and still am in so many ways. C'mon, you guys know that. Surely you'd agree!"

"We love you just the way you are," Lauryn responded. "You don't have to change for us."

"Well, maybe I need to change for me!" Emma shot back. "It's not like my life has been going that great the way I was. I mean, look at my track record. I never finished college, I have a dead-end job, I've already been divorced once. Nick is the best thing that's ever happened to me. And he loves me enough to be honest with me. That's more than you guys have ever done!"

No one responded. Chloe's eyes welled up with tears. Andrea's mouth dropped open, but nothing came out.

Emma looked around at the faces staring back at her, then, without a good-bye, she bolted from the room.

Heavy silence hung over the remaining four women after the hotel door slammed shut.

Finally, Lauryn spoke. "I didn't mean to say something to upset her."

"You didn't say anything wrong," Jocelyn assured her, still trying to figure out what exactly had just happened.

"What was that all about?" Andrea said, shaking her head. "You didn't say anything we all weren't thinking."

They sat quietly, trying to process Emma's sudden outburst. Then Lauryn, Jocelyn, and Andrea all looked at Chloe. She knew something—it was obvious by her silence.

"Chloe?" Jocelyn said softly. "Do you know what that was all about?"

Chloe swallowed, blinked quickly, and wiped at her eyes. "How would I know?"

"You're the only one who's met Nicholas," Lauryn said. "What's going on? Why is she so defensive?"

"Yeah," Andrea added. "She wasn't even being attacked, but she acted like we'd just told her we hated the guy."

"And why hasn't she told us about him? I mean, I knew they were dating, but I didn't know it was serious. Why hasn't she said anything?"

Chloe licked her lips then released a long breath. "She hasn't really said anything to me either, but I did meet him, only because I ran into them at the outlet mall one day." She ran her hands through her hair. "I didn't even recognize her at first. Don't get me wrong, I like her new haircut—not sure about the color, too harsh for her skin tones. Not to mention that she didn't even have me do her hair. I've done her hair since high school! She said that Nicholas took her to a salon in Vegas to get her hair done."

"Did she apologize?" Andrea asked.

"No. I mean, it's okay. I guess I would have just appreciated her letting me know so I didn't have to feel so awkward."

"What about Nicholas?" Jocelyn asked. "How was he?"

Chloe thought for a moment. "He is handsome. But there's something intense about him. He made me feel very uncomfortable. I couldn't wait to get away from him."

"Did he say something weird?" Lauryn probed.

"No, he was very charming. Said he was so happy to finally meet one of the Butterfly Girls that he'd heard so much about. I don't know how to describe it. His eyes are black, and they go right through you. Intense, you know. But also kind of creepy."

Andrea raised her eyebrows. "Creepy?"

Chloe covered her face with her hands. "Yes, I know. It's awful to say something like that."

"You can't help how he made you feel, though," Jocelyn assured her.

"I know! I didn't want to feel that way. I wanted to like him for Emma's sake. And I'm sure it's probably because I'm a little weird about men right now because of all this junk going on with Roger. So I shouldn't even be saying anything. I feel terrible."

"Listen," Lauryn said, "you don't need to feel terrible. Like Joss said, you can't help it if that's how he made you feel."

Chloe suddenly went on. "And to see her all different, you know, with this chic new hairdo and all this makeup, in clothes that were nothing like she'd wear. I mean, the words *Emma* and *bling* don't even belong in the same sentence. But she had on this hideous gold and black sequined halter top and black stretchy bell-bottomed pants with slits up the sides. She looked like she was in a costume."

Jocelyn opened her mouth to speak, but Chloe went on.

"And she pretended to be all okay with it and proud of how she looked, like she thought she looked as amazing as he thought she did, but I saw it in her eyes. Her head may be full of Nicholas, but I could see her heart through her eyes. She isn't convinced this is really her. I know it."

Jocelyn let out a whoosh of air and sat back with a slump. "I don't even know what to say. I mean, the Emma I know would never be caught dead in a halter or clothes like that. She was the first person to make fun of people who dressed like that!"

"I know. I mean, it's not like she's active in the Church anymore," Lauryn said sadly, "but she never presented herself like that, ever."

"What do we do?" Andrea said. "We can't talk to her because she doesn't want to hear anything negative."

"You can't go by what I'm saying either," Chloe said. "You should meet him before you form an opinion about him."

"I just hate to see her get involved with someone who's not good for her," Lauryn said. "She needs a guy who's going to treat her good, take her to church, love her for the wonderful person she is."

"I feel so bad that she's mad at us," Jocelyn said. "We have to fix that first. She has to know that we love her and are unconditionally there for her. Then maybe she'll trust us and open up."

"You're right," Andrea said. "She needs to know we're happy that she's happy."

"I'm not that good of an actress," Chloe said.

"So when it comes up, just don't say anything," Jocelyn advised. "That way you don't have to lie."

Chloe nodded. "I can do that."

"Okay, let's try and have fun and convince her that we really are on her side. I think we'll get further with her that way," Lauryn said.

"I agree," Andrea added.

"Me too," Jocelyn said.

"Good. Now, let's talk about something else," Lauryn said.

"Good idea," Chloe said. "Not about me, though. My life stinks. I've got circles under my eyes, my husband and I are separated; oh, and get this, I haven't even told you, my mother just got diagnosed with Alzheimer's!"

"What!" Jocelyn exclaimed. "No, Chloe. Really?"

Chloe wiped at her eyes again. "I'm going to need some chocolate real soon or I'm never going to stop doing this."

"I'm so sorry," Lauryn said.

"Me too," Andrea added. "When did you find out?"

"Just this week. We kind of suspected it for a few months, but she finally got diagnosed a few days ago. Suddenly, I realize that my mom is getting older. She is seventy-three. She's just so hip and fun, she never seemed old to me."

"How is she handling it?" Jocelyn asked.

"It's hard. She had a couple of really bad days, but now she's got her fighting spirit back. She's been all over the Internet looking at treatments and medications. She's determined to do everything she can to beat it or, at least, prolong the inevitable for as long as she can."

"I love your mom," Andrea said. "She was the best sleepover mom ever."

Lauryn laughed. "She was! I swear she was crazier than we were. I mean, she was the one who taught us how to TP a house."

They all laughed together. Then stopped when the hotel door opened.

Emma walked in and shut the door behind her.

Andrea got up and walked over to her and put her arms around her. "I'm so glad you came back. We're sorry."

Emma stood rigidly for a moment then slowly raised her arms and hugged Andrea. The other girls took the cue and joined in a group hug.

For now the crisis was diverted, but it was far from over.

Chapter Three

"I'm getting fat!" Chloe whined as she shoveled a spoonful of chocolate cookie dough ice cream into her mouth. "I shouldn't be eating this."

"You're not fat," Jocelyn said. "You're beautiful."

"You're such a liar. And I appreciate it. But let's face facts: I've been eating my emotions and they are the size of a giant hippo. It's all stupid Roger's fault. The worst part is, the way I look he's not ever going to want to come back to me even if I do decide we should get back together."

Jocelyn put her arm around Chloe and hugged her. "Don't be so hard on yourself. You've been through a lot."

"Yeah, Chloe, I'd say you're doing pretty good for all you've been through," Lauryn commended. "Besides, you got so thin after it all happened, you probably weigh the same as when it all started."

"That's true; I did lose a lot of weight right after I found out about all of that Internet garbage." She ate another huge spoonful. "It's so dumb. I feel good while I'm eating, but afterward I want to kick myself for doing it. Except I'm so fat my foot can't reach my rear end."

The girls laughed.

"Here," Emma said, "turn around—I'll kick it for you."

Chloe turned around but Emma gave her a hug instead, saying, "You are adorable no matter what you weigh. Maybe it's Roger's rear end we should be kicking!"

They laughed some more.

"So, now what? It's midnight—everything's closing. We shopped and ate all day, my feet are killing me, and my back," Lauryn said. "I think I'm ready to go back to the room and watch *Sabrina*."

"Sounds good to me," Andrea said. "I didn't want to admit it, but my feet are killing me, too."

"You? Miss Fitness?" Emma exaggerated her shock and surprise.

"Hey! After a full week of teaching classes and doing workshops, I'm wasted by the weekend. I am taking the whole month of July off, just to sit and do nothing," Andrea told them.

"That will last about a week," Emma predicted.

"I give it three days," Lauryn said.

"I know how to relax and do nothing," Andrea countered. "That was part of my therapy earlier this year—learning not to push myself so hard. I might go and visit my parents in Arizona for a week, too. Even though I hate the heat in the summer."

Jocelyn had been so happy to see that Andrea had put on a little weight and gotten help for her anorexia. She looked as fit as ever but so much more healthy.

"Well, you deserve a break, Andrea. You work so hard, you should take a month off," Chloe said.

"I've got the summer off," Jocelyn said. "We should hook up."

"That's right!" Andrea exclaimed. "The perk of being a school teacher."

"You two should come to New York on vacation," Lauryn suggested. "Jace would love to see you too."

"Hey," Chloe said, "what about me?"

"You come too! You need a vacation," Lauryn replied. "Emma?"

"Sounds fun. I'll have to see. I can't get away from work very easily. And I'd have to see what Nick says. He misses me tons when I'm gone too long."

Lauryn didn't miss a beat. "Okay." She gave Emma's hand a squeeze. "See what you can do. In fact, bring him along. That way we can finally get to know him."

Emma smiled. "That would be fun. I'll talk to him."

"Wait!" Lauryn exclaimed. "This might not work."

"Oh, are you too busy with your new line of gowns?" Jocelyn asked.

"No, Cooper has things under control."

"Cooper!" Andrea said. "How is Cooper? Did he end up dating that lady from your ward?"

Lauryn's expression turned sympathetic. "Yeah, sorry. They're pretty serious. He's taking the missionary lessons, too."

"Darn! I mean, great about the missionaries, but . . . I thought he was my soul mate," Andrea said with a theatrical sigh.

"Well, you never know. We'll have to see what happens," Lauryn said.

"So Lauryn, if it's not the gowns, what have you got going on that will prevent our grand adventure?" Jocelyn asked.

"It's not me, it's you!" Lauryn replied.

"Me?"

"What have you got going on, Joss?" Emma asked.

Jocelyn shrugged. "I have no idea what she's talking ab—"

"She might be moving to Milford Falls, Washington," Lauryn answered for her.

"What?" Andrea exclaimed. "Are you serious? When?"

"Why didn't you say something?" Chloe grabbed her hands. "I will miss you!"

"Oh, my gosh, you guys," Jocelyn flashed a displeased look at Lauryn. "I'm not moving."

"She might be. In fact, she wanted to talk about it with all of you," Lauryn said, staring back at her.

At the moment Jocelyn wished she could either shove a sock in Lauryn's mouth or go back home. She had meant to bring up her dilemma to everyone, but not like this.

"When we get to the hotel, she can tell you all about it," Lauryn said. Then she looked at Jocelyn with puppy-dog eyes. "Don't be mad, Joss. Between all of us we'll help you figure it out."

· * * *

They no more got through the door then everyone exploded with questions.

Jocelyn finally shut them up by explaining about the phone call from Mayor Duncan regarding her grandmother's house—the house she had owned for two years now.

"Wow, Joss," Chloe said. "I can see why it would make sense for you to go." She poked out her bottom lip. "But I will miss you so much if you do go."

"I'm not leaving you, Chloe," Jocelyn assured her.

"It doesn't make sense, though," Lauryn jumped in. "Do you know how lucky you are to own your own home? Besides, I think you need to go somewhere fresh and new. Meet new people."

"I.e., meet a husband?" Jocelyn clarified.

"Maybe," Lauryn answered.

"Hah! Then you've never seen Milford Falls. Besides, I don't think that's in the cards for me," Jocelyn told her for the benefit of all to hear. "I don't mind being alone."

"What's your biggest fear about moving?" Emma asked her.

"Um, let's see, not finding a job. Not liking it there. Having too much work to do on the house. I don't have much savings to put into fixing it up."

"But you'll still have your summer salary, and no rent to pay. Plus, you'll probably get a deposit back from your apartment, right? You know, you can do a lot yourself," Andrea said. "I love to go to Home Depot and figure out how to do stuff myself. Last summer I laid new tile in my bathroom. I did a fabulous job, too, if I say so myself." She stopped talking, but by the look on her face it was obvious her brain hadn't stopped processing her stream of thoughts. "Wait a minute! Oh, my gosh!"

"What!" Jocelyn said with alarm.

"I could go with you and help you. I have a whole month."

"No! You don't need to do that. I'm probably not even going."

"Joss, I think you need to think about this a little more," Emma said. "I agree with Lauryn."

"Oh, you do, do you?" Jocelyn said, understanding now how Emma felt earlier and thinking that it might be a good idea to run out of the room.

"We all know how frustrated you are with your job and with your apartment and basically with where your life is going," Emma said.

"I am?" Jocelyn said, gauging her getaway time.

"You've shared your frustrations with all of us," Emma reminded her.

"I have?" She could probably get out of the room in three seconds—four—if she stopped to grab her purse so she could go back home.

They all nodded. Even Chloe had joined the firing squad.

"Out of all of us, you know I depend on you a lot, Joss. But now that I think about it, without being completely selfish, I have to say, I think they are right. Even if you left for a year—or even just the summer—and ended up coming back. You need to get out of here and do something different, try something new."

"Why? My job is fine. I can find a new apartment—should've done it sooner, really. I can even take on a summer job to make some extra money so I can hire out the repairs done on my house. Then I could sell it or rent it out, maybe. Really, I'll be fine." Jocelyn tried to sound confident but suspected she wasn't convincing anyone, even herself.

The dubious expressions of her friends confirmed her suspicions.

"Just do it, Joss!" Andrea said. "I'll come with you. We can fix things up. Paint is relatively cheap, and we can do all the work ourselves."

"You'd do that for me?" Jocelyn said.

"Of course I would. It would be so much fun!" Andrea exclaimed.

"You guys really think I should do this? Honestly?"

"Absolutely!" Lauryn said without hesitation.

"No question in my mind," Emma said.

Chloe pulled a face of sadness, then said, "I can't believe I'm saying this, but yes, I really do. Just come back, at least to visit!"

Jocelyn bit her lip as the advice and enthusiasm of her friends sunk in. Was she supposed to move to Washington? Was this what the Lord wanted? And, if so, how had she not seen this coming?

"Guess I've got some praying to do," she said.

Her friends erupted in cheers and excitement. Their energy must have been contagious because to her surprise Jocelyn found herself feeling the beginnings of excitement in her stomach. The thought of a new adventure was exciting.

All the same, she felt like crawling into her bed and pulling the covers over her head, because on top of that tingle of excitement was a huge mound of fear.

Lauryn broke her thoughts by giving her a big hug. "Come on. You need to get your mind off of it for a bit. Let's watch the movie. We can talk later."

Chapter Four

Sunday morning Jocelyn, Chloe, and Lauryn went to church in Lauryn's home ward. It was fun for her to see old friends and catch up on town happenings. Emma had no interest in going, and Andrea had a headache bordering on a migraine so she'd taken a painkiller and gone back to bed.

When they got back to the hotel a little after twelve they weren't received with open arms.

"Wake up, you two!" Lauryn announced as they threw open the door to the dark, cluttered room. "We're starving!"

"Go away," Andrea said from under the covers.

"You need food. That will make your head feel better," Chloe said, sitting down on the bed next to Andrea.

"You too," Lauryn said, giving Emma a swat on the behind. "Get up!"

"Do you know how annoying perky people are in the morning?" Emma said, pulling the pillow over her head.

"Hey!" Lauryn exclaimed. "First of all, it's not morning. And second of all, it's not our fault you stayed up all night talking to Nicholas."

"Sorry. He missed me," Emma said. "He doesn't like it when I'm gone for long periods of time."

"You've been gone forty-eight hours. You'll be home in six," Lauryn complained.

"I can't help it if he's crazy about me," Emma said.

"Or just crazy . . ." Chloe gasped then clapped her hand over her mouth. "Did I just say that out loud?" she said in a muffled tone.

They all nodded.

"Thanks, Chloe," Emma said, throwing back the covers and storming off into the bathroom.

The tension brought Andrea from hiding. "Did you just say what I thought you said?"

Chloe now had her hands covering her face. "I can't believe I said that. What is my problem? I have no filter anymore. Is there any chance she might have taken that as a joke?"

"Probably not, but we'll help you smooth it over," Lauryn assured her.

"I shouldn't have said that—I know how sensitive she is about him." Chloe was beside herself with worry. She spoke quietly enough for only them to hear.

"We'll talk to her with you," Jocelyn said. "It will be okay." She turned to Andrea. "How's your head feeling?"

"A little better," she answered. "I don't do well if I miss a lot of sleep."

"Do you get migraines often?" Jocelyn asked.

"No, thank goodness, but when I do"—the bathroom door opened—"they really wipe me out."

Emma looked at her friends sitting on the two beds then went straight to her pile of clothes and suitcase and started packing.

"What are you doing?" Lauryn asked.

"I think I'm going to check out early. I have a lot of stuff I need to do at home."

"Emma, don't leave!" Chloe exclaimed. "I'm so sorry. I don't know why I said that."

"Said what?" Emma replied. She set aside a pair of capris and a T-shirt then shoved the rest of her things in her suitcase. "Really, I had a hard time getting away this weekend. I just need to get home."

"I don't believe you," Chloe said.

Emma shrugged. "You don't have to believe me. Doesn't make my work go away, though."

"Emma, please. I know you're upset because I made that remark about Nicholas. I didn't mean anything by it. It just popped out of my mouth," Chloe pleaded.

"Now that you mention it, I guess that remark did sting a little." She stopped shoving her belongings into her bag and looked at each of them. "What really hurts, Chloe, is that you don't even know him, yet you are judging him. I don't mean to rub salt in your wound, but look at Roger. You knew him for over a year and look at what happened with him. There's never a guarantee with a relationship. You have to follow your gut and listen to your heart. That's all you can do. Nick is the most thoughtful, loving, tender person I've ever known, and if you gave him half a chance, you'd find that out for yourself."

She grabbed her change of clothes and started for the bathroom.

"You're right," Chloe said. "You're absolutely right. I was only around him for a few minutes. I want to get to know him. I'd love to have a chance."

"So would I," Andrea added.

Jocelyn and Lauryn echoed their sentiments.

Emma stood stiff and unyielding.

"I really am sorry. I have such a sour taste in my mouth right now for men, my judgment is completely impaired. I just want you to be happy. I can't bear to see you get hurt again." Chloe ended in a whisper as her voice broke with her emotions. "I just want us all to be happy."

Emma stared at Chloe, who had one hand on her forehead and wiped at her cheeks with her other hand. Her resolve crumbled at the sight of her friend in tears.

"Oh, Chloe," she said, taking a step toward her. "Don't cry. I'm not mad."

"Yes, you are," Chloe cried. "You have your mad face on."

"My mad face?" Emma couldn't help but smile. She looked at Jocelyn, who just shrugged like she didn't know what Chloe was talking about.

"Yes, your mad face. You used to have the same expression every time Mr. Wilkey gave us a pop quiz in algebra. Or if one of us ever ate your last Milk Dud at the movies."

"How would you know? It was dark," Emma said.

"It was there. I could still see it," Chloe said, laughing shakily through her tears.

Emma put her arms around Chloe to calm her down.

"I just want us all to live happily ever after," Chloe cried. "Is that too much to ask?"

Emma patted her back. "No, sweetie, it's not."

"Please, forgive me. You've got to stay. We haven't done the Butterfly Box yet."

"All right, I won't leave." Emma shook her head and rolled her eyes.

Chloe stepped back. "And I would love to meet Nicholas and spend some time with him. I'd love to hear about Greece and his family."

"You really would?" Emma asked.

Chloe nodded. Jocelyn, Lauryn, and Andrea expressed a desire to meet him.

"He doesn't get back until late tonight," Emma said. "Maybe we can find a way to come and visit each of you. He flies his own plane."

"He does?" Andrea exclaimed. "Dang, girl. He's sounding pretty incredible to me. Does he have any brothers?"

"Actually, he does have a brother in Greece," Emma said. "He's close to forty, but he's very handsome and wealthy. And married. Sorry."

"A cousin? Nephew? Gardener?" Andrea said with desperation.

The other girls laughed, and the tension in the room lifted.

"I'll ask and see," Emma said. "I wouldn't be surprised. He comes from quite a large family. They are very close."

Andrea smiled and raised her eyebrows. "Oh, well that's nice."

For no particular reason, the conversation came to a halt. They all looked at each other then burst out laughing.

"Other than sleeping, I think that's the first time since we got together that one of us hasn't been talking," Jocelyn said.

"I know," Lauryn said. "Weird, huh?"

"I think it's time to do the Butterfly Box," Andrea suggested. "It is getting late, and we do need to check out soon."

They all agreed and began clearing off a space on the bed to sit.

"Ugh," Emma groaned as she tried to cross her legs. "This used to be so easy for me."

Andrea, on the other hand, looked like a yoga goddess in the lotus position.

Emma scowled at her.

"What? I work out, so sue me."

"I've never been able to do that," Chloe said, giving it one attempt and giving up. "Besides, my legs are so chubby they can barely bend."

"Stop with the fat comments already," Lauryn said. "You look great, Chlo."

"In high school I used to be able to shop in the children's section. I'm on my way to petite plus sizes!" she moaned.

"You really need to stop getting so down on yourself. Take it from someone who's been at both ends of the spectrum—who you are on the inside matters way more than the exterior. And your health is what counts anyway, not your weight. Are you following that workout plan I made for you?" Andrea asked.

Chloe looked down, like a child who'd forgotten to do her homework. "No."

"Even if you only work out three days a week you'll start seeing a difference," Andrea told her. "And not only that, it will give you an emotional boost, too. I know women who have been able to go off depression meds just by exercising regularly."

"I know. It's just so boring," Chloe said. "But I'll try. I promise."

"I've been trying to go walking a few times a week," Jocelyn said. "It's boring, but it does make me feel better."

"You look like you've been working out," Lauryn said.

"Yeah," Emma echoed, "you've lost weight, haven't you?"

"I had, until this weekend," Jocelyn answered. "I've probably gained it all back."

"I need to do something good for myself instead of eating chocolate icing from a can," Chloe said.

"So," Lauryn said, "should we get started? Since I had the box last year, I'll go first."

Placing the box in the middle of the circle, Lauryn lifted the lid then paused and set it back down.

"I know Ava's case went cold again last summer, and maybe we'll never find the answers we want about her death. But I am so grateful that the rest of us have stayed so close all these years.

"This last year has been unbelievably amazing. I know that the box doesn't have any magical power, but I have to say, I've had some incredible experiences while it's been in my possession. More than ever before. So, thank you for all the faith and prayers you offered on my behalf," she said. Then she reached in and pulled out the first item . . . the tiara.

"It's still so beautiful!" Chloe exclaimed. There was never a year during the ceremony that she didn't have to put on the crown, if only for a moment.

Lauryn handed it to her.

Chloe looked at the sparkling headpiece in her hand.

"Go ahead," Lauryn urged.

"I don't feel much like a princess," Chloe said. "Roger certainly isn't my prince anymore." She handed it back to Lauryn. "I think I'll pass this year." She blinked quickly as tears filled her eyes.

"Oh, Chloe," Jocelyn said, giving her another hug. As long as she'd known Chloe, she'd never seen her cry more than she had the past three days. "It's going to be okay. We'll help you through this."

Chloe sniffed. "I know. Thanks. It helps knowing I'm not alone." She wiped her eyes and said, "Sorry. I think I'm PMS-ing. Go on," she told Lauryn.

Lauryn gave her a sympathetic smile then took the movie they'd already watched and held it out. "Are we sick of this yet?"

They others answered with a resounding, "No!"

"Okay, just checking," she added, looking at the tiara in front of her. "Guess that's all."

"Joss, you still remind me of Audrey Hepburn," Chloe said. "In fact, you're just like Sabrina. You actually seem to get prettier as you get older."

Jocelyn laughed. "I do?" Her friends had always complimented her on her looks, but she had never considered herself the pretty one in the group. She knew she wasn't bad looking but getting *prettier?* At thirty-one?

"It's true," Chloe said.

Jocelyn shook her head. "I have started wearing a little makeup again, but I don't know what you're making such a big deal over."

"Girl, you're gorgeous no matter what, but I'll never convince you of it, I guess." She took a big, cleansing breath. "Can I go next? Before I start crying again?"

"Sure." Lauryn turned the box toward her.

Chloe pulled out a silk bag, opened the top, and pulled out the rhinestone clippie. She looked at it for a moment, her face registering the emotion of all the memories the clippie held. Jocelyn watched closely, prepared to hug her again if needed.

With eyes shut and a deep breath, Chloe battled the onslaught of emotion that threatened. Then she opened her eyes. "Someday I want my daughters to wear this on their wedding day."

Jocelyn relaxed, thankful that Chloe had found her resolve and was staying strong. She knew that inside Chloe's petite frame was a giant of a spirit, strong and determined. Life wouldn't get her down; she wouldn't let it.

"And, of course, there's always that piece of Ava we get to keep with us." She pulled the baggie of Ava's hair from the box and passed it around.

"Isn't it funny how something like this can bring back memories and suddenly make Ava seem so close?" Emma said, passing the baggie to Andrea.

"Even after all these years," Andrea said, passing it to Lauryn.

"It's funny how in the strangest moments I'll find myself thinking of her," Lauryn said. "Something will trigger a memory, like certain foods—"

"Like pizza," Emma said.

"Or movies or music," Lauryn continued.

"Like the theme song to *Friends,*" Andrea said. "Or that Celine Dion song . . ."

"'Because You Loved Me,'" Jocelyn called out. "Such a good song! Remember when we went to that Celine Dion concert?"

"And Ava was determined to get up on stage?" Chloe said.

"And almost got kicked out!" Emma reminded them.

"Her sense of adventure and fearlessness were what made her so fun to be around, but she was nuts sometimes," Lauryn said. "She really was. It was like it didn't occur to her that she wasn't supposed to do something or say something. Even if it meant getting in trouble. Or offending someone."

"A lot of kids at school really hated her," Emma said.

"She was kind of mean to some kids," Chloe said.

"That's an understatement. I wanted to die some days, the way she would treat people. I'm surprised she didn't get her tires slashed or her house egged more often," Andrea said.

"That's because she was friends with the right people. No one dared mess with her because they knew half the football team would pile on top of them," Emma said.

"Maybe, but she didn't ever care what people thought about her. I've never known a person since with that much self-confidence," Jocelyn said.

"My friend Cooper comes close. He manages to be friends with just about everyone he meets," Lauryn said.

"Ah, Cooper!" Andrea said, patting her hand on her heart. "Please . . . if he breaks up with his girlfriend . . ."

"I promise I'll let you know," Lauryn said, grinning. "I'm sure he'd love to see you anyway, all of you, in fact. You really should come to New York this summer. And if that doesn't work, how about September? We have our first show then. You should all come. This time I won't make you work behind the curtain like last year. You can have VIP seating."

Everyone chimed in about how fun that sounded, and for a while they swapped stories from their visit the previous summer.

As the talking died down, Chloe said thoughtfully, "Remember how Ava always wanted to be an actress and be on Broadway?"

"She probably would have done it too, as aggressive as she was," Emma said. "When she wanted something you just had to stay out of her way!"

"Well, you had to hand it to her, she knew what she wanted and she went after it. It was that same fierceness that made her so loyal. No matter what, she was a good friend," Chloe said. "I still miss her. Don't you guys?"

Everyone answered except Jocelyn. She never really knew how to respond to that question. Her relationship with Ava hadn't been so positive. She loved Ava, but it was because of Ava she'd had the greatest challenge of her life.

"Jocelyn, you're next," Lauryn said.

Jocelyn swallowed then nodded. She kept her comments to herself. She had all these years. None of them really knew what was in her heart regarding Ava.

"Well"—she pulled the necklace made of boondoggle string and colored beads out of the box—"we all remember girls camp and all the fun we had each summer."

"Maybe next year we should go camping for our Butterfly Girls reunion," Lauryn suggested.

"Camping?" Andrea said. "Are you serious? I wouldn't know the first thing about putting up a tent."

"We could stay in cabins," Chloe said. "I know the perfect place."

Lauryn's eyes lit up. "What do you think?"

Emma shrugged. "Sure, okay."

"Cabins would be good," Andrea said. "Just make sure they have showers. Hot showers."

"That would be fun," Jocelyn said. She liked the idea of mixing it up a little. "Just no snipe hunts or canoe rides."

"Agreed," Lauryn said.

The others watched as Jocelyn pulled the white box out and placed it on her lap.

Jocelyn knew they wanted her to divulge the contents. Every year they waited with anticipation. Every year she wondered if this would be the year she finally did it, when she would finally be ready. But she wasn't. She didn't know when she would be, but it definitely wasn't today.

"I'm done," Jocelyn said, putting the box down, even though she could see their disappointment.

"Okay, then," Andrea said, breaking the moment of awkward silence. "So, of course there's this." She pulled out the bottle of sanitizer. "Funny," she said, her eyebrows raised, "I notice how many of you now carry one of these in your purse."

Lauryn nodded. "It's true. I admit I won't go out without it. But when you're riding subways and in taxis you can just feel the germs on your skin."

"At school with all the kids and colds and flu and stuff," Jocelyn said, "I probably put it on my hands ten times a day."

"I'm washing my hands all day long, so I don't need it as much, but I use it on my girls all the time," Chloe said.

Andrea smiled triumphantly. "Glad you can finally see where I'm coming from and don't just think I'm such a germaphobe. I remember looking through those microscopes in Mr. Heplar's class and seeing those creepy germs growing. I never got over that."

"That *was* gross," Emma agreed. "Ew! And my lab partner was that creepy Herbie Finke."

"Oh, yuck. He was creepy. I don't know what it was about him, but he had this way of staring . . ." Andrea shuddered.

"In third grade he used to turn his eyelids inside out and chase us around the playground," Jocelyn recalled.

"I remember that!" Lauryn said. "That gave me nightmares."

"He told me he had a crush on me," Jocelyn said. "And when I said I didn't like him, he put a dead bird on my desk that he'd found outside."

"What? Really?" Chloe said. "Why would he do that?"

"Ooh, that reminds me of the time we dissected frogs in eighth grade," Emma said. "I remember watching Herbie's face when he was cutting the frog open. He seemed to get such a charge out of it. It was so freaky." She shrugged up her shoulders and shivered.

"Wonder what he's doing now?" Chloe asked.

"Guess if any of us ever went to the class reunions we'd know," Jocelyn said.

"I guess," Chloe said. "You know, I'm not sure which would cause more gossip: Roger and I getting a divorce or Roger and I patching things up."

"Maybe it's time we made an appearance at our next reunion," Emma said. "We'll all be with you, Chlo—you don't need to feel uncomfortable."

"I don't know. We'll see," Chloe said.

"Well, we can decide about the reunion later," Andrea said. "Let's finish the ceremony. It's time for the official changing of the Tootsie Rolls." She took the old bag out of the box and held up a new bag. "Anybody want one?"

"Me!" Chloe said. "I promise, I'll start my diet tomorrow. I'm starving, though."

They all were. No one had eaten breakfast yet.

They passed around the open candy bag, then finally it was Emma's turn.

She pulled the tightly folded T-shirt from the box.

"The bungee-jumping shirt," Lauryn said. "Oh, wow. I can't believe I ever did that. I can't even stand at the top of the Empire State Building and look down. I get so dizzy."

"I still can't eat nachos," Chloe said, pulling a face of disgust.

They all laughed.

Emma pulled out the envelope that contained the picture of all of them, with Ava, standing in front of the D on graduation night.

Every year without fail, they all grew silent as tears surfaced and the memory of pain and loss engulfed them.

"As I say every year," Emma continued, "Ava always lived life to the fullest and dared to dream bigger than anyone I know. This is a reminder for us to dream big and go after those dreams. She would want that."

"And that means taking chances," Lauryn said, looking at Jocelyn.

Jocelyn squeezed her eyes shut tightly and groaned. "I know," she said. "But it's so hard!"

"Good grief, girl, you went on a mission. That took some guts," Andrea said. "What happened to that brave girl we used to know?"

"I think she died," Jocelyn teased sarcastically. "Her bungee cord broke last time she jumped."

"I think Jocelyn needs the Butterfly Box," Andrea suggested.

"I agree," Emma added.

"Me too," Lauryn echoed.

"No," Jocelyn said. "Chloe needs it worse than I do."

"It's going to take more than a Butterfly Box to fix my problems. I need something more like an industrial sized Butterfly Cargo Bin filled with miracles or something," Chloe said.

The girls laughed.

"I feel guilty taking it when some of you could use it more than I could," Jocelyn said.

"Take it!" Emma told her. "We want you to have it."

"Okay, okay," Jocelyn said, putting her two items inside. "Thank you."

The other girls added their things, and the box was closed and locked for another year.

Chapter Five

Jocelyn's back ached from the long drive from Boise, where she'd stayed the night to help break up her trip to Milford Falls. It wasn't much farther, though, and soon she would be at her grandmother's house. Her new home.

It had been thirteen and a half years since Jocelyn had been to Milford Falls. Her grandmother's funeral had been held in St. George so family and old friends could attend. It was her grandmother's wish to be buried there, next to her husband, Jocelyn's grandfather, who'd died before Jocelyn was born. After her grandmother's passing, her house had been thoroughly cleaned by the Relief Society sisters, then locked up and left vacant for over two years now.

Before Jocelyn left St. George, she'd been so busy packing and taking care of moving details that it had been easy enough to block out the magnitude of what she was doing. Now, with long hours of driving across the states of Utah, Idaho, and Oregon, she'd had plenty of time to realize exactly what she was walking away from and how little she knew about what she was walking into.

Her stomach turned over. Again.

She was crazy! Crazy to listen to her friends who were so convinced this was the right thing for her to do. Crazy to give up a perfectly good job. Crazy to leave her hometown and her life, even though it was boring and predictable. What was wrong with predictable and boring anyway?

She sighed and turned on the headlights. The sun had set, and she was afraid of hitting a cow or woodland creature that might dart out from the thick, pine tree–lined highway.

Milford Falls was south of Seattle, nestled in the middle of rolling green hills, near Lake Edmund. It had a population of around nine thousand people and was growing due to the fact that many families were moving to Milford Falls, willing to commute the distance to Seattle, in order to raise their children in the small-town environment. According to the chamber of commerce website she'd checked prior to moving, Milford Falls was a mix of old and new, of small-town residents and newly transplanted professionals.

Jocelyn checked the MapQuest printout to make sure she didn't miss the turnoff. She was too tired to get lost and find her way back.

A road sign announcing nineteen miles till Milford Falls gave her a welcome boost of energy. She was almost there!

Homes sprinkled amongst pine trees, and dirt roads began to appear more often. Actually, the term *dwellings* was probably more appropriate because many of the structures were merely mobile homes with rickety carports attached. Broken down automobiles, children's toys, and old bicycles were strewn about the yards in disarray. Occasionally a small home with a nicely manicured lawn and yard would surprise her, especially as she got closer to town.

It was green, just as she remembered it. Thick pines and fir trees blanketed the rolling hills, shadowed darkly by the disappearing sunlight. She supposed it could be eerie, but she found it beautiful.

Her headlights cut a swath of light through the dusk, guiding her along the final stretch of road as she neared her destination. A sign appeared in the distance: WELCOME TO MILFORD FALLS.

She zoomed past the sign and thought about how nice it was to finally be there.

Her glance darted to the rearview mirror as a flash of lights caught her attention.

"Shoot!" she exclaimed as the blue and red lights urged her to the shoulder of the road. She glanced quickly at her speedometer, which read fifty-eight, and wondered what the speed limit was, not recalling a road sign along the way.

Immediately she signaled right and slowed to pull over. Just as she feared, the police car followed.

Once she was stopped, she rummaged through the glove compartment for her registration and dreaded showing the officer her driver's license. It was time for a new picture. This one was taken long enough ago that her hairstyle was laughable, a product of listening to her friends, yet again during a Butterfly Girls reunion. The reminder made her groan. Her friends were supposed to give her good advice, not advice that made her do dumb things like bad haircuts and uprooting her life.

"Good evening, ma'am," the officer said when she rolled down the window.

"Good evening," she said, thinking that *good* was not the word she would have chosen. "I'm sorry, officer, I wasn't expecting the city limits to pop up like that so quickly." She tried to keep her tone light, hoping it would lighten his mood too.

"I clocked you going thirteen miles over the speed limit."

"Really?" she replied, glad it wasn't more.

"Speed limit's posted two miles down the road," he said, accepting her license and registration papers. "Forty-five, right there in black and white."

She squinted at his name tag, imagining that Officer Goodrich liked sitting right there by that welcome sign. There was no doubt in her mind that she wasn't the first person he'd "welcomed" to town.

He directed his flashlight to her driver's license then beamed it on her face.

Her hand flew up to shield her eyes as her vision blurred and purple images danced before her eyes. "What the—"

"Sorry, ma'am, just doin' my duty. You might want to update your license. Have your eyes checked while you're at it." He took another look at her, sparing her the interrogation light this time. "Remain in your car while I run a check."

"Good grief," she muttered under her breath as he walked away. In the dim evening light, she guessed the officer to be in his midtwenties. Obviously, he had a little too much power for a young punk like him to handle.

Moments later he returned. He handed back her license along with a pink slip of paper. "The directions to pay the fine are on the back. If you want to dispute this ticket you need to call the number listed and set up a hearing."

She looked at the ticket and shook her head. This was the last thing she needed!

"Have a nice evening," he said, dipping his chin. "By the way, welcome to Milford Falls."

Shoving the ticket into her purse as he walked away, she slammed the registration papers back into the glove compartment then rolled up her window.

Resisting the urge to spray the officer with gravel as she pulled onto the road, she signaled nicely and slowly accelerated back onto the highway. *Welcome to Milford Falls, my foot*, she thought.

* * *

A light rain fell as she drove down the lane that led through a white picket fence to the driveway of the Tudor-style, white stucco and brown-beamed cottage, complete with a shake-shingle roof, dormered upstairs bedrooms, and overgrown ivy.

The house reminded her of an English cottage, which as a little girl made her feel like a princess in a fairy tale. Her grandmother's wildflower garden with lawn gnomes and lily pond had sparked her childhood imagination, allowing her to spin tales of fantasy and adventure. Her family had only visited a few times during her childhood, but the memories would last a lifetime. Looking at it now, as the headlights illuminated the yard and home, she was reminded of how much she'd loved it as a child. The whole town seemed a bit out of place and time, like a charming village from a Jane Austen book against the backdrop of a lush green Washington landscape.

The sight of the house caused her stomach to knot, triggering memories to flood her mind. In spite of the difficulties in her life, she'd cherished the time she'd spent with her grandmother after her junior year of high school, finally knowing how it felt to be loved and treasured by an adult, something she had yearned for from her mother. Having never known her father, she'd struggled, along with her two brothers, to find comfort and contentment in her family. Being with her grandmother had given her a sense of the caring and unconditional love that a family could provide. Her brothers had never had that chance to spend an extended period of time with their grandmother like Jocelyn had, and she didn't think it was a coincidence they both had ended up making choices and living their lives in a way that only brought heartache.

David, her brother just three years younger, had experimented with drugs and had consequently ended up in jail for a minimum of ten years. Jocelyn tried to comfort herself with the thought that at least she knew where he was now and that most likely he was clean and sober.

Once she got settled she would write to him and let him know where she was.

Her youngest brother, Mikey, had joined the military, having been given a choice between that and jail. He'd gotten involved in some sort of gang activity and messed up one too many times. He was serving as a medic in Iraq. She was amazingly proud of him and the man he'd become. The army had basically saved his life, since she wasn't sure he would have survived much longer hanging around with the gang he'd hooked up with. Her fear was that now that he was in a good place in his life, being in the military would also be responsible for taking his life. In his e-mails he often shared experiences that took her breath away or gave her nightmares.

She was as close to her brothers as circumstances allowed, and she loved them with all her heart. They in turn were devoted to her. Not just because she was their sister, but she'd also been a mother to them when their mother was either busy waitressing or off with one of her many boyfriends.

Jocelyn hadn't spoken with her mother in months. Usually her mom only called when she was in need of money. Mikey tried to help their mom financially when he could, but she was always needing something, and her current husband hadn't held a job as long as they'd known him.

With a deep breath, she decided it was time to get out of her car and step foot inside her home and her new life. Before she left, she'd visited with her bishop about her decision. He was the closest thing she had to a father figure, and she relied upon his counsel as such.

He'd been encouraging and supportive and had given her a priesthood blessing, something she never took for granted. As a missionary she'd gained a strong testimony of the power of the priesthood and knew the great blessing it was in her life.

Words from the blessing crossed her mind now, helping calm her nerves and bolster her courage. *Even though you are facing this new opportunity in life by yourself, know that you are not alone. Angels have been assigned to be at your side, and the Savior's love will uphold you. This journey won't always be easy, but you will have the strength to face whatever challenges come your way and the faith to know that this is the Lord's will.*

There was no other explanation for the way things had fallen into place for her. To her surprise, the local middle school even had an opening in the art department that she had interviewed for via phone last week—not that she knew whether she'd gotten the job yet, but it did seem like a good sign. Yes, this was the Lord's will. For some reason she was supposed to be right here, right now.

Was it to put her past to rest? Was it to give her a chance to find joy and fulfillment in her life?

She wasn't sure. But she was ready to face whatever lay ahead of her.

* * *

Sunshine peeked out from behind the clouds and shone between the café curtains of the upstairs window. Last night she hadn't thought to close the blinds, and this morning she was grateful. It was a glorious morning.

Jocelyn got up, showered, and got dressed then headed downstairs. The first order of business today would be a trip into town to buy a few essentials.

Andrea had been planning on joining her for a week to help get her settled and do a little home improvement with her, but a job opportunity in Los Angeles had come through and Andrea wasn't in a financial position to turn it down. Her exercise endorsements and video sales had dropped, so she was trying to find a steadier job in the fitness industry.

Jocelyn had told herself she wasn't too worried about making the move alone, but now that she was here, the emptiness was a little too . . . empty.

She looked at her surroundings, at the worn furnishings in her grandmother's house, and at her few boxes of belongings and felt a pang of loss and regret. Her life in St. George wasn't the most exciting and adventurous, but a comfort zone, even a boring one at that, was better than being lonely and separated from familiar surroundings.

Lying open on the kitchen table were her scriptures from the night before. She'd been studying them like she did every night. Last night she'd been looking for passages that would give her some help in coping with this new change in her life.

She had felt very anxious arriving at the house the night before. She had been flooded with memories and feelings, some joyous, some very painful. As she'd battled homesickness, loneliness, and feelings of inadequacy, she'd found some comfort in several scriptures, the first being John 14:18: "I will not leave you comfortless: I will come to you." The other scripture was Hebrews 13:5: "I will never leave thee, nor forsake thee."

Jocelyn had known for years that the first place she needed to turn to in order to overcome loneliness was the Savior's outstretched hand.

Sometimes in the middle of trials she forgot things she knew, things she believed in, things she had a testimony of. The Lord had promised to send the Comforter, whose influence she knew was always with her and would heal the hurt in loneliness. The Lord couldn't remove her burdens completely, but He would send comfort.

She wasn't alone—something she needed to remember every hour of every day.

Moving her scriptures to the side, she smiled as she saw the note that had been there when she arrived: *Sister Rogers, When we heard you were coming, we took the liberty of giving your home a quick touch-up cleaning. We hope you don't mind the intrusion. Here's your grandmother's key back. We look forward to meeting you. Love, the Milford Falls Relief Society.*

Maybe it had been a little presumptuous, but she was grateful all the same. With renewed energy she continued her list of things she might need to tide her over the weekend then headed to town.

She had noticed last night that the outskirts of the town consisted mainly of large homes. But as she got closer to the main part of old Milford Falls, the homes were mostly quaint Cape Cods, Tudor cottages, or bungalows. No fast-food chains or stores were allowed within a certain radius of the town center. That's what made Milford Falls such a charming town. Most of the five-block city center was vibrantly eclectic, with an assortment of diners, boutiques, and shops surrounding the large grassy town square that featured a massive white gazebo and a statue of Lewis and Clark.

Food was first on her list. After all the junk she'd eaten on her long trip from southern Utah, she was anxious to have a meal that didn't come out of a cellophane package and taste like cardboard.

Jocelyn found a parking spot on the street, backing in and then out of the spot several times before she parallel parked adequately.

The day must have started off with rain, but the sun had broken through the clouds and washed down on the rain-kissed sidewalk, causing steam to rise from the pavement. The grass was vivid green, the sky a vibrant blue.

The beauty of the bright sun illuminated the lush, gardenlike surroundings. There were flowers everywhere: in yards, in pots, hanging from light poles in baskets, and even in window boxes. The fragrance was intoxicating.

Digging through her memories she vaguely recalled a diner being on one of the corners across from Moose's Market. Hopefully it was all still there. She recalled them serving up delicious, home-style meals, especially their apple pie.

Even though it had been roughly fourteen years ago, not much had really changed. The relaxed pace of the town seemed to settle into the people as well as the traffic, if one could call three cars on the road "traffic."

"Good morning," an elderly man said as he walked out of Frank's Barber Shop.

Jocelyn noticed how he dipped his chin when he greeted her. Such a gentleman. She gave him a smile and returned the greeting.

In front of Darvill's Bookstore, a woman was setting out a table with clearance books for sale. Jocelyn stopped to look and noticed several books she had been wanting to read.

"Two for the price of one today," the lady said, giving her a warm smile. "I'd buy some, but my husband will kill me if I bring one more book home."

Jocelyn laughed and nodded sympathetically. She herself had realized what a pain it was to move books—she'd brought three boxes of them with her. But they were a love of hers, and she figured there were worse things to be addicted to. To indulge her addiction, she'd decided to build a library of classics.

Picking up *Wuthering Heights,* by Emily Brontë, and Steinbeck's *The Grapes of Wrath,* she went inside the store and realized she was likely to become a regular here. In the front of the store were new releases and current titles. In the back were used books on shelves stacked high to the ceiling. Darvill's was her new favorite store.

"Ahh," the man behind the counter said. He was probably in his midfifties, bald on top, with black-rimmed glasses. "A girl after my own heart. You like the classics."

"I do. I'm trying to build my library but on a budget. I've been wanting these books for several years."

"Sure glad we had what you were looking for. You'll have to come spend some time hunting through our used section. I'm sure you could find more of the same." He completed the transaction and handed her the receipt.

"I'll do that. I have a feeling you'll be seeing me a lot. I don't even own a TV anymore," she said.

"Good for you! You just made my day. Except for news programs and a few sports shows, I never turn the thing on. Are you new to

Milford Falls?" he asked, slipping the books into a bag and handing them to her.

"I am. I'm living in what used to be my grandmother's house. Did you happen to know Cora Randolph?"

"Cora? Of course I did. I can see where you got your love of books. She was one of my best customers. She wasn't one to keep books, though. Usually read them and brought them back for me to sell. Sweet lady. Intelligent, too. And you're her granddaughter?" He reached a hand toward her. "It's nice to meet you . . ."

"Jocelyn," she said, accepting his handshake.

"Welcome to Milford Falls, Jocelyn. I'm the owner of the bookstore, Warren Darvill. And I'll tell you what—next time you're in the neighborhood, drop by. I'll keep an eye out for some books you might like and keep them in the back for you."

Jocelyn's mouth dropped open a bit. "Wow, you'd do that for me?"

"I do that for all my favorite customers," he said with a twinkle in his eye.

"That would be great. Anything by the Brontës or Austen. And I'd love a copy of *Moby Dick* or *Silas Marner.*"

Mr. Darvill laughed. "Why don't you make a list and drop it by. Then I'll have it to refer to."

"Thank you, Mr. Darvill," she said, feeling truly grateful. "I'll come back soon, then."

"You can call me Warren," he said.

With a wave she left the bookstore, feeling a little bit more comfortable in her new town. Excited about the discovery of the bookstore and her recent purchases, she headed down the sidewalk, hoping the diner was still where she remembered it. Mentally she began making her "wish list" to leave with Warren.

Her thoughts were disrupted by a commotion from around the corner.

"Listen, Karl, you can't give me a ticket for jaywalking. You aren't on duty!" a voice yelled.

Jocelyn slowed her pace as she walked past Moose's Market and neared the corner.

"Can too," a voice responded. "And I'll add obstructing the law if you don't let go of my arm."

"I'll let it go when you decide to tear up that ticket. Either that or let me show you how recycled paper tastes."

"Now, there's no need for threats! But what's the point of being a deputy sheriff if I don't have authority to give tickets when citizens break the law?"

She rounded the corner and saw two men. The first appeared to be the officer who had given her a speeding ticket the night before. The other one was a scruffy bearded, ponytailed man wearing a plaid flannel shirt.

"Karl!" the bearded man threatened.

"What's going on out here?" A man the height of a small fir tree and as broad as a bull ducked through the doorway of the grocery store and stepped outside. "Now, Moose. You know I'm just doing my duty," the fellow name Karl said.

"Why in tarnation did the mayor go and make you a deputy in the first place?" Moose shook his head. "Don't you have somewhere else you need to be?"

"Actually, no."

"Karl," Moose said, drawing the young man's name out in a slow, threatening tone, "tear up the ticket and get on home. Your mother's probably got your lunch ready."

"Actually, she's at her weekly canasta meeting at Flora Bronson's house. The girls get together once—"

"I don't care what they do!" Moose's voice boomed. "Just move along, will ya? You're blocking the entrance to my store."

"But—"

"Tear up the ticket first," Moose said.

Karl looked at the ponytailed man and said with a snort, "Next time use a crosswalk." He then tore up the ticket and, unable to find a garbage can close by, shoved the shreds of paper into his pants pocket. He stomped off down the street, nearly plowing into an elderly woman who was walking her dog. The dog barked wildly at Karl, who promptly said, "Oh, pipe down, Fifi. I don't need any grief from you, too!"

Jocelyn didn't realize she was staring until the man in the apron turned and looked at her. The amused smile on her mouth faded, and she quickly turned and went directly into Moose's Market.

She'd planned on going to the diner next but figured as long as she was here, she might as well pick up a few things to tide her over for the weekend. She still had a cooler in the car from when she moved, so the refrigerated items should stay cold enough for a little while.

With a shopping basket looped over her arm she located cereal, milk, bread, peanut butter, jelly, some bananas, and a few frozen dinners that claimed to be healthy. Then, unable to help herself, she grabbed a bag of cinnamon bears, one of fun-size Snickers bars, and some peanut M&Ms. She could go to a larger grocery store for more once she got settled. For now, this would do.

Moose, or Mr. Moose—she wasn't sure what to call him—was at the cash register waiting to check her out.

"How are you today, miss?" he asked. His low baritone voice was much softer and friendlier than a few minutes ago.

"I'm well, thank you," she said.

"Will this be all?"

"For now, yes," she answered, adding a pack of gum to the pile.

"Are you just visiting Milford Falls?" He began ringing up the items and putting them in a bag.

"No, actually, I just moved here."

"Well, how about that! Welcome to Milford Falls. What brings you to our little town?" he asked as he weighed the bananas.

"My grandmother passed away a couple years ago, and I'm living in her house," she explained, glad there weren't a lot of customers around to hear the conversation. She didn't mind explaining her situation, but she wasn't one to draw attention to herself. Already the thought of going to church and meeting a whole ward of new names and faces made her feel panicky and sick to her stomach. She knew she might have met many of them fourteen years ago, but, frankly, the thought of seeing people she'd known then was even more terrifying than meeting new ones.

"Wait a minute. Are you Cora's granddaughter?" he asked.

"Yes. She left the house to me when she passed away."

"She did, did she? I'm sure sorry about your grandmother. Cora was quite a character. Sad to see her go."

"Thank you," Jocelyn said, handing him her debit card.

"You getting settled?" he asked, swiping her card.

"It will be a slow process," she answered. "The house needs some work." A bell jingled as another customer walked through the door. Moose greeted the woman with his friendly but booming voice.

Glad to have an interruption so she could leave graciously, Jocelyn shoved her wallet back into her purse and grabbed her three bags of groceries.

Moose turned his attention back to her, and before he could start up any further conversation, Jocelyn said, "Well, nice to meet you. I guess I'd better get going. Got a lot of work to do."

"Good luck! Thanks for coming in," Moose said.

Jocelyn nodded her head and hurried out the door then stopped once she was outside. Maybe instead of going to the diner, she would just go home. She had food, some good books, and plenty to do.

She took one last look around to make sure she wasn't forgetting something before she got all the way home.

Next to Moose's was the fix-it shop and there, across the street on the other corner, was the Sunflower Diner. She paused, trying to decide if she wanted to eat there or not. The thought of eating real food and a piece of hot apple pie and ice cream for dessert made her mouth water.

That did it. The possibility of pie was just too much to resist. She decided to put her groceries in the car and go to the diner.

She stood on the corner to cross, waiting for the only two cars on the street to turn, when she heard a man across the street from her say to another fellow, "Okay, Mayor, I'll keep that in mind."

"Yikes!" she exclaimed under her breath. It was Mayor Duncan. He was the last person she wanted to run into. And now he was coming her way!

Chapter Six

Without thinking she turned and darted into the nearest open doorway.

She stood back against the wall, praying that the mayor wouldn't come into where she was hiding.

A pounding noise in a back room caught her attention. She looked around, wondering where she was.

Her breath caught as the front door opened.

She tried to fade into the woodwork, but there was too much light inside the store.

The older lady she'd seen earlier walked through the door carrying Fifi. Relief flooded Jocelyn and she slowly released her breath. She tried to appear busy looking at what she quickly determined were wood stain samples. She realized she must have stepped into the fix-it shop.

Fifi's owner stood at the counter, waiting for someone to help her, and after a few moments, she grew impatient. "Hello?" she called. "Yoo-hoo, is anyone there?"

The curtained doorway parted, and the bearded long-haired jaywalker stepped through.

"Mrs. Davenport, how are you? Sorry to keep you waiting. I can't hear over noise in the back sometimes."

"Good morning, Jack. I was in town and thought I'd check to see if my picture frame is ready."

"I finished it this morning," he said. "I'll be right back."

Jocelyn peeked out the window to see if the mayor was out of sight so she could make her getaway. She could have pie later. Right now she just wanted to get home and away from Mayor Duncan. There was no doubt he would rake her over the coals again for letting her grandmother's house fall into disarray. She'd already had to deal with him over the phone more than once in the past couple weeks.

"Here it is," he said, presenting a lovely carved picture frame of dark mahogany wood.

"Look at that." She set down Fifi then examined the frame, front and back. "My goodness Jack, you can't even tell it was broken. You do fine work. How much do I owe you, dear?"

"Nothing, Mrs. Davenport. This one's on me."

"Absolutely not. I want to pay you for your time and your beautiful work. My sweet Harold gave me this frame on our fiftieth anniversary with our wedding picture in it. It's not that valuable, just very sentimental."

"I'm glad I was able to fix it. Here, let me put that in a bag for you so you can carry it more easily." He took the frame and wrapped it in tissue then slid it into a plastic bag. "Do you need any help getting it home?"

"No, dear. It's not heavy. I can make it."

"All right, if you're sure." He stepped from behind the counter. "Let me get the door for you."

Jocelyn was surprised to see how kind and gentle he was with the older woman—very much unlike the man she'd seen trying to get out of a ticket earlier.

The man named Jack held the door open for Mrs. Davenport and her dog then turned to Jocelyn and asked, "Can I help you?"

"Oh!" she exclaimed, feeling like a dunce. Up close she realized he was younger than his beard made him look, probably about her own age. "Um, actually . . . I, um . . ." She looked out the window, gasped, and said, "Oh, crud!" She jumped back and hid behind the display.

Mayor Duncan walked by the window and paused right in front.

"Are you okay?" Jack asked. Then he looked closely at her. "You're not, like, an escaped prisoner or something, are you?" He was half joking, but she didn't think it was half funny.

"No, of course not," she said. Then she glanced down. She was wearing a black-and-white striped shirt with her black capris. Okay, it was *a little* funny. She looked back up. "I can see how you might have gotten the idea, but no. I promise."

"You didn't rob a bank did you?"

"Milford Falls has a bank?" she asked sarcastically then held up her grocery bags, which were terribly heavy by now. "Just TV dinners and bananas, I'm afraid. And I paid for them. I have the receipt to prove it."

The man named Jack shrugged. "Mayor Duncan isn't everyone's favorite person in town, but I've never seen anyone react like this before." Jack craned his neck toward the window. "I think you're safe. He's gone."

"How do I know you're not lying and you just want to see me get busted so you can find out why I don't want to run into the mayor?"

"Hmm, now that you mention it, I should have tricked you. I guess I am a little curious."

"Actually, I, myself, am curious about something," she said. "If the mayor isn't everyone's favorite person in town, then how did he get elected?"

"No one else ran for mayor. Well, except Karl. We had to choose between a pompous windbag and an idiot. Who would you vote for?"

She nodded. "I see your point."

"Karl's consolation prize was being made deputy sheriff. Personally, I'd rather have him as mayor—he'd probably be less annoying than Duncan."

Jocelyn laughed. Since this town was the Mayberry of the Pacific Northwest, then Karl apparently was the Barney Fife of the town. She wondered if he carried a gun but had no bullets like Barney.

She relaxed and shifted her bags to the other hand. "You sure I'm safe to go?"

"That depends," he said.

"On . . ."

"On whether you're going to tell me why you're avoiding Mayor Duncan. My curiosity is now too strong for me to resist. Not that I don't avoid him myself, but unless I'm mistaken, you don't even live here. How do you know to avoid him?"

She introduced herself and briefly explained about her grandmother's house and the phone call from the mayor.

"So you just arrived here last night?" he asked.

"And received a grand welcome from the official Milford Falls welcoming committee."

"We have a welcoming committee?" he asked.

"Karl gave me a speeding ticket as I drove past the Welcome to Milford Falls sign."

Jack rolled his eyes and shook his head. "You're kidding."

"According to him, I was going thirteen over the speed limit."

"Ah! You're a menace to society! Keep up that kind of behavior and you will find yourself in prison," he teased. "I'm sorry about that. Karl discovered that little speed trap by accident. The highlight of his day is to patrol it each night. You won't have to pay that ticket."

"I won't?" she asked with surprise.

"No, just take it to Natalie at the city office building on Monday, and she'll take it off the record. If he had you listed going twenty-five over they would cite you, but you weren't actually in the forty-five-mile-an-hour zone yet."

"How do you know?" she asked.

"Everyone here knows. Karl hits on poor defenseless tourists who are in a hurry, so they just pay the ticket and get on their way. I'll have to say, though, our town's revenues have almost doubled due to his efforts. We have some pretty big blow-out celebrations with that money."

"He does it knowing they really aren't breaking the law?"

"Oh, Karl doesn't think of it like that," Jack explained. "He is fully convinced that they should anticipate the speed limit and could be a hazard to the town's safety if they haven't slowed down by the time they hit the sign. He's been trying to get the speed-limit sign moved for years."

"Thank you for the information. I'll go visit Natalie on Monday." She glanced at the window one more time to make sure it was safe before she left. "Karl's not going to give you a ticket for harboring a fugitive, is he?"

"He can try."

"I saw him try to give you a jaywalking ticket earlier."

"He won't make that mistake again, I assure you. And don't be too worried about Mayor Duncan, either. His bark is much worse than his breath. I mean, bite."

Jocelyn giggled.

"The mayor always seems to be stirring up controversy somewhere. His new plan is to update the town square by giving a makeover to all the stores that surround it."

"Really. I like it the way it is," Jocelyn said.

"So do I. He wants to bring in more tourists, but the reason I like living here is the fact that it is small and isn't a tourist trap. Who wants more riffraff to come to town?"

"Riffraff, huh?"

"Believe me, we get all kinds of crazies here. From tree huggers and hippies to professors and professionals. Quite a range of townsfolk."

"I hope that means there's a good chance I'll fit in somewhere," she said.

"Oh, so you're not just here to fix the house? You're moving in?" He seemed slightly alarmed.

"That's right."

"Oh."

"Well, I guess I'd better be on my way," she said after an uncomfortable pause. "Thanks again."

"Sure. Nice to meet you . . ."

"Jocelyn."

"Jocelyn."

She approached the door.

"Oh," he said, "sorry about your grandmother. She was quite a character. I miss having her around."

"Thank you," Jocelyn answered, realizing that her grandmother had been an integral part of this town. She wondered if she would ever feel like this was home to her. Certainly the people were nice and friendly, albeit a little odd. But then, to some she was probably a little odd too, so maybe she would fit in after all. Time would tell.

Chapter Seven

The gravel-covered lane leading to her grandmother's house—her house now (she was having a hard time getting used to that)—was a straight shot to the main road, with a long line of oak trees on either side, their branches touching in the middle. The green canopy kept the road shaded from the sun and created a mythical vision of horse-drawn carriages and headless horsemen. At least that's what she'd thought as a young girl the few times she'd come to visit her grandmother. At the end of the fantasy lane was her storybook cottage.

As a girl, her imagination had transported her into fairy-tale imaginings and stories with princesses and princes, godmothers, and enchantment.

Reality had a strange way of stomping on a little girl's imagination. But Jocelyn had managed to keep her daydreams and fantasies alive in her art. She painted the enchanted scenes, bringing to life magical places and times.

As she pulled up to the house and went to the trunk to unload her groceries, she wondered when she'd next have time to spend on her own art. There were just so many other projects ahead of her. Lost in thought, she didn't notice the car coming up behind her until it stopped right next to her.

"Good afternoon," the woman said through the unrolled window. "You're not Cora's granddaughter, Jocelyn, are you?"

With surprise Jocelyn answered, "Yes, actually, I am."

"Wonderful! We've been waiting for you to move to town."

Jocelyn smiled. In a town this size she needed to remember that her business was everyone else's.

"I just got here last night," she answered.

"Oh, my goodness! Are you getting settled all right? Do you need help unloading? I've got a couple of sons who would be happy to move boxes."

"I really didn't have that much," Jocelyn told her, knowing the woman wouldn't believe how little she'd brought with her. She'd given away most of her stuff in St. George. All she had left were her boxes of books, clothes, school and art supplies, and a few sentimental items. Nothing else she'd had seemed worth hauling all the way up here. Almost everything she owned had fit into her Corolla; the rest she'd been able to ship in just a few boxes.

"Are you sure?" The woman got out of her Jeep Cherokee and leaned up against it. "By the way, my name is Mary Jane Gentry. My friends call me MJ. I own the hair salon in town. I'm also the Relief Society president in the ward. I guess you could say that's why I appear to be stalking you. We talked about you in PEC last week, and I've been on the lookout."

Jocelyn's face must have registered shock because MJ quickly added, "Not that we have been *talking* about you. Oh, dear, that didn't come out right."

Jocelyn laughed. "I understand. And I want to thank you for the cleaning done here. It sure made it easier on me after that long drive."

"We just wanted to make sure you felt welcome and that you had help if you needed it. I want you to know how much we miss your grandmother. She was such a fun lady. We miss her humor in Relief Society."

"Thank you. I miss her too."

"She used to come to my hair salon every Thursday morning to get her hair done."

A sudden surge of emotion hit Jocelyn unexpectedly.

MJ was quick to notice. "I'm sorry. I'm sure it's hard to talk about it."

"I know it's been two years . . . It's just that being here gives me constant reminders that she's gone."

"I can see how that would be hard." She changed the subject by gesturing to the back of her vehicle, which was cluttered with quilt frames, fabric, and a jumble of other unidentifiable objects.

"We are getting ready for our Super Saturday activity tomorrow. You'll have to come if you have time. You can meet all the sisters. We get together, have lunch, do crafts and projects, and just have fun. I think you'll enjoy the ward."

"That does sound fun. I'll have to see how much unpacking I get done."

"Are you sure you don't need help?" MJ asked anxiously.

"Thank you, but most of it I need to do myself. I might start going through my grandmother's things and try to decide what to keep and what to get rid of."

"Sounds like a big project."

"Probably. I really don't know how big until I start going through closets and storage. Everything is pretty much the way it was when she passed away," Jocelyn explained.

"I would have thought your family would have come for her things already," MJ said.

"Well, Grandmother didn't have anything very valuable, really. The house is probably the only thing she had that was worth anything, and it could use some work."

"Were you quite close?"

"Yes," Jocelyn said, "very, though most of the time just through letters and phone calls." Jocelyn didn't tell her that her grandmother had been more like a mother to her than her own mom. Her grandmother was the one who instilled values in her, encouraged her to get an education, to go after her dreams. Her grandmother was there for her during the most difficult times of her life. "I miss her a lot. And I feel bad I let her home become a bit run-down in the last couple years."

"It's such a lovely place. With some tender loving care you can really make it beautiful. Such a large yard, too. How big is it?"

"Two acres, I believe."

"What in the world are you going to do with two acres! I hope you have a riding mower."

"I'm not sure what she's got. I need to do something about the yard, though. Mayor Duncan isn't very happy with me."

"Please don't tell me he's stopped by already and bothered you about that."

"Actually, he called me in St. George when I lived there. He's part of the reason I moved. He said there'd be steep fines if I didn't get the house and yard fixed up. He suggested I sell the place."

"Good grief. I can't believe him. I'm so sorry."

"It's okay. I really think it helped me face up to some decisions in my life. I was ready for a change. Maybe it will all be for the best."

MJ gave her a warm smile. "I hope so. I'm really happy you moved here. You'll love Milford Falls. It's a beautiful place, and the people are really warm and friendly—well, except for Mayor Duncan."

And your crazy sheriff's deputy, Jocelyn thought.

"Actually, we have some colorful characters here in town, but it makes living here more interesting." MJ opened her car door. "Try and come tomorrow if you can. Church starts at eleven on Sunday morning. I didn't know if you knew that or not. Oh, just a minute." The woman shuffled through a stack of books and papers on the backseat. "Here it is." She produced a small pamphlet and handed it to Jocelyn. "This is a list of ward phone numbers, including the bishop's and his office at the church. At the top is the name and number of each auxiliary president."

"Thank you," Jocelyn said. "And thank you for stopping by. It was wonderful to meet you."

Jocelyn waved good-bye as MJ drove away. She had to admit she'd certainly met a lot of people in a short amount of time. The people were definitely friendly, but they also seemed to be very curious about newcomers. She'd even been the topic of conversations in the ward. That made her a bit uncomfortable.

Just as she was about to go inside, the sound of yelling caught her attention. A man's voice was coming from behind the house.

She dropped her bags on the front porch and walked around to see what was going on.

Suddenly, the muffled bang of gunshot stopped her in her tracks.

"Blasted rabbits!" the man yelled. "I'll hunt you down if you don't leave my garden alone!"

She wondered whether she should run for cover or stay in one spot so she didn't startle the man by approaching him.

"Who in the Sam Hill are you?" the gruff voice asked.

Well, she wasn't going to startle him. He'd already seen her.

"Uh, I'm Jocelyn Rogers, Cora's granddaughter," she called out.

The man, who looked rather elderly, kept his gun trained on the thicket of trees and brush but turned to look at her.

"How do I know you're not a burglar?"

"Well . . ." She thought for a moment. "I doubt a burglar would move stuff *into* the house," she said.

"Hmph!" He scanned the woods for any more creatures. Satisfied they had been driven away for the time being, he lowered the barrel of the gun. "So, what are you doing here?"

"I've decided to live in my grandmother's house. She left it to me in her will."

"She did!" He walked toward her, cradling the gun in his arms. As he got closer, Jocelyn realized it was a BB gun. Her brother had one just like it when he was a little boy. "You're not the same girl that lived with her a few years back, are ya?"

Try thirteen years, she thought. She'd foolishly hoped that she could avoid any of the people who'd known she had lived with her grandmother back then.

"Um, yes, I am," she said with a nod.

"I see." He looked at her. "Guess it makes sense she'd leave the house to you."

"I guess so," Jocelyn replied, not sure where he was going with this but hoping he'd drop the subject.

"Y'know, you're the only family she had who ever visited her. To my way of thinking, none of the others deserved anything from her."

Jocelyn had to nod in agreement. Her mother had only taken her and her two brothers to see their grandmother three times that Jocelyn could remember. Every summer they asked to go, but their mother immediately shut them down. Eventually Jocelyn understood it was because her mother couldn't handle submitting to the "house rules" at Grandmother's, even for a week or two. Her mother's lifestyle was horrible at best. The woman smoked and drank and had a chain of unsavory boyfriends. Jocelyn never knew who she'd wake up to find in the house some mornings. Luckily she had a lock on the door of her bedroom, but that didn't mean some of the creeps didn't make advances toward her.

She shivered just thinking about it.

"I loved my grandma very much," Jocelyn told him.

"Hmph. Well, even you should have come to see her more often," he grumbled.

"I wish I could have." She didn't bother defending herself further. She knew she had done her best, and she knew her grandmother knew that, too.

He gave her a doubtful glare. "Guess it will be nice to have someone in the house finally. Mayor Duncan has been out several times and isn't happy that the place was left vacant."

"Yes, I know. He spoke to me," she confessed.

"He did, did he? Well, I don't know what he said to you, but don't worry too much about the mayor. He's not as important as he thinks he is."

Does anyone in this town like the mayor? she wondered.

"He did threaten to fine me if I didn't clean up the yard and fix up the house within thirty days."

"That old son of a goat!" he exclaimed. "I wish we could boot his sorry rear end out of office, but no one wants to go up against him. If I were younger I'd do it myself."

Jocelyn chuckled.

"If he gives you any trouble, you just let Harold Murphy know about it," the man said.

"Who's Harold Murphy?" she asked.

"Why, I am!" he exclaimed. "But you can call me Harry. Most people do."

"All right, Harry. I will let you know. I plan to avoid him as long as possible, though, just in case."

"Then you're going to fit in nicely here in Milford Falls," Harry said.

She nodded toward the gun. "Guess we've got a rabbit problem?"

"I got a hole in my fence, and the blasted nuisances keep coming in and eating my garden. Cora never let me take care of the problem when she was here. Didn't like seeing them hurt. I'm not going to sit around watching them eat my plants, though."

"Maybe you should get a dog," she said.

"Had one," he said. "Bumble headed canine ran into the road and got himself killed."

"Oh, I'm sorry," she said.

"I'm over it. Can't say I mind having a little target practice now and then, anyway. If Mayor Duncan comes sniffin' around, just give me a holler. I'll get rid of him for ya." He lifted the gun and raised his eyebrows.

She laughed, seeing the teasing twinkle in his eye.

"I sure will," she said. "Thank you."

"Guess I'd better call someone to come out and take a look at my fence and get that hole fixed." He gave her a nod of his head and walked back to his house.

Jocelyn found herself laughing at the absurd image of Harry shooting BBs at the mayor and the mayor running down the lane to get away.

Happy to be home, if not just to get a break from the "colorful" characters of Milford Falls, she went inside to cook a frozen dinner and tackle some boxes.

* * *

In her sleep Jocelyn dreamed she was a young girl, visiting her grandmother. She was on her grandmother's couch, taking a nap, but her brothers were bothering her by flipping her face with their stinky socks.

"Go away, I said!" she exclaimed, batting them with her hands. "Leave me alone!"

Then she realized it was a dream and woke up, only to find two birds fluttering around her.

"Ahh!" she screamed, covering her face with her arms and rolling off the couch onto the floor with a loud *kerplunk.*

How in the heck had birds gotten into her house?

The bigger question was, how the heck did she get them out?

Shivers ran down her spine as she remained on the ground, watching the frantic birds fly around her living room, one of them actually slamming into the window, leaving a smear of bird gunk behind.

"Ugh!" she exclaimed.

She had to get them out, but she was afraid. Did birds really attack, like on the Alfred Hitchcock movie? She imagined them pecking at her arms, head, and eyes and shuddered again.

Army crawling across the floor, she headed for the box labeled "coat closet & misc."

She lay on the ground next to the box and slid her arm inside, fishing around for the handle of her tennis racket.

There it is!

She also grabbed a hooded coat and slipped it on, pulling the hood over her head. She was ready.

Crawling to the door, she watched the birds, waiting for them to fly to the far side of the room. Then she quickly yanked the door open, throwing it so hard it banged into the wall.

Hoping she hadn't made a dent, she moved slowly to her knees then forced herself to stand, letting out a nervous whimper. "Please don't peck me to death."

Arming herself with the racket, she faced the birds and formulated her strategy. If she could get behind them she could maybe get them to fly out the open door. Of course, they seemed to have zero sense of direction, so she knew it was a long shot. Still, she had no choice: it was either them or her.

Sliding along the wall, she held her gaze on the birds, which were still flapping about, and dug deep for the courage to swat them if she needed to.

"I can't believe this is happening," she said as she pulled the racket into position, guarding her face with the strings.

She noticed bird feathers falling all around as the birds continued to bump into the ceiling and walls. "C'mon you silly birds, go out the door."

She had hoped it wouldn't come to this, but they clearly needed her help, so finally she found the courage to take action.

With a scream and a swing of the racket she startled the birds, causing them to swirl in a mad fervor. The results were not as she had hoped. She squatted down and covered her head with her arms. There was an increased fluttering of wings and whooshing, when suddenly she heard a loud "BAM!"

Peeking under one arm, she saw one of the birds lying on the tile near the doorjamb.

"You've got to be kidding!" she said, trying to keep an eye on the downed bird while looking around for the other one. But the second bird was gone. She listened intently, wanting to make sure it wasn't just perched somewhere, watching the fate of its misguided friend, but as far as she could tell, it had indeed made it to freedom.

Content that one of the birds had survived the ordeal, she next addressed the bird on the floor. Shouldn't it be moving by now? Surely it was just knocked senseless . . . *Oh, no! What if it's dead?* She watched for a while, holding her breath, but it didn't move at all. Poor, stupid thing.

She felt bad for it but didn't know how she could have done things differently to help it. She sighed. And now she had to get its body outside and into the trash. But how did she pick it up without touching it?

Glancing around, she spied her toolbox. She could use a hammer to slide the bird onto the racket, then she could carry it outside.

Approaching cautiously, she held the racket close to the bird then leaned down to slide the body onto it with the hammer.

Just as she touched the hammer to the bird, it burst into a frenzy. Jocelyn screamed, dropped the hammer, and ran outside with the bird following her. Still holding onto the racket, she spun around on her front lawn waving her arms about her hooded head until she dared to stop and see if the bird was finally gone.

The bird was gone, but she made a worse discovery. She wasn't alone.

A pickup truck with the words *Jack's Repairs* was parked in front of her house, and Jack was watching her from the cab, an amused expression on his face.

Chapter Eight

"Crud!" she said under her breath. She probably looked like she was certifiably insane. What was he doing there anyway?

"Everything okay?" he called through the open passenger-side window.

She reached up and slid the hood off her head, giving her hair a quick finger combing. "Uh, yeah. Just had a little bird problem in the house. They're gone now."

"*In* the house, you said?"

"Yes." She felt ridiculous standing there in her coat in the June sunshine, but she didn't really want to draw more attention to it by taking it off.

"They're probably coming down your chimney. You need to put a mesh covering over the top so they can't get inside. The old cover must've gotten loose somehow."

"Mesh covering?" she said. "Uh, okay. Thanks."

"By the way, have you seen Harry? Your neighbor? He called to have me come look at his fence, but he's not at home."

She glanced at her watch. After her lunch she'd taken a nap—that is, until the bird attack. It had easily been two hours since she'd seen him.

"Not recently. Did you check his garden? He was outside earlier."

"Yeah, I checked. Thought maybe he was out and about. Guess I'll try him again later. If you see him would you mind telling him I came by? My name's Jack, in case you don't remember."

"Right," she said. "Like it says on the truck."

"By the way, I'd get that chimney covered soon or you're bound to get more visitors."

"Thank you," she said flatly. She had no idea how she was going to fix this. She couldn't imagine climbing up on her roof trying to cover the chimney. She didn't even know if her grandmother had a ladder anywhere.

He drove off, leaving her melting in the summer sun.

With a groan, she went back in the house to clean up after the birds and hopefully regain some of her dignity.

* * *

"Who are you?" Jocelyn said, trying to hide the fear in her voice. "What do you want?" She looked around the dark alley, but there was nowhere to run, no way to escape. The only exit was blocked by the stranger, the man who'd followed her as she'd walked home from school. She'd taken what she thought was a shortcut, but there was no outlet through the alley.

The man didn't answer. He just took several steps toward her, heightening the terror she felt inside.

Her instinct told her to run, to fight, to do whatever it took to get away, but her fear kept her feet bolted to the ground.

His eyes were filled with pure evil; his smile sent chills down her spine. If she didn't do something fast, she knew she wouldn't survive his attack.

"Do something!" *the voice inside of her shouted. She tried to move her legs, but she couldn't; they felt as heavy as lead. He took another step closer, and then another.*

"Please, no," she whimpered, and he lunged at her.

"Stop!" she screamed, bolting upright in bed. Her arms flailed as she clawed at the sheet that was over her head. A layer of cold sweat covered her, and her breath came in gulps. She looked around the room in a panic, disoriented for a moment, then realized she was safe and sound in her grandmother's house.

It was morning, the sun shone, the sky was blue, and she was fine. Except she wasn't really fine. She was tired of this nightmare, the one she'd had for years, the one she usually had when she was upset or under a lot of stress.

She should have known she would have it. Not only because of the move but because of the bird incident yesterday.

Her breathing returned to normal, and her heartbeat slowed to a calm, steady rhythm. Sunshine poured into the bedroom and bathed her room with warm light.

She shook her head to clear the remaining effects of the nightmare then looked over at the clock on the nightstand that read 9:43. She'd stayed up until two in the morning unpacking boxes and making a "change or repair" list. It had grown to three pages long by the time she went to bed. Some of the items on the list were just cosmetic: paint, countertops, tile, etc. But some were bigger: leaks, sagging rain gutters, broken kitchen drawers, cracked windows. She knew that many of the changes were nonessential and mostly wishful thinking, but some had to be addressed as soon as possible. What little savings she had needed to be split between repairs and an emergency fund in case she didn't find a teaching job. That didn't give her much to work with for now.

A lot of the repairs were just going to have to wait. She needed to put them in priority and then start getting them fixed one by one. First would be to do something about the chimney. She didn't want any more feathered visitors inside.

Before climbing out of bed, she glanced around the room to make sure nothing with a pointy beak was perched nearby, waiting to attack. *You can't be too careful,* she told herself.

She rejuvenated herself with a hot shower—grateful something worked—and enjoyed a resurgence of optimism and enthusiasm. No matter what, it was her home. She didn't have a house payment, rent payment, or outstanding debt. At least she had that going for her.

After eating a bowl of cereal she slid her feet into a pair of hot pink flip-flops and pulled on a pink hoodie. Luckily she'd managed to set up her computer on her own, so she quickly mapped the directions to the nearest home improvement store and set out on her next adventure.

* * *

On the way to Home Depot, she saw notices tacked up on telephone poles and at stop signs along the way, advertising a town meeting to be held the following Thursday. She thought it would probably be a good idea to go and try to get involved. Her natural tendency was to be a hermit and hide in her hole, but she had recently vowed that she would fight those tendencies. This was her chance for a new beginning, and she was going to make the most of it.

When she got to the store, the parking lot was packed. Jocelyn groaned. Saturdays were the worst for stores like this. She was tempted to leave, but she knew she had to fix her chimney today or live in fear until she did.

Eyeing an empty cart near the entrance, she hurried to grab it before someone else did. But she was too late. A woman with bleached-blond hair, high heels, short shorts, a skimpy tank, and plenty of body to fill it out intercepted the cart, ignoring Jocelyn's outstretched hand. She was busy talking on her phone and far too involved to notice anyone or anything around her.

"You're welcome," Jocelyn said in a low voice as she entered the store.

Just as she expected, the cart stall was empty. She would have to watch for an abandoned cart somewhere in the store. Grabbing a basket from the stack, she looped it over her arm. Her stuff would never fit in there, but it was a start.

Keeping an eye out for a store employee so she could ask for help with her chimney, she began at the nearest aisle and started looking for items on her list. Light bulbs, tools, spackle, sandpaper, and various odds and ends went into the basket. She picked out colors for her living-room walls, trim, and ceiling, then left some paint at the mixing counter to pick up later. She still hadn't found an employee to ask about the chimney.

Actually quite glad she didn't have to try and maneuver a cart around the store with its overcrowded aisles, she lugged her heavy basket as she searched in vain for an employee who was available to help her.

Lost in the lumber section she felt her cell phone vibrate in her pocket. Transferring the basket to her left arm, she answered the phone.

"Hey, Joss, how's everything going?"

"Andrea, hi! I'm at Home Depot right now. It's crazy in here."

"Are you lost yet?" Andrea asked. "It can be overwhelming there. When I got ready for my tiling project last year, I had to get an employee to help me find pretty much everything. It's just so huge!"

"I'd much rather be somewhere else, but I don't have a choice. My grandmother's house is sort of falling apart . . . and I have birds inside."

"Did you say birds? Inside?"

"Yes, I had two attack me yesterday. It was very Alfred Hitchcock creepy."

"Joss, are you serious? I would have nightmares forever."

"It was like a nightmare. I slept with the sheet over my head all night last night. I'm trying to find someone to help me figure out how I can fix my chimney."

"You poor thing. I should be there with you. I hate birds, but I'd at least help you fight them off. Did you get pecked?"

Jocelyn shifted the basket to her other arm. It was really heavy, and she wasn't sure how much longer she could carry it. "No, thank goodness."

"I'm so sorry. I feel terrible."

"You should!" Jocelyn teased.

"If it helps, though, I got the job."

"Andrea, that's great. I'm happy for you."

"Thanks. Me too. Now I can afford food. I wish I could be there with you."

"Me too," Jocelyn said, spying an employee who was actually free. "Hey, let me call you later. I gotta talk to someone about the chimney."

"Okay. Call me!"

Jocelyn hung up and hurried over to the man in the orange apron.

"Excuse me," she said, out of breath and in desperation. "Can you please help me?"

"Of course! What can I do for you?"

"Birds are coming into my house. Through my chimney."

He pulled a face. "I hate birds. I was attacked by a wild turkey when I was young. Consequently, I hate Thanksgiving."

Is he serious? "Yes, well, I have to do something about it."

"Do you have a screen in front of your fireplace?"

"Yes," she answered. "They pushed through it."

"I see. They really wanted to get inside. It sounds like you need a screen on the opening outside."

"What kind of a screen exactly?"

"Let me show you," he said. He started walking and she followed. The young man was short and chubby but moved at a rapid pace. She had to walk fast to keep up, which wasn't easy with the overloaded basket in the crowded store.

He turned a corner and disappeared.

Jocelyn flew around the corner and collided with two men coming the opposite direction. Stuff flew out of her basket and into the aisle.

She looked up. *Oh—it has to be him!* "Hello, Jack."

Jack the repairman looked down at her, the lines of annoyance in his face softening. "Sorry about that," he answered in a controlled tone. "It's Jocelyn, right?"

The other man with him stooped down to pick up some of her things.

"I am so sorry," she said. "I was trying to keep up with . . ." The employee was long gone. "Dang it!"

"Here you go." Jack's friend handed her the items he'd retrieved. He had reddish hair, a quick smile, and friendly eyes. "Have you ever thought of playing football? You'd make a great lineman."

She smiled. "Thank you," she said, putting the things back in her basket then standing up.

"I'm Lenny, by the way. You need some help?" the friend asked.

Jack shot him an unappreciative glare.

She glanced down the aisle, wishing her aproned friend would come back for her.

"Uh, no," she answered. "It's okay."

"You look like you're taking on a lot of projects. You sure you don't need help?"

"If you could just point me to the aisle where I could find some screen-type stuff, that would help me a lot."

"Screen-type stuff," the friend said. "Uh, well, I'm not exactly sure what that is, but I bet if you try—"

"There you are!" a voice called.

With relief, Jocelyn saw her little Home Depot helper scurrying her way.

"I lost you somewhere along the way, and then someone needed to ask me a question," he explained.

"Thank you for coming back for me," she said. "I had a collision." She looked at Lenny and said, "Thanks for your help. I think I'm good now."

"This way, ma'am," the young man said.

Without another look, Jocelyn followed the guy in the apron and left the other two men behind. She imagined that living in a small town she was bound to bump into people quite often, but she seemed to be crossing paths with Jack the repairman every time she turned around.

Armed with supplies and rudimentary instructions to fix her chimney, Jocelyn found an abandoned cart, returned to the paint counter, then took her place in a long line at one of the busy checkout stands.

While she waited her turn, she thumbed through a basic do-it-yourself manual, hoping it was the "for dummies" version. She needed everything spelled out for her, including pictures and step-by-step instructions, and this book had both.

She had noticed a slow drip under the master bathroom sink, so she started to look at the chapter on vanity plumbing but was distracted by the sound of laughter in the next line over.

She glanced up to find Jack the repairman and his friend laughing together. She couldn't figure Jack out. Yesterday he'd been so friendly at first, and then he'd gotten kind of distant, and then he'd warmed up again. And today he'd been cold with her, but he was clearly having a very nice time with Lenny, just minutes later. What was Jack's problem?

Looking back at the diagram in the book but not really studying the text, she soon found herself glancing over at the two men again and discovered the woman with bleached-blond hair and short shorts—the woman who'd stolen Jocelyn's cart earlier—approaching the two men.

The woman batted her heavily made-up eyes at them, gave the friend a hug, then gave Jack a longer, more lingering hug.

As the three stood and chatted, occasionally laughing, Jocelyn noticed the woman's arm stayed around Jack's waist.

So, he has a girlfriend, she thought then wondered, *so why isn't his arm around her waist?* Not like she cared. She was just bored and curious.

Her turn came to check out, and she loaded her items onto the counter. After paying for her purchase, she grabbed her cart and headed for the exit just as Jack, friend, and Blondie were heading out the door. Not wanting to bump into them, she stopped to admire some indoor plants. Their voices and laughter followed them outside and, after waiting a few moments to make sure they were gone, she left the store.

The early afternoon sun had broken through clouds and intensified the lush green of the surroundings. Growing up in the desert of St. George, she wasn't used to the mild summer temperatures and rich plant life that was abundant in Milford Falls and much of the surrounding area.

Enjoying her surroundings, she pulled in a long, deep breath then walked to her car and stowed her purchases in the trunk then climbed in behind the wheel. Across the parking lot she noticed Jack and Blondie having a conversation next to Jack's pickup truck. Blondie was leaning back against the truck, posed like a flamingo, with one leg bent back on the running board.

Upon closer inspection, Jocelyn couldn't help noticing by Jack's body language that he seemed bored to tears and anxious to get into his truck.

Jocelyn didn't get it. Nor did she understand why she was wasting time watching the couple in their parking lot display.

You need to get a life, she told herself.

The drive home was filled with more awe and wonder at the beautiful scenery surrounding the town of Milford Falls. Tall fir trees towered thickly along side the road and rolling hills. Jenkins Creek meandered along the highway, which crossed the creek several times before entering the town itself.

Once she arrived home she made herself a peanut-butter-and-jelly sandwich then was ready to get to work. The first project was covering the chimney. She didn't want to go another minute worrying about bird attacks.

While she'd been talking to Harry the day before she'd noticed he had a ladder in his backyard and hoped he would let her borrow it. Not that she was excited to climb onto the roof. She was terrified of high places, but she didn't have a choice. It was either getting on the roof or turning her home into an aviary.

She knocked lightly on Harry's door at first then pounded a little louder when she didn't get a response. Soon she heard the shuffling of feet.

Even though his face had the appearance of grouchiness, she noticed a little light in his eyes when he opened the door and saw her.

"Well, well. What brings you to my door?"

"I hate to bother you, but I need to fix my chimney and I wondered if I could borrow your ladder."

"My ladder!"

She jumped at his quick, unhappy response.

"You shouldn't be getting up on a ladder," he lectured. "It's not safe."

"It's more safe than being attacked by birds," she told him.

"Birds. You were attacked by birds?" His face was scrunched with confusion.

"Yes. Inside my house. They came down through the chimney. It was terrifying." She knew she sounded dramatic, but it *was* terrifying to her. "I have some mesh stuff I need to put over the opening of the chimney so they won't come in again."

"I don't like the idea of you climbing up on your roof."

"I appreciate that, but I don't have a choice. I'll be careful," she assured him.

"Guess it needs to be done. Can't say I'd like birds coming into my house either, poopin' and flappin' all over. All right, you can borrow my ladder. It's right here in the carport."

The ladder lay against the wall, along with some two-by-fours and some PVC pipe. It was long but not heavy.

"I'll take one end," he said.

"No, Harry. I don't want you lifting this. I'd hate you to hurt your back."

"Oh, fiddlesticks!" he shot back. "Who do you think got it out and put it away just yesterday? Grab your end and let's get going."

She did as she was told, and together they carried the ladder back to her house. The shortest approach to the chimney was near the steepest part of the roof. Harry helped her set up the ladder then stood there, waiting.

"Well?" he said impatiently.

"I'm sorry?" she said, filling a bucket with all her supplies. She figured that was the easiest way to transport what she needed to do the job.

"I'm going to stand here and make sure nothing happens."

"You don't have to do that," she said. "I'll be fine."

His look of concern didn't change.

"I promise I'll holler if I need any help," she told him.

"You're as stubborn as your grandmother," he said.

Jocelyn smiled. "Thank you," she said.

He shook his head and turned to leave, muttering, "She's gonna fall and break her blasted neck. I just know it."

Jocelyn laughed nervously then looked up to the rooftop that seemed much higher than before and felt her stomach turn over.

Pulling in several deep breaths, she stepped back to take a better look at her approach. Maybe it would be better if she came up the back where the slant on the roof wasn't so severe.

Picking up the ladder she balanced it as she walked around the corner to the back of the house. The trees were filled with chirping, happy birds. She prayed that none of them decided to seek revenge on her for terrorizing their feathered friends.

Convinced the ladder was secure, she went back for her bucket. Hopefully the job would be as easy as the man at Home Depot said it would be.

Looping the bucket handle over her arm, she stepped up on the first rung and closed her eyes for a moment. *Please don't let me fall, Father.*

With a deep breath she began to climb and got about halfway when she heard Harry's voice.

"Hold on, hold on!"

She turned and saw him scurrying toward her.

"Crud!" she exclaimed, wondering what he wanted now.

"Just hang on a minute," he said, out of breath.

"I appreciate your concern, Harry, but I really do have to climb up there, even if neither of us is happy about it."

"I'm sorry, I just don't have a good feeling about you going up there. Your grandmother told me if you ever came to live here, I needed to watch out for you."

Jocelyn took a step down the rung. "She did?" she asked him.

"Yes, yes. She said she hoped you would come since you were the only relative she wanted to have live in her home."

"Thank you for telling me that," she said, feeling peace with the knowledge.

"Now, I'm pretty sure she just—"

"Hello?" a voice from around the side of the house called.

"Back here, Jack," Harry answered.

Jack? Jack! What is he doing here?

Harry exchanged glances with Jocelyn. "I thought you could use some help."

Chapter Nine

The bearded repairman walked around the corner before she had a chance to respond.

"Jack, thanks for coming so fast," Harry said, as Jocelyn reached the ground.

"You said it was an emergency," Jack said, giving Jocelyn only a quick glance.

"Did I?" Harry answered. "Well, I suppose it would be better to say I was trying to avoid an emergency. You see, my new neighbor, Jocelyn, is climbing up on her roof. She had birds in her chimney."

The comment struck her funny. "Sounds a bit like I have bats in my belfry, doesn't it?" she said to Harry.

Harry chuckled and so did she. Jack, however, didn't find it amusing.

"I'm not sure how this involves me, or an emergency," Jack said, clearly annoyed.

"Jocelyn needs to cover the chimney, and I don't feel good about her going up on her roof. I would hate to see her fall. Her grandmother told me that she would haunt me forever if something happened to her granddaughter."

Jocelyn's mouth dropped open. "She actually said that?"

"Yes. And if I know Cora, she meant it!" Harry replied.

"I'm sorry . . . Jack," she stumbled over his name like she wasn't sure she was allowed to address him directly in this conversation or not. "You really don't have to help me. And Harry, my grandmother won't haunt you, because I'm not going to fall."

Jack reached for the bucket. "I'm already here. I might as well give it a shot."

"I apologize. I had no idea Harry had called you."

"It's not a big deal," Jack said. "I'm sure it won't take long."

He looked at the bucket, shook his head, then began to climb up the ladder. "Harry, why don't you hold that for me so it doesn't tip," he commanded.

Harry held one side, and Jocelyn held the other. As soon as she thought Jack was out of earshot, Jocelyn said in a low tone, "I could have done this. You didn't need to call him."

"I didn't want you to fall. And you'll note that Jack *did* want someone to hold the ladder for him," Harry said, raising one eyebrow.

"Point taken."

"Besides, Jack needed to come out here anyway," Harry said.

"He's not too happy about it," she said.

"Aw, don't mind Jack. He's got a heart of gold. Don't let him fool ya. If you'd fallen he would have been mad at me for not callin' in the first place. I just decided to skip the part where you fall."

"Well, thank you," she said. "But next time give me some warning . . . and I'll try not to act so much like a three-year-old."

"Deal," Harry said. Then he called to Jack, "How is it going up there?"

"Just fine," he answered. "The covering over the flue is torn. That's how the birds are getting in. I've put the new mesh over it, so there shouldn't be any more visitors."

"Thank you," Jocelyn called out, not sure whether he cared whether she appreciated it or not. He was hard to read.

After a bit more banging and thumping, he finished the project and started down the ladder.

He descended quickly and was on the ground a moment later.

Again he explained, "It looks like there was some old mesh still up there, but the birds probably tore a hole in it. You shouldn't have any more trouble."

"That's good, because some birds attacked her in her house just yesterday," Harry said.

"I actually was here when it happened," he said.

"You were?" Harry responded. "And you didn't help her?"

"She seemed to have things under control," Jack said, giving her a quick glance with a raised eyebrow.

The vision of how she must have looked with the tennis racket and wearing a hooded jacket popped into her head.

"Well, it doesn't matter now. The problem has been fixed. Jack, thank you for your help," Harry said, patting the taller man on the shoulder. "And you," he turned to Jocelyn, "I don't want to see you up on the roof or on any other structure. You ask for help when you need something. You hear me?"

"Yes, sir . . . I mean, Harry." She felt like a child, but still, it was nice to have someone care about her welfare, haunting grandmother or not.

"Glad to help," Jack said.

"Yes," Jocelyn said. "Thank you. How much do I owe you?"

"I'll take care of it," Harry interjected. "I'm the one who called him, and he's on his way to my house to take care of some things anyway."

She didn't want to be a burden. "No, you don't—"

"I know I don't, but let me anyway, just this once."

She nodded appreciatively. "That's very kind of you."

"I'll carry the ladder back to your house," Jack told Harry. Harry gave him a nod, and Jack picked up the ladder. "I guess you're all set, then," Jack said to Jocelyn.

"Yes. And thank you. I believe I could have done it, but given my inexperience, he's right. I could have easily fallen."

"Don't thank me, thank Harry."

Jocelyn gathered up the tools and supplies then paused to watch Harry make his way back to his house. She was grateful that her chimney was fixed, but she wasn't sure she appreciated getting that Jack person involved. He had seemed so nice at first, but now it was like he had an emotional brick wall around him that was reinforced with barbed wire and cut glass. She didn't know what the guy's problem was, but she made a note to stay out of his way. She had enough problems of her own.

* * *

With the chimney taken care of and off her list, she began her next project: painting the living room. She knew it wasn't a crucial repair, but she'd decided that freshening things up could help give her the energy she'd needed to learn how to fix the rest of the stuff.

She pulled the front room furniture into the center of the room and covered it and the hardwood floor with drop cloths. There wasn't much furniture to move, actually. Her grandmother lived sparsely and never fussed about worldly possessions.

Jocelyn was frugal but did like to surround herself with beautiful things, even on a budget. She had only truly indulged her extravagant side once in all the years she'd been working—and not only had her grandmother encouraged her, she'd made it possible. After Jocelyn had been saving for several years to buy a painting by her favorite artist, her grandmother had offered to help. She would always be grateful for that—not just the financial support, but her grandmother's understanding of how much the painting meant to her. Jocelyn had taken an art class her sophomore year in college in which she studied different artists and different genres of art. There had been one contemporary artist, Pablo Bocelli, whose work she had fallen in love with.

Bocelli painted landscapes of the Tuscan countryside, and every time she looked at one of his paintings she felt a remarkable sense of peace and serenity. He used the rolling hills as backgrounds then filled the painting with color from vineyards, orchards, and flowers such as poppies, lavender, and ivy geraniums. His sunlit archways with Romanesque architecture, romantic villas, or stucco breezeways that led to bright blue waters carried her away. So, at the age of nineteen, she had made two goals: to one day travel to Italy so she could visit Tuscany up close and personal and to own a Bocelli original.

For years she'd watched for his artwork to become available at a price she could afford, and when *Verona Poppies* became available, she knew it was worth every penny and more—except that the price was more than she had in her savings. She told her grandmother how sad she was that she was still a little short, and to her surprise her grandmother insisted on paying the difference. Thirty-five hundred dollars later she was the proud owner of a Bocelli original. She knew it was worth much more now, perhaps double the price she paid for it, but to her it was worth more than just money. And she had her grandmother to thank for making it possible.

The painting now rested against the living-room wall, where she would hang it once she had the walls done. Being able to hang her framed work of art on a wall in her grandmother's living room was one of the factors motivating her to get the room painted. She wanted to make it look as charming as one of the Tuscan homes out of a Bocelli painting.

Maybe she could find a thrift store and pick up a few pieces she could cover up or refinish. She wanted a more comfortable couch and chair, and, if possible, she'd like a prettier end table and coffee table.

Unfortunately she knew that even thrift store furniture was out of the question until she could get some repairs done and reexamine her financial situation.

After getting a fresh coat of paint on the ceiling, she took a break with a cold bottled water and a handful of Goldfish crackers.

Between bites, she checked her phone and found a text message from Andrea. Instead of texting back she decided to call. She was in the mood to talk to someone, and she wanted to know how Andrea was doing. After four rings, Andrea's voice mail clicked on. Jocelyn didn't bother leaving a message since they had talked earlier that day anyway.

She got the same response from Emma, which was no surprise. Emma rarely answered her phone anymore. Jocelyn left a message asking Emma to call back. She really wanted to see how she was doing. Jocelyn didn't know what to think about her boyfriend, but if he made Emma happy she would find a way to like him.

Chloe's machine also picked up. Jocely left a cheerful message and told Chloe not to worry about calling back. She didn't want to add anything else to Chloe's to-do list.

She was convinced Lauryn would be out with Jace on a Saturday night, but she tried her phone anyway. At least her friends would know she was thinking of them, even if they weren't thinking of her!

"Hello."

"Lauryn, hi. It's Jocelyn."

"Joss! It's so good to hear your voice. How are you? Are you getting settled?"

Jocelyn heard music and talking in the background.

"Slowly. My grandmother's house needs a lot of work."

"You found a place to work? That's great. Where did you say it was?" Lauryn asked.

"No, I said my grandmother's house needs a lot of work."

"Oh, sorry. Jace, honey, can you come and get this platter?"

"I've caught you at a bad time," Jocelyn said. "I'll let you go."

"We just have a few friends over," Lauryn told her. "But I really want an update. Can I call you tomorrow?"

"Sure, I'd like that," Jocelyn answered. "Give my love to Jace."

"I will, sweetie. Can't wait to hear about everything."

They said good-bye, and Jocelyn hung up the phone, wondering what she'd do now.

She decided to tape off the baseboards and other trim so she could paint them next. That chore took longer than she expected, so by the time she was done, she decided to call it a day and go to bed.

After checking the locks on the doors and turning out the lights, she paused by the chimney before she went upstairs. To her relief, all was quiet. Hopefully her problem was solved.

Once she changed into her Hello Kitty pajamas—a gift from Chloe's daughters—and washed her face and brushed her teeth, she was about to turn off the light when she stepped in something wet. Had she splashed that much water when she brushed her teeth? She opened the cupboard under the sink with trepidation.

"Crud!" She ran downstairs and grabbed her bucket then dashed back upstairs. The less water that dripped, the less mess she had to clean up.

"I can't believe this has gotten worse in just two days," she muttered. "I guess it's a good thing I got that home-repairs book."

She moved away the little dish she'd placed under the pipe the day before, mopped up the puddle with a towel, then slid the bucket under the leaking pipe and made sure it was positioned to catch the increasing drips.

Realizing she would have to address this problem first thing Monday, she approached the bed with a sigh. She was ready to collapse.

Kneeling in prayer, Jocelyn found that she had to really stretch to find things to be grateful for. She was grateful that the people of Milford Falls had been friendly—mostly, anyway. She was grateful that she wouldn't have birds swooping in on her in her sleep and pecking her eyes out—assuming that this Jack character had done the job right. She was grateful she had a home—even though it was falling apart. She was grateful for a chance to have a new beginning and a new adventure—kind of.

She then asked that Heavenly Father help her adjust quickly to her new life, that the job at the school would work out, and that she wouldn't feel so alone.

Closing her prayer she climbed into bed and thought about her situation. For some reason everything seemed worse at night, and tonight was no exception. She began to doubt her decision to move. Was she really up to this? She'd never been a risk taker, and this had been the ultimate risk. She thought about her friends and their encouragement and support in this decision. Where were they now?

Tears gathered in the corners of her eyes. It wasn't just the present situation that was making things hard. Just being there, knowing that her grandmother was gone for good, made it difficult. She would never see her grandmother outside in her garden or hanging clothes on the clothesline because she preferred the outdoor freshness to the smell of laundry sheets. Her grandmother would never bake her special chocolate chip cookies for her again or sing hymns as she peeled potatoes for her delicious potato salad.

Her heart ached as she recalled memories, both good and difficult, inside that home. Some of her best experiences had been there, but so were some of her most challenging. Being there made her recall both, and they were equally as painful.

She began to wonder if she was really supposed to stay there long-term. Maybe her whole purpose in coming had been to realize how much work her grandmother's house needed and that she just needed to sell it.

Feeling overwhelmed, Jocelyn wiped the tears from her cheeks with her sleeve and noticed the silhouette of her scriptures on the nightstand. Turning on the bedside lamp, she reached for her triple combination. She'd recently read a talk about having strength during struggles and had marked several scripture references provided. She turned to the first one, hoping it would give her some comfort.

In Doctrine and Covenants 38:7 she read, "I say unto you that mine eyes are upon you. I am in your midst and ye cannot see me."

She wanted to believe that He was there, but she was having trouble seeing His hand in her life. Of course, getting help with her chimney today had been a blessing, even though that Jack guy had acted like it was such an imposition. But Harry—he definitely was a blessing.

She turned to Doctrine and Covenants 88:63–64. "Draw near unto me and I will draw near unto you; seek me diligently and ye shall find me; ask and ye shall receive; knock, and it shall be opened unto you. Whatsoever ye ask the Father in my name it shall be given unto you, that is expedient for you."

Was that part of the reason she was supposed to be here? So she would rely more upon the Lord?

Finally she turned to Ether 12:27. As a missionary this had been her favorite scripture. "I give unto men weakness that they may be humble; and my grace is sufficient for all men that humble themselves before me;

for if they humble themselves before me, and have faith in me, then will I make weak things become strong unto them."

Jocelyn felt ashamed that she had gotten weaker instead of stronger over the years. As a missionary she'd been focused, unwavering. Now she was filled with doubt and uncertainty. Was this one of the reasons she'd felt she was supposed to move? So she could be humbled and exercise more faith so she could become strong?

She closed the book as new tears surfaced. She didn't want to go through what it would take to make her strong again. It was too hard.

Yet she did want things to get better. She did want to improve. But what did He expect from her? She wasn't sure she had what it took left inside of her.

Regrets churned in her head, causing her to feel agitated and upset. Why had she uprooted herself like this? Her home was in St. George. At least there she was around friends, people who knew her, and familiar faces and surroundings. At least there she didn't have to be alone and miserable. And cold. She pulled the covers up to her chin. It got chilly at night here.

What were you thinking? she asked herself. She knew the answer as quickly as she thought it. She was thinking that it was time for a change. It was time to step outside her comfort zone, challenge herself, and grow. Comfort zones were boring, right? Well, she'd give anything to be bored back in St. George right now.

Chapter Ten

Either the water was rising or Jocelyn was sinking, she wasn't sure. But water was almost up to her nose, and she couldn't hold her breath any longer.

With a gasp for air, Jocelyn sat straight up in bed, covered in a cold sweat.

She continued to pull in gulps of fresh air, wondering if she'd held her breath during her dream.

Lately her dreams had become terrifying, and this one was no exception. It had seemed so real. She'd always had a fear of drowning, and now, to have a dream about it, freaked her out. Had she dreamed about it because she was feeling so overwhelmed and out of control at the moment?

It certainly made sense. She did feel like she was drowning in some respects. But to hold her breath like that while asleep . . . scary.

She shook her head, remnants of the nightmare troubling her. It was the sound of water she wanted to be free of—the sound of running water. But the sound wasn't just in her head. A quick glance outside told her that it wasn't rain.

"My bucket!" she yelped then flew out of bed, only to come to an abrupt stop at the bathroom door. The floor was completely covered in water, and when she opened the cupboard door, the bucket was overflowing from the steady stream coming from the pipes.

She needed to shut off the main water valve, but where could that be?

Calm down, she told herself. She needed to think. It couldn't be that hard. It had to be on the main floor somewhere.

She raced down the stairs, her wet feet slipping as she turned the corner into the kitchen where she skidded to a halt, her body slamming into the table and chairs, bruising her hip and thigh.

The ceiling was dripping a steady stream of water, and portions of the drywall had crashed to the floor.

"Ahh!" she screamed in panic. Now what did she do?

She grabbed her cell phone and prayed that Harry was home. Five rings later his machine picked up and an automated voice asked her to leave a message. Where could he be?

Time was of the essence. Another clump of ceiling fell and landed with a heavy splat.

Frantically she looked for the ward phone list. She hated having to call, but she couldn't think of a better option.

First she tried the bishop's house, but there was no answer. Then she tried the Relief Society president. Again, no answer. It was only an hour before church—they probably had some sort of meeting. So maybe someone would be at the church building.

As much as she hated bothering people with her problems, this was an emergency.

She dialed the bishop's office.

On the fourth ring, a man answered.

"Hello," she said, fighting to keep her voice controlled, "my name is Jocelyn Rogers and I just moved into the ward. I'm Cora Randolph's granddaughter."

"Sister Rogers, how are you? This is Lenny Hewitt, a member of the bishopric."

"I am so sorry to bother you, but I have a huge problem." She fought to keep control of her emotions, but she was on the verge of tears. "My upstairs bathroom flooded, and my kitchen ceiling is caving in. I don't know where the main water valve is to shut it off."

Without waiting a second, Brother Hewitt said, "Sit tight. I'll have someone there in two minutes!"

As soon as she hung up the phone, she tore herself away from the horrors of watching her disintegrating ceiling and ran back upstairs. If she could empty the bucket and catch some of the water, it might help a little. Luckily she had her grandmother's towels as well as her own, so she had plenty to throw on the floor to soak up some of the mess.

Barely able to lift the bucket, she sloshed over to the bathtub and dumped the contents. Water splashed everywhere, but at this point it didn't matter.

She shoved the bucket under the sink again, and water flowed into the bucket in a steady stream.

Pulling towels out of the closet, she threw them all over the floor, hoping to soak up as much water as she could. They were immediately drenched, but hopefully they would prevent water from pouring onto the kitchen floor below.

A banging at the front door caused her to jump, and she sped back downstairs. She yanked the door open and saw an unfamiliar man in a suit and tie. Behind him was MJ and . . . Jack? Alongside Jack was his friend Lenny, the guy she'd seen with him at Home Depot. Connecting the dots she realized this was the same Lenny who'd answered the phone at the church.

"Come in!" she exclaimed. "I don't know where the water main is—I guess that's the first thing we need to figure out."

"I'm Bishop Wilson," the unfamiliar man said. "Welcome to the ward." He flashed a quick but sympathetic smile at her and started heading through the house. "I think your valve is by your washer and dryer hookups. I had to shut it off once for your grandmother a few years back."

"Thank goodness." Jocelyn followed him into the laundry room and, sure enough, behind a small cupboard door was a shut-off valve.

Just to have the source turned off was a relief.

"Now," the bishop said, "let's see what's going on."

"I feel terrible pulling you away from church."

"When the ox is in the mire, you don't just leave him there," the bishop said. "Don't worry about it. We can get this mess cleaned up in a hurry."

Lenny examined the damage to the kitchen ceiling while MJ started cleaning up the soggy drywall with a dust pan and some towels.

"Where's Jack?" the bishop asked.

"He went upstairs to find the leak," Lenny said. "I just hope he doesn't come crashing through the ceiling." He looked overhead then took a wide step sideways.

Jack did appear but came by way of the stairs, thank goodness. By the look on his face, the prognosis wasn't good.

"What do you think?" the bishop asked.

"The plumbing in this house must be over fifty years old, and it looks like it's not all copper. You've got some rust and rotting pipes. You're lucky that you just had one leak. I'm guessing there's also some leaking behind the shower wall."

The news didn't surprise her. Why not have rotting pipes? It perfectly matched her rotten life.

"Oh, honey." MJ put her arms around Jocelyn's shoulders. "Don't try and think about all of this right now. Let's just get things cleaned up, and then we can talk about how to get it all fixed later."

"You will have to make some decisions soon," Jack said matter-of-factly. "You can't use that upstairs bathroom until the pipes are fixed, and I'd worry about damage being done elsewhere in the house."

Thank you, Mr. Sunshine! she wanted to say.

"You must be freezing in those wet clothes," MJ said. "Why don't you go change. I can clean the rest of this mess, then we can take care of the bathroom."

Jocelyn was horrified. She'd forgotten that she was running around in her Hello Kitty pajamas.

In her room she changed into sweats and a pair of crosstrainers.

The three men's voices stopped when she came back downstairs. They looked at her with guilty expressions. She guessed they were talking about what an ignoramus she was. And they were right. What was she thinking, coming here and living in this house? She should have sold it the minute she became the owner of it.

Before coming to Milford Falls she hadn't felt ready to sell her grandmother's house, but she was ready now. She couldn't imagine why she'd been so reluctant about it before. It was just a house, after all. Besides, Grandmother had always just wanted her to be happy, and Jocelyn was pretty sure that living here was not going to bring her anything but anxiety and distress.

While the two women mopped up the mess, the three men examined the rest of the house as best they could. She heard some pounding, which made her more than a little nervous. On the bright side, they said they'd shut off all the valves in the upstairs bathroom so water could still flow to the rest of the house, which gave Jocelyn a main floor bathroom with a tub. It wasn't ideal but it was functional at least.

Twisting the top of a black trash bag, Jocelyn fastened a tie around it to hold the waterlogged remnants of her kitchen ceiling. She began to drag the bag across the floor to put it outside the back door until garbage day, whenever that was.

"Here," Lenny said, "I can get that for you." He carried the bag outside then joined everyone back in the kitchen.

"From what we can judge," Bishop Wilson said, "you need some extensive pipe work done. And this is also going to require some substantial holes in your walls and ceilings to get the job done."

Jocelyn swallowed. That didn't sound cheap, nor like something she could do herself.

"You can pay a professional plumber," he said, "or Jack here said he can work on it in the evenings."

"It will probably take a couple of weeks, unless we find some surprises," Jack said then added, "like mold, termites—"

"Now, now," MJ said, putting her arm around Jocelyn, who felt like crumbling to the floor. "Don't give her more to worry about." She gave Jocelyn a squeeze. "They won't find anything else," she assured Jocelyn. "Don't you worry." But Jocelyn was worried, and now, a little nauseated. She doubted she could afford to fix the plumbing—plus anything else they found. And she wasn't sure she would be comfortable having Jack there every evening.

"Jack here's the best," Lenny said. "He won't charge you an arm and a leg, either."

She smiled awkwardly. "I'd want a bid on the cost, and I'll need to think about it before I commit," she told them. "If that's okay."

MJ gave her another one-armed hug. "Of course it is. And why don't you plan on coming over to my house after church and having dinner with us. You could probably use a home-cooked meal. We can talk about the situation then and help you figure things out."

"Oh no," she declined. "You don't need to do that. I'm fine."

"I won't take no for an answer. Jack, why don't you come too? You can help us come up with a plan."

He didn't refuse fast enough.

"I—"

"Be there about two thirty," she instructed both of them. "And Jack, why don't you pick up Jocelyn here and bring her with you, since she doesn't know the way to my house?"

Jack opened his mouth to speak then closed it again. It wouldn't do him any good.

"Hey, what about me?" Lenny asked.

"Your wife probably wants you home to eat with your family," MJ told him.

"If she's making meatloaf again, I'll be over with my kids too," Lenny replied.

"Not a big meatloaf fan, huh? Well, I'm sure it's delicious anyway. The brownies she brought yesterday were to die for. Now, I've got to get back to the church before Relief Society starts. Jocelyn, would you want to come? I can wait while you change."

Jocelyn couldn't see why not. There was nothing to be done here that couldn't wait. "Sure. Thank you," she said, then she looked at the bishop and the other men. "And thank you all for your help. I didn't know who to call."

"Happy to help," the bishop said as Lenny nodded in agreement.

"Course, Lenny here will do anything to get out of Sunday School, won't you, Len?" Jack said.

"I'm sorry, but can I help it if I have low blood sugar and need to get something to eat before sacrament?"

"Ding Dongs and Peanut M&M's?" Jack asked.

"That's why they call it *low* blood sugar. I need to get sugar back into my system fast."

"We have sacrament meeting last," MJ explained to Jocelyn. "We seem to get a better attendance that way."

"Come on, counselor," the bishop said, "let's get you back to church before you collapse. I've got some cookies in my office from interviews on Thursday."

"You got cookies Thursday? I don't remember seeing any."

"You were in the gym playing basketball instead of doing interviews, remember?" the bishop said.

"Oh," he said with a frown.

"Guess we'll see you at church," the bishop told the two women.

They left while Jocelyn ran upstairs to change again. Even though she felt like crawling back into bed and pulling the covers over her head, she knew she'd be better off at church.

Wishing she'd had a chance to shower and get cleaned up, she pulled her long hair into a ponytail, slipped a white sweater over her wrinkled, light blue linen dress, slid her feet into white ballet flats, and called it good. At least her first impression would be pathetic enough that anything from this point would be an improvement.

In the car, MJ assured Jocelyn again she'd done the right thing in calling the church.

"Bishop Wilson is such a great guy—really caring—the type who would do anything for you."

"I was so surprised a busy bishop would show up on a Sunday morning like that."

"That's just the way he is."

"And Lenny is one of his counselors?" Jocelyn asked.

"Yes. Hard to believe, I know. He's as bad as a teenager sometimes. But then again, he relates to the youth. They really love him," MJ explained.

"I bet; he seems really fun. And what about Jack? Is he also in the ward?"

"Yes, though I know he doesn't look it. Jack's an all-around great guy. He's very private, almost prickly sometimes, but he'd do anything for anyone, too. He's usually the first to show up for a service project. He grumbles a lot, but that's just a smoke screen for how kind his heart really is."

Jocelyn nodded thoughtfully. That did fit with what she'd seen so far.

"You know, I really don't want to become the ward service project."

MJ laughed. "You don't know our ward. We love having things like this to work on together. You should have seen the Saturday the ward put a new roof on Brother Murphy's house. We had so many bodies there we had to come up with other projects to do. He got his garden weeded, his lawn mowed, and some shutters painted. The Relief Society always feeds all the volunteers. It's more fun than work most of the time."

"Please don't get me wrong, all of that sounds great, but I'm wondering if I should scrap my plans to live here and just sell it."

"Sell it! You just moved here! It's a charming home. It's just old and needs some improvements."

"That's the problem. I may not have the resources to fix it up, and I definitely don't have the know-how."

MJ turned the car into the church parking lot. "Well, don't put up a For Sale sign just yet. We might be able to get a lot of the labor done by the members."

Jocelyn knew that MJ was trying to be helpful, but maybe this whole leaky pipe thing was a sign that she was supposed to go back home to St. George. Is that what the Lord had in mind for her? She wondered if she could possibly sell the house as is. Somebody out there had to be looking for a fixer-upper. Didn't they?

"Come on," MJ said. "Let's go introduce you to the members. You're going to love our ward."

* * *

Grateful the first two meetings were over, Jocelyn followed the crowd as members made their way toward sacrament meeting.

She had been welcomed briefly in Sunday School, and then the teacher focused on the lesson, but in Relief Society MJ had fussed over her and insisted she stand. Jocelyn couldn't bring herself to say she might not be staying permanently, so she smiled and nodded as the sisters welcomed her with enthusiasm. She was surprised to see the blond woman from Home Depot—the one she suspected was Jack's girlfriend—sitting toward the back of the room. The woman was beautiful in some ways, but her platinum hair, fake-and-bake tan, heavy makeup, and tight-fitting clothes seemed incongruent in a Relief Society room.

Jocelyn wasn't sure if it was her imagination or not, but as she was getting introduced she thought she had seen Sister Blondie give her a very calculating glare. At least that was how Jocelyn had felt when the woman's eyes were on her.

No matter what, Jocelyn was just glad most of the initial welcomes were over. As a missionary, she'd had to get over her fears of being in charge, having all eyes on her, and being the focus of people's attention. Adjusting to new areas, new wards, and new companions was all part of missionary life. But in the years since, she'd built up the walls of her comfort zone to high levels again, and it was very difficult stepping outside those boundaries.

There were many things she'd done as a missionary that now, looking back, amazed her. Where had that outgoing, take-charge person gone?

She entered the chapel where she saw MJ waving her over and patting the spot next to her on a bench. Next to MJ were two teenage boys.

Jocelyn smiled and made her way to the bench, but not before several members shook her hand and welcomed her. She had to admit she'd never felt so welcome, though it was almost to the point of suffocation.

"Glad you made it," MJ said when Jocelyn sat down next to her. "I didn't mean to leave you behind."

Jocelyn assured her that she hadn't felt abandoned. Even though she was amongst a sea of unfamiliar faces, she couldn't deny that the feeling and the spirit of the meeting were the same she'd felt back in St. George.

Settling back into her seat, she felt a peaceful relaxation take over. Prelude music from the organ bathed her nerves, and the congregation began to calm down in anticipation of the meeting getting started.

Just as she felt all the tension subsiding, she was jarred out of her tranquility by the face of a man staring at her. It was Karl Goodrich, and he was smiling at her.

She swallowed hard and smiled weakly in return. Luckily the bishop stood, and she shifted her glance forward.

The meeting got underway with an opening song and prayer followed by a few announcements, including plans for the Fourth of July festivities. It sounded like town events and ward events were closely intertwined, which sort of surprised her.

Finally the sacrament was administered, and Jocelyn spent her time in prayer and meditation, trying to find out what the Lord's will for her was. She received no promptings, but decided to ask the Lord again after she'd had a chance to further study out her options.

After the meeting was over, Jocelyn felt like kicking herself for not driving to church in her own car. She was ready to get out of there, but MJ apparently felt compelled to continue showing her around.

After introducing someone from the Young Women organization and a couple of women in Primary, MJ said, "You'll have to meet my husband at dinner. He's on the high council and had to speak in another ward. You're probably anxious to get home. I just need to turn in these receipts then we can leave. I wish my oldest son, Jeffrey, was here; he could give you a lift home. He went to Seattle last night and ended up staying over with friends."

She stood in the foyer, waiting for MJ, whose sons had hitched rides home with friends. This was the last time she would get stuck waiting on another person, she assured herself.

She was surprised but also relieved that she hadn't run into Jack yet. Maybe he was avoiding her. She wouldn't blame him if he was.

"Well, well, what a nice surprise," a man's voice said.

She turned to see Karl Goodrich walking toward her.

Forcing a smile, she prayed that MJ would hurry up.

"You don't happen to need a ride home, do you?" he said.

"Actually, no, I don't. Sister Gentry is giving me a ride."

"I think she's busy in the bishop's office. I'm going your way. I'd be happy to take you."

"Ah, well, I . . . I'm . . ." She didn't think quickly on her feet.

"I feel it's the least I can do after giving you a ticket. I feel pretty bad about that."

"Oh, well. I was speeding, after all." *She couldn't believe she was saying that.*

"It's possible I could reduce your ticket to a warning."

She appreciated his offer but just couldn't find herself accepting it. She didn't want to feel obligated to him in any way.

And why was he being so nice to her all of a sudden?

"It's no trouble. I have the power to change it."

She tried not to smile at his puffed-up use of the word *power.* Maybe he was just being nice and had no ulterior motive. But he seemed to have more in mind than just being nice, and she wanted to avoid giving him the wrong message. He just wasn't her type. Of course, she didn't really have a *type,* but that was beside the point.

Before he could make any more peace offerings, MJ came rushing down the hallway.

"Karl!" she exclaimed. "What are you still doing here?"

"I had a short Sunday School presidency meeting. I'm the official bell ringer," he told Jocelyn proudly, then turned back to MJ. "I was just offering our new ward member a ride home."

"That's sweet of you, but she's coming with me."

Jocelyn gave him a shrug, like it was out of her hands, and said, "Thanks anyway."

"Tell your mom I'll call her about visiting teaching this evening," MJ told him.

"Fine," he said, disgruntled. Then he turned and walked out the glass doors.

MJ shook her head. "Bless his heart. A little odd, but such a nice young man."

Together they walked to MJ's car. The day was beautiful and clear. Jocelyn stopped to take in a deep breath of the pine-scented air, so fresh and clean.

She opened the door and stopped. Two butterflies near the back of the car had caught her eye. They danced and swirled around each other in the air, a floating waltz of color and grace. She couldn't look at butterflies and not think of her friends, of their prayers and support, and not feel hopeful. Maybe everything wasn't as dismal as she'd been telling herself.

"So, how did you like the ward?"

She smiled, her heart feeling light for the moment. "Very friendly. I've never been so overwhelmed with welcomes. It felt like everyone in the ward made a point to meet me."

"We're like a family, so to them you are like a new member of the family," MJ told her. MJ turned onto the lane leading to Jocelyn's grandmother's house then said, "I talked to the bishop about arranging for some help to do the repairs on the house. He's going to call the elders quorum president and see what we can do." She explained about all of the talented people in the ward that would most likely be able to help.

"Oh, I really don't want to be a burden—"

"Nonsense. We want to help you. Of course, we won't force ourselves on you, but just think of all the blessings we could get helping you. You wouldn't want to rob us of those, would you?" MJ gave her a wink and pulled up in front of her house.

"I'm just not used to accepting much help, I guess," Jocelyn confided. "I don't really know how to handle it."

MJ patted her hand. "Listen, sweetie, we all loved your grandmother very much, and she spent a great deal of time serving and giving to everyone around her. This is our chance to give something back to her." She tilted her head and studied Jocelyn for a moment. "You're a lot like her. I can tell you're smart and independent and that you have a good heart. We don't want to step on your toes, but we also don't want you to do this alone."

Jocelyn swallowed and cleared her throat as an unexpected rush of emotion caught her off guard. "Thank you," she managed to say.

"You're very welcome. Now, I'll see you for dinner a little later. I believe Brother Emerson said he'd pick you up."

"Brother Emerson?"

"Sorry. Jack Emerson, the fellow who was here at your house earlier."

"Oh, right. I didn't catch his last name before. You know, I don't want to put him out. I could drive if you just gave me directions."

"It's a little tricky," MJ said. "And I'm sure he doesn't mind."

"Don't take this question the wrong way, but I take it he's single, then?" She wasn't asking out of personal interest; she figured it would be wise to find out. She'd had enough awkwardness to last a lifetime.

"Yes, he is. Many have tried to change that, but I don't think he dates much, if at all. I think it has something to do with his first wife."

"He's divorced?" She hoped she didn't sound like she was prying.

"No, the poor soul. He lost his wife and daughter in a car accident. That's really all I know. Jack moved here about ten years ago. He is a convert, and that has helped get him out of his shell a bit."

Jocelyn nodded as she took in the information. "I guess I'll see you later, then. You certainly don't need to do this."

"I always make a large Sunday meal. I love to invite company over to eat. Sometimes it's the missionaries and their investigators, sometimes it's visitors to the area. I love to cook and entertain."

"Can I bring anything?" Jocelyn asked automatically then kicked herself.

"Heavens, no. Just your appetite."

"I'm glad you said that, because all I could offer is half a bag of fun-size Snickers."

MJ laughed then drove away with a wave.

Chapter Eleven

Jocelyn nervously paced around the room, waiting for "Brother Emerson" to pick her up. She really wished that she hadn't agreed to go to dinner. Already she felt awkward and she wasn't even in his truck. The man made her feel uneasy.

She glanced up to the ceiling in her kitchen and groaned again. What a mess. Monday morning she'd call to look into getting her old job back and then track down a real estate agent to find out what selling the house would entail. Maybe she could get the house fixed and sold and be back in St. George by the end of summer so she could get back in time to start school. She also needed to remember to thank her friends for their advice . . . their *bad* advice.

A movement out the window and the flash of a maroon vehicle caught her eye.

He's here.

She had a perfectly good TV dinner in the freezer. Why had she accepted MJ's invitation so readily?

As he knocked she realized she hadn't brought down her shoes. She answered the door, silently berating herself for her mindlessness.

"You ready to go?" Jack asked.

She nodded. "Yes. Well, mostly. Come in. I just have to grab my shoes."

He came inside the living room and stood while she ran upstairs to get her shoes, worried the whole time that he was going to be angry for having to wait for her.

Shoving her feet into her shoes, she hurried back down the stairs and found him studying her Bocelli painting.

"I'm really sorry you got stuck having to pick me up. I offered to drive myself, but MJ wouldn't hear of it."

"It's no problem. It's a little tricky getting there," he explained. "By the way, this is a really nice painting."

"Thank you," she said, surprised but pleased at the compliment. "It's an original Pablo Bocelli. I love his use of warm colors and how he draws you in with his . . ."

His head was tilted as he listened. She felt stupid for running off with her mouth.

"Sorry," she said. "I get overenthusiastic."

"No, go on. It's interesting."

"Well, I feel like Bocelli's style is like an invitation, like he wants you to join him in admiring, appreciating, even experiencing what he experiences when he's painting one of his pictures. Whether it's a landscape like this one or just a flowered archway in a villa, you get a sense of what it would be like to be in the picture, to feel the warm sun on your face, to smell the fragrant flowers, or feel the brush of the breeze against your skin."

Again, she was rambling.

"Sorry."

"No need to apologize. I never really listened in art class. Guess I was missing something. The way you're talking about the painting really helps me appreciate it on another level." Suddenly he turned and walked to the front door. "Guess we'd better get going."

For a moment Jocelyn had actually felt like Jack was someone who might become a friend. And while that might be true, she could see that becoming friends might be a long, rocky process.

Pulling the door shut behind her she climbed into the passenger side of his truck—no easy feat since the truck was three feet off the ground and she was still in her church clothes.

As soon as she got the door shut, he put the truck in drive and took off. She quickly fastened her seat belt and tried not to tip over as he turned the corner.

She reminded herself of his painful past and tried to imagine how hard it would be to have lost the two greatest loves of his life. She didn't know how she would deal with something like that. If he wasn't into dating, he probably really didn't appreciate having to pick her up for dinner. Not that it was a date, but MJ seemed to be the matchmaking type.

They didn't speak for several minutes. She wanted to break the ice, but she wasn't sure what to talk about and was afraid of being rebuffed.

Finally Jack asked, "So, did you have any more leaking after we got things shut off?"

"No," she said, not sure if he wanted conversation or just an answer. "I can't tell you how much I appreciated your help this morning. I think I panicked."

"Wasn't a problem," he said. "I'm sure you didn't know what to do when you woke up to all that water."

"And my ceiling on the floor."

He actually flashed a sympathetic grin, or was he in pain? She couldn't tell.

She wanted to talk to him about the situation but really hated bothering him. Still, she needed to straighten something out.

"I know you got volunteered to help fix my pipes, but I want you to know you don't have to. I'm sure I can find someone to do it."

"Let me bid it out. I can't promise it will be cheap, but I can promise it will be a lot less than anyone else. Most plumbers will charge you an arm and both your legs," he told her.

She didn't mean to grimace, but she did. She didn't have much money nor an arm and two legs to spare.

"I'm not technically a plumber, but I am a licensed contractor—bonded and insured, in fact." He gave her a wry grin. "I actually have some experience in doing exactly the sort of work your place needs," he said.

"You do?"

He nodded as he turned the truck onto a dirt road that went through a field. "I had to do the same thing to my house a few years ago. I was able to catch the leak before much damage was done, though."

"Are our houses about the same age? Do you know?"

"I'm guessing they are. Similar styles, too. Yours is bigger, though, and your property is twice as big as mine."

"I don't know what I would ever do with all of this property if I were to stay."

"You're thinking about not staying?" he asked.

She shook her head. "I'm not sure my original plan makes sense. I'm afraid I've bitten off more than I can chew here. At least in St. George I have friends to help when stuff like this happens. I hate imposing on anyone, let alone strangers."

"Like I said, it's not that big of a deal. I'm free most evenings after I close up shop."

"I'm not sure . . ." She swallowed. How did she say this? "Depending on the total . . . I may not have . . ." She shut her eyes and tried to find some words that would work.

"No hurry. You can pay me whenever, even after the house sells, if you'd like. Do you think you could come up with money for parts?"

"Yes, that shouldn't be a problem."

"Then we can get started."

"Do you think it makes sense to make the repairs if I'm not even staying in it?"

"Yes," he said. "You'll get a better price for the home if the repairs are made."

"I'm sure you're right," she said, wishing she had some idea of what kind of money this was going to take. But in spite of her mixed feelings for the man, she fully believed that having him do the repairs would definitely save her some money. "Thank you, Jack, I think I will take you up on your offer."

The truck rumbled through a cow pasture and over a bridge, then he took a sharp right through the open gate of a white rail fence they'd been following.

She had to put her hand down on the bench seat to prevent her from falling over.

"Sorry, almost missed it."

With a smile she pushed herself upright and straightened her sweater.

Two large dogs came running, barking in a frenzy around her door.

She recoiled and remembered the time a German shepherd had attacked her while she was babysitting at a neighbor's house. His bite had barely broken the skin on her forearm, but it had instilled a healthy fear of dogs. And, of course, now she was also scared of birds. What was next, snakes? No, she already hated snakes.

Jack pulled the truck to a stop, and Jocelyn kept a tight hold on the door handle. She didn't want it open until it was safe.

A man at the front door called the dogs, and they yelped as they obediently ran around to the back of the farmhouse.

"Dang dogs!" he exclaimed as he came toward them and greeted Jack, who was already out of the truck.

The two men shook hands, then the one she didn't know came to open Jocelyn's door. She smiled weakly then glanced at the corner of the house to make sure the coast was clear before bravely stepping out.

"Welcome," the man said. "I'm Brian Gentry, MJ's husband. You must be Jocelyn, Cora's granddaughter."

"I am," Jocelyn said. "Nice to meet you." They shook hands, and he showed them inside the house, where Jocelyn finally relaxed.

"I understand you had a little trouble at your house today," Brian said.

"I did. I guess I've got some rusty pipes that started leaking." She looked at Jack as if to check her explanation. He confirmed it with a nod.

"That's a crummy deal for you. Did your grandmother mention anything about the pipes?"

"No, nothing. But then we didn't usually talk about her house. Maybe if I'd known it would someday be mine I would have asked some questions like this."

"Not the sort of thing you plan on, I suppose. Sounds like you've got the best man on the job, though."

She looked over at Jack, who rolled his eyes and shook his head.

"Don't let him fool ya," Brian said, giving Jack a slap on the back. "This guy can do anything. He built me a shed that, I swear, if we ever have a natural disaster, that's where I'd head for cover. It'll withstand just about anything, it's so solid."

MJ whirled into the room with her apron tied firmly about her waist and a hand towel thrown over her shoulder.

"Hey, guys. Glad to see you made it. Bri, honey, why don't you have our guests sit down."

"I was getting to it," Brian replied. "Good heavens, woman, go stir your gravy. I've got this covered."

"Isn't he darling when he's grumpy?" MJ said, giving him a little snap on the thigh with her towel. She scurried out of the room before he could retaliate.

"You two have a seat and relax a minute. I need to add a few more chairs to the table."

"You need some help?" Jack offered.

"Nope, it'll just take a sec."

Brian was off, leaving them there on the couch.

After a few minutes of silence, Jocelyn decided it was her turn to start the conversation.

"So, how long have you lived in Milford Falls?" It was all she could come up with, even though she knew the answer.

"About ten years," he said.

"I see." She was hoping he'd expound a little, but he didn't. "What brought you here?"

"Not really sure. I just drove through one day and liked how it felt. Can't really explain it."

"Huh. That's kind of unusual."

"You might want to stay a little longer, give the town a chance," he said. "It would grow on you."

"I haven't ruled it out entirely," she said. "But seriously, I don't know what I was thinking coming here."

"It's a good thing you were in the house when that pipe broke. You could have had some irreparable damage."

She hadn't thought about that. "I guess so." Not wanting to think about that right now, she asked, "So, where are you originally from?"

He didn't answer right away. In fact, he paused so long she wasn't sure if he'd even heard her question, or maybe he was ignoring her.

"I was living in LA before I came here, but I grew up in a suburb of Chicago. How about you? Have you lived in St. George all of your life, until you moved here?"

She couldn't believe he was finally making an attempt to further the conversation.

"Mostly, but I went to college in Orem, Utah, and spent eighteen months in Jamaica on a mission."

"Jamaica! Wow, that had to be crazy," he said.

"Actually, it was. Crazy and wonderful. I survived two major hurricanes, but I think driving on the roads there was even more dangerous."

He shook his head with wonder. "I can't imagine what it was like. I almost went there on . . ."

She waited for him to continue.

He backpedaled and said, "I was supposed to go there once but changed plans because of the threat of a hurricane."

"Hey, maybe it was while I was there. I was in Kingston during the worst one, so we weren't hit quite as hard, but some of the towns along the coast were wiped out."

"How was missionary work there?"

"Incredible," she answered. "I met some of the most amazing people. I have some pictures of some of the baptisms being performed in the ocean."

He nodded. "That had to be something to see."

"It was. Unforgettable."

"It's pretty cool you served a mission. I bet your family was proud."

How did she tell him that they didn't really care, especially her mother, who wrote her a total of six times the entire time she was there and once to ask if she had any money!

"Uh, well, not really. None of my immediate family are active. They thought I was crazy for going. But my grandmother supported me, along with my ward and friends."

His expression caught her off guard. He actually looked impressed, or something like that.

"Do you think they'll eventually come around? Your family I mean?"

"You mean, like become active? Probably not, but I still hold out a little hope."

This wasn't a topic she was fond of discussing. She felt uncomfortable explaining about her mother the addict and her other brother in prison. Her youngest brother, who was in Iraq, was living a productive life, but he had nothing to do with the gospel. The discussion was unlikely to go anywhere positive.

They sat for a moment in silence. It was obvious dinner wasn't quite ready, but whatever MJ was cooking smelled heavenly and made Jocelyn's stomach growl.

"You want me to go see if MJ has a piece of bread or a roll or something?" he offered.

She was embarrassed he'd heard her stomach. "Thank you, I'm fine. With all the excitement this morning I forgot to eat."

"I'm sure it won't be much longer." He crossed his ankles and leaned back against the couch cushion. "So, what is it you do for a living?"

"Before I came here, I taught school in St. George."

"Really? My mom was a schoolteacher. What grade do you teach?"

"I'm an art teacher," she said, "most recently in a middle school."

One of MJ's son's came into the room. "My mom said she was sorry it took so long, but we're almost ready now if you want to come on in."

Jocelyn and Jack got to their feet and followed him into the kitchen and dining area.

MJ's husband had a woman's apron tied around his waist. He was stirring something on the stove and whistling a Church hymn. One of her sons was filling water glasses, and the other one was carving a large pot roast. Jocelyn couldn't help but pause for a moment and drink in the sight of the family working in harmony to put the meal together.

She caught Jack looking at her and quickly flashed a smile then said, "Mary Jane, is there something I can do to help?"

"That would be great. Would you mind putting that pan of rolls into this basket? Jack, go ahead and take a seat. Here," she handed him a bowl of steamed green beans, "put these on the table for me."

The meal quickly came together, and soon all of them were seated around the feast.

"We're so happy to have both of you here with us today," MJ said. "Honey," she said to her husband, "do you want to ask someone to give the blessing on the food?"

"I think its Ben's turn," her husband said, directing his comment to the older of the two boys.

Ben folded his arms and bowed his head, waiting a moment for everyone to follow suit.

Again, Jocelyn was touched by the goodness of this family. To see teenage boys helping out in the kitchen, praying when asked, and being kind and respectful was an unfamiliar sight to her, at least compared to her home life.

The young man offered a short but sweet blessing on the food, even remembering to be thankful that Jack and Jocelyn were there.

Jocelyn was touched.

As soon as they all said amen, the table came alive with chatter and motion. Bowls of food were passed around, as small talk about the weather, neighbors, and town activities and events were shared. Jocelyn felt less like a guest and more like family as they included her in their discussion.

She noticed how often MJ and her husband exchanged loving glances and laughed together at comments and how interested they were in both of their sons' summer activities. Whenever her family sat down for dinner together, a very rare occasion, it never failed that an argument would erupt.

"Hey, Jack," the youngest son, Tyler, said. "When you goin' fishin' again?"

Jack raised his eyebrows and said, "When does football camp start?"

"Not for another week," Tyler answered.

"How about tomorrow?"

Tyler looked quickly at his mom. "Can I?"

"What about me?" Ben added.

MJ was thoughtful for a moment. "You can go but only if you don't come home and sleep till noon. You boys are supposed to clean out the garage tomorrow."

"We won't sleep all day," Tyler said. "Will we, Ben?"

"How early are we going?" Ben asked Jack.

"Not too early. Five thirty." Jack poured a puddle of gravy onto his potatoes and meat.

Ben's excited expression faltered for a moment.

"Come on, Ben," Tyler said. "Don't be a wuss."

"I'm not a wuss," Ben argued. "I just hate getting up early."

"Well, we're going. Huh, Jack?" Tyler confirmed.

"You bet, buddy," Jack said. "What about you, Brian? Are you coming?"

"Can't," Brian answered. "I gotta go to Seattle in the morning for meetings. Next time, though."

"I guess I'll pick you up at five fifteen, then," Jack said to Tyler.

"I'll think about it," Ben said.

"Maybe if you didn't stay up all night talking on the phone to Amanda you wouldn't mind getting up early."

"I don't stay—"

"Boys!" MJ said sternly.

The two boys immediately stopped their arguing, and the topic was changed to the major surge in the growth of their town and a new subdivision being developed.

"I hate to see it happen," Jack said. "Part of the reason I moved to Milford Falls was because of its size. I like the small-town feel."

"Next time you see Mayor Duncan, let him know," MJ urged. "If enough people speak up, maybe he'll listen."

Jocelyn noticed Jack mixing his corn in with his mashed potatoes. She was a little surprised, because as unusual as the combination was, that was exactly how she liked to eat her corn and mashed potatoes.

"So, Jocelyn, tell me about St. George. I've never been there," Brian said.

Jocelyn explained to them about the beautiful red hills and black lava rock beds that surrounded the burgeoning community. With the mild winters and hot summers, it was a vacation destination as well as the perfect place for retirement, not to mention an outdoor paradise, especially for golfers and bikers.

"Sounds like a beautiful place," Brian said. "What compelled you to move to Milford Falls?"

She told him about her grandmother willing the house to her and how Mayor Duncan had called, threatening to fine her if she didn't come and fix it up.

"That man is such a pain," Brian said. "But it's great that you're improving your grandmother's place."

"Did you visit your grandmother a lot before she passed away?" MJ asked. "It seems like we would've seen you around town."

Jocelyn shifted uncomfortably in her chair. "I visited several times, but my mom didn't bring us kids here very often."

"Did your mom grow up here?" MJ asked.

"She grew up in St. George," Jocelyn said. "My grandfather had a business there. But he had a heart attack and died when my mom was in high school, and my grandmother decided to move here, closer to where she was raised. My mom was having some problems in school, and Grandmother thought it would be good to get her away from her friends. But when they got here, Mom decided that she didn't want to stay. She dropped out of school and went back to St. George and lived with a friend."

Why did I have to tell them all that? Jocelyn asked herself.

"That must have been hard for your grandmother," MJ said.

"I'm sure it was," Jocelyn said.

"But it sounds like you two were close," MJ said.

"Yes. In spite of our physical distance, she was always there for me." Jocelyn knew it wasn't a good idea to continue the conversation because she'd end up in tears.

"What kind of work do you do?" Brian asked.

Jocelyn wasn't used to being the center of attention. "Uh, well, I'm an art teacher. I've taught in middle school and high school."

"You're an artist?" MJ exclaimed. "That's wonderful!"

"Well, I paint with water colors and dabble in oils, but I haven't had time to do much for a while. I'd like to start painting more, but the only painting I'm going to be doing this summer is the walls in my house."

"You need to find time to paint. And I don't mean walls," MJ said. "I believe every woman needs to develop her talents, not only to share with others, but because it does so much for them personally."

Jocelyn nodded. She agreed, but it had been hard to feel like painting when she felt like her life was going nowhere. She had hoped that this move would help spark her creativity again, but now that didn't seem likely.

"Are you going to be teaching here in Milford Falls?" Brian asked.

"I did a phone interview at the middle school here, but I haven't heard anything. To be honest," she said, deciding to just come out with it, "I may only be staying this summer while I fix up the house and try to sell it."

"Please tell me you're not really considering that!" MJ exclaimed. "Our presidency was so excited to have you in Relief Society—in fact, I told the bishop I had dibs on you. I wanted to make sure we got you before any of the other auxiliaries."

"I'm sorry," Jocelyn said. "I think I just jumped into a whole new situation without really understanding what I was up against."

"Surely it's just a case of cold feet. Are you missing your family? Your job?"

Hardly, she almost said. "Well, no. None of my family is there anymore. My job was fine, but I quit it to move here."

"See," MJ stated matter-of-factly, "you're supposed to be here with us."

Jocelyn didn't know what to say, so she just smiled and shrugged. MJ was a wonderful person but a little too persistent for her.

"Brian, have you thought more about adding onto the house?" Jack said quickly. His eyes shifted to her for a brief moment then back to Brian.

He did that to get Mary Jane off my back.

An unexpected warmth washed over her. So Brother Jack Emerson did have a heart.

Once everyone had eaten their fill, Jocelyn helped clear dishes while MJ got dessert ready. The men were still discussing the family room Brian wanted to add on to the house, and the boys had been excused because most likely they both had better things to do than sit around and talk with boring adults.

Delicious bowls of vanilla ice cream topped with raspberry sauce were served, and as Jocelyn took the first bite of one of the tart, plump raspberries, she shut her eyes and felt like she'd died and gone to heaven.

"Those raspberries are fresh out of my garden," MJ said proudly. "I think I'm going to have a bumper crop this year."

"These taste better than anything I've ever had from a store," Jocelyn said.

"Why, thank you," MJ said. "I'll tell you who knew how to grow raspberries."

Jocelyn took another bite of raspberry sauce.

"Your grandmother."

"My grandmother?" Jocelyn said with her mouth full. She quickly swallowed. "I knew she liked to garden, but I didn't know she had raspberries. I'm afraid I haven't taken a good look around the backyard yet. It's still too overgrown."

"Oh yes. Cora always had the most beautiful garden. Her raspberries, though, were to die for. I think she started about . . . eight years ago? Then each year she'd plant more and more of them. In fact, she was considering turning all that back property into a berry farm. You know, the kind where people could come and pick their own. Those are very popular around here. We have the perfect weather and soil for berry farms."

"Really?" Jocelyn said, wishing she'd been able to spend time with her grandmother before she passed away. There was so much about her she never knew. Her grandmother had always had a garden, but Jocelyn never knew about her plans to start a berry farm.

"It's a great summer business," MJ said. "You know, for a teacher, it would be ideal. Since you have your summers free, you could teach during the year and have your berry farm during the summer. Some of the early varieties start producing in June, and if you plant several varieties you could have berries all summer long. Plus, there are farmers markets all over you could take your berries to."

"MJ," Brian said, trying to rein in his wife's exuberance, "she may not be staying, remember?"

"I'm just saying *if* you did decide to stay, you could turn quite a profit with all your property," MJ added.

"I can't imagine growing anything better than this," Jocelyn said, raising her spoon to MJ. It wasn't that she didn't think MJ's idea wasn't good, because it was. It was just that she was pretty sure she wasn't going to be around to plant anything. She just needed to get the plumbing fixed and the yard cleaned up so she could put the house on the market.

Then she would go back home.

Chapter Twelve

Monday morning Jocelyn awoke with a start. She pulled the covers off her head and peeked out. Satisfied there were no birds, she relaxed. Next, she listened for the sound of running or dripping water. Nothing. All she heard was the quiet sounds of morning: birds chirping in the trees—where they belonged—a dog barking in the distance, the sound of a lawn mower. She breathed a sigh of relief.

Outside the warm covers of her bed the air was brisk. Already she could tell it was cloudy, but she actually didn't mind having it rain today. After she ran to town to take care of her speeding ticket, she was going to make a couple phone calls then finish what she'd started and paint the trim in the front room. It was something she could do without a fix-it manual, at least.

After a bowl of cereal and a shower, she pulled on a fleece jacket, and with the ticket in hand, she got in her car. A misty rain was falling, making the air smell fresh and clean. The flowers in the yard were especially bright, and the surrounding lawn, bushes, and trees were brilliant shades of green. *Lush* was the only word to describe it.

She started the car, put it into gear, and pushed on the gas. After a short pause the car engaged and she shot backward. *That was weird.* It had been slipping a lot lately, and she knew she needed to get her car into a shop for servicing, but it had never done this before.

She put the car into drive and again pushed on the gas. The car didn't move for several seconds, then it grabbed onto the gear and jumped forward.

She drove toward town, feeling an occasional slip as the automatic transmission changed gears when she accelerated. Car trouble on top of everything else? Perfect!

For a while the car cruised along without incident, but after she stopped at the stop sign at the end of her lane, she accelerated to pull onto the main road into town, and again the car stalled slightly, then the transmission grabbed and the car lurched forward.

Wanting to cry and telling herself over and over that it was nothing, she drove through neighborhood streets filled with well-manicured yards, small cottage-like houses, and large trees lining the road. The rain created a misty, surreal image, like a photograph in a magazine.

She turned into the town square, slowing her speed to accommodate all the pedestrians walking with colorful umbrellas. It was breakfast time, so most of them were either heading for the diner or leaving the diner.

Hoping it wouldn't take long, she found a parking spot right in front of the city building and hurried inside. She didn't have an umbrella, something that was definitely a must in this part of the country. She needed to buy one after she was done here. Moose's would probably have one.

The woman in the clerk's office was friendly and helpful, telling her to submit her request to have the traffic court judge review her case and that they would contact her. "But," the woman assured her, "I doubt you'll end up having to pay for it. Between you and me, Karl is more of a menace to society than anyone in town."

Shaking her head as she left the office, Jocelyn went back to her car then decided to just walk across the park to Moose's. The rain had let up, and it felt brisk and refreshing outside.

Somewhere music was playing—granted, it was an elevator-music version of current hits, but it was as if a movie soundtrack were playing while she made her way across the square, like she was a character in a reality show about what it was like to live in a small town with quirky characters.

A bell jingled when she opened the door to Moose's, and Moose himself looked up from the register and greeted her.

"Well, it's the newest member of Milford Falls. How can I help you this morning?" he asked cheerfully.

"I need an umbrella, something small that can fit in my purse."

"Right there on aisle six, halfway down," he said. "Holler if you need help finding what you need."

She walked down the aisle and saw the rack of umbrellas of various shapes and sizes. Finding a small, compact purple umbrella, she made her purchase and promised to come back soon then went back outside.

A small bakery caught her eye, and she decided to stop in to see what they had, wanting something for now and something for later. Lost in thought as she walked, she was surprised when she reached to open the door to the bakery and Jack walked out with a bag in one hand.

"Oh!" she exclaimed, stepping out of the way before they collided. She almost didn't recognize him in his baseball cap.

"Jocelyn," he said. "Hello."

When she didn't respond right off, he held up the bag and said, "Betty's breakfast croissants beat Cheerios any day."

"Wish I'd known that before I had a bowl," she said.

"I'm glad I bumped into you. Is tonight still a good time for me to come and see what I'm going to need for your pipes? I know you're anxious to get started on this project."

"Tonight would be great," she said. She didn't want him to feel pressured, but she appreciated him being sensitive to her situation.

"Great. I close shop about five. I can be over right after."

She gave him a nod.

"Try one of her apple turnovers," he suggested. "They're her specialty."

"I will," she said. "Thanks. Oh, how was fishing?"

He smiled. "We couldn't pull them out fast enough. The fish were practically leaping into the boat."

"Really?"

"They love the rain."

"I've never seen anything like that," she said.

"Maybe . . ."

She waited for him to continue.

"I can take you sometime, before you leave."

She dipped her chin. "Yeah. I'd like that." *Did he just ask me out? No, this must just be one of his friendly moments.*

"Well, I'd better get to work," he said abruptly, looking down the street and shutting off the warmth that had accompanied the conversation up to that point.

Nope, definitely not a date. He seemed to have regretted even asking. He took off down the sidewalk, and Jocelyn watched him go. In his well-worn denim jacket, jeans, and boots, she thought he looked more like a farmhand than a repairman. But then she didn't know that many repairmen to compare him to.

After making her purchases, she stepped back outside the bakery and quickly pulled out her umbrella before she left the safety of the awning overhead. Rain was falling again.

Making a dash for her car, she managed to step in a puddle and soak her foot on the way. Soggy and cold, she climbed inside and started her car, cranking the heater up as high as it would go.

Ready to head home so she could change into warm, dry clothes and shoes, she put the car in reverse, but it didn't move. Revving the engine a bit, she rechecked the position of the gear shift to make sure it was in gear. It was.

Shutting her eyes, she prayed that her car would work, but nothing changed. The thing was not going anywhere.

If she were back home she would know exactly who to call about this. And she wouldn't be wet and freezing either.

After taking a few minutes to feel bad for herself, she decided it was time to take action. With determination born out of frustration, she climbed out of the car and went back into the city office building.

"Hi, again," the receptionist said when Jocelyn approached her.

"I wondered if you could help me," Jocelyn said. "Do you happen to know where I could find a mechanic? I'm having some trouble with my car."

"Oh, I'm sorry," the girl said. "I actually do know a good mechanic. My boyfriend, Wade. He works down the street a few blocks. You want me to give him a call for you?"

"Would you?"

"I'm sure he can take care of the problem."

Jocelyn forced herself not to think about the amount of money it was going to take to get her car fixed. Maybe she would get lucky and would just need some transmission fluid or something.

The thought almost made her start laughing. Her? Lucky?

"Is your car drivable?" the girl asked.

"No," Jocelyn answered. "I put it into gear, but it won't move."

"Sounds like the transmission," the girl said into the phone. She listened for a moment. "Is it right out here in front?" she asked Jocelyn.

Jocelyn nodded.

The girl hung up. "He'll be down in a few minutes to take a look. They can tow it back to the shop if they need to."

"Thank you so much," Jocelyn said.

"Hey," the girl said, "Wade will take good care of you, and he won't overcharge you. I'll make sure of that."

"Thank you," Jocelyn said. "This couldn't come at a worse time."

"Car problems tend to do that," the girl said.

"Maybe I should go outside and wait for him?"

"It's too wet and cold. He'll call when he gets here. Stay inside where it's warm and dry."

In spite of her frustrations, Jocelyn couldn't help admiring how cute the girl's haircut was and how pretty the color of her hair was. It was so natural looking she almost wondered if they were highlights from a salon.

"Is everything okay?" the girl asked.

Blinking, Jocelyn realized she was staring. "I'm sorry, but your haircut is so cute. Where do you get it done?"

"Just around the corner at Sassy's Salon. If you're interested in getting your hair done, that's the best place to go."

"I'll have to remember that." *If I stay around long enough to need a haircut.*

Jocelyn felt as if the dark clouds overhead were bringing more than just rain.

"Ask for MJ. She's the best. But she only works two days a week—"

"Wait a minute, did you say MJ?"

"Sure did. You know her?"

"I met her a couple of days ago."

"She's the only one I'll trust with my hair. I have this really annoying natural curl, and MJ's the only one who knows how to do it," the girl explained. "So are you new here? I'm Natalie, by the way."

Jocelyn introduced herself and told Natalie about her grandmother's house, the birds, and the pipe disaster. "I'm sorry, I didn't mean to unload all of this on you."

"Are you kidding? I can't imagine having all of this happen within the first three days of moving to a new town." Her phone beeped. "That's Wade. He's probably outside. I'll walk out with you."

The rain had stopped so the two girls walked out the front doors where a large truck with flames and the words *Top Notch Auto Repair* were painted down the sides. The driver's side door opened, and a large, burly man stepped out.

"Hey darlin'," he said when he saw Natalie. He gave her a hug that lifted her off the ground. "Don't you look spiffy this mornin'."

Jocelyn liked him already.

"Wade, sweetie, this is Jocelyn. She's new to town."

Wade turned to her and gave her a big smile. "Nice to meet you Jocelyn. Are you the one having car trouble?"

"Yes. Thank you so much for coming to help me."

"No problem. Glad to help. That's not your car right there, is it—the one with the parking ticket on the windshield?"

"What!" Jocelyn shrieked. She turned, and there under the windshield wiper was a pink ticket stuck to the wet window.

"You have got to be kidding!" Natalie said. She yanked the paper from the windshield and opened it. "Just as I thought. Karl!"

"The same guy who gave me my speeding ticket?" Jocelyn asked.

"Yes. We've told him a million times to quit doing this. I've never seen anyone get so excited about giving a ticket. He loves it when he catches someone doing something wrong."

"What did I do wrong?" Jocelyn asked.

"The parking spaces around the town square are only an hour. Around the corner, off the main square you can park all day."

Had she been gone a whole hour? She checked her watch and realized that it was about four minutes over an hour. What was this guy, the traffic stalker?

"Are you okay?" Natalie asked her.

"That guy had to have been watching for me. He probably knew I didn't know the parking rule."

"First of all," Wade said, "Karl's harmless, just so ya know. And second of all, I wouldn't put it past him to do something like that."

"Don't worry about it," Natalie said. "I'll put this with your other ticket. You won't end up having to pay either of them."

"Thank you," Jocelyn said. "I really appreciate it." She turned to Wade. "How much do you think it will cost to fix my transmission?"

"I'll give you the best deal I can," Wade said, "but I can't be sure until I take a look at it. If it's the transmission it will most likely be at least nine hundred."

Jocelyn swallowed hard. "Really?" she managed to eke out.

"Yeah. Now there is a chance your filter is just plugged. If that's the case you just have low hydraulic pressure and that's why your car won't shift into gear. That would be a quick and easy fix, really inexpensive."

Jocelyn shut her eyes for a moment, offering a plea heavenward. *Please let it be just a plugged filter.*

"I'll have one of my guys tow your car to the shop, and we'll take a look," Wade said.

Jocelyn nodded and tried to remain optimistic. Hopefully luck would finally be on her side.

* * *

While waiting to find out the prognosis on her car, Jocelyn read the *Seattle Times.* The arts and entertainment section boasted a wide selection of performances and gallery shows. She was particularly interested in an article focusing on Italian artists. As she read the article further she discovered a potential solution to her financial problems, one that she hated to even consider.

The only thing she owned of any great value was her Pablo Bocelli painting. Apparently, ever since his art had been discovered in the states, Bocelli's artwork had skyrocketed in value.

Just the thought of selling her painting to a dealer made her sick inside, but she knew it was an option she might need to consider. "Well, I hate to have to tell you, but your transmission is shot." Wade's booming voice filled the room.

Jocelyn responded with a forced smile. "So, how much am I looking at in repairs?"

"We can probably keep it under fifteen. I'll do some of the labor myself and give you the parts at my cost."

She took a steadying breath and fought to keep her cool. "Fifteen hundred," she said, just to clarify.

"I'll try and cut costs wherever I can," he said.

"I really appreciate that, Wade," she said.

"I can have one of the boys give you a lift home, and if we have all the parts we need, we can probably have this done for you first thing in the morning."

Holding on to her emotions, she managed another smile and thanked him.

"Ed!" he yelled to the back room. "I need you to give a customer a ride home." He turned back to Jocelyn. "He'll be right with you."

After he left the room, Jocelyn shut her eyes and rested her face in her hands. Really, what else could go wrong?

A young man, probably in his late teens, with teeth too large for his mouth and long bangs that nearly covered his eyes, entered the room. "Are you the one needin' a ride?"

"Yes," she answered, hoping he could see the road well enough to drive but relieved it was a younger guy at least. She was rarely comfortable being alone with strange men. She followed him to the parking lot where he motioned toward an old Chevy pickup truck.

"So, you new in town?" the kid asked.

"I am," she answered, not in the mood for chitchat.

"Where'd you move from?"

"Southern Utah," she said, keeping her gaze out the window.

"Oh yeah? What brought you here?"

Her emotions caught in her throat as she opened her mouth to answer. She had to clear her throat several times before she could talk.

"My grandmother left her house to me when she passed away. I came to get it fixed up so I could sell it."

"Ah," he said with a bob of his head. "You're just here for the summer, then?"

Hopefully not that long, she thought. "Maybe just a month," she said. "Depends on how long it takes to get the repairs made."

"That's too bad," he said. "That yer movin', I mean."

"Oh?" she said, a little surprised by his comment.

"Yeah, you would really like it here. Best place in the world."

She couldn't help smiling.

"Have you always lived here?" she asked.

"Sure have. Born and raised. Never want to leave. I can't imagine being anywhere else."

She had to admit his love for his town was sweet. Of course, she was feeling the same way about St. George now that she was gone.

"Wade will give you a call when your car is done," Ed said, pulling up in front of her house. "I'd be happy to pick you up and give you a lift back to the shop then."

With a quick thanks, she stepped out of the truck and hurried up the walk to her front door. The out-of-control yard called to her, its overgrown bushes and weed-infested garden in serious need of care, but she needed to go inside and take something for the screaming headache that was pounding inside her head.

The disaster inside the house perfectly matched the one in the yard, and now with her car trouble she felt as if another weight had just been added to her shoulders. It was too much. She couldn't handle all of this.

Throwing back a couple pain tablets, she sat down on the couch and rested her head in her hands. Tears of frustration filled her eyes. The decisions, plans, and solutions were all up to her, and she had no idea what to do.

The more she thought about her predicament, the lower she sank. A quicksand of disappointment sucked her in deeper and deeper until she collapsed back onto the couch in a heap of sobs.

She didn't know how long she cried, but finally the tears dried up and she lay still, listening to the pitter-patter of raindrops on her window. The sound was calming, and even though she felt weaker, she also felt more clearheaded.

With a fresh approach she looked at her options. First, she could just sell the house the way it was and go back to St. George with whatever she could get for it. Second, she could fix up the house and sell it for more and then move home, but it would take longer and require money—money she didn't have. Third, she could fix up the house with money she didn't have, find a job, and live here.

The first option was the most appealing.

The decision was made. She would contact a Realtor and put the house on the market as soon as possible.

She still needed money for her car repairs, but since she wasn't going to spend anything on house repairs, she could cover the auto shop bill with her savings. She could continue to live here rent free until the house sold, and she'd have another paycheck coming in July from her old teaching job.

As she gazed out the window, the sun suddenly broke through the clouds. The bright rays lifted her spirits further. Things were going to work out.

Needing some fresh air, she pulled on her jacket and walked out the back door. A pair of weathered wooden chairs sat on the cement pad, facing what used to be her grandmother's garden.

Half of the property was on a small hillside, bordered by the edge of a pine forest. Beautiful wildflowers bloomed, offering bursts of color against the backdrop of verdant greenery. These were some of the most breathtaking surroundings she had ever lived in.

The scent of rain still sweetened the air, and she pulled in several deep breaths. There was a sense of serenity and solace out here. Her grandmother had always told her how therapeutic the outdoors were and how much she had loved her home and yard. She felt a pang as she remembered she was selling all this. But it was for the best, she told herself.

She smiled as a delicate, white butterfly fluttered just above the deep red blooms of a rhododendron bush. Moments later, another one joined it, and then another one.

She watched as the three butterflies swirled and danced in the air, carefree and lively.

A warm, happy feeling tingled inside of her, and she shut her eyes for just a moment to offer a quick prayer of thanks. She was certain that her friends were thinking of her and praying for her at that very moment.

When she opened her eyes the butterflies were gone, but the warm feeling inside remained.

She stayed outside for a while, thinking and planning, mentally making to-do lists and trying to come up with a plan. Finally, she realized she needed paper and pen to write everything down.

Inside, she sat down at the table and began to write then noticed her phone indicated that she'd missed a call. She didn't recognize the number, but there was a new message.

"Hi, Miss Rogers. This is Marilyn Michaels at Milford Falls Junior High. I was calling to see when you would be available for an interview with Mr. Clark, the principal. And just between you and me, this interview is pretty much a formality. Mr. Clark was so impressed with your phone interview he's ruled out everyone else unless you have taken a different position elsewhere. Please call me at your earliest convenience. He does have some time in the morning, if that would work for you."

Jocelyn looked at the phone as if she didn't trust it, like somehow it was playing a joke on her.

She thought it was ironic that this call came right after she'd made the choice to leave.

The job prospect was intriguing, but it didn't make sense to go to the interview if she wasn't staying in Milford Falls. In fact, if anything, she needed to make a call to her old school in St. George and see what they had available there.

She knew the number by heart and dialed it even though it was already five. With the hour time difference there was no way anyone would still be in the office, but she knew she could leave a message for the office manager.

"Mountain View Middle School, this is Cindy," the voice on the other end said.

"Oh! Hi, Cindy. This is Jocelyn Rogers. I'm surprised you're still there."

"Jocelyn! Is that you? My goodness, how are you? I'm just working late to get things organized so I can leave for vacation in a couple days. So tell me, how is Washington?"

"Well, that's actually why I'm calling. Things aren't working out here with my grandmother's house, so I'm going to sell it after all and move back to St. George. I wanted to see what the situation was with teaching positions."

"Oh, wow. I hate to tell you, but we've actually got a surplus of teachers in the district this year. As far as I know, all the schools have filled all their positions, and there are still a lot of applicants hoping something will open up."

"Really?" Jocelyn said, trying not to sound desperate. "So, I guess it's a little too late to try and get my old job back, huh?"

"Yeah. I'm sorry. That was filled days ago. I can take down your information and pass it along, though. It wouldn't hurt to get your name on the list. I just can't guarantee something will open up before school starts."

"I see. Well, my phone number is still the same. You can just call me if you get any openings."

"Okay, sure. Gosh, Jocelyn, sorry things didn't work out. It would be great to have you at the school again. Who knows, maybe something will open up."

Jocelyn felt the quicksand sucking her under again. "Okay, thanks Cindy. I'll keep my fingers crossed."

She tossed her phone onto the couch cushions and collapsed in a heap next to it.

There were no tears left to cry, just feelings of frustration and disappointment. She felt like she was standing on one side of a drawbridge over a big river. She wanted to cross to the other side, but the bridge had lifted and separated in the middle. She didn't know how to connect the two sides of the bridge back together so she could cross.

So now what did she do? She still didn't want to stay here, but going home wasn't going to be a picnic, either.

She wondered how fast she could sell her grandmother's house. That would give her enough money that she could live comfortably in St. George while she waited for a teaching position. Maybe she could even substitute teach if she had to.

Her thoughts were interrupted as a loud banging sounded on her front door.

Wondering who could be at her door, she stole a glance through the sidelight and got a glimpse of a man's backside.

At first thought, she worried that the mayor had decided to drop in, but the man on her porch was in jeans and a gray, hooded sweatshirt. Mayor Duncan was more of a Dockers and cardigan type. Then she realized who it was and wondered briefly if it was too late to hide so he'd go away.

Jack.

Feeling like a deflated balloon, she forced herself to open the door and hoped she could mask her complete lack of enthusiasm at having to talk to him.

"Hi," she said.

His forehead creased and brows narrowed. Wow. How had she not noticed before how intensely blue his eyes were?

"You okay?" he asked.

She realized she probably looked like a train wreck after all her crying and moping.

"Yeah, I'm fine," she said.

"I can come back later," he said.

"Why are you here?" she asked, wishing that her comment hadn't sounded quite so snippy.

The lines in his forehead deepened. "We talked about having me come over to assess the damages and come up with a cost for repairs. Didn't we?"

"Oh yeah. I guess we did. Um, I don't think I'm going to make any repairs."

He raised an eyebrow but didn't speak.

"I'll just take my losses and sell the house as it is."

"You've decided, then, after four days, you're done?"

"Yup." She leaned against the door frame and crossed her arms.

"You're going back to southern Utah?"

"It looks that way," she said.

One side of his face scrunched together, his head tilted in confusion.

"What?" she asked with annoyance.

"My neighbor, Marilyn Michaels, told me that the school was interested in offering you a position. Maybe I misunderstood her."

"No, they called and left a message. It was flattering, but it doesn't make sense to take a job here if I don't want to live here."

"I guess not. So, are you going back to teach in St. George?"

"Um, well, not exactly. They've already filled my old position. That's why I need to get back soon, so I can get something lined up as soon as possible."

"Okay, then," he said with a nod, "I guess that's that."

"Guess so."

"Well," he paused, "I guess I'll be on my way, then."

"Thanks for coming over," she said.

He dipped his chin then turned and walked off the porch. She shut the door and sighed.

She jumped as a loud knock came at the door.

Pulling the door open, she saw Jack standing in front of her.

"Listen," he said, "I know you've had a bad time of it since you arrived, with the house and . . . your car."

"You heard about that?"

"It's a small town." He licked his lips then said, "Listen, I was just on my way to the diner to grab a bite to eat. I just wondered if maybe you'd want to join me, unless you already have other plans. It's my treat. Well, actually it's the diner's treat, since they're running a two-for-one special tonight."

"Hmm, I don't know. That means I'd have to skip my frozen meatloaf dinner."

He pulled a face that made her laugh.

"If you want meatloaf, Milt makes the best around, though his fried chicken is my favorite."

Her hollow stomach seemed to be signaling her mouth to say yes. Finally she couldn't resist any longer.

"That actually would be nice," she said. "Do you mind if I take a minute to freshen up?"

"No problem," he said.

"Why don't you come in and have a seat. I won't be long."

He came inside and took a seat on the couch while she hurried upstairs. She appreciated Jack's thoughtfulness, even though he was a mystery to her.

After smoothing her hair back into a clean ponytail and pulling a V-neck sweater over her T-shirt, she took a look in the mirror and decided that she needed a little color to her face. Quickly she swiped on some tinted lip gloss, gave her cheeks a dusting of blush, then added a few strokes of mascara.

Grabbing a jacket out of the closet, she hurried down the stairs and found Jack checking the pipes under her sink.

"Oh, hi," he said, closing the cupboard door. "I just wanted to see if you had any leaking under the sink."

"And how does it look?"

"Looks fine. I didn't see any signs of leaking."

"Gee, that's refreshing," she said.

"I'm sure it's not as bad as it seems," he said, getting to his feet and brushing off his hands.

"I don't know. Sometimes I think this house must have been built over an old cemetery or something."

He laughed and together they walked out the front door.

Chapter Thirteen

The diner wasn't crowded, but it was filled with delicious aromas. The décor was simple and inviting. Walls of pale blue, shelves filled with antique kitchen items, chairs and tables in bright red, and a large fireplace at the end of the room gave patrons a sense of home and hearth.

A young woman showed them to a table situated near the toasty warm fireplace.

"Jocelyn, this is Celeste," Jack said, "Marilyn Michaels' daughter."

"Nice to meet you, Celeste," Jocelyn said.

"You know my mom?" Celeste asked. She was tall, with thick brown hair and a warm smile.

"Uh, no, not really," Jocelyn said.

"Your mom called her about a teaching position at the middle school," Jack said.

"You'll love teaching there!" Celeste exclaimed. "I work in the office part-time, and I absolutely love it. The principal is so awesome, and the kids are the best. What subject do you teach?"

"Art."

"Wow, that's wonderful. The other teacher, Mr. Harding, was such a grump. He finally retired, thank goodness," she added in a whisper. "Anyway, they need a good art teacher and you are so young and pretty, the kids will love you."

Jack and Jocelyn exchanged looks, but neither said anything about Jocelyn not staying. Celeste's enthusiasm was too overwhelming.

"Here are your menus," she said. "Could I start you off with something to drink?"

They both asked for ice water, and Celeste cheerfully rushed off to get them their drinks.

"Is she anything like her mom?" Jocelyn asked.

"Identical. Marilyn is a go-getter, really energetic and involved. The kids in town think she's pretty cool."

Jocelyn knew from experience how important the office staff at the school was to the students and to the tone of the whole school, really. When the office workers were fun, kind, and helpful, the students responded in a positive way.

They looked over the menu, and Jocelyn decided on the chicken pot pie. Jack surprised her by ordering the meatloaf, saying that once she'd mentioned meatloaf he couldn't get it out of his mind.

"So," Jack said, after their order had been placed, "I'll admit, I'm still a bit confused about why you're leaving. Fixing your grandmother's house would be a big project, but it's doable. It sounds like your car will be ready to go tomorrow, and you pretty much have a teaching job secured. What has St. George got that you don't have here?"

She was just trying to formulate an answer when a woman's voice interrupted.

"Jack! What a surprise!"

Jocelyn recognized the blond woman from Home Depot and church rushing toward them. She was dressed in tight-fitting jeans and high-heeled boots, with an even tighter fitting T-shirt that dipped a little too low in front. Her platinum hair was teased and sprayed to four times its normal size, and she had hoops dangling from her earlobes and bangles jangling on her wrists.

With dramatic movements she gave him a giant hug, nearly knocking him from his chair. Judging by his expression and reluctance to hug her, he was far from excited to see her.

"And how nice to see you again, Jacqueline," Blondie said.

"It's Jocelyn," Jack corrected before Jocelyn had a chance.

"Oh, sorry. Jocelyn. What a pretty name. I'm Lacey. Lacey Bloomquist. How do you like our quaint little town?" Her tone was tinged with sarcasm.

"It's beautiful here. And—"

"That's wonderful!" she interrupted. "So, Jack, I hear you're on the Fourth of July celebration committee. Guess what? I am too! I can't wait. We can work together. We should probably have a meeting soon, don't you think?"

"Actually I've already started," Jack told her. "I've got a committee, and we've already had our first meeting. Sorry. I'm sure Duncan has something planned for you, though."

"Oh pooh!" she said. "I was hoping we could work together."

"Unless you can work a band saw, nail gun, or want to paint"—he looked at her sculptured nails—"you probably should stick with one of the other committees."

"I guess. We always have so much fun together, though," she said, stroking his sleeve with her finger then resting her hand on his shoulder for a moment.

He shrugged. "Sorry. I just do what Duncan tells me to do."

Her bottom lip curled out in a pout, then she turned it into a smile that looked unnaturally sweet. "Well, maybe I can talk Duncan into putting me on your committee. I'm sure there's something I can do to help."

"Make sure you wear a heavy pair of work gloves," Jack said. He turned toward Jocelyn, essentially shutting out the woman. It took a few seconds for her to get the hint that the conversation was over. Jocelyn felt embarrassed for her. Why didn't she give up and move on?

"I guess I'd better get going," she said. "Enjoy your dinner." She flashed a tight, icy smile at Jocelyn then turned with a sweep of her long, bleached mane of hair. Her high heels clackety-clacked as she walked away.

Jocelyn tried hard not to stare, but she couldn't help it. Lacey Bloomquist had just secured a spot on Jocelyn's people-I-want-to-avoid list. She was dying to know more about Lacey but wasn't sure this was the right time to ask.

Celeste delivered their meals before they had a chance to resume their conversation. Jocelyn's mouth watered at the sight of the steaming chicken pot pie in front of her as well as a side salad with large wedges of tomato and slices of cucumber in it.

Jack grabbed the salt and sprinkled some on his meatloaf, mashed potatoes, and green beans.

"I have to admit," she said, "that doesn't look anything like the stuff in my freezer."

"You want a taste?"

"No, that's okay. I didn't mean—"

"Here," he said, "try it." He lifted his plate toward her and held it there, waiting for her to dig her fork in.

With a flush of red washing over her and silently berating herself for drawing attention to his dinner, she speared a small corner of the juicy meatloaf and put it into her mouth. The full flavor and blend of spices exploded in her mouth.

"Oh, my gosh," she said, chewing as quickly as she could so she could talk, "that's incredible."

He smiled with satisfaction. "I know. Want some more?"

"No, really," she began to say automatically. Then she shocked herself by saying, "Actually, yes, I do."

With a laugh, he lifted his plate again and held it toward her. This time she took a bigger portion.

"You have to understand, I am not a big meatloaf fan, but I am amazed at how good this tastes."

"I'm more than happy to share, but the way you love this, I'm thinking I should order another one. You can take your pot pie home with you for tomorrow."

"You don't have to do that," she said. But it was too late. He'd already signaled for Celeste to come over.

The new order was placed, and within minutes Jocelyn had her own steaming plate.

"I'm sorry," she said between bites. "I'm not usually this weird."

"Weird? I wouldn't go that far," he said with a teasing twinkle in his eye. "Unusual maybe, but definitely not weird."

She smiled and took a bite of the creamy, garlic-flavored mashed potatoes.

"To be honest, it's nice to see a girl eat like a normal person," he said.

"Well, thank you," she replied. "I could always eat my two brothers under the table."

He nodded. "Very impressive. So you have two brothers? Any sisters?"

"Nope, just me."

"Is your family back in St. George?"

She shook her head. "Actually, one of my brothers is in Iraq, and the other one is, well, he's . . . in jail." She paused and wiped her mouth with her napkin. "I don't know which one I worry about more."

He seemed unfazed by her revelation. "And your parents?"

"Um, well . . ." She paused. How much did she really want to say? It wasn't like she needed to worry about gossip—she wouldn't be in town long enough to care. But there was also no need to overwhelm the man with details. Over the years she'd come up with a pat answer, which was usually enough to answer the question and not encourage more questions. "I never knew my dad, and my mother and her husband live somewhere in Nevada. We aren't close."

He nodded. "I understand."

"Oh?" She didn't expect that comment.

"Yeah. My parents are separated. I can't keep up with how many wives my dad has had, and my mom has decided that being alone with her cats is better than having a man in her life. We don't have a whole lot in common. Neither of them is too keen on the fact that I joined the Church, so they don't really talk to me much. My brother and two sisters are pretty cool about it—they don't really care which religion I am or if I even belong to a religion. My brother is agnostic, one of my sisters is into that Kabbalah stuff that a lot of those movie stars are into, and my other sister is . . ." He was thoughtful for a moment. "Actually I don't know what she is."

Jocelyn felt an unexpected connection with him. His family life was far from perfect, just like hers. They actually did have something in common.

"We get along pretty well one on one, but we don't do well as a group. I've given up on trying to bring our family together. They don't understand my efforts, and I come off as some kind of kook to them."

"How did you get introduced to the Church and end up getting baptized?" she asked.

His warmth suddenly left. "I joined a couple of years after I moved here," he answered in a tone that left no room for further questions. He motioned for the waitress.

"Oh," she said, wishing she hadn't asked but not understanding why the question had put him off so suddenly.

"How is everything?" Celeste asked. "Can I get anyone anything? Would you like a dessert menu?"

They both declined. Celeste cleared their plates and promised to be back with the check and a box containing Jocelyn's leftovers.

Shifting uncomfortably in her seat, Jocelyn wished she hadn't asked about his conversion. Usually that was a safe question but apparently not for Jack.

They shared small talk, but the awkwardness remained.

Climbing back into his truck, Jocelyn clutched her purse on her lap and wished that she understood what had just happened. There had been an open communication and connection during their conversation, then *bam*, Jack slammed the door shut.

Twisting the strap of her purse as they drove, Jocelyn tried to focus on the road ahead. Then Jack cleared his throat and asked, "So, is your decision about moving final?"

"Yes. I'll just tidy things up and pick out a real estate agent. Hopefully we can get a sign up by the weekend."

"I see. So you seriously don't want me to come and work on it?"

"No, you don't need to."

"What about all the holes I made in the walls when I was trying to locate the problem?"

"I'm hoping that someone looking for a fixer-upper will buy it, so I don't suppose it matters." She didn't know what else to say. Maybe it wasn't the wisest choice, but it seemed like the best one for her situation.

He was thoughtful for a moment, then he said, "Listen, I would be happy to come and at least patch up the holes where I know the pipes are fine, just to clean things up a bit. No charge."

"That's nice of you, but—"

"Hey, I'm the one who made the holes. The least I can do is patch them up."

She sighed, not wanting to put him out.

"You really don't have to, but I guess it might help to have some of them fixed."

"I could also give you an idea of the extent of the damage, just so you can let prospective buyers know what they're dealing with."

With a nod of her head, she thanked him then turned and looked out the window at the darkening sky.

"So," he said, breaking the silence. "What have you got waiting for you in St. George?"

"Well, I have some friends," she said, but even as she said it, she realized she really didn't. Emma was involved with her boyfriend, Andrea was back in California, and Lauryn was busy in New York with her design house. Chloe was the closest friend she had, but she lived forty-five miles away, so they didn't even see each other that often. "I mean, most of my best friends are actually spread out all over . . ."

He waited for her to continue.

"And, well," she tried, but she couldn't come up with much else.

"I can see why you're anxious to get back," he teased.

"I know. I guess it doesn't make sense. But at least there I'm comfortable and familiar with my life."

"Well, let me ask you one more question, and I'm completely serious: what have you got *here?*" he asked.

"Hmm." She thought for a moment. "I have . . . my grandmother's house that's falling apart, a broken-down car, a huge lot full of weeds, and . . ."

"A job offer. A chance to meet some great people and fit into a wonderful community. A new start."

"What are you saying?" she asked, wondering why he even bothered trying to persuade her.

"I'm just saying that you kind of remind me of myself," he said. "And I think you owe it to yourself to give things a try here. Something brought you here."

"Yeah, a threat. From Mr. Duncan."

"You didn't have any other reason to come?"

"I don't know. Yeah, I guess. Maybe. You see, I didn't think I had the courage to sell the house. My grandmother meant a lot to me, and I had memories there. I couldn't afford to just keep it here vacant, so moving here seemed like the logical solution. I tried to be prayerful. I wanted to do what the Lord wanted me to do. I thought I was following a prompting, but now I have to wonder if it was just desperation."

"The fact is, you're here. Aren't you even curious to find out for sure if this is where you're supposed to be? I know you've had a lot of problems in the four days you've been here, but isn't it kind of soon to just give up, especially if you really were following a prompting to come?"

Why was he making sense to her? He was practically a stranger, yet he was talking to her like an old friend or a concerned family member.

"You're right. I guess I need to think about it a little more."

Jack pulled up in front of her house.

"Maybe you should go to that interview tomorrow and see how it feels. Who knows? That could give you your answer."

She pulled in a deep breath. "Okay. Why not? Like you said, it's not like I have anything waiting for me in St. George." She opened the door to get out. "Thanks for the dinner; it was delicious, as promised."

"I'll come over tomorrow after work and take a look at things and get some of those walls patched. Here," he said, handing her the boxes of leftover food. "Don't forget this."

"Oh yeah." She took the food and went to shut the door then stopped. "Um, Jack?"

"Yeah."

"Thank you. I appreciate your help and advice. I feel like I owe you for a therapy session."

He laughed. "I'm just glad I didn't offend you. You could've just told me to get my nose out of your business."

"No, really—it was advice I needed to hear."

"Well, good luck tomorrow with the job interview. I hope you decide to stay."

* * *

That night, lying in bed, Jocelyn thought about her situation and pondered her options again. Her prayers had again yielded no confirmation one way or the other. If she was supposed to be here in Milford Falls, then why in the world did everything have to be so blasted difficult? It took forever to fall asleep because her mind kept spinning a hundred miles a minute.

When she awoke the next morning, her head throbbed and she felt as if she'd been slammed with the worst jet lag on record. Dragging herself to the downstairs bathroom, she cringed when she saw her reflection in the mirror. She'd never looked worse in her life.

Perfect for a job interview.

But then, maybe that was for the best. Maybe she wasn't supposed to get the job anyway.

She phoned the school to set up her interview, doing her best to avoid getting caught up in a long conversation with the enthusiastic Marilyn. She ended the call with relief then remembered that she needed to get her car out of the shop before she could drive anywhere.

Dialing the number, she hoped that the repairs would be finished and that she would be able to afford the final bill.

She was wrong on both counts.

"Wish I had better news for you. The more I looked the more I found that it's not just your transmission that's giving you problems," Wade told her. He began to list the problems her car had: a cracked this, a broken that, a damaged something else. The list of what was functioning in her car would have been shorter.

She could barely speak when he told her the cost for repairs would be between twenty-five hundred and three thousand dollars.

"Wouldn't it be better just to buy a new car?" she asked.

"You could do that, but you've got an awesome engine. Once you make these repairs, your car will be just like new. You'll be good for at least another hundred thousand miles," he said. "It will take until the end of the week before I can get all the parts in and make the repairs. I've got a car here you can use for a loaner until we get your car done. No charge. You just take care of the gas."

"Thank you," she said, still in shock.

"I can send one of my boys to come pick you up when you're ready, if you have things you need to do today. The loaner car is here and ready to go."

"I have an appointment in about an hour and a half. Maybe they could come in about an hour?" she asked.

"Will do," he said. "I want you to know, I really am trying to keep costs down as much as I can."

"I appreciate that," she answered.

With the arrangements for her ride to town made, she hung up and went back upstairs to change her clothes and get ready for her job interview. By the time she got to her room, though, the tears that threatened finally found their way to the surface. She fell onto her bed, sobbing. How would she pay such a huge bill?

After ten minutes of solid crying, she finally ran out of tears and remained frozen on her bed for several more minutes, trying to pull herself together. The next thing she did was slide to her knees by the side of her bed and unload her burden in prayer.

She'd learned on her mission that she could get through anything as long as she had the Lord with her. Now she asked Him for guidance and wisdom and for help. Between her house and her car, she was left with nothing of worth. Except for one thing.

Tears stung her eyes as she thought about selling her painting. She might have a chance to buy it back when she sold the house, but there were no guarantees it would still be available.

But what were her other options? She had a couple credit cards but had always paid off the balances monthly; she didn't feel comfortable charging something if she didn't know when she'd be able to pay it off. As for the possibility of a mortgage, she suspected a loan officer wouldn't be too thrilled about the fact she was unemployed.

After continuing to pray and after several moments of pondering and deep thought, she pushed herself to her feet, knowing exactly how she would pay for the repairs—and feeling surprisingly peaceful about it.

Robotically, she dressed and fixed her hair and makeup so she would look presentable for her job interview. Next she found bubble wrap and completely covered her Bocelli painting in plastic to keep it safe.

She was ready to go just as the car from Wade's showed up.

The driver this time wasn't as outgoing and friendly as the first guy, but she wasn't in the mood for chitchat.

At the repair shop Jocelyn got a few directions on how to get to Milford Falls Junior High, then she drove the old Chevy Malibu out of the parking lot and down the road.

The school smelled a little old and musty, but she liked the open hallways, polished floors, and warm and welcoming front office.

A middle-aged woman with a trendy short haircut and funky earrings looked up and smiled.

"Hi, can I help you?"

"My name is Jocelyn Rogers," she replied. "I'm here for a job interview."

The woman's smile broadened. "Jocelyn, it's so nice to meet you! You're as pretty as I expected."

"Oh?"

"Your voice sounded like it belonged to a pretty young woman, and I was right!" the woman said proudly. "I wasn't in Relief Society when you were introduced on Sunday, but I heard we had a new ward member."

I feel like I'm back in Utah! Everywhere I go I'm meeting members!

"I'm Marilyn, the office manager," the woman continued. "I'm the person who left the message on your phone. How are you?"

You don't want to know. "Just fine, thank you."

"Mr. Clark is anxious to meet you. Your references spoke very highly of you."

Jocelyn smiled. "That's wonderful to hear," she said.

"Have a seat and I'll let him know you are here."

Colorful posters and positive sayings about education and achieving dreams hung on every wall. Brightly colored cabinets gave the room an energetic feel. Jocelyn responded to color and contrast, and she felt a surge of optimism grow inside of her.

"Jocelyn, Mr. Clark will see you now."

Swallowing, Jocelyn stood and pulled her shoulders back. She wanted to appear confident and capable, even though that wasn't how she really felt. She still wasn't sure she even wanted this job, but after Jack's advice last night she was trying to keep an open mind.

The principal stood when she walked into the room and greeted her with a warm smile and a firm handshake. He was a nice-looking man with graying brown hair and kind, hazel-green eyes. "Please," he said, "sit down."

His demeanor had a calming influence. Jocelyn took a seat and felt herself relax.

"So, are you all settled now in Milford Falls?" he asked.

"Yes, more or less. It turns out my home needs quite a few repairs, including new plumbing."

The man nodded. "That can be a big job," he said. "Have you got someone reliable to help you?"

"I think so," she answered, thanking her lucky stars for Jack and the other ward members who had come to her rescue.

"Well, that's good to hear because we are in desperate need of an art teacher."

"That's wonderful," she said then realized how that sounded. "I mean, it's wonderful for me, not for you."

He smiled. "You would have the rest of the summer to come up to speed with the curriculum and lesson plans."

She smiled and nodded, realizing he was talking as if she had already gotten the job.

Mr. Clark explained the particulars about the school, apologizing for the modest salary. She didn't tell him that it was more than she had made at her other school. The possibility of smaller classes was appealing. And even though there wasn't a huge budget for supplies, it too was more than she was used to having, and she knew she would be able to bring some new options and ideas to the art program.

"I think you would fit well here at our school, Miss Rogers," he said. "Our faculty and student body are the finest in the state, and we pride ourselves on our high standards of education and test scores."

"It sounds wonderful," she said. And the funny thing was, it really did.

"I'll get back to you within the next few days, after I talk to the district. I don't foresee any problems, though."

Jocelyn found herself hoping that she would be approved for the position. She loved teaching and was surprisingly excited for the position and the added opportunity to grow.

But wait—wasn't she moving? Wasn't she heading back to St. George?

She waited for her heartbeat to quicken, her worries to start tumbling about her head. But it didn't happen. She felt calm yet excited.

"That's wonderful to hear," she heard herself saying. "I look forward to getting your phone call."

Did this mean she was staying in Milford Falls after all?

Chapter Fourteen

Glancing at her MapQuest driving directions, Jocelyn watched for her exit and prayed that she was doing the right thing. This wasn't what she wanted to do, but she reminded herself it was a blessing she even owned the painting so she could sell it.

Cars zoomed past her, but Jocelyn didn't care. She had to drive slowly to follow the directions. Finally, she found the street where the gallery was located and heaved a sigh of relief, letting the muscles in her shoulders and neck relax. She'd made it.

Pulling up in front of the gallery, she parked the car and turned off the engine, then closed her eyes and weighed her decision one more time.

She knew she had other options, but this was what had felt right. If she wanted the Lord's blessings, she needed to follow His promptings.

With her final decision made, she got her painting out of the car and walked into the gallery.

* * *

Jocelyn sat on her front step eating a raspberry yogurt and contemplating her yard and where to start. Weeds had overgrown the flower beds filled with out-of-control wildflowers. The lawn, if that's what it was, looked more like a field of hay, long and dried. Yet, as monumental as the task seemed and as hard as it had been to sell her painting, she felt surprisingly upbeat. The job interview had gone well, and she was 99 percent sure they would offer the position to her; and she was beginning to realize that as much as she loved St. George and the few people there she was close to, she was beginning to like it here.

Breaking into her musing, the sound of an engine roared up the lane before the actual vehicle came into view. To her surprise, Jack's truck appeared, heading toward her house.

He pulled up in front and gave a wave. Someone was with him.

Jocelyn smiled. It was Lenny.

They were busy talking and laughing when they got out of the truck.

"So the guy says, 'What if I choose not to pay it,'" Lenny said.

"Really? I bet that sent Karl into orbit."

"I thought smoke was going to come out of his ears."

"So what happened?" Jack asked.

"He told Karl to stick the ticket in his ear or send it to Mayor Duncan—that he'd know what to do with it."

Jack laughed. "I wish I could've seen the look on Karl's face."

"Priceless, I tell you. Absolutely priceless," Lenny said. "Then the guy got in his car and drove away. Karl was speechless."

"That's a first."

"No kidding. I thought Karl was going to start crying. Instead, he just wadded the ticket up and drop-kicked it then went and stomped on it. Then, Karl, being Karl, picked it up and put it in the trash."

"That guy needs to move out of his mama's house, out of town, find a real job, and find a wife."

"Why don't you tell him."

"I have!" Jack responded.

They had been so busy talking, they didn't see Jocelyn right off.

"Oh, hi," Jack said.

"Hey," Lenny said.

"Hi, you two." She smiled at the pair.

"We thought we'd take a look at your walls and see what supplies we needed for the repairs."

"Oh, great. Come right in."

She opened the door for them and stepped aside.

Lenny pointed out several holes and said, "Nice job," to Jack.

"Hey, it's pretty much a guessing game when you're looking for bad pipes."

"You're not a very good guesser, are you?"

Jack gave him a wry smile then nodded toward the first wall in the kitchen."You could do better? You have X-ray vision?"

Lenny didn't answer; instead, he got out a measuring tape and went to work looking at the damage.

"So," Jack said to Jocelyn, when Lenny was out of earshot, "how did the interview go?"

She smiled. "Actually, it went really well."

"Did you get the job?"

"I don't know for sure yet, but the principal said he didn't see any reason why I wouldn't."

Their gazes locked, and he gave her a smile. "That's really great. Does that mean you're staying?"

Her eyebrows lifted as she said with a nod, "I guess it does. I can't really commute from St. George."

He chuckled. "I suppose not. Sounds like we need to do more than patch walls, then. Here's a rough estimate based on what we saw Sunday—I made it just in case. And I just want you to know, you don't have to worry about paying me right now."

"Actually, that won't be a problem. I've taken care of the finances."

His eyes widened. "Oh? Well, okay, then, that's great. You still don't need to worry about it right now, though."

"I don't like owing money to people," she said. "It's okay. I'm just grateful you can fix it."

"We'll get started right away. Lenny is going to help me tonight, then I'll take it from there."

"That sounds great," she said.

"All right, then. I'll get to work."

* * *

Later that night her phone rang. It was Andrea.

"So, how's it going?"

"Things are going pretty good. I have had some challenges—that's for sure—but I'm working through everything. I can give you more details in a minute, but first, how about you? How's your job?"

"I think it's going to work out fine. You know how hard change can be."

"Ha!" she burst out. "You're telling me?"

Andrea laughed. "Yeah, I guess we're both taking on a little more than we can chew."

"You said it," Jocelyn answered. "Especially since I'm not even hungry!"

Andrea laughed again. "How's the house?"

Jocelyn explained about the repairs.

"So tell me about this repair guy. Does he have a name?"

"His name is Jack."

"And is Jack single?"

"Yes," Jocelyn answered.

"And do we like Jack?"

"Sheesh, Andrea, I've only lived here a few days."

"It doesn't take days to know whether you like someone or not."

"I'll just say he's a nice guy and he's being very helpful."

"Sounds to me like he likes you."

Jocelyn shut her eyes and shook her head, feeling the lateness of the hour catch up to her. "I couldn't really say. I get the feeling he's the kind of guy who helps everyone out. He's like the ward Good Samaritan. He just enjoys helping people. Besides, he's not my type."

"Oh, really? I didn't know you have a type," Andrea said with a teasing lilt to her voice.

An incoming call sounded on the line. Jocelyn took the phone away from her ear and looked at the number. It was unrecognized. Usually she didn't answer anonymous calls, but just in case . . .

"Andrea, hang on a sec." She pushed the button and answered the call. "Hello?"

"Miss Rogers, hi, this is Marilyn Michaels. I'm sorry to call so late."

"No problem. I'm still up."

"I know this could wait until morning, but I just found out Mr. Clark and I got our wires crossed earlier, and, anyway, I wanted you to know that your name was approved for the position. The district wants to hire you."

"That's great!"

"We're looking forward to having you join our faculty. If you can come to the office in the next day or two, you can sign all the paperwork and I'll show you around the school."

When they ended the call, Jocelyn felt like crying and laughing at the same time. She had a job! Quickly she clicked back to her other call. "Are you still there?"

"Yeah, I'm just sitting here in front of my TV watching *Decorating on a Dollar.* Have you ever watched it?"

"I love that show."

"You should go to some thrift stores and find some vintage furniture. You could fix your house up so cute."

"Yeah, maybe I will. That's right in my price range."

"You have such a good eye for decorating and style, you could have fun fixing up your grandmother's place."

Jocelyn had to admit, now that she'd made the commitment to stay, she was getting excited about the prospect of fixing up her grandmother's house and making it her own.

"I promise, if I get any time off I'll come and help. I would love to do some painting or anything else you need."

"Thanks, Andrea. You're welcome anytime. I'd love to have you or anyone else come and visit. By the way, have you talked to Chloe or Emma lately?"

"Emma! Ha! She doesn't answer her phone or return my calls. I don't know what to think of her. Chloe is hanging in there. They haven't gotten back together, but they also haven't decided to get a divorce."

"I'll give her a call tomorrow and see how she's doing," Jocelyn said.

"Sounds good, Joss. I'll stay in touch. Tell Jack hi from me."

"Ha, very funny," Jocelyn said. "Thanks for calling."

"Send a picture of him to my phone," Andrea added.

"Good night, Andrea," Jocelyn said.

"Ask him if he has a brother," Andrea added before she signed off.

Jocelyn hung up with a laugh.

A yawn crept up on her, and she decided to call it a night. She would take one of her books to bed and read for a little while.

After checking the locks and pausing by the chimney to listen for any chirping, she brushed her teeth and washed her face in the downstairs bathroom then went upstairs to her bedroom.

Soft flannel pajamas helped ward off the chill in the air, and she pulled down the covers, ready to climb inside. Then she stopped.

On top of the dresser was the Butterfly Box. Of course, she knew that her friends loved her, thought of her and prayed for her, but for some reason, as she looked at the box, knowing that the butterfly on top represented change and taking risks, she felt their support, and the strength of Heavenly Father with her.

A few things had gone badly these last few days. In fact, it had felt like anything that could go wrong had gone wrong. But now, with the job offer and the repairs started, things in her life were slowly being rebuilt.

Within her a warm tingling began until it filled her entire being. Could it be that really and truly this was where she was supposed to be?

She ran her fingers lightly across the smooth surface of the box, feeling the cool jade inlay of the butterfly. With the prayers and support of her friends, and with faith and strength from Heavenly Father, she knew she could meet whatever challenge came her way. It was time to quit doubting and get to work!

* * *

The next morning Jocelyn hit the ground running. She wasn't sure where all her energy had come from, but somehow her change of heart and attitude fed her desire to accomplish something positive. She was tired of whining and feeling sorry for herself. It was time to do everything in her power to make her situation better and leave the rest up to the Lord. That's how she'd done it on her mission, and that's how she was going to do it now.

With the money she had from the sale of the painting, she budgeted out the expense for car repairs and the most urgent home repairs. Even leaving her small savings account intact, it looked like she would have several hundred dollars left for some furniture. If she was going to live there, she might as well make her grandmother's house her own.

A bell tinkled as she stepped through the door of the thrift shop. It was a charming little place just off the town square and looked like it might have a few interesting pieces for the house. She started looking around and realized this place could be a gold mine.

"Good morning," a man said. He looked like he was about her age. "My name's Danny. Can I help you?"

"I noticed that there aren't a lot of prices on the items. I'm interested in this coffee table and that chair."

The pieces needed some refinishing, but they were solid and sound, just in need of a little cosmetic work.

The young man told her the prices of each piece, and she had a hard time containing her surprise at how inexpensive it all was.

"For twenty-five dollars we can deliver this for you," Danny said.

Even better! She'd been wondering how she'd get everything home.

While he moved her selections to the loading area, she continued browsing through the store for any other treasures. There was plenty of junk, but she'd learned enough over the years to recognize quality craftsmanship and classic design.

A standing lamp with a burnished antique finish caught her eye. With a new shade and a little touch-up paint, it would look like new and be just the perfect accent for her bedroom. She added it to her growing pile of purchases and kept looking. She felt like she was on a treasure hunt!

Just when she thought she was done, she found the greatest treasure of all. Her breath caught in her throat. The chandelier was magnificent, with three tiers of dangling crystal prisms.

But she didn't need a fancy fixture for her formal dining room. She'd decided to turn that room into a home office and—hopefully—art studio. The piece would look out of place in her breakfast nook, so that wasn't an option either. Wait! What about her living room? It had a nice, high ceiling. It would be the crowning touch to the room, making everything else look that much more elegant.

"We just got that in last night," Danny said, coming up behind her.

"It's pretty," she said, trying not to appear too anxious and cause him to raise the price.

"We get a lot of stuff from estate sales. It's missing a couple of crystals, but I think we could find some to replace it that are pretty close."

"How much?" she asked.

Because she was buying so much, he told her he would give it to her for one hundred and fifty-five dollars. With that much crystal she would have expected it to cost three times as much.

"I'll take it," she said.

He nodded and smiled. "Good choice. My wife saw it and fell in love with it. She wanted it for herself, but we just don't have anywhere in our house to put it."

"Lucky for me," she said. Maybe her streak of bad luck had finally ended.

"I'll load it on the truck. Let me know if there's anything else you find."

Feeling like a kid in a candy store, she rummaged through boxes and piles, hoping to find anything else she could use to decorate her house. Danny told her he'd give her a call if a nice area rug or bookshelf came in.

They arranged a time to meet for the delivery first thing Thursday morning when the driver would be available, and she left the store with her spirits soaring. Excitement coursed through her veins as she visualized the house with new paint and refinished furniture. She couldn't wait to get started.

With a rush of adrenaline, she charged out of the thrift store and ran smack into . . . Mayor Duncan.

"Well, well, if it isn't the newest resident of Milford Falls," he said.

She groaned inwardly and gave him a weak smile. "Mayor Duncan."

"I hear you've had a few challenges with your grandmother's home. How is all of that coming? You've got Jack Emerson on board for repairs? Good choice. Jack does a fine job."

Stunned that he already knew so much about her and what was going on in her life, she had to pause before answering. She wasn't sure how she felt about being the topic of people's conversation. Actually she did know. She didn't like it a bit!

He didn't even wait for her to respond. "I guess it's a good thing you moved here when you did. No telling how much damage would have occurred had you not caught the problem in the early stages."

"I guess so," she answered.

"We're happy you are fixing the place up," he said. "The pride of our town is what makes it such a gem of our state. We've received numerous awards for our fine city."

She wondered who "we" were exactly. Not that she didn't want the city to be lovely and award winning, but his tactics made playground bullying look harmless and fun.

Not knowing how to respond, she thanked him, and as soon as he said good-bye, she made a quick getaway. The man unnerved her, probably because he had no problem telling people what he thought, no matter how tactless he was.

In the safety of the car, she sped toward the middle school, hoping she didn't need to make an appointment. She was anxious to see her classroom and get an idea of what she could do to personalize her room and make it a stimulating learning environment.

Marilyn, the school secretary, was on the phone when Jocelyn walked into the office. Her eyes lit up and she motioned Jocelyn inside.

It felt good to be wanted and to have someone so happy to see her. Jocelyn knew it was silly to be so needy, but she couldn't help it. Her emotions had been a bit fragile the last few days, and she needed all the bolstering she could get.

"Jocelyn!" Marilyn exclaimed when she hung up the phone. "I was just thinking about you." The woman rushed over and gave her a quick hug. "I'm so excited you accepted the position. I'm looking forward to getting to know you, and the kids are going to love having you for a teacher. I was hoping you'd find time to stop in today. I'm sure you're anxious to see your room and get familiar with the school."

"I am," Jocelyn said. "I want to get an idea of the space so I'll know how to decorate."

"Ah! A woman after my own heart. Some of our teachers don't even bother putting things up on the walls or fixing up their rooms, but the children respond to a stimulating environment."

"That's how I feel," Jocelyn said.

"Then I will take you to your room first; we can tour the school afterward. Let me just tell my daughter I'm stepping away from the phone so she will answer it." Marilyn disappeared into an alcove and spoke to someone then walked out with someone behind her. Jocelyn recognized her at once.

"Celeste!" she exclaimed.

"Jocelyn!" Celeste responded.

The two girls laughed when Marilyn looked at them with a puzzled expression on her face. "You two have met?"

"At the diner. She came in the other night with Jack Emerson."

"Oh?" Marilyn raised one eyebrow. "Really?"

"No, we just . . ." Jocelyn started.

"Mom, it wasn't a date," Celeste said in Jocelyn's defense, then she looked at Jocelyn. "Was it?"

"No," Jocelyn answered. "He's going to do some work on my house. He came to give me a bid and we were both hungry. That's all."

Marilyn nodded. "I see." She winked at Celeste.

"Mom!"

"I'm sorry. I've hoped for years that Jack would find a nice girl like Jocelyn."

"She just moved here!"

Marilyn shrugged. "I'm just saying . . ."

"I'm sorry," Celeste said. "She thinks she has the gift of matchmaking."

"My record speaks for itself," Marilyn said. "I've introduced five couples to each other, and they are all now happily married."

The phone rang. "I'll get it," Celeste said. "Mom, please, Jocelyn doesn't need your help."

Marilyn held up both hands. "I won't butt in where I'm not wanted," she said.

"Good." Celeste picked up the phone, and Marilyn took Jocelyn by the elbow and steered her out of the office.

"You'd think she was my mother, not my daughter," Marilyn said.

"She's a wonderful girl," Jocelyn said. "She works two jobs?"

"Yes, she's trying to get as much money saved as she can before her missionary comes home."

"Is he one of your . . ."

"Matches? Actually, no, Celeste met Nick through mutual friends of theirs. He's a wonderful boy, very considerate, hardworking, loves to laugh."

"He does sound wonderful."

"They dated for three years before he left on his mission."

Jocelyn's eyes widened. "That's a long time."

Marilyn nodded. "Yeah, if I didn't know them both, I'd think so too. I mean, she's dated him since he was sixteen. I liked the boy, but I was worried about them getting too serious, you know? But after a few months I realized that they were still making sure to go out in groups or double date or hang out around one of the families. They were very mature about everything—way more than I would have been. Anyway, this boy really is a keeper. Get this . . . when they first started dating, he gave her two gifts: a patchwork quilt he made himself and a custom puzzle piece that had part of some text on it that he had written. He told her to keep the piece and that he would give her more as they had more *special* days together. Well, from that point on, he would give her a piece of the puzzle on days like Valentine's Day, Easter, Christmas—he even gave her one on Canada Day."

"So what does the puzzle say?" Jocelyn asked, completely hooked by the story.

"That's just it—it doesn't really make any sense. It seems like some kind of instructions or something, but we don't have it all figured out. He's even sent a couple of pieces from his mission. Needless to say, we are very anxious to find out what the message on the puzzle says and what it all means."

"That's quite a story."

"He's quite a guy," Marilyn said. "He's the kind of boy you pray your daughter will meet."

"When does he get home?" she asked.

"Middle of July."

They turned the corner. "Here we go. This will be your room."

They entered a large room that had big windows on two walls. There were two rows of tables with five rectangular tables in each row. One wall had cupboards from floor to ceiling; the other was bare—ideal for hanging artwork or posters.

"It's perfect," she said, immediately getting flooded with ideas on how to arrange the tables and configure the room so she could make each student feel included and valued. Her goal as a teacher was to focus on the individual. She realized that every student came to class at a different level and that each student learned at a different pace. She was determined to make each one feel important. She got excited as she thought about the boxes of resource material she had packed in hopes of being able to use it once again in a classroom.

"I'm sure you'll like it even more when you decorate it the way you want it," Marilyn said.

Her heart dropped. Her painting. She'd been so excited to bring her original art piece to school to show her students.

"Jocelyn? Are you okay?"

Jocelyn cleared her throat. "Yes." She nodded, knowing she had to block it from her thoughts or she'd start crying.

"Something's wrong, I can tell. Is it the room? Are you disappointed it isn't bigger?"

"Oh, no, this room is wonderful. I couldn't ask for a better room. It's just that . . ."

"Honey, what is it? Is there something I can do? Some way I can help?"

Jocelyn looked away, embarrassed that she was so easy to read. She wasn't sure if it was being in the room or being with Marilyn who was so kind and caring or exactly what it was that had uncorked her, but her emotions bubbled right to the surface. Before she knew it she was telling Marilyn about her car and having to sell her beloved Bocelli painting.

Marilyn slid an arm around Jocelyn's shoulders. "I'm so sorry. That must be so hard on you."

"I know it's for the best," Jocelyn said. "Thanks for listening."

"Well, sweetie," Marilyn gave her another squeeze, "I'm always there if you need me. I've raised three daughters, and I have learned how to listen when one of them needs to talk. Believe me, I know how good it feels to let it out. Don't you feel better?"

Jocelyn smiled. "Actually I do. I never had a mom to listen to me like that."

"That's a shame. But you just remember, I am always there if you need a friend, or"— she smiled—"a surrogate mom."

"Thank you, Marilyn," she said.

"I won't try and suffocate you, but I tend to be a mother hen to all my teachers. Of course, some don't always appreciate me fussing over them, but I can't help it, it's just the way I am."

Jocelyn smiled. "I think it's wonderful."

"It will all work out, honey. You'll see."

* * *

The next order of business was to go back home and try to get some work done on the yard. The day was clear and beautiful, and she knew that she had to take advantage of good weather. The problem was, she wasn't really in the mood to weed flower beds.

In the mood or not, she put on her ragged jeans and a Dixie State College baseball cap and went outside to tackle her overgrown yard.

With sweat trickling down her forehead and neck, she worked tirelessly, finding that once she began, she really didn't mind being outside in the pleasant weather, feeling the soft breeze on her face and getting a breath of fresh, pine-scented air. In fact, she felt energized and pleased as she surveyed her progress. She still had a lot to do, but it looked much better, especially in the front yard.

"Not bad," she said, wiping her cheek on her shoulder. She wheeled the lawn mower back to the shed, wondering how much a riding mower cost.

Putting away the rest of the equipment, Jocelyn went inside and poured herself a tall glass of lemonade then took it outside and sat in the shade to relax and enjoy the moment.

From his backyard, Harry called, "Hey, neighbor, you trying to make me look bad?"

She laughed. "Actually, I'm just trying to keep Mayor Duncan off my back."

"Wise move. You did a nice job. I have an edger if you want to borrow it."

She'd never used an edger before. She thought it might add a nice finishing touch, but she was too tired to do it today. "Maybe tomorrow," she said. "Thank you."

He began walking away.

"Hey, Harry, do you have a minute?"

He stopped and turned. "Sure, what's on your mind?"

"Is it true my grandmother wanted to turn her land into a berry farm?"

A smile grew on his face as he walked toward her. "She talked about it often. Why?"

Putting down her glass of lemonade, she stood and met him where their properties joined. "I don't know anything about growing berries, but I just got a job teaching at the middle school, and I thought it might make a good side job for the summer."

"A few years back she was very serious about doing it. I looked into it and discovered that having our land slope on the east like it does provides a perfect area to plant berries."

"*Our* land? Does this mean you were also thinking of doing it?"

"When Cora came up with the idea, I thought she was off her rocker, but the more research I did, the more I came to see that it wasn't as harebrained of an idea as I thought. In fact, there is a lot of potential in growing berries and having a U-pick farm. I've never grown berries, but I did grow up on a farm and know a thing or two about taking care of crops. It would involve more of your land than mine, but it would make use of both properties."

"Would you still be interested in doing it? I'm a little intimidated with the thought of tackling something like this by myself."

"I had money put aside to get the farm started, but when your grandmother got sick, well, of course, plans changed. It's all still there, ready to get things started."

"That's great! I have a little cash I could put into it, but I guess I don't know how much I'd be looking at."

"Don't worry about it. If we do this together, we can pool resources and be partners."

"You'd do that?"

"Sure. I really think this could work and, I'll be honest, being retired isn't all it's cracked up to be. In fact, retirement is for the birds! My back is good, I have plenty of energy, it would get me outside of the house . . . why not?"

"You know I'll pay you back for any of the money you put into it, right?"

"I'm in no hurry. We can work all of that out."

Jocelyn smiled. She wanted to hug the man.

"I'm not ready to start on this quite yet, but I'm excited about the idea. Give me a couple of days to look into it, okay?"

"Of course!" he exclaimed. "It's a bit involved, but nothing we couldn't handle."

Jocelyn loved how he included her. "I think it sounds great. I probably should just research it a little to find out what I'm getting into, though."

"Not a bad idea. Seein's how you're a teacher and all, most likely you'll be the brains behind our little venture."

"Ha! Don't look at me to be the brains. Remember, I'm an *art* teacher. Believe me, when it comes to math and finance, I know diddly."

Harry chuckled. "We'll figure it out. Let me know when you're ready to talk business."

Worn out but excited about the prospect of starting a business, Jocelyn went inside to take a shower. She felt a great deal of satisfaction as she thought about her accomplishments so far that day. For the first time in a long time she felt as though she was finally moving forward instead of backward.

* * *

By the time she'd showered off the garden grime, her stomach was growling insistently.

One look inside her fridge told her she was out of luck and out of food. She could go to the grocery store and buy something then bring it back and make it, but that would take too long—she was hungry now. She'd half expected Jack to come and start work, but since he didn't show up, she figured something had come up. She wasn't about to call and pressure him since he was already doing her a favor.

"That's it," she said as her stomach growled again. "Time to go to the diner."

She grabbed a light denim jacket and pulled it on then threw her purse strap over her shoulder and headed out the door. Even though she needed to watch her spending, she hated having to cook for one. Maybe she could invite Harry over once in a while. She imagined he felt the same way about meals.

The day continued clear and beautiful, and she paused to look at the yard one more time before getting in the car. The lawn had several brown spots, and the bushes were in need of trimming, but having everything tidied up made all the difference. As a little girl she had loved the little cottage, and now she realized she could fall in love with it all over again.

With her spirits high and her appetite raging, she drove down the canopied lane to town, where she parked off the main square. She wasn't about to risk a ticket again.

Most of the businesses had closed for the day, so most of the people in the square were either those who were doing the same as she was—looking for a place to eat—or those who were out for an evening stroll, enjoying the beautiful, clear evening.

She drank in the atmosphere as she cut across the square and made a beeline for the diner. A small bell jingled in greeting, but it was the aroma of delicious food that welcomed her.

Pausing by the counter where a sign read PLEASE WAIT TO BE SEATED, she scanned the booths, sort of relieved there was no one she knew eating there that night. She was fine dining alone and happy to be left to her own thoughts.

"Hey, Jocelyn," Celeste said, grabbing a menu from the pile on the counter. "How are you? What did you think of the school?"

"I'm excited to get my room ready and get my lesson plans figured out. Your mom told me my budget for the year and I was shocked."

"That bad?" Celeste motioned for her to take a seat in one of the smaller booths out of the way.

"No, good. It's more than I've ever had to work with. I barely know what I'll do with all that money to work with."

"Just make sure you spend it all, or they'll adjust it down next year," Celeste advised.

This was a challenge Jocelyn was thrilled to take on.

Celeste didn't have to wait for Jocelyn to decide what she wanted—something caught her eye right away. The menu was full of delicious options that would take weeks to try, but this time she wanted a bowl of cheddar potato soup in a sourdough bread bowl.

To start off the meal, Celeste brought her a lemonade and a dinner salad.

Jocelyn speared a tomato as she pulled out her notebook and began jotting down thoughts and ideas for her classroom and for the house.

"Excuse me, is this seat taken?"

Jocelyn didn't even notice anyone standing by her until Jack had spoken. She looked up with a start.

"I'm sorry. I didn't notice you were busy. I didn't mean to interrupt."

"No, you're fine. Please." She pointed to the seat across from her.

"You're sure?"

She nodded as he slid into the booth.

"Sorry I didn't make it over tonight," he said.

"No problem. I figured something came up." She wrote down a final thought on her list and closed the cover of her notebook.

"I love living here, don't get me wrong," he said, "but it would be nice if every time the town needs something built or repaired they didn't come to me. The mayor's office called and said they needed me to come and take a look at something, and I ended up spending my entire afternoon there, fixing a wall in the mayor's office that he just happened to make a hole in while practicing his golf swing."

"What!" Jocelyn exclaimed with a laugh. "He hit the wall with his golf club?"

"Not exactly. He knocked over a large lamp that fell into the wall and made a big hole, completely breaking the lamp. I had a hard time not laughing when I saw it."

"I bet. Did he come out and tell you how it happened?"

"He wasn't even there when I arrived. His secretary filled me in. She said that's just one of the many things that's happened that she could tell me about."

"Oh, really? That's sounds intriguing."

"Believe me, I didn't even want to know. Mayor Duncan's private and public life are really no interest—" Jack groaned like he was in agony. "Oh no."

"What's wrong?"

"Don't look now; keep your head down. Maybe he won't see us."

"Who?" she asked bending down her head.

"The mayor!" he hissed.

"He's here?" she barely spoke, not wanting to draw any attention to them.

"Yes," he replied in the same soft tone.

"So glad this is about you and not me this time," she said.

The mayor's booming voice disturbed the quiet atmosphere of the diner.

"Good evening, all. Just want to personally invite you to the town meeting tomorrow. We have some important issues on the docket and need the people of this fine town to come and discuss some decisions that need to be made regarding our town square as well as whether or not we should grant the Three Holy Heirarchs Church access to their parking lot from Fir Street. We also need some more volunteers for our Fourth of July celebration. In fact," he paused, "I think I see one of our dedicated committee members right now. Thank you, everyone. I'll see you tomorrow!"

Jack ducked his head down farther but couldn't escape Mayor Duncan, who was now standing right next to him.

"How's our stage coming for the big celebration, Jack?" he asked, completely oblivious to Jack's efforts to avoid him. The mayor's face lit up when he noticed Jocelyn sitting across from Jack. "And a big hello to our newest town citizen."

Jocelyn smiled, hoping she could avoid any part of the conversation. Her goal was to avoid the mayor as much as possible.

"The stage is fine, Duncan," Jack said. He was clearly the type who didn't like someone breathing down his neck to get a job done. Jocelyn was the same way. If someone gave her an assignment, she liked to be left alone to do her work. Having someone hover about was distracting and annoying.

"And—" he turned to Jocelyn "—am I right in the fact that you have just been hired as the new art teacher at Milford Middle School?"

Jocelyn groaned inwardly. She cleared her throat. "Yes, that's right," she answered.

"Wonderful! We need a backdrop painted for the stage. Something with a patriotic theme. Something grand and glorious," he said, sweeping his arm in a large arch. "You're just the person to do it. You and Jack can discuss the dimensions and come up with some ideas then get back to me. We only have two and a half weeks until the big day. I'd like to have all of this in place in the next week and a half so we have time to make adjustments and changes."

Neither Jack nor Jocelyn attempted to counter his demands. She felt completely bulldozed and unable to say no to the man.

"Wonderful, then," he said, "glad I stopped in. Celeste!"

The waitress jumped when he said her name.

"Cut me a piece of apple pie to go," he ordered then turned back to the booth.

"I'm also thinking we need to have a town cleanup. I expect plenty of state dignitaries to visit our celebration, and we want our city to look its finest." He turned to Celeste, who had a foam container ready to hand to him.

"Thank you, my dear. Just put it on my tab." He took his pie, his booming voice, and his overbearing presence and left. Jocelyn thought she heard a collective sigh of relief as he exited the diner.

"That man is insufferable," one woman said rather loudly.

"It's our own fault. We need to elect someone else as mayor," her husband said, glancing around at the other customers.

"Don't look at me," another man said. "I don't like the man either, but I don't want to be mayor."

No one in the room seemed to have a desire or the backbone to do anything about the mayor.

"Looks like we're stuck with him," Jocelyn said to Jack. "Why don't you run for mayor?" she said to Jack.

"Me!" Jack said with surprise, then he burst out laughing. "There's not enough money in the world to entice me to do that."

"People really seem to respect you," she said. "I think you'd do a great job."

"I'm not very diplomatic."

"And Duncan is?"

"No, but he likes being in charge. I don't."

"So we're stuck with Duncan," she said.

"Looks that way," Jack said. "Sorry you got roped into working on the celebration committee."

"He doesn't even give you a chance to say no."

"That's part of his charm."

She smiled, wondering how long it would really take to paint the backdrop. "So how big is the stage?"

"Don't know. I haven't even started it yet."

"You haven't?"

"It won't take long. I was planning on working on it this weekend. I need to get over and get started on your place first. I should be able to make it tomorrow night."

"That should work fine," she said.

Celeste showed up with Jocelyn's soup bowl.

"That looks good enough to eat," Jack said. "Could you bring me one of those?" he asked.

"Sure thing, Jack," Celeste said. "Jocelyn, what about you? Is there anything else I can get you?"

"Just a backbone," Jocelyn said.

Celeste and Jack laughed.

"I wouldn't mind helping with the painting," Celeste said. "I don't have any artistic talent, but I am willing to help if you could use it."

"I would love your help," Jocelyn said. "Thank you for offering."

Celeste smiled and left to get Jack's soup.

"Well, that was easy," he said.

"Let's just hope it all goes that smoothly," she said. "I'd feel better if I'd done something like this before."

"You'll figure it out. I'll get the plans drawn up tonight so I can give you the dimensions when I come over tomorrow."

Celeste brought his soup, and, for the next half hour, they brainstormed on ideas for the scene in the backdrop. Jocelyn was surprised at the range of creativity Jack had. He was a man of many talents.

Since the evening had grown dark while they'd been in the diner, Jack walked her to her car.

"Wow, look at that," she said, pointing at her loaner car.

"I don't see anything."

"Exactly!" she exclaimed. "I managed to park without getting a ticket."

Jack laughed.

Jocelyn was surprised at how comfortable she was beginning to feel around him. This wasn't like her at all. Being around men, especially alone, made her very uncomfortable. Not Jack, though.

As they said good-bye, she found herself looking forward to seeing him again the next night.

Chapter Fifteen

A loud banging on the front door brought Jocelyn out of a deep sleep. She was disoriented and immediately covered her face with her hands, still subconsciously nervous about a possible bird attack.

The doorbell rang several times in succession.

"My delivery!" she exclaimed, jumping out of bed and scrambling for a hoodie to pull on over her T-shirt.

She charged down the stairs and yanked the door open just as the guy was walking away.

"Sorry!" she exclaimed. "I didn't realize you were coming so early."

"You Jocelyn Rogers?"

"I am."

"You expecting a delivery?"

"I am."

"Where do you want it?"

"Um, well . . ." She decided not to worry about specific placement yet. She hadn't finished painting, and, anyway, this guy seemed like he wasn't in the mood to wait for anyone or anything. "Just inside the front door is fine."

"Okay," he said with a huff. "We'll bring it in." He whistled to another man sitting inside the cab of the truck, and the guy climbed out.

Jocelyn propped the screen door open then made sure the path was clear for them to bring her purchases inside. In spite of the grumpy delivery men, excitement bubbled up inside of her.

Huffing and puffing, the two men brought in her chair, coffee table, headboard, lamp, and, finally, with crystal tinkling as they clomped up the walk, they brought in the chandelier. It had to be turned on its side to go through the front door, and she held her breath, praying that none of the crystals would fall off and break.

"Here." She pointed at a spot on the floor already covered with protective plastic. "Just set it on here."

For a couple of brutes, the men were actually quite gentle with the glittering fixture, which would be a crowning touch for the living room.

After the men were paid and had left, she sat in her new chair and visually arranged the furniture several times before she finally decided on an arrangement that felt right. Once she got the new pieces cleaned up and finished and the walls painted, the room would have her personal stamp on it and feel like her own.

Since she'd finished her last coat of white on the trim the night before, she was ready to remove that tape and start taping off the ceiling and trim so she could paint the walls.

Listening to her iPod while she worked, Jocelyn sang along with the music, feeling energized by the fun of giving the room a face-lift.

She took a short break after she got the taping done and grabbed a bite to eat. It was barely noon, and she'd already gotten a lot accomplished. Eyeing her new furniture she decided to put off painting the walls just a little longer.

Putting her earphones back on, she turned on some tunes, keeping her choices to upbeat songs that kept her energy up and drove her to keep going.

First, she cleaned the floor-lamp base. Next time she had a chance she would buy a new shade for it, and it would look charming.

Next she got out the vacuum and gave the chair a good cleaning. The fabric wasn't worn, but it had spots on the arms and a couple on the cushion that needed cleaning. Luckily, the deep red and cream–striped fabric didn't show the marks, but she still wanted to remove them, so after vacuuming, she spot cleaned the areas that were stained and was able to get most of them out.

Her next project was to tackle the coffee table. It was oval shaped and stained dark. She liked the chunky legs and scrolled edges, but the finish was badly nicked and scraped, and she wasn't excited about refinishing the entire thing. Then she had an idea.

In the shed her grandmother had a few tools. Jocelyn was thrilled to find a power sander. Even if her idea didn't work out, the sander would help her get the table ready for refinishing.

She covered the floor of the porch with an old sheet and carried out the table, then, with sander in hand, she clicked the switch and went over the surface and edges of the table, taking it down to the bare wood in some places and just smoothing out the finish in other places.

Every so often she'd stop and examine her work, liking how it was beginning to look. Singing along with one of her favorite songs by Seal, "Kiss from a Rose," she wiped off the sanded areas with a cloth to remove the dust then stepped back to admire her work. She would just coat the carefully distressed table with a matte varnish, and it would be perfect in the room. Swirling the rag and swaying to the beat of the music, she sang along, loving the table and thrilled that she'd found it.

Then she froze midsentence. There was Jack, a giant smile on his face.

"Crud," she muttered under her breath, feeling the heat of embarrassment flush her face red. She hadn't realized it was so late.

She yanked off her earphones and gave him a half wave. "Hey, Jack."

He just smiled more broadly.

"Um, you mind giving me a hand with this?" she said, wishing she could disappear.

"That's one of my favorite songs," he said while picking up the table and carrying it inside.

She couldn't tell if he was teasing or serious.

"You've got a nice voice."

She rolled her eyes. She never sang in front of people, ever.

"I didn't mean to catch you off guard."

"Wasn't my plan either," she replied.

"I called to let you know I was coming."

She hadn't heard her phone because of the music and the noise of the sander.

"You don't need to be embarrassed. I sing to my iPod too."

"When someone else is listening?" she asked, feeling the heat finally leave her face.

"Not if I can help it," he said.

Their gazes connected, and they both started laughing. It felt good to let all the tension go.

"So, what's all this?" he asked.

"I found some great stuff at the used furniture store."

He looked at the chair, lamp, and table she'd been working on and nodded. "I like it. I've been in there a few times and have never been lucky enough to find pieces like this."

"But wait, you haven't seen the best part." She slowly lifted the plastic covering from the chandelier.

His eyes opened wide. "Okay, that is amazing."

"I know! I couldn't believe it when I found it. They'd gotten it in just the night before."

"Talk about being in the right place at the right time."

"Do you think it will be hard to install?"

"Shouldn't be. Lenny's the guy to ask. He does electrical stuff all the time."

"I hope he can. I really love it."

"It fits you," he said.

"You think?" She smiled, loving the idea.

"Yeah, it does."

Again their gazes connected for a moment, then he quickly said, "So, I'm ready to get to work on your pipes and walls."

"Great. I sure appreciate you being willing to do this," she said.

"I'd just go home and sit on my couch all night watching TV if I didn't," he said.

"How come I doubt that?" she said, knowing all the service he did for others. "Do you need my help?"

"Nah, I pretty much know where to start and what to do. I'll holler if I need anything."

"Want to borrow my iPod?" she joked.

He broke into a smile. "You're probably kidding, but actually, I would. I want to check out what you listen to. So far I like your choice of songs."

Surprised, she handed him the device and earphones, and he put them in his shirt pocket then picked up his bag of tools and went up the stairs to her bathroom.

If felt good to have company, someone else in the house to fill up the emptiness. Not wanting to get paint spattered all over her right before the town meeting, Jocelyn decided to start reorganizing the kitchen cabinets rather than painting the living room.

She smiled as she worked, hearing Jack whistle to tunes from her playlist. She was tempted to peek in on him but didn't want to be a pest. Maybe he was thirsty, though. Certainly it wouldn't hurt to take him a drink.

With an icy cold glass of lemonade in her hand, she climbed the stairs, the sound of his whistling growing louder as she got closer. She stopped when his whistling turned into singing, and she stopped to listen for a moment, his soft voice smooth and pleasant.

Jack had an awesome voice!

She didn't want to disturb him unannounced, so she backtracked to the bottom of the stairs and yelled up, "Hey, Jack, would you care for something to drink?"

The singing stopped, so she yelled up again and asked.

"Sure, that'd be great."

She paused so he wouldn't know she'd been hovering by the bedroom door, then she climbed back up the stairs and went into the room. A large portion of the wall separating the bed and bath was torn open, the pipes and electric wiring exposed.

Her expression must have registered a bit of shock because he quickly said, "I promise, it will look good as new when I'm done."

With a nod, she handed him the drink. "This is quite a project, isn't it?"

"The hardest part is locating the problem." He took a long drink from the glass then wiped his mouth with the back of his hand. "S'good, thanks. Well, I guess I'd better go clean up before the town meeting. Will you be going?"

"Absolutely. Wouldn't miss it."

After Jack left, she made herself a sandwich, pulled on a pair of jeans and a T-shirt, then grabbed her jacket and purse and headed to town. She wanted to arrive in plenty of time so she could blend in with the crowd rather than chance making a late entrance.

Apparently town meetings were a big deal because the square was packed with cars and people. She found a parking spot around the corner off the main square and walked to the town hall building. A couple of familiar faces jumped out at her but no one she felt comfortable talking to.

Her eyes scanned the crowd to see if Jack was there yet, but she couldn't locate him.

With time to spare, she entered the building and followed the crowd into the meeting room where rows of chairs had been set up and were quickly filling up.

She paused at the back of the room, looking for a place to sit, when she saw Marilyn and her daughter Celeste, already seated, waving her over. In case Jack didn't show up, she decided to join them, rather than risk sitting alone. She would save the seat next to her, just in case.

"I was hoping you'd come," Marilyn said when Jocelyn approached. "How are you? You're looking gorgeous tonight."

"I'm great. Thank you." Jocelyn accepted Marilyn's warm hug and a quick hug from Celeste.

"How's your house coming?" Marilyn asked.

"Right now it looks like it should be cordoned off with yellow caution tape, it's such a disaster."

"We'll have to come see it when you're done," Marilyn said. "Actually, if you need help, we'd love to come spend an evening or a Saturday."

"Saturdays work best for me," Celeste said. "I'd love to come and help."

Jocelyn smiled at the two women, feeling her heart grow warm inside of her. "Thank you. That's so nice of you to offer."

An abrupt tapping with a gavel interrupted the chatting as Mayor Duncan brought the meeting to order.

"Citizens of Milford Falls, welcome. We have a full agenda, so we will begin our meeting. We'll dispense with the reading of the minutes from our last meeting, but they will be posted outside for your perusal."

Jocelyn quickly scanned the crowd for any sign of Jack but didn't see him. She hoped he hadn't gotten hung up doing something involving her repairs.

"As you all know, preparations for the Fourth of July celebration are in full swing. Most of our committees are staffed and underway, but there are still many slots for volunteers that need to be filled. Karl, will you start the clipboard please?"

Karl, dressed in his official deputy sheriff gear, stood and presented a clipboard with a pen on a string tied to it. Before handing it to the crowd, he said, "Last time we had a few jokesters in the crowd who thought it would be funny to sign as Disney characters and other more . . . shall I say, colorful . . . characters. This will not be tolerated. This clipboard is official city business, and we request that the names of actual town citizens be listed. Thank you."

Jocelyn pursed her lips together to not smile, though it was hard.

"Thank you, Karl," the mayor said as he took the floor again. "You'll notice that we need quite a few more volunteers to help with publicity. We'd like a big showing this year, and our goal is to make the Milford Falls Fourth of July celebration one of the biggest in the state of Washington. Of course, the Lewis and Clark dress-up contest has already put us on the map, and we expect an even bigger turnout for that, but I'd like to see our pie-baking and pie-eating contests as well as the fishing derby double in size.

"Of course, we'll have the usual game and food booths, and we're even going to increase the size of our fireworks display, but this year we thought we'd add something to our Fourth of July program. Following the parade, where we'll unveil our new town fire engine, we'll come back here to the town square where we'll have the grandstand set up for our program. Townspeople and visitors will be able to meet our new police chief and receive a special gift."

"What's the gift, Mayor?" a voice called out.

"Well," the mayor rubbed his palms together with excitement, "I guess it doesn't need to be a secret, but we will be handing out invisible ink pens, with which to mark your valuables in the event of burglary."

The revelation produced an impressive response from the audience.

The mayor beamed with the reaction, then continued. "I am proposing that we launch, starting this Saturday, a Milford Falls clean-up effort. We want our city to sparkle and shine as we welcome visitors from all over the state to our celebration."

A small rumbling erupted, and the mayor held up his hand to quiet the crowd.

"I sense some dissension. I'm happy to discuss the issues."

Karl was on his feet, giving the audience a level glare, as if daring anyone to get out of line.

"It's just that we had our annual spring cleanup barely a month ago," a balding man said.

"Yeah," another voice in the crowd agreed.

"What do you want us to do, Bernie? Vacuum the sidewalks?" yet another voice chimed in.

The group laughed and other comments were made.

"Please, people," the mayor said. "Do I need to remind you that this is one of our city's shining moments and we want visitors to feel welcome and comfortable here? Beautifying our city will make people want to stay and spend their money."

"Listen, Mayor," a woman with black hair exclaimed. "I don't have time to do all of this cleaning again. I have a business to run, not to mention my assignment for the Fourth of July celebration."

"Yeah, me too," a gentleman sitting a few rows behind her said.

"I agree with Lark. It doesn't make sense to clean before the celebration anyway," another woman said. "The whole town gets trashed."

The woman named Lark gave a nod of appreciation toward the others.

More townspeople voiced their agreement with the opposition, and Duncan's expression became gloomy.

"Listen, Duncan"—a male voice from the back of the room spoke up—"the town is clean enough. We need to spend our energy on getting ready for the celebration." Jocelyn recognized the voice and turned to see Jack standing at the back of the room. Next to him was Lacey. Jocelyn's heart sank when she saw them together.

Lacey stood next to Jack, smiling as though she'd won an Oscar. Of course, with her desperate performance at the diner, she probably could be nominated for one.

The rest of the audience agreed with Jack, many claiming that they barely had time to get everything ready as it was.

Mayor Duncan finally acquiesced. "Citizens, please, I can see that this is one of those issues that will require a compromise. I'd like to propose, then, that perhaps each business owner be responsible for at least making their storefront as attractive and inviting as possible and that maybe we could recruit our Scout troops to do a final sweep of the town square to pick up trash and make sure our lovely town is presentable for the festivities."

"Agreed!" Jack said, speaking for the group.

A hearty cheer went up, and for a moment, the crowd chatted with excitement and fervor.

Marilyn leaned over to Jocelyn and said, "You have to understand that when Mayor Duncan wants the town cleaned he doesn't just mean sweeping sidewalks and picking up litter. He wants everything washed down, even the streets; he wants all street signs cleaned and touched up; trees, bushes, and shrubs all have to be trimmed; even bricks have been vacuumed at his insistence. The man is OCD about cleanliness."

"What a waste of time," Jocelyn said. "You can't keep the outside clean, because . . . well, because it's outside!"

"Exactly!" Celeste said.

"His mother must have been psycho while he was growing up. The man is insufferable, and this whole cleanliness thing is abnormal,"

Marilyn said. "I swear, next time we have an election I'll run for mayor before I vote Duncan in again."

The discussion about the Three Holy Heirarchs Church gaining access to their parking lot from another street ensued, and Jocelyn found herself quickly losing interest. She began scanning the room, recognizing a few of the members from her ward, a couple of the store owners she'd met, and then her glance took her back to Jack and Lacey. Jack leaned against the wall, his arms folded across his chest, while Lacey stood so close that several locks of her fried blond hair rested on his shoulder.

Jocelyn turned back around, listened briefly to the boring banter about parking lots, access, and zoning, and realized she was ready to leave.

"I think I'll slip out," she said to Marilyn. "I don't really know much about what's going on, and I'm about ready to fall asleep."

"I'm right behind ya," Marilyn said.

"Me too," Celeste echoed.

Crouching down as they left their seats, they tiptoed down the aisle to the closest exit. Jocelyn found herself worried that Duncan would notice them and order them back to their seats. Relief filled her when they made it safely outside.

"Whew, made it!" Marilyn said. "I don't know why I even bother going to those meetings. Well, actually I do. It does get pretty heated in there, and Duncan turns this bright shade of red when he gets mad. He's like a geyser getting ready to erupt."

"This parking lot thing wasn't a hot enough topic to get Duncan that mad, or we would have made you stay," Celeste told Jocelyn. "Trust me, it's worth it."

Jocelyn laughed. "Gee, that's something to look forward to. I knew I moved here for a reason."

"And people say small-town life is boring. Well, they've never been to Milford Falls," Marilyn said.

"The cleanest city in America!" Celeste added with raised fists.

The three women parted ways, and Jocelyn slung her purse over her shoulder and strolled back to her car.

The evening was perfect, fresh, and cool. There was still a blush in the sky from the setting sun, and the air was filled with a combination of floral scents. It was intoxicating.

Even though she hadn't been there long, Jocelyn was beginning to feel comfortable in Milford Falls. She still yearned for the familiarity of

St. George and the comfort zone it provided. But she was beginning to feel like maybe, at least for now, she was where she was supposed to be.

That night, back at home, she got on the Internet and began to research berry farming and what it would take to turn her backyard into a working farm. The more she learned, the harder it sounded but also more lucrative. Berry farms were big business, and it fit in perfectly with her teaching schedule. She started writing down notes and ideas and questions for Harry.

Before she went to bed she sketched out a couple of ideas she had for the grandstand backdrop. She didn't know why they couldn't just have a couple of banners and some balloons, but Mayor Duncan had his mind made up and apparently whatever Duncan wanted, Duncan got.

Ready for bed, she got down on her knees and spent some time in prayer and meditation. She tried to process all the challenges she had faced the last week. The part that amazed her the most was that she'd gotten through them all and actually felt stronger and more independent than she ever had in her life. Of course, compared to many people, her challenges were nothing, but to her they were big and had required a lot of effort and sacrifice.

It felt good to know she had made it this far, and it helped her feel less apprehensive about her future. She didn't know what trials were in store for her, but she did know that with faith, prayer, and the help of wonderful friends, new and old, she would make it through.

Chapter Sixteen

Friday morning she picked up her car from the repair shop. It was excruciating writing out the check, not only because of the enormous expense, but because she equated it with the loss of her beloved painting. She had to remind herself that it had been the right thing to do and that at least she still was debt free.

After spending the rest of the morning grocery shopping and doing a little yard work, she'd gotten estimates to replace a few cracked window panes. For her hard morning's work she rewarded herself by doing a little reading, but by midafternoon she'd regained enough energy to get a first coat of paint on the living room walls. She'd chosen a caramel color, wanting to keep a neutral palette but add warmth and richness to the room. The result was exactly what she wanted. The hardwood floor was beautiful dark maple, and the tones of the floor complemented the wall color beautifully, especially when offset by the creamy white of the baseboards.

Jack had called to say he'd be a little late coming over that evening so he could buy some needed parts and materials. Jocelyn was pleased he hadn't been calling to cancel.

When he arrived she followed him upstairs as he explained the repairs he was making. She really had no idea what he was talking about, but she thought it was nice of him to act as if she did. Just the fact he was spending his evenings at her house was kind. It occurred to her he probably hadn't even stopped for dinner before coming over. "You know," she said, "I was about to make a big pot of homemade chicken noodle soup. I finally did some real grocery shopping this morning. Have you eaten yet? Or do you have plans for dinner?"

"No on both counts. You don't have to feed me, though."

"I know," she said, "but it's nice to have someone else to share it with. I had been planning to freeze most of the soup for later. I hate cooking for one."

"Me too. In fact, I never cook for myself, although I actually enjoy cooking."

She smiled at the revelation. "Really?"

He nodded. "I watch cooking shows all the time. I like Paula Dean's style but without all the butter."

She continued to smile.

"Of course I'll deny it if you tell anyone I said that."

"Your secret is safe with me," she told him, thinking that he managed to impress her the more she got to know him. "But now that poses a problem."

"It does?"

"Yeah. I'm nervous to cook for someone who knows what to do in the kitchen."

He laughed. "Don't be nervous on my account. I said I *like* to watch cooking shows and I *like* to cook. That doesn't mean I'm any good. I can do a few different pasta dishes and I'm pretty good with a grill, but that's about the extent of it."

"Hmm. Maybe I should just get a pizza delivered."

"Tell you what, you cook for me tonight and I'll cook for you sometime, maybe next week. I'll show you that I'm not that great."

"Gee, that sounds so enticing."

"No, I didn't mean it that way. The dish I want to make is good, but it's about the only thing I do well."

"All right," she said with a nod, "I accept." Her homemade chicken noodle soup was her grandmother's recipe. Her mouth watered just thinking about it. She just hoped Jack liked it.

Before long Jocelyn had the process well underway. With the chicken simmering in the pot, she added all the chopped vegetables to the water then rolled out the dough for the homemade noodles. With a sharp knife, she cut long thin strips and set them aside. Once the vegetables were tender, she would put the noodles in to cook.

Keeping an eye on the pot, she set the table with her best two bowls and bread plates. She'd bought a sourdough baguette that would taste delicious with the soup, so she sliced that up and put it in a basket.

Testing one of the larger slices of carrot, she decided it was time to throw in the noodles. Giving the pot one last stir, she went upstairs to tell Jack dinner was almost ready.

"How's it going?" she asked when she found him with white dust covering his arms and hands. "Had to cut more, huh?"

"Sorry. I really am trying to be conservative about how much I destroy."

The hole was nearly the size of the doorway.

She shrugged. "Do what you've got to do. I don't want to have to ever do it again."

"That's what I figured."

"I just thought I'd let you know that dinner will be ready in a few minutes."

"Thanks. I'll be right down."

Jocelyn returned to the kitchen to put ice in the glasses and fill them up with water when her phone rang. It was Andrea.

"Hey, girl, how's it goin'?"

"Things are going great, actually. I've been getting some painting done finally, and I found some furniture that I'm refinishing."

"Serious! That sounds so fun. I'd much rather be with you than stuck here in LA," she said.

"What's going on? Don't you like your new job?"

"I can't decide yet. There are a couple of girls who are making me crazy."

"Like how?" Jocelyn filled up the glasses with water and put napkins next to the silverware, suddenly wondering if it would look too much like a date. It wasn't a date—they were just friends sharing a meal. She decided she was overanalyzing. "It's just that, well . . ." Andrea stammered and restated a few things several times until she finally burst out, "Okay, basically I hate them because they are young and beautiful and getting all the attention."

"Andrea!"

"I do. I hate that I'm getting old."

"You . . . we," she corrected, "are not old!"

"In my business, I am. For Oprah, fifty may be the new forty, but in the fitness world thirty might as well be sixty! And the thing is, I've never felt healthier or in better shape in my life. But these girls are wrinkle free, sag free, and cellulite free, and I can't compete."

"Then don't. Andrea, you have proven yourself in that industry. You are highly respected, and you have created a name for yourself. You're a celebrity, for crying out loud! It's time to start acting like it."

"Whoa, Jocelyn," Andrea replied.

"I don't mean act like a spoiled diva. I mean, carry yourself with confidence. You know who you are and how hard you've worked to be where you are. Don't let them make you feel any other way."

"Hey, Jocelyn," Jack's voice echoed through the kitchen, "mind if I wash up in the bathroom?"

"Not at all," she said. "There should be clean towels hanging up."

"Hold the freaking phone!" Andrea exclaimed. "Is that who I think it is?"

Jocelyn laughed. "Yes."

"What is going on? Tell me everything."

"I can't at the moment," Jocelyn said, "but I'd be happy to call you later."

"You'd better! Oh, my gosh, Joss, this is so exciting! You totally deserve someone awesome!"

"You're jumping to conclusions," Jocelyn said in a calm tone, but inside her concerns were reawakening. What was she thinking! She'd never made dinner for a man before.

"Call me as soon as he leaves!"

"You can count on it," Jocelyn said and hung up the phone.

She noticed her hand trembling as she put her phone on the counter. Andrea's call had succeeded in making her realize exactly what she was doing. She'd been so comfortable with Jack that she'd actually been brave enough to invite him for dinner, a dinner she herself had prepared.

Suddenly she was sick to her stomach.

"Something sure smells good," Jack said as he came back into the kitchen.

Jocelyn stopped and looked at him, not answering. Last week she had looked at Jack as someone to be avoided, then she saw him as a ward member, and finally she'd considered him a friend. But until this moment she had never looked at him from a romantic perspective. Suddenly she was very aware of how attractive she found him. He was tall, lean, and strong, with very blue eyes and dark, wavy hair. With his ponytail and beard he had a rugged, backwoodsman look about him, like he should be wearing buckskin pants and a fringed leather jacket.

"Jocelyn?"

She snapped out of her trance. "Oh, sorry," she said. "I was just trying to remember if I added salt to the soup."

"Why don't we find out?" he said. "I'm starving."

"Good idea."

She quickly turned to the stove and dipped the ladle in and gave the noodles a stir. Her stomach was swirling as much as the contents of the pot, and she told herself to calm down and relax. They were just friends, and they were eating dinner together. They'd done it before. Nothing was different.

But something had changed. The emotions she felt were unfamiliar to her, yet she knew exactly what they were. She was developing feelings for Jack. She didn't just like him, she *liked* him.

Going through the motions, she ladled several large scoops of the soup into a bowl.

"Here," he said, coming up behind her, so close she felt his elbow brush her arm, "let me help."

"Thank you," she croaked then swallowed hard to clear her throat so she could sound more like a human—*if* she dared to speak again.

She filled another bowl, which he also took, his closeness making her feel light-headed. The sudden recognition of her feelings for him seemed to increase her awareness of them. She needed to get a grip . . . fast!

The basket of sliced baguette was on the table and so were the drinks. She had no chance to escape for a moment so she could get her breath back.

He looked at her and smiled.

She returned his smile and sat down in her chair, fumbling for her napkin. "I hope you like it. I can't make any promises."

"If it tastes as good as it smells, I won't have any complaints."

They both sat in awkward silence for a moment, the steam from their bowls bathing their faces.

"Should we pray?" he asked.

"Yes, that would be nice."

His forehead wrinkled as he studied her for a moment. "Is everything okay?"

She laughed nervously. "Of course. Why wouldn't it be?"

"I just wondered if something was wrong. You seem different after that phone call."

"No, everything's fine. I'm just hoping everything tastes good. I've never cooked for a . . ."

He looked at her, waiting for her to finish.

She swallowed, wondering why she'd started talking. Big mistake. She was such an idiot! *He's waiting for you to say something.*

"I don't usually cook for other people," she finally said.

"I'm sure it will be fine. I would have ended up eating ramen noodles tonight. It's got to be better than that."

He was so sweet to try and make her feel better.

"Why don't I bless the food since you did all the work to make it?"

He was so thoughtful!

They bowed their heads, and he said a quick prayer on the food but caught her off guard by saying that he was grateful for the time they could enjoy together that evening.

Her heartbeat quickened and her head spun. This was ridiculous! She was acting like a love-struck teenager. But that was exactly how she felt.

He picked up his spoon and dipped it into the bowl. She held her breath with anticipation.

He blew on the soup to cool it then ate it.

"Does it need salt? I forgot, didn't I?"

He shook his head. "It's perfect. Delicious."

"You're sure?" she asked.

He nodded and took another bite. "It's really good."

Jocelyn tasted one of the noodles and some of the broth. She wished she would've let the noodles cook just a bit longer so they weren't quite as chewy, but they were still good and the broth was flavored with just the right spices. Regardless, they couldn't keep talking about the soup. She searched her mind for a safe topic of conversation.

"So, how do you think my pipes started to leak?" she asked.

"My guess would be that they probably froze during the winter and damaged the pipes. When you started using them again, the pipes couldn't handle the water pressure."

"I didn't think it got cold enough to freeze here."

"It usually freezes a few times during the winter, but last winter we had a few weeks of unusually cold weather. We even got snow. It caused a lot of problems for a lot of people. I've had plenty of practice. I'm sorry you've had this happen right off the bat."

"Me too. And I'm so glad you're able to help me. I really appreciate it," she said. Did she sound gushy? *Stop worrying so much and just move on!* "My grandmother would be happy that I'm fixing up the house. She'd also be thrilled about the idea that Harry and I have come up with."

"What's that?"

She told him about the berry farm idea.

"I know of a couple of small berry farms north of Seattle that are very successful. With you having summers free I think it's a great idea. See, you're fitting right in here in Milford Falls."

An unexpected knock came at the door.

Jack and Jocelyn looked at each other. "Were you expecting someone?" he asked.

"No." Then she had a horrible thought. "You don't suppose it's the mayor, do you?"

"I wouldn't think so," he said, but his tone wasn't convincing.

She got up from the table and went to the door, pausing before opening it. "I'm scared," she said to Jack. "What if it is him?"

"If we're lucky maybe some birds will attack him," he joked.

Jocelyn laughed.

The knock came again.

With dread, she turned the knob and opened the door to find Lacey standing at her door. Between the snug top and clunky high heels, the woman looked like she was wearing clothes she'd worn ten years and ten pounds ago. It occurred to Jocelyn she could still use those birds. They might like Lacey's hair for their nest. Jocelyn cleared her throat to prevent herself from giggling. "May I help you?"

Lacey peeked around her to look inside her house. She lit up when she found who she was looking for. "Jack, I was hoping I'd find you here."

Jocelyn stepped back as the woman barged her way into the house.

"Oh, Jack," she said with desperation. "I need your help. Dylan's run away from home."

"Again?" Jack asked, seemingly unworried as he took another bite of soup.

"Yes. He hooked up with some older boys he met at the bowling alley, and they invited him to go to Seattle to a concert. Of course, I told him he couldn't go, but when I got home from work he was gone and I can't find him anywhere. I think he's gone to Seattle with them."

"Do you know their names?" Jack asked.

"No."

"Do you know where the concert is?"

"No."

"Do you know what kind of car they're in?"

"No."

"How do you suppose we find him, then?"

Lacey lifted her hands helplessly. "I don't know. I don't know what to do!"

"Have you contacted the police?" he asked, still not moving from his seat.

"I don't want to until I know for sure he's gone to Seattle."

"Have you checked with all of his friends, gone to all the places he hangs out?"

"Yes, all of that."

"Then I don't see what else you can do. You need to contact Sheriff Williams and tell him what you suspect has happened."

"Jack, can't you please come and help me? I'm frightened something is going to happen."

"Dylan is smarter than you give him credit for, Lacey. He's just trying to get attention."

"Well, he certainly got it!" Lacey exclaimed. "I'm at the end of my rope with him. What do I do?"

Jack shut his eyes briefly, letting his head slump back. "All right, fine." He put down his spoon and wiped his mouth with his napkin. "I'll meet you at the bowling alley in ten minutes."

Lacey stopped her theatrics, her expression of stress turning into a triumphant smile. "You will?" her voice oozed with sweetness. "Oh, Jack. You are such a sweetheart." She tugged at the hem of her shirt and wiggled her shoulders back, giving her hair a toss. "I will have to think of some way to thank you."

"Please don't," he said. "I'll see you at the bowling alley."

"See you in a few," she said over her shoulder to Jack, throwing one last glance Jocelyn's way, as if to make sure she was aware of her claim on Jack. Jiggling her way out the front door, Lacey left, leaving Jocelyn standing at the door in amazement.

"Guess you'd better get going," Jocelyn said, not knowing what else she could say. "Sounds pretty urgent."

Jack looked at her with one eyebrow raised.

It was obvious Jack didn't feel a sense of urgency at all.

"I'm only going in case she isn't crying wolf. Dylan's a half-decent kid. I'd hate to see anything bad happen to him. I'm their home teacher, and I know Lacey milks that for all it's worth and then some, but I still have to try to help out where I can."

"Well, before I forget, thanks for all the work you did tonight." *Her home teacher,* not *her boyfriend.* Jocelyn suddenly felt so much lighter that she was almost giddy

"Thanks again for dinner. The soup reminded me of my mom's. Actually, it was even better than hers."

"Ah . . ." She waved a hand at him. She knew he was just being nice, but she started to blush.

"Sorry to have to run out like this."

"Not a problem," she said.

He fished his keys out of his pocket. "I tried to leave your bathroom in some kind of order, but it's just a messy job."

She took a step toward the front door. The last thing she wanted was to have that woman come back and see what was taking him so long, something Jocelyn wouldn't put past her.

He paused at the door, as if he wanted to say something, then changed his mind and turned the knob. "See ya," he said. Then he was gone.

Jocelyn stood in the middle of her front room, looking at the closed door, thinking about the evening, mostly about the fact that she'd had the tenacity to invite Jack to dinner, that he'd stayed to eat with her, and that she found herself having feelings in a way she'd never had them before. She preferred not to think about that woman who'd interrupted their time together. Besides, he clearly wasn't excited to go. That thought brought a smile to her face.

Deciding that she was too tired to do any more that day, she cleaned up the dinner dishes then curled up on the couch to relax and read. It wasn't until her phone rang that she remembered she'd promised to call Andrea.

"So? How did it go?" Andrea asked anxiously.

"Good, I guess."

"You guess?"

"Yeah, it's hard to say. I feel really comfortable with him."

"That's good."

"It is good. But we were interrupted by this woman—I think she and Jack used to date, or still do date, or . . . I don't know exactly."

"What do you mean you were interrupted?"

"She came to my house to ask Jack to help her find her son, who apparently took off with some friends and she couldn't find him."

"Really?"

"Yeah. Jack didn't seem too worried or anxious to leave. It was weird. I don't know what to think."

"But the time you had together was good?"

"Yeah," Jocelyn said wistfully, "it was. He's a really great guy."

"Joss, this is so wonderful. I knew this would happen for you eventually. I'm so happy for you."

"Thanks, but it's not like we have anything going on. He's working on my house. I made dinner for him."

"But you have feelings for him?"

Jocelyn didn't answer for a moment. Acknowledging her feelings to herself was one thing, but admitting them out loud to someone else was another.

"Joss?"

"Yeah, I guess I do. But that doesn't really mean anything. It's not like he has any for me."

"You don't know that yet. You just have to take a risk, put yourself out there, take a chance."

"You know me. I haven't ever met a guy who seemed worth the trouble. I've never even wanted to play the dating game," Jocelyn said. "I don't know how to be anything but myself."

"Joss," Andrea said, "being you is enough. We're too old to have to play games and pretend we're different than we really are anyway."

"I never got that back in high school, y'know?" Jocelyn said. "I'd watch Ava or Emma flirt with guys and act so stupid sometimes, and I just never understood it. I figured if that was what it took to have a boyfriend, then I didn't want one."

"I know. But I'm guilty of it too. Remember when I was dating Derrick, the football coach?"

"Of course I do. We were convinced you were going to marry him."

"So was I," Andrea said. "I was totally infatuated with him. He was single, good-looking, successful, and active."

"Remind me what was wrong with him?" Jocelyn asked.

"We had absolutely nothing in common. He was a football addict and beyond that, there was nothing else in his life. At first, I wanted to like football because I wanted to like him. So I went to his games, I listened to him talk about it, I sat and watched games on television. We even went to a playoff game, and then I started to realize that we never did anything I liked to do. We didn't go to movies unless they were about football or sports. We never went out to eat. He didn't even ask me what was going on in my life or what was important to me. When I finally got honest with myself I realized he just wasn't right for me."

"Sad."

"It was sad. It was so hard breaking up with him. And, of course, he was clueless. He had no idea anything was wrong. The clincher was that when I asked him to tell me what I did for a living, he didn't really have any idea. He hadn't cared enough to know and understand me and what was important to me."

Jocelyn thought about Jack. He seemed very interested in finding out more about her.

"You're doing it right, Joss. Just be you. Whoever you end up with needs to love you for who you are because you are an amazing woman. You don't have to change for anyone."

Jocelyn felt her throat tighten and her eyes tingle. These weren't familiar words to her. Growing up, the only people who told her she mattered were her friends, her grandmother, and her Young Women leaders. She'd had to learn for herself that she mattered to Heavenly Father, but sometimes it was nice to hear it from someone else.

"Besides, it's so exciting that you've met someone you're interested in. This is a big step for you."

Jocelyn cleared her throat then had to laugh. No truer words had ever been spoken. She'd mostly had bad experiences when it came to men. Other than bishops, her mission president, and occasional school teachers who had been kind and caring, she hadn't been around any men who were positive influences for her.

Jocelyn said, "I'm surprised myself. We met by accident, and it just evolved before I even realized what was happening."

"Well, I hope things keep progressing. Maybe it's a good thing I didn't come and stay. You might not have been forced to get to know people like you have."

Jocelyn hadn't thought of it like that before. Andrea was right. She usually kept a safe distance. It wasn't like her to get close to someone so quickly. Jack had taken her by surprise.

"I still want to come and visit sometime. I'm dying to see your house," Andrea said. "But I won't lie. I'm dying to meet Jack even more."

"Don't come too soon. The house is a wreck, and as for Jack, there's nothing going on between us."

"Yet," Andrea added. "It's time to take a chance on love, Jocelyn. Don't be afraid to let him into your life."

"I'm going to try," Jocelyn said.

"Good luck with everything. I love you, Joss."

"Love you too," Jocelyn said. "And thanks, Andrea. I'm really glad you called earlier."

Feeling like she'd gotten a second wind, Jocelyn changed into her painting clothes and got a second coat of paint on her living room walls.

She had just finished cleaning up her supplies when her phone rang.

"Hi, Jocelyn. It's Jack."

"Oh, hi!"

"I forgot to tell you, but we have a Fourth of July committee meeting tomorrow. Are you free around ten in the morning?"

"I should be," she said, knowing she had absolutely nothing else going on.

"We want to start construction on the grandstand. You'll have free rein on the backdrop, and you'll have some committee members to help you."

She felt like his warmth from earlier was gone. His tone was businesslike, not open and friendly like before. Had something happened with Lacey?

Trying to hide her concern, she said, "I've got a couple ideas planned; I don't think they will be too difficult. So, where are we meeting?"

"At the empty building behind the town hall, but we'll build the grandstand right in the town square."

"Okay, see you tomorrow."

She hung up, trying to ignore the worry she felt. Why had she dared even think he would be interested in her?

Exhausted both physically and emotionally, she switched off the light in the kitchen and went upstairs, wishing she could switch off her feelings so easily.

Chapter Seventeen

Wondering why she'd accepted the assignment to work on the grandstand backdrop, Jocelyn walked into the empty building where a small group of people were talking around a pile of lumber.

"If we buckle down we should be able to get the frame up today. We will build it on site, so we'll need to move this lumber over to the town square. Hopefully you brought work gloves." Jack gave Jocelyn a nod when he noticed her join the group.

He fielded a few questions from members of the committee, then the lumber loading began. Jocelyn hadn't brought work gloves—they usually weren't required for painting.

"Hi, glad you could make it," he said to her.

"I'm sorry. I wasn't told we needed gloves," she said.

"I didn't mean for you to help load."

"I don't mind, really."

"You have your own project to work on."

"I'm not exactly sure where to begin. I brought my sketches . . ."

He pointed to the other side of the room where a large roll of white canvas stood in the corner.

"Once we get this lumber out of here, you can roll out the canvas and measure it for the grandstand. I've got the dimensions right here. If my guess is right, you should be able to cover the back with three widths of fabric, thirty feet long."

It was a bit larger than she'd expected, but she could adjust her scale to fit the measurement without too much trouble.

"I found a couple of people to help you with the painting. You already know both of them. The first one is Mary Jane Gentry and the other one is . . ."

Don't say it, she thought.

". . . Lacey."

No! Jocelyn didn't want to cause a problem, but the last person she wanted to work with was Lacey.

"You know, Jack," she said, "I don't see this being that big of a job that I would need two people to help me. I can sketch the pattern onto the fabric, and the other person can start painting. It will go fairly quickly. If you need one of my people—say, Lacey—you are welcome to have her help you."

"That's very generous of you, but I have plenty of help, probably too much even. No, you'd better keep her."

There it was! She saw it. A flicker in his eye. He was teasing! He didn't want Lacey helping him any more than she did. She was positive. Maybe things weren't as dismal as she had thought last night.

"How about swapping one of your committee members for one of mine, then?" she asked.

"Sorry," he said. "I really can't help you."

"I'll throw in a plasma-screen TV and a new Porsche."

He raised his eyebrows with interest then said, "Nope, sorry. Still not worth it."

She laughed. "Name your price."

He thought about it for a moment, then said, "Since our dinner was interrupted the other night, maybe we could try it again."

"Dinner? That's it?" She laughed. "You got it. Anything you want."

"All right. I'll get back to you on that. Now, I just need to find Lenny to let him know he has a helper. He knows how to handle Lacey."

"Thanks, Jack."

"I expect dessert, too," he said.

"Of course," she replied.

He smiled. "Okay, then. Glad that's settled." He turned to leave then stopped. "You probably could still use some help, though."

"Yeah, kinda." Then she remembered something. "Wait, Marilyn and Celeste offered to help. Once I get the sketch drawn onto the canvas, they can help paint."

"You sure?"

"Absolutely. I'm good." She held up both hands as if to stop him from any further assistance. "Just for the record, you know—in case Karl is looking for an assignment, or heaven forbid, Mayor Duncan."

Jack burst out laughing. Jocelyn couldn't help joining him.

Just then Lacey walked in and saw them. A look of displeasure crossed her face. For some reason, that made them both laugh even harder.

"Excuse me," she said, "I was told I was supposed to report to the backdrop committee." By the tone of her voice it sounded like she was headed for a firing squad.

"Actually, you've been reassigned," Jack said, wiping at the corners of his eyes. "You'll be helping on the grandstand."

Her face brightened. "With you?"

Jack's gaze slipped quickly to Jocelyn's face then back to Lacey's. "Uh, yeah. That's my committee."

"Sounds good to me," she said warmly. "I'm happy to help wherever you need me."

Jocelyn had to fight to not roll her eyes. This woman wasn't for real, was she?

"I'll meet you over in the square," Jack said. "Just find Lenny and tell him to put you to work."

"Okay," Lacey said in her syrupy sweet voice. "Don't be too long."

Without acknowledging Jocelyn, Lacey turned and strutted out of the room.

Jocelyn was stunned by the woman. She looked at Jack to read his expression, but he was busy texting someone on his phone. He pressed the send button and said, "Just giving Lenny a heads-up so he'll play along. Guess I'd better get over there and make sure everyone is doing their job. We really don't have much time to get this together. MJ should be coming anytime. She called and said she'd be a few minutes late."

"I'll call Marilyn and make sure she and Celeste are okay to help."

"Let me know if they're not. There are a few others we can call."

He took off in a rush and left her to assess the backdrop. The first course of action would be to get the fabric cut and stretched out on the floor. They could figure out how to connect the pieces later.

Not wasting any time, Jocelyn placed the call to Marilyn. She had to leave a message since Marilyn didn't pick up. She hoped that she didn't sound too desperate, even though that was how she felt.

"Well, if it isn't our own Milford Falls Michelangelo." MJ's voice echoed through the room. "How's the masterpiece coming along?"

"Now that you're here, I'm sure it will be great!" Jocelyn was thrilled to see MJ, and the two women hugged briefly before discussing the first step.

Jocelyn was immediately filled with gratitude to have the woman on her committee.

"I have a heavy duty sewing machine," MJ said. "I can sew the pieces together. I used to make draperies and bedspreads, so I know it can handle this fabric. Also, we can just take your sketch, project it up onto the backdrop, and trace it on, then paint it. That would be much easier than doing it by hand."

"MJ, you are brilliant!" Jocelyn said.

"Not really. I just happen to have been placed on the right committee."

"So glad it was mine!"

"Me too. Let's roll this out and get to work."

Another reason Jocelyn was glad MJ was on her committee was the fact that the woman didn't mess around.

They were busy rolling, measuring, and cutting when her phone rang. It was Marilyn, enthusiastically accepting the invitation to help on the backdrop. Celeste was at work but would be happy to help as much as she could.

They set up a time to meet later, after MJ had the fabric sewn and her husband could bring over a projector for them to use.

Doing all they could do for now, Jocelyn and MJ left and planned to return that afternoon. Jocelyn decided to spend some time in the yard, since the day was clear and sunny.

After weeding the flower beds—and wondering how weeds grew so fast—she pulled out some trimmers to tackle the shrubbery. She was contemplating the bushes in the front of the house when Harry appeared.

"Hi, Harry. I've been meaning to talk to you."

"I just wanted to tell you I've found a place to buy the plants. They will give us a volume discount and even send someone out to show us how to prepare the soil. They are just out of Seattle."

"Wonderful! I have been researching U-pick farms on the Internet, and even though growing berries seems a bit complicated, I think it sounds like a really great idea. I learned that the berries are ripe the middle of June to the end of July for summer bearing, and August through September for fall bearing. Except for the weeks in September when I'm in school, it works out with my teaching schedule."

"I won't lie to you—it will be a lot of work," Harry said.

"Knowing it was my grandmother's dream makes me want to pursue it. I would like to do this for her."

His eyebrows lifted, causing his whole face to light up. "She would be very happy to hear that. And I'm pleased you've done your homework." He nodded thoughtfully. "So, are you saying that you want to go ahead with the raspberry farm?"

"I do. Yes! If you're sure you want to."

He blinked several times then grinned, reaching out for her hand. With a nod of his head, he gave her hand a squeeze. Jocelyn had the feeling this farm meant a great deal to him. Probably not as much financially as a way to stay active and involved.

"We probably should draw up some kind of an agreement—who's paying for what, that sort of thing."

He patted her hand. "I trust you. I'm in for more than just the money, anyway."

Just as she'd thought.

"I figure I can pay for all the plants. And since we are using mostly your land for the farm then I think we're both contributing to the success equally."

She hadn't thought of it that way before. Without the land he couldn't even plant the raspberries.

"You do realize that I have absolutely no clue how to raise raspberries," she said. "I am willing to work hard, though."

"I've talked to several owners of other berry farms, and they've said it's not bad once you get the routine down."

With the verbal agreement in place, the plan was set in motion. As Harry walked away, Jocelyn felt an immense joy fill her soul. Was this yet another reason why she was supposed to move here? To help Harry? Or for him to help her?

She closed her eyes and sent a quick prayer heavenward. Either way she was grateful for the way things were settling into place and making sense. She kept her expectations low—life had taught her to do so—but she felt optimism about the future.

Feeling lighthearted and happy, she pulled in a breath of pine-scented air and started to trim her bushes. It felt great to be alive!

* * *

"I want to die," Jocelyn said as she tried to push herself out of bed the next morning. Her neck, her shoulders, her back, and her arms screamed with the slightest movement.

MJ, Marilyn, and Celeste had all joined her to work on the backdrop late yesterday afternoon, and after five hours of work they'd succeeded in getting the entire thing sewn, sketched, and outlined with paint. The next time they got together they would just finish the painting and be done.

Right now that satisfaction did nothing to alleviate her sore muscles. She found it ironic that of all the things she'd done this week, it was the art that ended up being the most painful.

She attempted to turn her head to look at the clock on the nightstand and groaned. Was it possible to get whiplash from looking up at a wall for five hours?

"I hate Mayor Duncan," she said as she inched her way to the stairs then slowly made her way down to the main floor bath. "And I hate my stupid pipes."

She stopped in the kitchen to take some ibuprofen, hoping it would kick in soon, then started the water running in the tub. Maybe after a long soak in the tub she would get some relief. Luckily she had plenty of time before church started.

While she waited for the tub to fill, she checked her phone and found she'd missed a couple messages.

The first message was from some guy whose name she didn't remember, asking her to call him back regarding updating personal information for their class reunion. Their class had a reunion every five years, and they weren't due for another one for two years, but Jocelyn assumed someone was just being thorough. None of the Butterfly Girls had ever gone to their reunions, but they had decided that they would all attend the fifteen-year reunion together.

She made a mental note to call him back after church.

The other message was from Chloe. She didn't say much other than that she too wanted Jocelyn to call back.

Jocelyn planned on returning the calls, but the first thing she needed to do was climb into the tub and get some relief from the soreness.

Sinking into the steaming hot water, she relaxed her sore muscles, massaging the tight knots in her neck and shoulders.

Even though she was sore, she had to admit that she enjoyed being part of something, being included in a project, and feeling needed. St.

George was her home, but she had always felt like she was on the outside looking in. Here, she realized, people reached out and drew her in, some of them gently, others by force, but still, she felt more at home here than she had in St. George. It didn't quite make sense to her, yet that was how she felt.

She thought about the trials she'd experienced right off the bat and could see that they had forced her to reach out and to let others reach out to her. Normally she stayed to herself, choosing not to bother others with her needs or problems and consequently not really getting very close to anyone, whether in her ward, her neighborhood, or her job. But here, she'd had no choice when things started falling apart. And she was learning a lot about herself through the process.

She closed her eyes, soaking in the warmth of the water and feeling the tension and soreness melt away.

Her thoughts drifted lazily from starting the raspberry farm with Harry, to spending time with MJ, Marilyn, and Celeste on the backdrop, to recalling how delightful it had been to see Jack show a lack of enthusiasm at Lacey's blatant attempts to get his attention.

Things weren't perfect, but her life was pretty darn good right now.

The trill of her cell phone brought her out of her hypnotic state with a jolt.

"Good grief!" she said as she watched the wave of water slosh over the rim of the tub, dousing her towel.

She wiped her hand off on a dry corner and gingerly picked up her phone.

"Chloe?" she said into the receiver.

"Joss, I've been trying to reach you. Did you get my message?"

"Well, yeah, I noticed you'd called. I planned on getting back to you."

"Has anyone else called to tell you?"

"Like who? Calling to tell me what?"

"I didn't want to scare you in my message, but they're reopening Ava's case again. I wanted to make sure you knew before you heard from someone else."

"What is it, Chloe?"

"I guess they got an anonymous tip or something. They think that whoever tried to kill Ava thought that all of us would be in the car with her!"

Jocelyn nearly dropped her phone. "What?" she whispered. "But who would want to do that?"

"That's what I want to know. I'm still trying to process all of this myself."

"Chloe, if someone did try to kill all of us, whoever it was could still be out there."

"I know. It's freaking me out. I don't dare go outside or let my girls outside."

Jocelyn's mind began racing. Who would possibly have that much hate inside of them that they would actually attempt to injure or kill all of them? And, the bigger question now was, would that person come back after them?

"Are we safe?" Jocelyn asked.

"I don't know. I mean, what if the person found out that the case has been opened up and he or she decides to strike again?"

"What are the police saying?"

"They'll be contacting us to question us again."

"We aren't suspects, are we?"

"I think because none of us was in the car with her, it's possible that we are. You will probably get a call soon."

"Wait a minute," Jocelyn said. "I got kind of a weird phone message about our class reunion. The guy said he's trying to update our contact information, but I didn't know his name, and it seems a little soon to be working on it."

"Yeah, I got one of those calls too. You don't think . . ."

"I won't erase the message so that when the police call I can tell them about it and let them hear it, just in case, you know, it's him, wanting to find out where we live!" Jocelyn felt fear clutch her heart.

"Oh, Joss, I'm scared."

Suddenly Jocelyn wanted to make sure all her doors and windows were locked tight. And she wanted to go get a dog, a German shepherd.

"Listen," Chloe said, her voice calming down, "this is silly. Even if the police think they have a lead, we certainly have no new insights on the case. If someone wanted us dead, he's had thirteen years to do it. I'm sure we're fine."

"Yeah, I guess that makes sense." Jocelyn wanted to believe it, but she couldn't deny she was freaked out now.

"Ah!" Chloe yelped into the phone.

"What's wrong!"

"Sorry, someone just rang my doorbell. I think it's my home teachers. I asked them to give me a blessing. Between Roger and this, I'm a basket case. I'll call you later."

Jocelyn didn't know what to do. Panic was her first reaction, but she knew that wouldn't help. If someone wanted them dead, he would have done it years ago, wouldn't he? It was crazy to think someone was out there waiting to kill all five of them after all these years.

Which made her wonder who would even hate them so much that they'd resort to murder? Her mind couldn't wrap itself around the concept. Either she was in denial, or it just plain didn't make sense to her.

She went through the motions of getting dressed and driving to church, but she was incredibly distracted and worried.

Luckily, in the meetings this week, there wasn't much of a fuss made about her. She only had to introduce herself to a few people. The rest treated her as if she'd been part of their ward for years. It felt wonderful.

The lessons and talks did a great deal to take her mind off Chloe's phone call and help her feel safe and calm again. Still, she didn't want to take any chances and found herself figuring out things she could do to make her home safer.

Catching her off guard, Lacey and an elderly woman approached her as she made her way out of the chapel. Her breath caught in her throat. What could Lacey possibly want from her? And who was this woman?

"Jocelyn," Lacey said, looking her up and down, "there's someone here who wants to meet you."

Jocelyn tried to smile at the woman whose expression seemed anything but warm and friendly.

"This is my mother, Iris Beaumont. She was a good friend of your grandmother's."

"Oh, hello, Sister Beaumont," Jocelyn said, "it's nice to meet you."

"What did you say your name was?" Iris asked, not breaking her cool expression.

"My name is Jocelyn Rogers."

"Hmm," the woman thought for a moment, "I believe we've met before."

"Oh, I'm afraid I don't recall that," Jocelyn said, hoping that would satisfy the woman's curiosity.

"You don't look familiar," Sister Beaumont said, "but I'm sure we've met."

"Well, it's certainly nice to meet you again, then," Jocelyn said.

Sister Beaumont gave her another critical once-over then said to her daughter, "I need to stop by the bishop's office for a minute before we leave."

"Yes, Mother," Lacey said, not quite hiding the annoyance in her voice.

Jocelyn watched both of them walk away then closed her eyes for a moment while she breathed deeply to calm herself down.

Coming back to Milford Falls was a risk. She'd hoped enough time had passed since she was last there. When she'd lived there with her grandmother, she hadn't gone out much. She didn't remember any of the people, even Harry, but somehow Iris thought she remembered her.

She sighed. Just when things seemed to be finally moving forward . . .

Chapter Eighteen

Jocelyn did hear from a St. George police detective on Monday, but she doubted she told him anything that wasn't already in the file. He politely thanked her for her time and assured her she needn't take any more than the usual safety precautions, but all the same she was left feeling unsettled and helpless.

On Monday and Tuesday, Jack came and worked on her house. Jocelyn felt guilty making him spend his evening there, but truth be told, he didn't seem to mind.

Wednesday he called, begging off for the rest of the week so he could work on the grandstand.

"Of course. No problem," she said but felt disappointed all the same. She would miss his joking and the way he whistled as he worked.

* * *

Between working on her house, her yard, and the Fourth of July backdrop, Jocelyn stayed busy enough that she was almost surprised when Saturday rolled around again.

"That looks incredible!" Marilyn exclaimed as she stood back to take in the full effect of the backdrop. "I can't wait until we can hang it up."

Jocelyn also thought it had turned out well. The vivid red, white, and blue of the flag and the contrast of the spread-winged eagle in the corner had a powerful impact.

"Do you think the mayor will like it?" she asked, tracing the upper edge of the eagle's beak one more time. She still wasn't quite satisfied with it.

"Who cares," Marilyn said. "The man wears stripes and plaids together; clearly he has no taste. And the eagle looks perfect."

"Are you sure?"

"He can't help but love it," MJ said. "You've done a fantastic job, Jocelyn."

"I didn't do it. You two did most of the painting," Jocelyn argued.

"An idiot could have done what we did," Marilyn said. "Without your artistic eye and talent it wouldn't have turned out. Don't be so humble—you are immensely talented. I'm so glad we got you to teach at our school."

"I just wish one of my kids were that age in school so they could have you for a teacher," MJ said. "Hey, you ought to teach private art lessons."

"That's a great idea!" Marilyn said. "Celeste has always wanted to take art lessons."

"I'll think about it," Jocelyn told them, but she was pretty sure she'd never have the time, especially if she started painting again herself.

The outside door creaked open, and Jack poked his head inside. "Hey, girls, how's it going in here?"

"If I weren't married, I'd definitely go after this guy. He's a major hunk," Marilyn said under her breath, looking directly at Jocelyn.

Jocelyn's eyes grew wide, and she felt her face flush red. She hoped he hadn't heard her. MJ started laughing, which added more color to Jocelyn's face.

"We've almost got the stage—" He stopped dead in his tracks when he saw the completed backdrop. "Wow. This is fantastic."

"Turned out pretty incredible, didn't it," MJ said.

Marilyn piped up. "Jocelyn's quite talented. It's not fair that someone so smart and beautiful is also so talented, is it MJ?"

MJ caught on immediately. "Not fair at all. I've never met anyone as—"

"So," Jocelyn blurted out loudly, "is this what you wanted, Jack?" She gave MJ and Marilyn scathing looks, but they both just smiled at her innocently.

"This is incredible. Not that I doubted your talents, but under the circumstances, I honestly had no idea it would turn out this good."

"How soon until we put it up?" Marilyn asked. "We're anxious to see it hanging."

"We're working on the back panel right now. Maybe by the end of the day we can hang it. Is the paint dry?"

"Most of it is," Jocelyn said. "But it would be good to wait a few hours to transport it, just so it doesn't smear. Tonight will be great."

"I'll call you when we're ready, and you can be here when we put it up," he said to her.

He looked up from the mural to Jocelyn, and their gazes locked for a moment. She knew she had a goofy grin on her face, but she couldn't help it. Marilyn was right; he was a hunk.

"All right, then. Guess I'd better get out and crack my whip a little harder so we can get this up tonight." He looked directly at Jocelyn. "I'll call you."

She smiled as he hurried away and back outside.

Marilyn didn't miss a beat. "Something's going on between you two, isn't it?"

"What?" Jocelyn said with surprise.

"Well, if it isn't, it should be, the way you two were looking at each other," MJ said.

Jocelyn put her hands on the sides of her face to try and hide her flaming cheeks. "Nothing is going on."

"I guess it's possible you two don't see it quite yet."

"Or haven't admitted it yet," MJ said.

"Right," Marilyn added, "but you two have some pretty serious chemistry going on."

Jocelyn covered her whole face. She felt like she would die of embarrassment, yet she loved what they were saying.

"Can you really not see it?" MJ asked.

Jocelyn split her second and third finger and peeked at MJ. "See what?"

"The way that man looked at you," Marilyn added. "Jocelyn, he had bigger stars in his eyes than the ones on the backdrop."

"He did?"

"Yes," MJ confirmed. "And the way your face lit up when you saw him was priceless."

"It did?" She covered her face again.

"Sweetie," MJ said, "don't you dare be embarrassed. This is exciting. Jack deserves a wonderful woman like you."

"And you deserve someone as wonderful as Jack. In fact, it is so good to see a sparkle in his eye. He hasn't had one since he moved to Milford Falls. You did that to him," Marilyn said.

Jocelyn tried not to smile, but the urge was too big, and it broke out all over her face. "I don't know what to say."

"You don't have to say anything; your face says it all," MJ said.

"Sure does," Marilyn said. "I remember what it was like to feel that way. So exciting. So thrilling."

The three women said their good-byes in high spirits. The other two weren't sure if they could make it back for the hanging of the backdrop, but they would try. In the meantime Jocelyn did some grocery shopping, visited her friend Warren at the bookstore, then took everything home and put it away.

The day was clear and sunny, and she couldn't help but open her windows to let in the fresh air and soft breeze.

She was just putting a half gallon of milk in the fridge when her phone rang. A sudden, sick feeling came to her. She'd pushed her fears about Ava's death to the back of her mind, but unexpected calls, curious looks from strangers, even cars driving past the house at a slower pace than the speed limit sent chills up her spine.

She didn't recognize the number, but it had a Washington area code, so she knew it was local.

"Hi. This is Danny at the thrift store. I'm just calling to let you know that we got a piece of furniture you might be interested in."

Immediately she thought of her bank account and knew she needed to be careful. She didn't have a whole lot of available cash to spend on furniture. Still, he'd been kind enough to call. It couldn't hurt to hear what he had to say.

"What is it?"

"You mentioned earlier that you were looking for a bookshelf. You didn't mention a color or size, but a tall one just came in that is white, with attractive molding along the top and only a few dings, which gives the piece character."

Why did he have to say white!

"How much are you asking for it?"

"I was going to ask fifty, but since you've already bought so much from me I'll drop it ten dollars."

"I'll take it," she heard herself say. There was no way she could turn it down for that price. "Can I see it first, though?"

"You bet. Come on down. We're open until seven."

"I'm coming to town a little later, so I'll stop by." She loved how people in small towns looked out for each other.

"I'll keep it in the back till you get here. I have a feeling it will get snatched up fast if you don't want it."

She wasn't sure she could justify the purchase except that a white bookcase up in her bedroom would be ideal. The room was decorated in pale blue and white with strong red and yellow accents. The bed was black wrought iron and had beautiful scrolls and lines and was topped with a plump down comforter. The room had a vintage feel about it, and a bookshelf next to the overstuffed chair and standing lamp would really complete the room.

Over the next few hours she worked hard to finish the touch-ups in the living room so she could put the room back together. The furniture she'd refinished had turned out beautifully; the tone and style of the room were exactly what she wanted.

With the furniture in place and a beautiful light coming through the windows, she stood back to admire the room that now felt fresh and new.

It took a little effort to control the ache that was left by the empty wall where her Bocelli should have been hanging, but one day she would own another one. In the meantime, she'd keep her eye out for something inexpensive, maybe at the thrift shop. *Or I could paint something myself.* The thought filled her with excitement and a little nervousness. She didn't usually put her artwork on display for everyone to see. *Why not?* She resolved to start a new painting just as soon as she set up her studio space in the former dining room. So, other than a lack of artwork, all that was left in the living room was to get the chandelier hung. Maybe Lenny could come over and put it up for her. She owed favors to half the town by now. She couldn't move for ten years just to give her time to return all the kindnesses she'd received since living there.

While she was in her garden gathering a bouquet of wildflowers, her phone rang. Her heart skipped a beat when she saw Jack's number come up.

"Are you busy?" he asked.

She glanced at her watch. It was much earlier than she'd expected.

"We're ready to hang the masterpiece."

"Oh, that's great. But when are you going to put up the backdrop?"

He laughed. "We've already moved it onto the stage and are putting up ladders. Can you come down?"

"I'll be right there," she said, trying not to sound as anxious as she felt.

She quickly sent a text to Marilyn and MJ then rushed inside to put the flowers in a vase before she left. Catching a glimpse of herself in the mirror, she decided to change into a nicer shirt and put on a little makeup.

Her friends had always told her that she looked like Audrey Hepburn, but she didn't see the resemblance. Still, she found herself trying to channel her inner Audrey by playing up her large eyes and long lashes. She had pulled her hair into a high ponytail and put on a pair of crystal drop earrings. Again she wondered if this was how all her friends in high school had felt when they got all dressed up for what seemed like no reason whenever they went to the mall or even each other's houses. Whether it was or not, she still decided to keep her mind and heart open and allow herself to enjoy the experience, knowing full well her balloon could crash land at anytime. She felt ready to take the risk.

Once she was parked, she nearly ran to the town square where the large grandstand stood.

Jack noticed her right off and gave her a smile while he finished talking to one of the men holding several boards in one arm and a hammer in the other.

He had his baseball cap turned around, which Jocelyn thought gave him a boyish look. She couldn't help noticing how his light blue T-shirt hugged the muscles in his shoulders and how at-home he seemed with his tool belt slung low on his hips.

Consciously dragging her attention away, she refocused on the grandstand. The enormous structure astounded her, and she began to move toward it to better appreciate the craftsmanship and hard work that had been put into it. Her moment was short-lived when Lacey came around the corner carrying an armload of scrap lumber, her grim expression turning to one of disdain upon seeing Jocelyn.

As Lacey continued in her task, Jocelyn gave her a smile, not wanting to be part of her game, knowing full well that this was about Jack. She didn't blame the girl for trying. Especially if they had a history, Lacey most likely felt she'd staked her claim on Jack and Jocelyn was moving in on her territory. In the past, any kind of personal conflict would have scared Jocelyn away, but she didn't feel that way now. She was enjoying the thrill of romance—or whatever this was—for the first time in her life. She was seventeen years later than her friends, but she didn't care. It was exhilarating, like waiting for a thrill ride at an amusement park. She just hoped there were more ups than downs ahead.

"Hey, there," Jack said, catching up to Jocelyn. "What do you think?"

"Jack, this is incredible! I can't believe how awesome it is." She noticed how he smiled at her praise.

"You probably can't tell, but it separates into sections and is fairly simple to take apart and put back together so it can be reused each year."

She smiled at him. "I don't know what to say. You're brilliant!"

He shrugged, unable to hold back his own smile. "I got tired of reinventing the wheel every year." Someone on the stage called his name. "We're ready when you are."

Jack turned to her. "Are you ready?"

She tensed up with excitement and nodded.

"Okay, Stan," he yelled to the man, "go for it!"

Someone actually turned on the "Star Spangled Banner," and as it played over the sound system, the backdrop was slowly raised into position. The giant flag and eagle unfolded in grandeur as the music swelled in a powerful crescendo that raised the flesh on Jocelyn's arms and the hair on her neck. Tears stung her eyes, which she quickly blinked away.

The mural, fully stretched, rippled gently in the breeze, giving movement to the depictions on it, adding life to the patriotic theme. It was a thrilling moment.

When the song ended, there was a brief pause of silence, then the crew began to clap and whistle, the entire group sharing in a moment of reward for their collective efforts and hard work.

"I didn't expect that," she said to Jack as she dabbed at the corners of her eyes with her fingertips.

"That was MJ's idea," he said. "I think we should start the festivities the same way at the breakfast devotional on the Fourth."

"You think Mayor Duncan would go for it?"

"It's worth a try."

"Hey, Jack," another man yelled. "Can you come take a look at this speaker?"

"I'll be right back," Jack said, giving her arm a quick squeeze.

Jocelyn felt a jolt of electricity from his touch and told herself to calm down and act her age.

Jack left her side, but she was soon joined by MJ, Marilyn, and Celeste.

"That was so amazing!" Jocelyn exclaimed as she hugged each woman. "I'm so glad you were here to see it."

"It is really magnificent," MJ said.

"Thank you for your help," Jocelyn told the women who had already become dear friends to her. She turned to look at the mural and froze. "Uh-oh, do you think the star on the upper left corner is lopsided?"

"Jocelyn," Marilyn said in a motherly tone, "it's perfect. We've told you that a dozen times."

She knew she had a tendency to be a perfectionist about some things, but it was so important to her to have it just right.

"You're right. I'm sure I'm the only one who can see the flaws."

"We did good, girls," Marilyn said, putting her arm around Celeste's and Jocelyn's shoulders.

"Sorry I didn't help more," Celeste said.

"Well, it's hard to find time when you're working two jobs," MJ said. "By the way, how's your missionary doing?"

Celeste blushed and smiled. "Amazing. He sent me another puzzle piece today."

"He's got us puzzled, that's for sure," Marilyn said. "When it comes to romance and surprises, this kid's got everyone beat."

"Lucky you," MJ said. "Brian's idea of dinner and a movie is sitting on the couch watching TV. Men . . . gotta love 'em."

Jocelyn laughed.

"Speaking of Brian, I'd better get going. He's going to be wondering where his dinner is."

"Me too. My husband acts like he is incapable of pouring himself a bowl of cereal or making a sandwich."

"It's because you've pampered him, Mom," Celeste said.

"Well, don't make the same mistakes I did when you get married," Marilyn said. "I love your dad, but sometimes it feels like I have another child around."

Jocelyn smiled at the women, knowing that their teasing was in fun. She'd seen both of them with their husbands, and they were both very happily married and very much in love.

"Thanks for coming back," Jocelyn said to them, giving each of them a hug as they left.

"We'll see you tomorrow at church," MJ said.

"I'll save you a seat," Celeste said.

"That would be nice, thanks," Jocelyn said.

"Bye, sweetie," Marilyn said. "Come visit us at school soon."

"I will. I have some ideas for the classroom."

The three women left, and Jocelyn decided it was probably time to get to the thrift store before it closed. She was anxious to see the bookshelf.

In spite of the few little flaws only she noticed, the mural was quite powerful and really did add to the patriotic atmosphere they were trying to achieve.

"Hey," a voice called as she started walking away.

She turned to see Jack taking long strides toward her. Her heart fluttered, and her breath caught in her throat. *You're like a schoolgirl with a crush,* she told herself.

"Where ya goin'?" he asked.

"I need to run over to the thrift store. They're holding a bookcase for me. It just came in."

"You need some help getting it home?"

Was he offering?

"Last time I paid them to deliver," she explained.

"I can help. In fact"— he turned back to look at the work crew that was slowly leaving—"if Lenny is still here he could help too, then he could take a look at your chandelier."

"Really?" She was dying to get that thing up. "That would be great."

"Hang on." He took out his phone and texted something. "If he's still here I'm sure he won't mind. His wife and kids are gone for the weekend to a family thing. He had to stay for some work stuff and to help today. Actually," he said in a lower tone, "I think he was looking for excuses not to go." His phone buzzed.

He checked the message. "Yeah, he's good. He'll meet us over there."

"Should I follow you in my car?"

"You can leave it here and I'll bring you back to get it," he said.

She shrugged. "Sure. Okay."

"Thanks, Stan," Jack hollered and waved to one of the men as he was leaving. The rest of the group was putting away tools and cleaning up the remaining pieces of lumber and plywood.

Together they walked to his truck, discussing the mayor's possible reactions to the grandstand, when out stepped Lacey.

She had a sickeningly sweet smile on her face. "Hi, guys."

"Hey, Lacey," Jack said, fishing in his pocket for his keys then beeping the doors to open the truck.

"Jack, do you have just a moment?" she asked.

"I'm kind of—"

"It will just take a minute," she said, her eyes flashing quickly toward Jocelyn then back at him.

"Do you mind?" Jack said to Jocelyn.

"Not at all," she said, sensing his reluctance to speak to the woman.

She got inside his truck and pulled the door shut, situating herself so she could catch their reflection in the mirror. Jack had his back to the mirror, and she could only see Lacey's shoulder and arm as they talked.

Without anything interesting to observe, she noticed how tidy Jack's truck cab was. She liked that. She'd grown up never taking anything for granted, which meant taking good care of the few things she did have. She liked that quality in others.

She glanced back at the mirror and gasped. They were hugging.

Quickly she looked away, but curiosity forced her to look again.

Crud!

Wondering what that was about, she reminded herself that they'd known each other longer than she'd known him and that he was Lacey's home teacher. She had no right to care.

But she did.

* * *

"Hand me that screwdriver again," Lenny said.

Jocelyn handed the screwdriver to Lenny, who was up on a chair, while Jack stood below, lifting the chandelier.

"You about got it there, Len?" Jack said through gritted teeth.

"Hold your horses," Lenny said. "You can't rush these things."

"This chandelier isn't light," Jack said.

"Actually, it is a light." Lenny laughed at his own joke and Jocelyn giggled.

"Just hurry," Jack said.

"Almost got it," Lenny said, twisting the two last wires together and screwing on a little yellow cap over them. "I think that does it. Okay, go ahead and lift so I can hook it."

With a groan Jack hoisted the chandelier up a little higher and helped Lenny attach the dangling crystal fixture onto the hook, then Lenny slid up the little antique brass cover and secured it onto the ceiling.

"That should do it." He checked one last time to make sure it was solid then said, "Go ahead and give it a try."

While Lenny got off the chair, Jocelyn went to the utility room to switch the breaker. Then she came back and turned the switch on. The light illuminated the whole room, sending crystal sparkles around like sprinkles of fairy dust.

Jocelyn took in a quick breath of surprised delight. "It's beautiful. Lenny, thank you so much. You too, Jack," she added. "I just love it."

"That's quite a fixture," Lenny said. "Don't let my wife see it. I can see her wanting one just like it."

"I gotta be honest, that's pretty awesome," Jack said.

Jocelyn gave a contented sigh. The chandelier was the perfect accent for the room and every bit as pretty as she'd hoped it would be.

"Hey," Jack said, looking around, "where's that beautiful Italian picture? I don't see it."

Jocelyn had to swallow before she answered. "I don't have it any longer."

"You don't?" His forehead crinkled with confusion.

"Yeah, it's a long story," she said in an effort to avoid the explanation. "I'll tell you about it sometime."

"Speaking of time"—Lenny looked at his watch—"I gotta run. If I don't get the house cleaned up before my wife gets home she'll tan my hide."

"She's only been gone two days," Jack said. "How dirty can it get?"

"Hey, the only time I can eat pizza and chips and drink pop is when Katie's gone. She's determined to make our family healthier. I'm telling you, tofu and wheat germ are what's going to kill me."

Jack and Jocelyn laughed.

"In fact, I think I'll grab a burger and fries on my way home, just to get one more hit of junk food before the health Nazi gets home. Katie's an awesome woman, but she never does anything halfway. We can't just start with whole-wheat bread and ease into this. She's purged our house of anything edible. I'm going to starve to death." He patted his ample stomach. "The other day she smelled chocolate on my breath and threatened to put me in time-out!"

Jocelyn knew by now that Len loved to exaggerate—that's why his stories were so entertaining. She'd met his wife, Katie, and she was absolutely darling, as were his kids.

"Well, thank you again," Jocelyn said. "I have a bag of peanut M&M's in my cupboard. Do you want them?"

"Are you kidding? Yes!" Then he thought for a moment. "I'll just have to make sure I gargle with Listerine before she gets home."

She grabbed the bag of candy out of her cupboard and handed it to him.

"Ahh." He closed his eyes and held the bag to his chest. "Like manna from the gods. I shall live yet another day."

Jack rolled his eyes and Jocelyn chuckled. He was as nutty as the bag of candy.

Len ripped the bag open and began chomping down on the candy. "See ya," he said with his mouth full.

Jack and Jocelyn watched him leave then burst out laughing when the door closed behind him.

"You don't think it's really that bad, do you?" she asked Jack.

"Are you kidding? Katie waits on that man hand and foot. She probably suggested he lighten up on the fried foods or something and, Len being Len, he turns it into a comedy routine."

"It was nice of him to come over and help tonight. I'll have to sneak him M&M's occasionally to thank him."

"That's all he needs," Jack said. "Speaking of M&M's, I'm starving. How about you? I know a great little Mexican place outside of town. Interested?"

"I've been craving Mexican food," she said. "That's one thing I definitely miss about St. George: my favorite Mexican restaurant, Durango's."

They talked nonstop while they drove to the restaurant. She told him about the Butterfly Girls and what each of them was doing, reminding herself that she hadn't talked to Emma in ages. She made a mental note to track her down when she got home, especially after what Chloe had told her about Ava.

"Hey, there," Jack said. "You left me for a minute. Is everything okay?"

She smiled, appreciating that he was so mindful of her. Definitely one of his top qualities.

"Yeah, it's great." She didn't want to burden him with all the details until she knew more about Ava's case.

They ordered dinner and continued to talk. Even though he was opening up to her, she still felt that he kept a wall up. She wished she could break it down but at the same time knew that she was no different; she had her own guard up to some extent. Slowly, though, the walls seemed to be crumbling, and she couldn't remember ever feeling so happy in her life.

* * *

Once the grandstand and backdrop were finished, both Jack and Jocelyn had a chance to focus on getting her pipes fixed and her walls repaired. Jack was both fast and efficient and ended up spending less time and money on the repairs than he'd originally planned. Nonetheless, when he gave her the grand total, it was obvious he wasn't charging her for his time, though he insisted he was just charging her a fair price. Once she insisted on itemization, he caved and admitted he was only charging for parts, but he still refused to accept more.

"I feel really guilty about this," she said, handing the check to him.

"Maybe I'm glad I had an excuse to come over," he said with a sly grin.

"Oh, really," she said, feeling her feet lifting off the ground. Was it normal to have butterflies in her stomach and clouds in her head? "Does that mean that something else at my house needs to break so you'll still come over? Of course, knowing my house, that's likely to happen."

He laughed then looked at her intently and said, "Your pipes don't need to burst to have me come over."

Words escaped her. All she could do was grin.

She thought about the Butterfly Box and the amazing power it had to bring good luck. Of course, she knew it was faith and prayer that was the real power behind it, but the symbol of the box was undeniable. She was so grateful for the good things that were finally happening in her life.

Moving to Milford Falls was definitely worth it.

* * *

"Emma, this is Jocelyn. I haven't talked to you in ages. This is like the tenth message I've left for you. I'm dying to hear what's going on with you. I have a ton of stuff to tell you. Call me. I miss you!"

Jocelyn hung up the phone. None of the other girls had heard from

Emma either. Lauryn was the only one who'd at least gotten a text from her telling her that she was extremely busy with work and with Nicholas and that she'd get in touch soon.

None of them knew what to do. Emma was the type that did what she wanted, when she wanted to do it. But she'd never completely blocked her friends out of her life like this.

As hard as they wanted to like Nicholas, it was difficult. He seemed to keep her sequestered from the outside world, especially her friends.

She glanced at her watch. The sun hadn't even risen, but the birds were singing like crazy in the trees. She was up early to go to the annual Fourth of July breakfast. Jack was meeting her there. He needed to be extra early to make sure everything on the grandstand was set up and ready to go. Mayor Duncan had made it plain and clear that there was no room for error. He wanted things perfect.

The light rain that had fallen the night before was still evident by the few remaining puddles on the road outside. But the sky was clear and free from clouds. It was going to be a beautiful day.

Still, she knew that it would be chilly until the sun finally broke through the trees.

Pulling on her jacket and tucking her umbrella in her bag just in case, she turned off the kitchen light and went out to her car. She paused to notice the fresh blooms on her wildflowers and the intoxicating pine- and rain-scented air. This place really was beautiful.

"Mornin' Jocelyn," Harry called from his backyard. He was stooped over his tomato plants.

"How are you, Harry? Are you going to the breakfast?"

"Naw, I don't really like crowds."

"Harry, you have to go. It's going to be delicious, and they have a wonderful program planned."

"I don't think so."

She wondered if he was hesitant because he didn't want to go alone.

"I'd love to have you come with me. You need to come see the backdrop I painted for the grandstand."

"Oh?" He pushed himself up to a standing position. "Didn't take long for Duncan to put you to work, did it?"

"Nope. As much as I try to avoid him, he somehow seems to find me."

"I s'pose I could join you. Will you be staying long?"

"I can leavc whenever you're ready."

"Good. I can't be around some of those people, especially Duncan, too long. He makes me want to tear out my hair, and I haven't got much to start with."

"I know how you feel. I'll drive over and pick you up."

"All right, then. Let me lock up the place."

She was glad she'd run into Harry. She often thought of asking him to go places with her, but she didn't know how much he liked being pestered.

They drove through the colorfully decorated town toward the main square where the morning festivities were happening. Banners, balloons, painted store windows, and hundreds of flags adorned the streets. Jocelyn couldn't deny that the town looked incredible. Pain in the neck or not, Mayor Duncan's vision had come to life and turned out amazingly!

The sidewalks were already packed with people walking to the breakfast. Patriotic music blasted from speakers posted on telephone poles. Jocelyn felt like she was heading to a presidential inauguration.

Once she found a parking spot, Jocelyn and Harry walked to the town square together. Most of the people were unfamiliar to her, but many of them knew Harry and greeted him warmly. Jocelyn was pleased to see him receive such a nice welcome. Maybe this would help him be more comfortable coming out to community events.

Jocelyn was happy to see MJ, Brian, and their family. The two boys said hello then took off to find friends.

Brian and Harry were both impressed with the grandstand and the backdrop and provided ample compliments to both of the women for their contribution.

The air was filled with the delicious aroma of sizzling bacon, eggs, and pancakes. Lines of people formed to fill their plates with the delicious food, and dozens of brightly decorated tables had been set up so they could sit and enjoy their meal and see the program on the grandstand.

The lines moved quickly, and soon Jocelyn's little group was sitting at a table, enjoying the food and the warm sun that had finally broken through the trees.

Jocelyn tried not to seem distracted, but she couldn't help constantly watching for a glimpse of Jack. He didn't seem to be anywhere.

Partway through their meal, a screech from the microphone caught everyone's attention, and Mayor Duncan walked up onto the stage.

"Welcome, dear friends, neighbors, and visitors, to the Milford Falls Fourth of July celebration!" he announced. "For those of you visiting our fair city, we hope you enjoy your day of celebration. We have many events and activities planned and have a booth where you can also meet Bob Jacobs, our new police chief, as well as receive your invisible ink pen."

"Get your pens right here," Karl shouted from the booth, waving to the crowd.

"Yes, thank you, Karl," the mayor said. "Moving on, the proceeds from the sale of tickets for the carnival rides will go toward constructing a new bell tower for the town."

He began to clap, so the audience responded with a lukewarm effort.

"Okay, well, more about that later," he said. "We'd like to begin with our national anthem, sung by our very own Lacey Williams. Would the audience please stand." He turned to the stairs where a bedazzled Lacey had been waiting. As she stepped onto the stage, the sun hit all the rhinestones on her white denim jacket and blinded the audience.

"Holy smokes!" Harry exclaimed, covering his eyes. "What in tarnation!"

Others in the audience had the same reaction, but it was clear, as Jocelyn looked around, that many of the men stood a little taller and sucked in their stomachs.

Lacey began to sing, and the audience went completely quiet. Jocelyn was completely shocked by the beautiful tone of her voice. With the delivery of a superstar and a voice to match, Lacey delivered one of the most amazing and stirring performances of the song Jocelyn had ever witnessed.

"Holy smokes!" Harry exclaimed again when the song ended.

The audience erupted into thunderous applause, and Lacey milked the audience for all the applause they were willing to give.

Mayor Duncan finally walked back onto the stage and put his arm around her.

"Hard to believe so much talent is contained inside such a tiny body," he said.

MJ and Jocelyn exchanged looks then started laughing. Jocelyn knew the mayor was single, but there was at least a twenty-year age gap between the two. Did the mayor have a thing for Lacey?

It didn't matter because Lacey shrugged his arm off of her and walked off the stage, waving like Miss America.

"Wow," Jocelyn said. "She has an amazing voice."

"She does," MJ agreed. "Such a beautiful gift. She sang a solo in our Christmas program at church, and there wasn't a dry eye in the congregation. She has done some community theater and really is quite talented."

Jocelyn shook her head in amazement. This was a whole different side of Lacey she hadn't known. She watched as the woman made her way through the crowd, receiving hugs and handshakes like a celebrity then finally making it to her seat. And there, to Jocelyn's horror, was Jack!

* * *

Harry and Jocelyn mingled with some of the townspeople after the program, but after a while, Jocelyn was ready to go home. Jack was no longer with Lacey and her son, but she still hadn't seen him and didn't know what to think. If he was interested in her, wouldn't he have come looking for her?

She got mad at herself for having expectations. She'd known of the dangers and risks. He was in high demand all over the city, and she wasn't the only woman after him.

She felt like such an idiot.

There were rules to the game of love, and she didn't know how to play. Heck, she didn't even know what the stupid rules were.

"You ready to go, Harry?" she asked. They were both standing, surrounded by people still eating and chatting and kids running wild.

"I think so. Are you?"

"I am."

"Did you ever find who you were looking for?" he asked.

"How did you know—"

"Your head rotated around your neck like the light in a lighthouse," he said.

She smiled. "I didn't realize it was that bad."

"I'm sure no one else noticed it but me," he assured her.

"Well, it doesn't matter. I'm ready to go." There was a lot more going on that day, but she didn't want to hang around. Without a backward glance, she left with Harry, never knowing what had happened to Jack.

* * *

Feeling out of sorts because of Jack's apparent snub, Jocelyn decided she needed to keep herself busy to keep him off her mind. She was confused and sad that he hadn't made any effort to say hi. Granted, he was busy, but was it too much to expect a hello, at least?

"I guess so," she said out loud as she went to the closet in her grandmother's bedroom on the main floor. She'd taken one of the guest rooms for her room and had left her grandmother's room just the way it had been. The décor hadn't been changed as long as Jocelyn remembered it, with the rose-pattern wallpaper, the white chenille bedspread, the sheer white swag curtains, the blond-colored chest of drawers and bed, and the oval shaped picture of her grandmother and grandfather on their wedding day.

She sighed, the heaviness of her heart causing an ache in her chest. She missed her grandmother terribly. She was someone Jocelyn could always call when she needed a listening ear or a boost when she was feeling down—or when something wonderful happened.

She'd been wanting to go through her grandmother's things to decide what she wanted to keep or put in storage and what she wanted to give away. Anxious to get her mind off Jack, she decided now was as good of a time as any.

First, she sorted through her grandmother's clothes, choosing a few special pieces that were sentimental to her. One item was her grandmother's fur coat. It wasn't fancy, but it was real, and it had been her grandmother's pride and joy. Jocelyn also kept a few of her house dresses, because they totally reminded her of her grandmother. She loved the colorful house dresses that snapped up and had big pockets in the front. Someday when she got old, she planned on wearing them herself.

Folding and stacking the clothes onto a chair, Jocelyn then moved on to her grandmother's shoes, which were two sizes smaller than Jocelyn wore, so she put all of them aside to be boxed up. On the shelf above the dress rack, her grandmother had some hats—all of which Jocelyn kept—and some folded Christmas sweaters—all of which Jocelyn gave away.

With all the drawers and the closet sorted out, she boxed up all the keepers and replaced them in the closet. Everything else she shoved into bags to take to Goodwill. She could do that tomorrow too.

Going on her third hour of organizing, Jocelyn worked on the storage closet under the stairs on the main floor. She was on a roll and making great progress. As much as she loved her grandmother, she knew it didn't make sense to keep all of her belongings.

Finally she attacked the pantry, sorting through shelves of fruit bottles, old cans of food, and household items that were either outdated, not working, or just plain unnecessary, Jocelyn did find a few wonderful items, like a hand wheat grinder, a candle-making kit, and several nice sterling silver serving pieces. The rest she either tossed or put in a box for Goodwill.

After the pantry was finished, Jocelyn sat down at the table and had a diet soda and a turkey sandwich. It was after four in the afternoon and she was exhausted.

She nearly choked on a bit of sandwich when a loud banging came at her door.

"Good grief!" she said as she jumped up from the table and darted around the side of the fridge. She wasn't going to open it until she saw who it was.

She peeked out toward the front door in case the person was standing by the sidelight windows. She couldn't see anyone.

Crud!

The banging came again.

Her stomach tightened and her heart began to race.

She had to see who it was.

Slowly, she peeked out again. There was a bearded face staring back at her through the window.

She definitely needed to get blinds. And a peephole.

Giving Jack an embarrassed wave, she came out from behind the fridge and opened the front door.

"Where have you been?" he said sternly, barging into the house.

"What do you mean? I've been here. Why?"

"I've been trying to call you. Did you get my message this morning?"

"No. What message?"

"This morning, just as the program started, the mayor got a call from the people in charge of the carnival telling him they'd had a break-in. All of their money for the carnival today had been stolen."

"Oh, dear! Do they know who did it?"

"Not yet, but the mayor was in such a tizzy, I had to help him. He didn't want to alarm the townspeople that there was a problem by taking the police chief away from the festivities, so Lenny and I went with him. I told Lacey to tell you where I was and that I'd call you later."

"Maybe that wasn't the best idea."

"You're right. That was stupid of me. Anyway, I watched for you before the program, but it got a little crazy getting everything ready. I was hoping you'd come and find me."

"I saw you, but you were busy. I didn't want to bother you."

His expression softened. "I'm sorry. I can't imagine what you were thinking."

"I figured you had other obligations," she said, not confessing her complete feelings.

"Can I ask what you were doing hiding behind the fridge?"

"Hiding? Is that what it looked like I was doing?" She attempted to laugh but knew she didn't sound convincing.

One of his eyebrows arched.

"I thought I saw—" She tried to come up with an excuse but had never been good at lying.

His other eyebrow arched.

She pulled in a deep breath. "Okay, I'm embarrassed to admit this, but I was frightened." As she thought about it, she realized that most murderers probably didn't knock at their victim's doors. She was such an idiot.

"Really? What were you expecting?"

"I thought maybe the Jehovah's Witnesses were going through the neighborhood."

His brow furrowed, then he started to laugh.

"Okay, honestly, it was the loud pounding on my door that frightened me. I get scared sometimes when I'm alone."

"I didn't mean to frighten you," he said with kindness in his voice and in his eyes.

"I know. Sometimes my paranoia gets the best of me when I'm alone. I'm still getting used to how creaky this house is."

"I guess that could get a little scary. Having those pipes fixed should help with some of the noise."

"Maybe so."

"So, are you interested in going back to the celebration?" he asked. "They have some bands and entertainment scheduled for the grandstand up until the fireworks start."

She acted like she was thinking about it, but she didn't have to—she'd been hoping he would ask.

"Sure. I'd love to."

"You might want a jacket. There's a bit of a breeze, and it will cool off when the sun goes down."

She grabbed her jacket and made sure the doors were locked before they left. It was around five o'clock when they walked outside. They could hear the sounds of the celebration in full swing even from a distance.

Once they got there, the smells of popcorn, hot dogs, and cotton candy struck Jocelyn full force. She hadn't eaten much that day, and, for some reason, those hot dogs smelled like heaven.

Jack must have noticed. "Hungry?"

"Yeah, kind of."

"Let's eat. I haven't eaten since breakfast."

She found out that, just like her, he was a ketchup-and-mustard-only kind of guy. No onions or relish. They each got an order of French fries with extra fry sauce, and for dessert they got churros. It had been a while since Jocelyn had eaten junk food, and it tasted heavenly.

A group of youngsters from a local dance studio was up on stage performing some kind of clogging routine to the song "Cotton-Eyed Joe," and a barbershop quartet was lined up to follow.

They sat together in the audience eating and watching each act. It was exactly what she'd expected from a small town.

Lacey was one of the last to perform.

As she sang "Hero" by Mariah Carey, Jocelyn had to admit the woman could really sing.

"She should do something with her singing," Jocelyn said. "She's good."

"She's got power but not a lot of control. She does well on the big notes but doesn't really carry soft notes very well."

Jocelyn looked at him with surprise. "It sounds like you're an expert."

"Are you kidding?" he was quick to respond. "I just, uh—oh, look, there's Lenny. Let's go say hi."

He grabbed her hand and pulled her to her feet.

They made their way over to the table where Lenny and his wife and three kids were eating. Their youngest son was covered in purple cotton candy.

"I told you we shouldn't have bought that for him," Lenny's wife complained, trying to wash some of the purple sugar off with wet wipes.

"Can I help it if the kid's hand-eye coordination is nonexistent? He gets it from your brother Rodney. That guy can't blink and talk at the same time."

"Lenny!" she exclaimed.

"Hey guys," Lenny finally said, licking the stickiness off his fingers. "Hungry?" He held up a soggy purple cone of cotton candy.

"We just ate," Jack said. "Have you guys been here all day?"

"Nah, we had a family reunion over at the park. We're all meeting back here for the fireworks. The kids wanted to go on some of the carnival rides and have some real carnival food."

"Disgusting," Lenny's wife said. "They'll probably all get stomachaches from it."

"That's what Pepto Bismol is for, honey," Lenny said.

Lenny's wife rolled her eyes at her husband and said, "How are you, Jocelyn?" They visited while she plowed through nearly a whole box of wet wipes. Her son had gone from purple to pink, she'd scrubbed him so hard.

"And how's the house coming? I hear you got a fantastic chandelier in your front room."

"I did. You should come and see it."

"I'd love to. We'll come some night when we've got a sitter for the kids. They would destroy your place."

"I doubt that. It's pretty much falling apart by itself. Without Lenny's and Jack's help it would have collapsed by now."

"Old houses can be overwhelming. It's such a quaint house. It reminds me of a cottage from a fairy tale. Like the one in *Snow White.*"

"Daddy, we want to go on the Ferris wheel," their oldest boy said, tugging on his dad's shirt. "Hurry!"

"Guess that's our cue," Lenny said, gathering up the leftover paper plates and cups to throw in the trash. "You two have fun."

Jocelyn and Jack told the family good-bye then began to wander out of the town square toward the city park a block away. Many of the festivity-goers were doing the same thing.

"How does this year's turnout compare to other years?" she asked, amazed at the mass of people.

"I don't like to admit stuff like this, but I think Duncan managed to at least double the turnout this year. If you want to see gloating on steroids, come to the next town meeting. That is, if any of us can fit into the room with Duncan's ego."

"What's the mayor's story? Was there ever a Mrs. Duncan?"

"Yes. She died years ago after battling cancer, and he's never remarried. Most likely that's why he spends so much time doing the mayor thing. He doesn't really have much else—I mean, other than his law practice. I don't think he gets an overwhelming amount of business from the town except for an occasional divorce or estate issue."

"Gee, knowing that makes me feel a little sorry for him."

"Yeah, it does. Still, he could tone down the intensity a bit."

It was dusk and the fireworks show was about to begin. Jack had remembered to bring a blanket so once they found a spot a fair distance from the masses, they spread it out on the grass and sat down.

The evening air was refreshing. Patriotic music played over loudspeakers, and occasionally a red, white, or blue balloon would escape and float gently up into the air.

"It's such a beautiful night," she said.

"Somehow we always manage to have good weather for the Fourth. Occasionally we'll get a little rain in the morning, which makes the breakfast a soggy mess, but I've never seen the fireworks get rained out."

Just then, the first explosion sounded, followed moments later by the burst of sparkling color in the air.

Set to music, the fireworks ranged in size and color, creating a breathtaking display in the sky.

Jocelyn had gone to watch fireworks with Chloe's family last year, just after Roger moved out. Watching the excitement on the children's faces had been more fun than watching the fireworks, but Jocelyn had always enjoyed a quality production, and the Milford Falls display was easily among the best she'd seen.

Several times Jocelyn gasped at the glorious magic happening against the darkened sky. She glanced over and caught Jack watching her.

"What?" she said, embarrassed.

"You look as though you've never seen fireworks before."

"They bring out the kid in me," she said with an apologetic shrug.

He smiled. "I can tell."

They were both leaning back on their elbows so they could look up into the sky. As she returned his smile, the flash and color above them reflected on his face.

He looked over and this time caught her looking at him.

They both smiled, keeping their gazes locked on each other as lights flashed and loud booms sounded. They were so close their shoulders nearly touched, so when he made the move toward her, she only had to move a few inches to meet him halfway.

With her heart pounding as loud as the cannon explosions, their lips met and she closed her eyes, losing all sense of everything around her except for the feel of his soft lips on hers and the charge of electricity rocketing through her arms and legs.

The kiss was soft, sweet, and tender and a full sixty seconds long. It was wonderfully unexpected and delightfully wonderful.

She kept her eyes closed for a moment after the kiss ended, not wanting the moment to be over.

Releasing a contented sigh, she finally opened her eyes and saw him looking at her from just inches away, a large smile on his face.

"Those fireworks got nothin' on you," she said.

"I was thinking the same thing," he said.

A fury of explosions sounded as the grand finale filled the air with bursts and sparkles of light and color. It was spectacular.

And then it ended.

There was silence and darkness for a moment, then the crowd began to clap.

Jack took advantage of the dark and kissed her again. She knew she could very easily get used to him doing that.

"Come on," he said, grabbing her hand. "Let's get out of here before we get caught in traffic."

Holding hands and taking off in a run, they got a head start on the crowd and slowed to a walk.

Exhilaration coursed through her veins, and she found herself feeling giddy and carefree. She wished the feeling would last forever—joy, excitement, and anticipation all rolled into one.

They hurried across the town square toward Jack's truck so they could beat the traffic.

Almost to his truck, they crossed the street, when out from the shadows stepped Lacey. How did she do that?

"Well, hello, you two," she said with a silky voice and a Cheshire cat smile.

"Lacey," Jack said, stopping short, squeezing Jocelyn's hand tightly to keep her close.

Jocelyn didn't speak, but something in her gut told her the woman was up to something.

"Enjoy the show?" she said. "Duncan certainly outdid himself this year, didn't he?"

Jocelyn wasn't sure what was going on or why Lacey was here. Couldn't she tell that she and Jack were together for the evening?

"The show was great. Did you get to watch it?" he asked.

"I saw enough," she remarked.

Jack was at a loss and didn't speak further. Jocelyn didn't know what to say or what the woman possibly could want. She felt awkward, yet more for Lacey than for herself.

"So, how did you enjoy your first Fourth of July in Milford Falls?" Lacey asked Jocelyn. But before Jocelyn could answer, she said, "Oh, wait. You've actually been here for one before, haven't you?"

Jocelyn didn't answer. Jack looked at Jocelyn, his own expression confused.

"You were here during high school, your senior year, wasn't it?" Lacey said.

"What's this all about, Lacey?" Jack asked.

"Why don't you tell him?" Lacey said to Jocelyn.

"I . . ." Jocelyn swallowed. "Well, I . . ."

Jack suddenly said, "I wish we could stay and chat, but we were actually in a rush." He pushed his way past Lacey, pulling Jocelyn behind him. In seconds he had the driver's side door open and had pushed Jocelyn inside. She immediately scooted across the bench seat.

"Why don't you ask her about the—"

Jack slammed the door, cutting her off, but Jocelyn was sure he heard the rest of Lacey's question, since the woman was now clearly repeating it, shouting it out for everyone to hear.

"That woman is psycho," he said, starting the engine. He didn't even look at Lacey as he put the truck in gear and pulled away from the curb. By that time hordes of people had made it to the square, and Lacey got swallowed up in the masses.

Jocelyn sat on her side of the truck, shaking, fighting the nausea in her stomach and the tears that threatened.

"I'm really sorry, Jocelyn," he said. "She has issues."

Jocelyn nodded, afraid to speak. She knew her voice would betray the emotions that she was trying to push back down. She could deal with them later when she wasn't with Jack.

"Are you okay?" Jack said, looking over at her as he waited at a stop sign.

Luckily it was dark, so he couldn't see her expression. She was sure if he could, he would see she was anything but okay. As much as she'd tried to deal with her past, it still came back to haunt her.

"I'm fine," she said, glad that her words sounded normal. "Lacey kind of unnerves me. I'm never sure what she'll say or do."

"That pretty much sums her up," he said. "You know, the sad thing is, she is very talented and dynamic. She used to be on the city council, and she was very involved in church and community things, but she's changed over the last few years. I'm not sure what's going on."

So maybe if Jack and Lacey had dated at one time, it was during her normal Dr. Jekyll phase, before she became Mrs. Hyde.

Either way, Jocelyn still didn't like the woman digging into her past and making it public knowledge. What right did she have to do that? And why was she doing it?

Already knowing the answer, Jocelyn sighed. Lacey had feelings for Jack, and she didn't like Jack paying attention to another woman.

Jocelyn couldn't blame her. He was worth fighting for.

The radio played softly, and Jocelyn strained to hear the lyrics to get her mind off the disconcerting encounter. A song she recognized came on—a tender, almost haunting, love song.

It had barely started when Jack reached up and abruptly shut it off.

They finally reached her house, and Jack pulled up in front, leaving the truck running.

The magic of their first kiss and the possibility of their relationship moving in a new, exciting direction was gone. Tension and awkwardness hung between them.

"Thanks for the ride home. I enjoyed *most* of the evening." She wanted to lighten the mood a little, but he seemed awfully distracted.

"Huh? Oh yeah. You're welcome," he said.

He didn't offer more than that, so she took it as her cue to get out. She'd hoped he would walk her to the door, to make sure the house was secure, but he showed no sign of doing so.

"Well, good night," she said and opened the door.

"Good night, Jocelyn." He looked at her briefly as she climbed out but didn't say more.

With a slam of the door, she walked away from the truck and to her front door. Glad she'd left a light on inside, she unlocked the door and went inside. As she shut the door she heard him drive away. Then, without another step, she dissolved into tears.

* * *

Jocelyn looked at the clock on the nightstand. 2:15. She didn't want to take a sleep aid, but she knew it was the only way she'd finally fall asleep. These events that triggered her memories were unexpected, and she never knew when she would have an episode. A doctor had told her she had a mild form of post-traumatic stress disorder and that throughout her life she would deal with it to some degree.

The sleeping pill would calm her nerves and settle her brain so she could sleep. Turning lights on as she went through the house, she found the prescription in the kitchen cupboard by the sink. The pills were old and past the expiration date, but she knew they were still potent enough to do the trick. She only took them when she absolutely couldn't help it, an occurrence that happened only once or twice a year, if that.

Twenty minutes later a numbing heaviness took over her brain and her muscles. She felt like she was melting onto her mattress. In a matter of moments, she was asleep.

"Who are you?" Jocelyn said, trying to hide the fear in her voice. "What do you want?" She looked around the dark alley, but there was nowhere to run, no way to escape. The only exit was blocked by the stranger, the man who'd followed her as she'd walked home from school. She'd taken what she thought was a shortcut, but there was no outlet through the alley.

The man didn't answer. He just took several steps toward her, heightening the terror she felt inside.

Her instinct told her to run, to fight, to do whatever it took to get away, but her fear kept her feet bolted to the ground.

His eyes were filled with pure evil; his smile sent chills down her spine. If she didn't do something fast, she knew she wouldn't survive his attack.

"Do something!" *a voice inside of her shouted. She tried to move her legs, but she couldn't. They felt as heavy as lead. He took another step closer and then another one.*

Out of the corner of her eye she spied a metal bar, a crowbar, just out of her reach. If she could get ahold of it, she might have a chance.

"You can do it!" *the voice inside affirmed.*

Without another thought she surprised her attacker by lunging for the crowbar just as he made a move to attack her. In one fluid motion she grabbed the bar, whirled back around, and connected with the attacker's rib cage. The man let out a loud groan of pain and doubled over. Not willing to give him a chance to strike, she swung the bar again and slammed it down on his back, forcing him to his knees.

Adrenaline coursed through her veins like liquid courage. All the years of being a victim, of backing down in the face of fear, of being a doormat and a passive participant in her life erupted like a geyser of strength.

Anticipating his next move she readied her weapon and took a pouncelike stance, ready to defend herself or to die trying.

Without warning the man's arm shot out, and he grabbed her right ankle and yanked. She fell sideways, oblivious to the pain of landing hard on her hip. The motion caused him to lose his grip, so she scrambled backward to add some distance and got on her feet. Holding his side, the man pushed himself up, his eyes full of fury.

Holding tight to the crowbar with both hands, she turned it around in her hand, the pointed end facing out. She would have one chance. She had to strike accurately.

The man growled, his frenzied expression and movements convincing her that she was dead if she missed.

Reflexes and senses in high gear, Jocelyn faced her attacker and prepared herself to do what she needed to do. This was the final face-off.

As if in slow motion, the man charged like an angry bull, each step and breath magnified by the measured movement, allowing her time to ready herself and take position. With her left leg forward, her body turned slightly sideways, she held her ground, her arms cocked and ready. Then, as he took that final step, closing the gap between them, she thrust the pointed end of the crowbar into his chest.

"Ah!" Jocelyn screamed out loud, sitting straight up in bed. She shuddered and shook her head, trying to clear the image from her mind. The thought that she'd actually killed someone in her dream was unsettling. She'd had this recurring dream for years and never before had she actually confronted her attacker.

She marveled that although she had felt fear in the dream, she'd also felt strong and powerful.

Confusion tumbled around her brain as she sorted through the events of the last twelve hours. Her feelings of being disappointed by Jack then being thrilled by his kisses, being frightened in her home and being confronted by Lacey, then confronting her attacker in her dream . . . What *did* it all mean?

Usually she felt upset and frightened whenever she had *the dream,* but this time in her heart she knew she would never feel that way again. The man in the dream had no power over her anymore. She had won; she had triumphed.

She got her drink then went back to bed, a smile on her face.

Yes! She nodded as she climbed under the covers. She'd won!

* * *

The Butterfly Box on the dresser glistened in the morning sun. Jocelyn dressed quickly, wanting to get a jump on the day. She was going to get the kitchen ceiling painted if it killed her.

Feeling empowered and energetic, she worked tirelessly, taping, priming, then rolling on a fresh coat of white.

By five o'clock her shoulders and neck ached from the constant movement of painting, but it was worth it. The ceiling looked good as new.

"You deserve to celebrate," she told herself as she hopped in the shower and let the hot water soothe her aching muscles. She was meeting Marilyn and Celeste at the diner for dinner. They had some catching up to do, and she was glad to have company. She hadn't heard anything from Jack all day, and she couldn't help but wonder what was going through his mind.

Blowing her hair dry then putting on makeup, she was ready just in time. They were meeting at six thirty, and she needed to stop into Darvill's bookshop before she went to the diner. Warren had called to tell her that he'd found a couple of books on her list and that she could pick them up.

Since it was after six she was allowed to park anywhere on the street around the town square. She wasn't going to give Karl a chance to leave another pink ticket on her windshield.

Another beautiful summer evening graced the quaint town, and she strolled up the sidewalk with her purse swinging with each step. She had on a cool cotton skirt that made her feel especially summery. She looked forward to spending time with Marilyn and Celeste and having a nice dinner.

When she got to the bookstore, Warren had left for the evening, but the young girl working there knew which books were Jocelyn's.

"He told me to give you 10 percent off," the girl said.

"How nice. Please thank him for me," she said. She thought back on that first day in town and how kind Mr. Darvill had been to her.

Carrying her bag of books in one hand and her purse in the other, she headed for the diner. She couldn't help but glance at Jack's repair shop, noticing that the door was closed and the lights were off.

Wishing she could see him and unable to forget the amazing but brief kiss they'd shared, she wondered what was going to happen next.

Inside the diner, she found a booth and settled in. Marilyn and Celeste weren't there yet, so she pulled out one of the books, *Crime and Punishment,* by Fyodor Dostoevsky. She'd started reading this book in college and had never finished it.

Opening the pages, she thumbed through the story, trying to remember where in the story she'd stopped reading all those years ago. She found a spot that seemed familiar and read a few paragraphs, then a few more, until she was pulled into the story, oblivious to the other customers or what was going on around her, until the sound of a man's voice caught her attention.

Jack.

By the way she was sitting with the book in front of her face, she wasn't surprised that Jack and Lenny hadn't noticed her. At least, she hoped that was the reason they hadn't said hello and not that they were trying to ignore her.

Keeping her face hidden behind the book, she felt her heartbeat slow down and realized she was holding her breath. Calming herself, she remained still, not sure what to do. She could hear what they were saying and didn't mean to eavesdrop, but she also didn't want to come out from behind the book and surprise them. She didn't know what to do.

"You aren't the type to run away from a challenge," Lenny said.

"I used to be a risk taker, and I lived to regret it," Jack replied.

"You can't compare what happened then with your life now," Lenny said. "You weren't living in the real world back then, Jack, and you know it. You were caught up in fame, fortune, and everything that went with it. You aren't that person now."

"I know, but I can never go through that again. Ever."

"Ever is a long time, man. I don't think that's what she'd want."

Jack was silent.

"It's all about forgiveness. Forgiving others and . . . yourself."

"I know that," Jack said, his voice tinged with anger. "I know."

Jocelyn was trembling. She didn't really understand what she was hearing, but if they knew she was there, they probably wouldn't be too happy about it. What did she do? What if Marilyn and Celeste came in just then and . . .

"Jocelyn!" Marilyn's voice called. "I couldn't see you for a minute."

Wishing she could melt into the vinyl seat, Jocelyn peeked over the top of the book at the two women then tried to nod discreetly toward Jack and Lenny so Marilyn wouldn't draw attention to them. But it was too late. She made eye contact with Jack, and he didn't look happy.

She felt sick. And sad. How could everything go from being so perfect to being so horrible in less than twenty-four hours?

"What are you reading?" Marilyn asked as she examined the book.

"I read this in school," Celeste remarked. "It was good."

"Yes, but that was an assignment. Why are you reading this?" Marilyn asked her.

"I just picked up some books at the bookstore. I'm trying to build my library of classics."

Marilyn pulled a face. "We need to get you out more, girl. You need to go shopping and to the movies. We need to go to Seattle and have some fun. A girl as beautiful as you are shouldn't be home reading. Especially depressing books like this!"

"Mom!" Celeste rested her forehead in her hand.

As amusing as Marilyn was, Jocelyn was unable to get her mind off the fact that Jack was in the next booth and now knew that she'd overheard his conversation with Lenny. She'd hidden behind a book, like she was sneaky and conniving. And she hadn't even meant to. She had to tell him; she had to explain.

But she wouldn't have a chance. Lenny and Jack got up to leave.

"Hey, guys," Marilyn said, not aware of what had just happened. "Where you going so fast? Come and join us."

Jocelyn wanted to kick her under the table. She couldn't bring herself to look at Jack.

"I can't. My wife will beat me if I'm not home to tend the kids while she goes to her yoga class," Lenny said.

"I knew it!" Marilyn exclaimed. "I could tell she'd lost weight. She looks amazing."

"I'll tell her you said that. We're going on a cruise in September, so she thinks she needs to get in shape. Which will only make me look bad."

"Maybe you should do a few sit-ups and lay off the peanut M&M's for a while," Marilyn said. This brought a chuckle from Jack.

"You too!" Lenny exclaimed. "What is it with you women? You know, in some countries being fat is a symbol of wealth and prosperity."

"In this country, it means laziness and overeating," Marilyn said bluntly.

Another laugh from Jack. Maybe he wasn't upset after all.

"Uh-oh." Lenny looked at his phone. "I'm late!"

The two men rushed off, and Jack didn't say anything or even look at her. Jocelyn's heart sank.

Marilyn and Celeste chattered back and forth so much they didn't even notice that Jocelyn had barely said two words. Celeste's missionary would be home next week, and he had told her there was only one more piece of the puzzle left. Both women were bubbling over with excitement.

Dinner was served, but Jocelyn barely ate, her stomach was so knotted with nerves. She had to talk to Jack.

"Okay," Marilyn said as they left the diner. "I mean it about going to Seattle. What are you doing Saturday? Celeste needs a new outfit to wear when Nick gets off the plane, and you need to do something fun."

Jocelyn didn't have a thing going on Saturday. Unless something else in her house fell apart. That would be the only way Jack would come over again.

"Saturday is great."

Marilyn erupted with excitement and gave her a hug. "It's a date. Save the whole day so we can do lunch, shopping, and a movie."

"Sounds fun," Jocelyn said.

"You okay?" Celeste asked, also giving her a good-bye hug.

"Yeah, just tired. I painted all day."

"We need to come see your house one of these days," Marilyn said. "We can do that on Saturday, too."

"Okay. I'll see you then," Jocelyn said, switching the heavy bag of books to her other hand.

They departed in different directions since they'd parked on opposite sides of the town square.

Jocelyn didn't know what to do. Did she just drive over to his house to talk to him? Should she call? Should she text?

She couldn't bear the thought of what he was thinking about her right now.

"Good evening, fair Jocelyn."

Jocelyn gasped and stopped short. Karl had appeared out of nowhere.

"You're looking quite lovely this evening." He was out of uniform and wore a pair of camouflage utility pants, an argyle vest in navy and red, and a button-down, light blue dress shirt. He looked like a confused army recruit from Yale.

"Hi, Karl. You startled me."

"My apologies. I wondered if I might carry that heavy bag for you. Are you on your way somewhere special?"

"Just to my car. I just had dinner with friends."

"Wonderful!" he exclaimed. "So glad to see you've found friends so quickly."

She smiled at him, not giving up her bags. She didn't want to encourage him.

"I've been meaning to speak with you," he said.

Her smile faded. Where in heaven's name was this going?

"Yes, I have to say, I feel a bit distraught over how I welcomed you to town. You know, the speeding ticket."

"And the parking ticket," she reminded him.

"Yes," he closed his eyes as he nodded. "And the parking ticket."

"Well, thank you, Karl. I appreciate that." She continued walking, wishing she'd parked closer. "I was getting a little worried about parking and driving around town."

"I assure you it won't happen again," he said with remorse. "Hey, are you busy tonight? A few of us, well, my mother and I, are getting the telescope out. It's been over a year since we've done any stargazing, but I'm finally over it."

"Over what?" she asked, hoping she didn't regret the question.

"Over the absurd declaration that Pluto isn't a planet. I was devastated for months. Pluto's always been my favorite planet. I mean, Disney even named a character after the planet, for crying out loud!"

Jocelyn stared at him in disbelief. She didn't even know how to respond to that.

"Actually, I have plans for this evening, but thank you," she said.

"Maybe another time, then?"

"Of course," she said, trying not to be too enthusiastic. She had a tendency to attract strange people. She wasn't sure why. Somehow she drew them to her like ants to sugar.

"You have made my day, m'lady," he said dramatically, placing his hand over his heart and bowing his head. Clearly, he'd missed his calling in the theater—or in the sixteenth century.

She was at a loss for a response, and frankly, she wasn't up to humoring him. She had other things on her mind, like Jack.

"Okay, well, thank you for your apology," she said. "I guess I'll see you around, then."

"You can count on it," he said.

She attempted to smile then walked briskly to her car, her heart filling with dread. She knew exactly where this would lead. He would continue to pester her about going out, and it would get awkward because she would refuse him, knowing that if she gave in and went out once, it would get extremely uncomfortable and eventually come down to her having to explain to him that she wasn't interested in him as a boyfriend and that she hoped they could just be friends. Crud!

Chapter Nineteen

The drive home seemed endless as her mind played the scenario with Jack over and over. It started off with their magical moment at the fireworks, an almost too-perfect first kiss, and ended with Lacey's confrontation.

She pulled into her driveway and sat inside her car for a moment as conflicting emotions churned inside of her. Anger, disappointment, and sadness mixed together, creating a build-up of energy that needed release. Some of her best cleaning and organizing was done when she was upset. The problem was, the house was clean and her closets were in perfect order. Starting a new home improvement project would likely bring more frustration than relief.

That left the yard. There was always something to do in the yard.

She quickly changed her clothes, then as the sun hung low in the sky, she attacked her flower beds, pulling out any plant, weed, or flower she took a disliking to. She yanked and dug as hot tears spilled onto her cheeks.

"Mother Nature tick you off?" a voice asked, startling Jocelyn.

She looked up and saw Harry, who had a strange-looking plant in his hand.

"I was going to offer you a start of moon plant, but maybe I'd better not. Looks like you've got a bit of an anger issue with growing things." He was teasing, but his voice also carried a sense of compassion.

She wiped at her cheeks with the back of her glove but realized she was only smearing dirt on her face. She yanked off the gloves and threw them on the ground then covered her face with her hands.

"Hey, there," Harry said, putting the plant on the ground. "It can't be that bad."

She wiped her face on the sleeve of her shirt.

"You want to talk about it?"

She considered that. It wasn't that she didn't trust him, she just wasn't ready to expose her wound. She was used to keeping her problems to herself.

"Maybe another time," she said, not wanting to close that door completely. "I'll be okay."

"If you ever need an ear to bend, you can always have mine."

"Thanks, Harry. That means a lot to me." She looked at the strange plant on the ground and wondered why he would offer her a weed. "What did you call that?"

"It's a moon plant."

"I've never heard of that."

"Well, some people call it evening primrose, but no matter the name, I think you'd really enjoy it. In fact, your grandmother used to come over at night in the summer, and we'd watch it bloom. She never wanted one in her yard, though. She said she was fine just coming over and watching mine."

"What do you mean you'd watch it bloom at night?"

"That's why it's called a moon plant. It blooms at night. Right after sundown you can tell which buds are going to bloom because they start to shake ever so slightly, and then, right before your eyes, they will open. It takes about fifteen minutes to half an hour. The blooms are beautiful. You need to come see mine. I haven't been able to count all the blooms some nights. I'd say upwards to ninety or a hundred."

"A hundred! Really?"

"Why don't you come on over. It's almost time."

They left her moon plant start by the flower bed where she was working and walked over to his yard. Harry's presence had helped her calm down and take a step back from the situation with Jack. She didn't feel great, but she was already feeling better.

Harry had a small wooden bench they could both sit on, and they perched themselves in front of the plant. It was about four feet wide and three feet deep against his house.

"What happens to all the blooms?" she asked, noticing there weren't any on the plant.

"Once the sun comes out, they wilt within fifteen minutes or so. I'll come out each day and pick off the wilted blooms, and the next night, it starts all over again."

She shook her head with wonder. "What a strange plant. I have to say, though, I'm intrigued."

"I think the Creator had a bit of fun when He created this plant, and the Grand Canyon. That must have been quite a show that day."

Jocelyn agreed. So many of the earth's creations were a marvel—it just took stopping long enough to notice and appreciate them. Something she didn't do often enough.

"There!" he exclaimed, pointing. "That one. And that one!"

She didn't see it at first, then, upon closer inspection, she noticed several buds quivering as though they were filled with excitement. Suddenly, the buds split and out peeked the pale yellow of flower petals. Then another bud quivered, and another, and several more.

Realizing that she was holding her breath, Jocelyn took in a gulp of air and flashed an astonished look at Harry. "This is incredible."

"Isn't it? I'm telling you, I've never tired of watching this plant bloom."

"I can see why."

"You just have to be patient and willing to watch long enough, then it will open up to you. I think that's how we get in life sometimes. We want the answers now. We want our problems solved now. But sometimes the good Lord takes His time giving us what we need because we're supposed to learn something important along the way."

He looked at her as if he knew her struggles, yet there was no way he could. Maybe she just needed to be patient with Jack until he was ready to open up. She didn't want to go over there and demand he tell her what was going on. And to be realistic, she needed some time before she was ready to be completely open with him as well.

They counted close to forty blooms that night. The blossoms were spectacular and seemed to generate a sense of peace and serenity. It was an unforgettable experience.

"Guess that's all for now," he said as a stillness settled in on the fresh blooms. "Not a bad show, was it?"

"Not bad at all. Thanks, Harry. I guess I'd better get my plant in the ground."

"I packed it well. It can wait till morning if you don't want to do it in the dark."

"That's a good idea. I am a little tired." She took one last look at the moon plant and smiled. "Thanks again."

"It was my pleasure. I've missed having someone to watch the plant with. Your grandmother was a good friend."

"I'm sure she felt the same way about you. I'm glad to know she had such a great neighbor."

He gave her a nod and got to his feet, taking a moment to straighten up. "Pulled too many weeds today. I'm going to be stiff tomorrow."

"I know how you feel," she said, thinking of the stiffness in her neck and shoulders from painting all day.

They bid each other good night. She noticed that Harry watched until she got safely inside her house before he went in. It gave her a good feeling to know he was watching out for her.

After securing the locks on the doors and windows, she got a drink of water before going up to bed. She admired her pristine kitchen ceiling and looked at all the other work she'd done the last few weeks. Even on a shoestring budget the changes on the house seemed drastic. She still felt the loving spirit of her grandmother there, but she was making it her home, with her own taste and personality coming through. She wondered what color she'd paint the kitchen—maybe yellow? Or how about a fresh green?

She was about to turn out the light when her cell phone buzzed on the counter.

She picked it up and noticed a call from Lauryn coming in.

"Hey there," Jocelyn said, "isn't it a little late for you to be calling?" It was ten thirty for her, which made it one thirty for Lauryn in New York.

"I've left a couple of messages for you." Lauryn sounded anxious.

"Is everything okay?" Jocelyn asked, her stomach constricting with worry.

"I'm fine," she assured her, "but I just got off the phone with Chloe. She's really worried about Emma."

"Emma! What's happened to Emma?"

"That's the trouble—we don't know. Chloe's been trying for over a week to get ahold of her without luck. Have you heard from Emma?"

"I sent her an e-mail yesterday," Jocelyn said. "She used to respond fastest to those because she e-mails from work, but I haven't heard anything from her since I've been in Washington."

"Chloe says that something doesn't seem right; she is really worried. Plus, she's really concerned about the investigation into Ava's death."

"That's kind of got me freaked out too," Jocelyn said. "I'm wondering if I should get a dog."

"Yeah, maybe you should. We already have an alarm system, but I feel antsy when I'm home alone. It just makes me nervous thinking that someone actually could have caused Ava's death—and maybe intended to hurt all of us. I hate considering that we might be in danger now."

"Me too. It doesn't help being alone."

"You definitely need a dog. A big mean one."

"So, what about Emma? What are you thinking?" Jocelyn asked.

"Well, that's kind of why I called. I'm going to a trade show in LA on Monday, and I was thinking I could fly west a few days early and stop in St. George. What are you doing this weekend? Could we have an emergency Butterfly Girls meeting?"

She was pretty sure Marilyn and Celeste wouldn't mind postponing their girls' day out, but she was reluctant to spend the kind of money it would take to buy a last-minute ticket. The prices would be exorbitant.

"Andrea said she could fly in Friday afternoon. I have plenty of frequent flyer miles to help you with the flight if the airline will take them on such short notice. If not, I'm more than happy to pick up the tab for you."

Jocelyn wasn't surprised Lauryn would offer; that was the kind of person she was. But it did underline just how important this get-together was to Lauryn.

"Lauryn, that's too generous. And I can pay my own way, really."

"Hey! I know how much you've had to fork out with house and car repairs. You need to save up for future projects. Besides, this get-together is my idea, so it's my treat. Please, let me do this for you. I really want you there. We really need to get together and talk about everything."

"I want to be there too," Jocelyn said. "How about you try out the frequent flyer option first, but if it doesn't work I'll pay you back for the ticket."

"It's a deal! I'll take care of it first thing in the morning and get the information to you. Hopefully I can get you out on a Friday afternoon or evening flight. Does that work for your schedule?"

"Yeah, that works great." She gave Lauryn all the personal info she'd need to book the flight.

The girls were both quiet for a moment. Then Jocelyn said, "What do you think is going on with Emma?"

Lauryn sighed. "I wish I knew, Joss. I keep thinking crazy things."

"Me too. It's not like her to not stay in touch. I don't think I've ever gone a week without some kind of contact with her, either a call or a text or e-mail. Something."

"Same here. Chloe thinks Nicholas has totally got her brainwashed or something and that he's a psycho who's so possessive and controlling that he's keeping her away from her family and friends."

"Her family hasn't seen or talked to her either?"

"No. Nothing. And when Chloe called her work to talk to her they just said she'd taken some time off and they weren't sure when she was coming back."

"Okay, now you're scaring me."

"I know. I don't know what to think," Lauryn said. "Listen, I've got a big meeting tomorrow, so I'd better get some sleep. I'll be in touch in the morning."

"Sounds good. Thanks, Lauryn. Give Jace my love. And tell Cooper hi."

"I will. He asks about all of you."

That made Jocelyn smile.

They hung up and Jocelyn double-checked her doors and windows one more time. She thought about Emma and her boyfriend and wondered what could possibly be going on. As hard as she tried to stop it, her mind conjured up all sorts of crazy, drastic situations that were completely off the deep end. Lately, there were enough weird stories in the news to think anything was possible. And no one knew Nicholas enough to know what he was capable of.

She spent a lot more time on her knees that night. Worries about Emma, worries about Jack, and worries about Ava's investigation filled her mind and heart, and she knew that she needed to get the peace that came only when she prayed.

She remained on her knees after the prayer, paying attention to her thoughts and impressions. Nothing came regarding Emma, but her feelings for Jack became crystal clear. She cared for this man. They hadn't known each other long, but she'd never gotten so close to a person as quickly as she had with him. She knew things might still work out between them, but it hurt to think that all of it might possibly be over.

Knowing that only time would tell, Jocelyn curled up under the covers and let the sound of the raindrops on her roof lull her to sleep.

* * *

Her stomach tingled with excitement as the plane landed on the runway at the St. George airport. Even though she'd only been gone three weeks, she felt like it was three months. So much had happened in her life; so many things had changed.

Just as they'd planned, Lauryn was waiting for her by the baggage claim. The two women hugged, and even though the purpose of the visit was a somber one, Jocelyn couldn't help feeling excited about being together.

Lauryn and Jocelyn recapped the information they knew about Emma, trying to figure out what they should do to find her. They both felt like the weekend could be intense.

"Andrea got in last night," Lauryn said. "She stayed with Chloe. She texted me and said that Chloe is not doing well. She's had to get a restraining order against Roger."

"This is so sad," Jocelyn said. "He's willing to lose everything for this addiction."

"Our friend who's an attorney was telling Jace that one in five divorces have some element of pornography tied to them."

"I can believe it. I really hoped that Roger could pull out of this. Chloe still loves him and wants their marriage to work out."

"By the time Roger realizes it, it will be too late. I think she's finally ready to move forward and make their separation final," Lauryn told her.

"Poor Chloe. She always wanted the whole 'happily ever after' fairy tale, but her prince turned into a frog."

"More like a toad," Lauryn said. "With warts."

Neither of them laughed. It was too painfully true to be funny.

"So, tell me how things are in Milford Falls," Lauryn asked. "How's the house?"

"I'm done painting my living room. The plumbing and drywall repair is finished, too."

"How's Jack?"

Jocelyn felt a sharp stab in her heart, just hearing his name. She'd thought to call him and tell him she was leaving, but she wasn't sure he cared. He hadn't called or made an attempt to reach her since he'd dropped her off Wednesday night. It had been going so well between them. Then things had changed so suddenly that she felt like she'd been hit with a meteor falling out of nowhere and landing right on top of her.

"I don't really know," she said. "He kissed me on the Fourth, but then his mood changed later and he hasn't called since."

"What? You kissed him?" The rental car swerved a little as she looked over at Jocelyn.

"Lauryn, be careful!" Jocelyn exclaimed as Lauryn corrected her course.

"Sorry, but I don't get it."

"I know. But really it's been a roller-coaster ride since we met, so I guess I shouldn't be surprised."

"No explanation?"

"Not really." She didn't want to get into her theories yet. First she had to tell all her friends something to help them understand better.

"I'm sorry," Lauryn said, reaching for her hand. "I felt so good about you two."

"I was starting to feel that way too," Jocelyn said.

They pulled into the hotel parking lot and found the room Andrea and Chloe had already checked into. The hotel door flew open, and out ran the two other women to greet them.

With hugs out of the way and suitcases unloaded, they all settled on the beds to come up with a plan.

Jocelyn was happy to see Andrea still looking healthy. Chloe, on the other hand, looked like she'd been hit by a Mack truck and backed over a few times. She had dark circles under her eyes, and she appeared to have lost ten pounds in the last three weeks. And her usual spark was gone.

"So, where do we begin?" Andrea asked, looking at the others. "I want to find that Nicholas and wring his neck!"

"With all of us leaving e-mails and messages on her phone telling her that we're meeting this weekend, I can't imagine she won't show up," Chloe said.

"Assuming she can," Lauryn added.

Chloe nodded.

"We can't let our imaginations run away with us," Jocelyn reminded them. "The explanation could be something as simple as Nicholas surprising her with a vacation and that she forgot her phone charger so her phone is dead."

All three of them looked at her like she'd just tried to convince them that grass was really purple.

"Well, I'm just trying to keep some perspective here," she said in her defense. "The truth is I'm terrified something horrible has happened to her."

"Me too," Lauryn said.

Andrea and Chloe nodded.

"I've made a list of places to check around town. We could even drive to Vegas and find Nicholas's house."

"Let's do it," Andrea said, ready to get started.

"Wait a minute," Lauryn said. "We need to come up with a story, a reason why we're doing this. I don't want to alert anyone to the fact that we are worried sick until we know for sure there is a reason to be."

"I agree," Jocelyn said.

"All right," Andrea said. "Let's just say that we had a chance to get together and wanted her to join us but were having trouble reaching her. It's basically true and seems harmless enough."

"I agree," Chloe said. "I talked to her mom this morning on the way. I tried to make our meeting sound like it was just for fun and that we hoped Emma could join us."

"What did she say?" Andrea asked.

"She said that they don't see her much because Emma has been so busy with work and Nicholas. She didn't sound worried. I tried to pull information about Nicholas from her, to find out what she thinks of him or if she's worried about him, but all she said was that they didn't really know him very well. They'd only met him once, and that was by accident at a restaurant."

"Really? She hasn't taken him to meet her parents? They had to meet him by accident?" Andrea said.

"I think that is really weird. If you love someone and are excited about them, you want your family to meet him, don't you?" Lauryn said.

"You'd think so," Jocelyn said, knowing that she would have loved her friends to meet Jack.

"I say we start at her apartment. Maybe we can find something there," Chloe suggested. "She gave me her key in case there was ever an emergency. I'd say this qualifies."

"We can look on her computer," Andrea said.

Lauryn shook her head. "I can't believe we have to do this. Why can't she just contact one of us and tell us what's going on?"

"Either she can't or she doesn't want to," Andrea said. "Neither excuse is good."

"All right, then," Lauryn said with a sigh. "Let's go get this over with."

They piled into Chloe's van and made the trip across town to Emma's apartment. Even though the tone was serious, the girls couldn't help spending time catching up with each other.

Jocelyn was relieved the topic of Jack didn't come up. She wasn't ready to tackle that one yet.

"Here we are," Chloe said, shoving the gear shift into park.

"I feel like we're doing something wrong," Jocelyn said. "Going in without her knowing, snooping around like this."

"Hey, I hope she catches us!" Andrea said. "I will be happy to let her know that we're only there because she's forced us to be snoopy."

Lauryn nodded. "It's true. We aren't doing this out of spite or curiosity."

"Let's get this over with, then," Jocelyn said, getting out of the car.

Luckily her apartment was at the end of the row, on the bottom. Since most of the people who lived there were single, it was likely they were either at work or at school, so the place was quiet.

"Hurry, Chloe," Andrea urged, looking around the complex like she was about ready to rob the place.

"I am. The key is hard to get in." Chloe wiggled the key into the lock and turned it then pushed the door open.

With a push from behind, Andrea rushed them all inside and closed the door behind them.

"Oh!" Lauryn exclaimed, pinching her nose. "What is that horrible smell?"

Chloe looked cautiously around as she made her way to the kitchen. "Just what I thought," she said. "The trash." Chloe pulled the container out from under the sink and pulled out the plastic liner filled with the offensive-smelling garbage.

"Hurry," Lauryn said, gagging.

Chloe rushed the bag outside and set it on the porch.

"Let's open some doors and windows to air the place out," Jocelyn said.

"That's been sitting there a while to smell that bad," Andrea said.

"Which means she hasn't been here for a while," Jocelyn said, pushing images out of her mind. She refused to think something bad had happened to Emma.

Chloe came back inside and took a good look around the place. "If she were home there would be dishes in the sink and clothes on the floor. Emma only cleans on Saturdays."

Andrea walked across the room to the bedroom door.

"Andrea, wait," Lauryn said.

Andrea looked at her with raised eyebrows.

"Let's go in together," she said. Her suggestion confirmed everyone's concern that their worst fear was about to come true.

"I can't look," Chloe said. "What if she's in there? You know . . ."

"Oh, come on, you guys," Andrea said, "you don't really think—" She swung the bedroom door open quickly and gasped.

Chloe screamed.

Jocelyn and Lauryn grabbed each other.

Andrea started laughing. "Sorry, I couldn't resist."

"Darn you!" Chloe said. "That's not funny."

Lauryn swatted Andrea on the shoulder. "I can't believe you did that."

Andrea kept laughing. "Sorry. I was just trying to lighten up the mood." She stepped inside the bedroom. "See, there's no one in here."

"I swear, you about gave me a heart attack," Chloe said. "If I die, the girls are stuck with Roger. And I'll come back and haunt you forever."

"I'm sorry," Andrea said remorsefully, "really."

"Hey," Lauryn said, "it looks like she packed a suitcase."

"How can you tell?" Jocelyn asked.

"See the flat spot on her bed right there?"

The down comforter had been flattened on the corner of the bed.

"And look," Lauryn said, slipping some shirts that were hanging out of a drawer back inside. "It looks like she packed in a hurry."

"I think she's right," Jocelyn said, going to the closet. Hangers still stuck out like clothes had been yanked off of them.

Lauryn sorted through the hanging clothes. "It's gone."

"What's gone?" Andrea asked, stepping over to the closet.

"The dress I sent her for her birthday. She said that even though she wasn't a *dress*-type girl, she loved it and wears it all the time."

"That's a good sign," Jocelyn said. "See, maybe they did go on a vacation."

"Still, why can't she just let one of us know?" Chloe picked up a couple of tops that had fallen on the floor and hung them back in the closet.

"I think if something fishy were going on, she wouldn't have packed a suitcase for it," Lauryn said.

"I agree," Jocelyn said, hoping she was right. She hated the thought of something happening to her friend.

Andrea shrugged. "I guess."

"So now what do we do?" Jocelyn asked.

"Not much we can do," Lauryn said. "We just wait until she contacts one of us."

"Great, then I say we go get something to eat. I'm starving." Andrea walked out of the room and left the others to follow.

"You guys hungry?" Chloe asked.

They both nodded.

Closing the windows before they left, they also tidied up a few things around the house, knowing that Emma had left in a hurry.

Andrea wrote her a note and left it on the table for Emma to see.

"*Hey, Emma! Remember us? Your friends? We're hoping everything's okay with you. Take a minute and give one of us a call so we know you're still alive.*" She signed it, *The Butterfly Girls.*

"I hope she doesn't get mad we came into her apartment," Jocelyn said.

"I don't care if she does," Andrea said. "She should know we would wonder what's going on if we don't hear from her for a month."

"You're right. It's been that long since I've heard from her," Jocelyn said.

"Me too," Lauryn said. "She just sent a text about the dress. I didn't even talk to her."

"Don't you think it's weird that she doesn't have pictures of her and Nicholas anywhere?" Chloe said.

"Yeah, for as long as they've dated you'd think there would be one picture." Andrea scanned the room. "Well, there's nothing else we can do."

They gathered their purses and left the apartment cleaner and better smelling than they'd found it.

* * *

"So, my agent is trying to get me to do one of those *Bachelor*-type shows next summer. He thinks it will give my career a boost," Andrea told them on their way back to the hotel.

"Does your career need a boost?" Lauryn asked.

"In my business the younger and hotter you are, the more in demand you are."

"You're thirty-one for crying out loud!" Chloe exclaimed. "Our world is so messed up!" She continued ranting about morals and media and models and the Internet.

The other three looked at each other, knowing that Chloe's venting was a result of Roger's continued struggle with pornography.

"Are you going to do it?" Lauryn asked.

"I don't know. I mean, I'd probably be the first one kicked off, so it wouldn't tie up my life for too long. I just can't imagine being part of a show like that. You know, as a Mormon."

"You'd get great exposure, and you could be one of the girls that doesn't bad mouth all the other girls. And I would design your clothes so you could have a drop-dead wardrobe," Lauryn said.

"I think you should do it," Chloe said. "Do it for all the girls who want to show the world that there are still women with values and integrity who won't sleep with a guy just to get him to like them. Even if you don't last long, you can still get that message out there."

"I think you would last longer than you think," Jocelyn said. "Come on. You're beautiful, smart, successful, funny—what more could a guy want?"

"Apparently something," Andrea said. "I haven't seemed to find anyone who wants me yet. By the way, Lauryn, how's Cooper?"

"He's great. He's working with some pretty sharp missionaries right now. Once he makes the commitment, he will be baptized. He's just making sure," Lauryn explained.

"Let me know, because I'll drop everything I'm doing and move to New York if I have to. I don't know what it is about him, but I can't get him off of my mind," Andrea confessed.

"He is memorable," Lauryn agreed. "He asked about you just the other day."

Andrea smiled. "He did?"

"Yep."

"Well, anyway, I have to make sure this TV show thing works with my schedule. It's quite a big time commitment."

"What's the show called?" Chloe asked.

"*Looking for Mrs. Right,*" she said. "It's a lot like *The Bachelor,* but I think he gets to do individual dates right off the bat, so you get to know the girls right away. And the country gets to vote, even though he gets the final vote who stays or who goes. I like the format."

"I hope you do it," Lauryn said.

"Me too," Jocelyn added. "The country would love you."

Andrea smiled. "Thanks, you guys."

"So, now what do we do?" Chloe said. "I can't believe Emma is standing us up."

"She'd better have a good excuse," Andrea said. "This really isn't like her."

"I know!" Lauryn exclaimed. "I miss all the silly e-mails she used to forward me. I can't remember the last one I got."

They sat and looked at each other, then Jocelyn realized this was as good a time as any. Even without Emma, she needed to do something, and she didn't want to put it off any longer.

"I brought the Butterfly Box," she said.

"You did?" Chloe said. "Why? It's yours for the year."

"I know," Jocelyn said. She took a breath and let it out slowly.

"Joss, are you okay?" Lauryn asked, reaching over and taking hold of her hand.

Jocelyn had her head down but nodded slowly.

She was going to lose her nerve if she didn't get it over with.

"Hey," Chloe said, slipping an arm around Jocelyn's shoulders. "What's going on?"

Jocelyn shut her eyes for a minute and prayed for strength.

"Sweetie, you know you can tell us anything," Chloe reminded her.

It would be all right, she knew that. It would feel so much better once she got it out. She'd been carrying this burden for too many years.

"The reason I brought the Butterfly Box with me was . . . well . . ." She swallowed. "There's something I need to tell you."

She saw the other girls exchange glances. It wasn't a secret that they had always wanted to know what was in the little white box, but they'd never pressured her to tell them. She appreciated their love, support, and patience with her. That's what made it possible for her to share her secret with them now.

She opened the lid of the box and sorted through the items until she found what she was looking for.

"It's time to tell you what's inside."

Chapter Twenty

She paused to gather her strength and thoughts. She needed to do this right.

"It's okay, honey," Chloe said. "Don't be afraid."

"I'm actually not afraid," Jocelyn said. "Up until now I have been. But I realize now that I'm strong enough and healed enough to tell you. That's why I know it's time."

Each of her friends looked at her with love and understanding. It would be okay.

She grasped the lid of the box and was about to lift it when a loud banging came at the door.

They all jumped.

"Who the crud is that?" Jocelyn said, feeling as though her heart had jumped out of her chest.

"I'll find out," Andrea said, getting to her feet.

She went to the door and peeked out the peephole. "Emma!"

She yanked the door open and let out an excited squeal. "It's about time you showed up! Where have you been?"

Andrea practically tackled Emma with an exuberant hug.

Jocelyn slipped the box into her pocket and joined the others to greet Emma.

Emma hugged each one of her friends and apologized for not staying in touch better.

"It's so good to see all of you. What is going on? Why are all of you here?" Emma asked.

Jocelyn couldn't help noticing Emma's snug-fitting, low-cut minidress and high heels. Jocelyn couldn't ever remember seeing Emma in an outfit like this. In fact, this was the type of outfit Emma normally would have said she wouldn't be caught dead wearing.

The four girls looked at each other, then Lauryn spoke up. "We were worried about you. It had been such a long time since anyone heard from you we didn't know what to think. Your family and your work didn't know where you were."

"You guys did this for me?" Emma said. Then her face scrunched up with her next thought. "What did you think had happened to me?"

Was that anger Jocelyn detected in her voice?

"Uh, we weren't sure," Andrea answered. "I mean, c'mon Em, it's not like you to go a week without contacting someone. And it's been longer than that since any of us had heard from you."

"It's true," Chloe backed up Andrea. "It's not like you to take off without saying something."

"So you guys naturally assumed I was in trouble or that something was wrong? I don't suppose it occurred to you that maybe I was just busy or had something going on that didn't involve you guys? I mean, we aren't all joined at the hip, you know."

Lauryn and Jocelyn exchanged brief glances before Lauryn spoke up. "Emma, don't get mad. We got worried, that's all."

"Gosh, you guys," Emma said, slipping her Prada handbag off her shoulder. "I can't believe this. What did you think happened?"

"Like Andrea said," Jocelyn piped up, "we weren't sure. You are usually the one who stays in contact the best out of all of us. Suddenly there aren't any texts, e-mails, or phone calls. How could we not get worried?"

That seemed to help calm Emma a bit, which helped them all relax a little. It was then that Jocelyn saw the diamond ring on her finger. "Emma, is that what I think it is?" She grabbed Emma's hand and lifted it. The others gasped.

"Is that an engagement ring?" Lauryn asked. "Oh, my gosh, Emma, are you engaged?"

Emma closed her eyes for a moment. She shook her head. "No," she said. "I'm not engaged. I'm . . . married."

"You're what!" Andrea screamed it so loud Jocelyn's ears rang for a second afterward.

Emma nodded happily, but her eyes searched the expressions of her shocked friends, clearly unsure of what to expect.

"Emma!" Chloe said, her voice cracking and eyes watering. "You got married without us?"

Lauryn was completely stunned, and Jocelyn was actually sick to her stomach. Jocelyn didn't feel like she knew this person standing in front of her anymore.

"I'm sorry," Emma said. "It all happened so quickly. Nick came to visit one weekend, and the night he was supposed to go back to Vegas he looked at me and said he couldn't bear leaving me again. He was tired of us living in different cities and commuting back and forth. He said he loved me and he proposed."

"Wow," Andrea said, her voice less than enthusiastic.

"Seeing each other on weekends was getting old, and I found I wasn't doing my job well anymore because I was so distracted during the week."

"So you two got married?"

She nodded, smiling broadly.

Jocelyn knew that the others were as shocked and concerned as she was, but their feelings wouldn't change the situation. Their job as friends was to love and support her now.

"Well, congratulations!" Jocelyn said, giving her friend a big hug.

Lauryn followed her lead, then Andrea. Chloe wiped at her eyes quickly before it was her turn. She managed to give a half-convincing performance of her excitement for Emma.

"I can't believe it," Jocelyn said. "I mean, I've never even met him. Where is he? Can we meet him now?"

"He went back to Vegas," Emma explained. "We took a two-week honeymoon and just got back. That's why I didn't get your messages. We were out at sea on a cruise in Hawaii."

"That sounds wonderful." Lauryn gave Emma a warm smile, showing her unconditional support. "So when do we get to meet the lucky man?" Lauryn asked.

"He'll come and pick me up when you guys go home. You can meet him then. We want to move some stuff out of my apartment anyway."

"You're moving to Vegas?" Chloe exclaimed. "You're leaving me?"

"I'm so sorry, Chloe," Emma said. "His work is down there, and I can do mine anywhere."

Chloe nodded, her eyes filling with tears again.

"I am anxious for you to meet him. He's such an incredible person. He can be a little intimidating at first, but he's really such a teddy bear."

"I'm looking forward to it," Lauryn said. "I'm sure he's incredible, much like that diamond. What is it, anyway—two carats?"

Everyone laughed, and then the other girls found something congratulatory to say about Nicholas and the marriage.

"As I scanned my e-mails"—Emma held up her touch phone—"I saw that note about Ava's case. What's that all about?" Emma asked, adjusting the strap on her dress and pulling it up in the front and down at her exposed thighs.

"That's something else we wanted to look into while we were together," Lauryn said. "Remember Joey Hutchinson from school?"

"Yeah," Emma said. "He's the jerk who copied off my history test then got us both suspended for cheating. Why?"

"Oh, I forgot about that," Lauryn said. "Well, anyway, he's a detective now for the St. George Police Department, and he said we could call him this weekend and he'd tell us what he could about Ava's case."

"How did you get hooked up with him?" Jocelyn asked. She'd forgotten all about Joey and, frankly, most of the other kids from high school.

"He knows Jace pretty well, and they connected on Facebook. He mentioned to Jace that our old football coach, Coach Drake, had a heart attack. Jace called him to get details, they got talking, and he mentioned something about Ava's case."

"We need to find out what's going on," Emma said. "I'm a little freaked about the thought that a killer might be running around with us in his sights."

"Me too," Chloe said. "I got the girls a dog. I thought with Roger being all unpredictable lately we maybe needed some extra protection anyway."

"I'm thinking of getting a dog too," Jocelyn said.

"He's actually a better companion than Roger ever was, and I don't have to pick up after him either."

"So," Emma said, looking at her cell phone for the fiftieth time, "other than talking to Joey, what else is going on?"

Andrea looked at Jocelyn.

It was hard to get back into the moment, but Jocelyn knew she couldn't take back what she started. The girls wouldn't let her off the hook now.

"When you got here I was about to share something with everyone," Jocelyn said. She pulled the box out of her pocket and showed Emma.

"Is that what I think it is?" Emma said.

Jocelyn nodded.

"Oh, wow. I'm so glad I came when I did." Then her eyebrows scrunched together. "Hey, you guys were going to do this without me!"

Andrea shrugged. "Next time answer your dang phone, then, or check your e-mail once in a while."

"All right. I know. I'm sorry." Emma again tugged her dress down to cover her thighs and pulled up the front to cover her chest.

Jocelyn couldn't stand it anymore."Emma, do you want to change into something more comfortable? I have a T-shirt and some pajama pants."

"I'd love to," Emma exclaimed. "Thanks."

Jocelyn pulled the articles of clothing out of her suitcase and handed them to Emma who quickly rushed to the bathroom and changed her clothes.

Emma charged out of the bathroom and plopped herself on the bed next to Jocelyn.

"Okay, I'm ready. I have to say, I've been dying to see what's in here since that day after the funeral." Emma looked at the others, but none of them said anything. None of them seemed sure what to expect.

Jocelyn took the box and decided to explain before she lifted the lid.

She took a deep breath."I don't know if any of you remember this, but one night, back when we were juniors, I was hanging out with Ava and she was determined to find some guys to hang out with."

"That doesn't sound like her," Emma said sarcastically.

"You know, out of all my friends, she got me into more trouble than anyone," Andrea said.

"I was grounded for a month one time—" Emma started then stopped and looked at Jocelyn. "Sorry. You were saying . . ."

"Anyway, you know I wasn't into chasing down boys, but she refused to take me home because she didn't want to go by herself. So after a while we ended up at the Frostop. You were there, Lauryn, and Jace. We came in to grab a bite to eat."

"I remember," Lauryn said. "I'm not sure why I remember that, but I do."

"Well, we met these two college guys, and Ava was totally throwing herself at them. And, of course, I was dying because I didn't want to go back to their dorm like she wanted to, so they said they would drop me off on the way.

"But they didn't drop me off. Of course, Ava didn't really care because she was getting her way, and all that mattered to her was the fact that this stupid college boy was paying attention to her. I decided that as soon as we got to their place I would just walk home."

Jocelyn fanned herself with her hand as she suddenly had a rush of perspiration. For a moment she wondered if she was really ready to do this, then she stiffened her resolve and pushed ahead.

"We get there to their dorm, and the guy who was stuck with me said he felt bad that they hadn't dropped me off like I wanted to, so he offered me a ride home."

"That was nice," Emma said.

"Maybe of him but not of Ava. That was pretty crummy of her to put you in the situation to begin with," Lauryn said.

"She was kind of a poop that way," Andrea said.

"What happened?" Lauryn asked.

"Well, like I said, he seemed really nice, and he started driving me home, but then, instead of taking me to my house, he drove up that road that goes up the canyon and pulled off on a dirt road."

"Joss, no," Lauryn said, putting her hand over her mouth.

"He promised he wasn't going to hurt me," Jocelyn said, feeling the surge of emotion and panic that always accompanied the memory. She'd spent years working through this. She knew she could do it. "He said he just wanted to talk, to get to know me better. He complimented me a lot and started to make moves on me. When I said no, he got angry but didn't stop . . . making advances. I didn't know what to do. I kept thinking I should try to get away, but I knew we were far from any help and he could run faster than me. I fought his advances anyway. I begged him and I prayed and I cried, but it didn't stop him. He raped me."

She glanced briefly at her friends, who looked at her with tear-filled eyes and horror-stricken expressions.

Jocelyn tried to hold back her emotions and kept going. "You know that movie, *The Hulk?* That's what happened. He seemed like a normal guy, nothing special. But he seemed to transform into this big, raging . . . monster," she choked out as hot tears trickled onto her cheeks. "I tried . . . so hard . . . to stop him," she whispered. She shut her eyes and shuddered with a wave of tears then pulled in a quick breath to get her emotions back in check. Her friends were frozen with shock.

"Afterward," she said, still unable to look at them while she talked, "he told me that if I told anyone what happened, he and his friends would hurt me." She laughed sardonically. "Like he could hurt me any more than he already had. He said it would be his word against mine and since he was there on a football scholarship and he was some kind of town hero or something, he wasn't worried a bit. He would be protected."

"Joss," Emma said in a strained whisper, "I can't believe this."

"Oh, sweetie," Chloe said. "You poor thing. You went through this all by yourself."

Andrea couldn't control her tears. "Joss, I am so sorry we weren't there to help you."

She went to Jocelyn and hugged her. The two women held each other while Andrea sobbed. Jocelyn cried with her, but her tears were not for herself anymore. She cried for the pain her friends felt for her.

When Andrea got her emotions calmed down, Jocelyn said, "I wanted to tell you guys, but I was so ashamed. It sounds illogical to me now, but I wondered if I'd done something to lead the guy on, and I was convinced that this was the way my life was going to be because, well, you know how my mom was. Heck, I don't know exactly what I thought. I was an emotional train wreck. But I didn't tell anyone for a long time. In fact, I missed a whole week of school because I felt so dirty and scared."

Jocelyn twisted the ring on her finger around several times, knowing that she had to finish the story. "It might have been different if I'd had parents, or at least a mom, that I could go to. But she wasn't even around then. She wouldn't have cared anyway. She was always calling me Miss Goody-Two-Shoes and Molly Mormon. For all I know she would have probably just laughed and told me to get over it.

"My Young Women leader, Sister Stevens, took me home from Young Women one night, and she could tell something was wrong. I finally broke down and told her everything. I refused to go to the police, but she convinced me to go to the bishop. I was so afraid to talk to him, but when I finally did, he really helped me a lot. I was glad they both knew about it, especially after what happened next."

"Oh, my gosh, Joss," Lauryn said, "there's more?"

"I know. I'm sorry I kept it from you. No one knew except the bishop and Sister Stevens. And my grandmother. I don't think I would have made it without her."

"Is that why you went to live with your grandmother after your junior year?" Chloe asked.

"That's part of the reason," Jocelyn said.

"What was the other part?" Lauryn asked.

Jocelyn couldn't speak for several seconds. It was hard enough to remember, let alone share, but she had waited long enough.

"This," she said, lifting the lid off the box.

Lauryn took the box from Jocelyn and looked inside then lifted out a tiny bracelet with pink and white beads. On it was a heart-shaped pendant that said, *Never in my arms but forever in my heart.*

Lauryn looked up at Jocelyn and swallowed. Chloe took the bracelet and read the pendant. She didn't speak either.

Andrea and Emma read it together. It was Emma who finally spoke. "You had a baby?"

Tears flowed like a steady faucet down Jocelyn's cheeks. She didn't even try to stop them anymore. The secret was out. And she was strong enough to handle whatever happened from this moment on.

"A little girl?" Andrea said.

"Oh, Joss," Chloe said softly. "Sweetie."

"That's why you went to your grandma's so suddenly," Lauryn said. "You were pregnant." She paused. "I hate to ask, but was the baby . . . okay?"

Jocelyn nodded. "She was perfect. But she went home with her new family."

"Wow, Joss," Emma said. "We had no idea."

"I know," Jocelyn said. "I'm sorry. I didn't want anyone to know. Especially . . ."

"Ava," Lauryn finished for her. "Look what her selfishness ended up doing to you."

"Lauryn!" Emma said.

"I'm sorry, but that's exactly what it was. Ava didn't care what was going on with Jocelyn to even stay with her and instead left her with that creep." Lauryn wiped at her own tears.

"It wasn't Ava's fault what that boy did," Jocelyn said. "He made his own choices. And, to be honest, the situation felt wrong to me, going into it. I knew in my heart I was making a mistake going with him. I should have called one of you to come and pick me up. I was so stupid. Fifteen minutes changed my life forever."

"Honey, we all can look back on our lives and see mistakes we've made that have altered our futures. Believe me, you're not alone. But you committed no sin here . . . In fact, you were very brave bringing that little girl into the world and then being able to move on with your life. You're a great example to me."

"Thanks, Chloe," Jocelyn said.

"We're proud of you," Lauryn said, putting her hand on top of Jocelyn's.

"I feel bad you went through it alone," Andrea said. "But Jocelyn, our friendship is unconditional. We all love you, no matter what." She added her hand on top of Lauryn's.

"I've always admired your strength and never understood how you were that way," Emma said. "I think you came out of this horrible trial a much stronger and even more compassionate person."

"It's true—trials do strengthen us and make us who we are," Lauryn agreed.

"It was the hardest thing I ever did. I knew I had nothing to offer that child. I had no home to take her to, no real support system to help me. People made it clear to me that I could have an abortion with a clear conscience under the circumstances, but I didn't feel right about that, either. The family who took her was able to give her a wonderful, happy life. I met the parents and felt really good about them," Jocelyn said. "I know she's happy."

"Do you stay in touch with them?" Chloe asked.

"Not really. Once in a while they will send a note letting me know how she's doing. They named her Allison Kate. Her dad calls her his little alley cat," Jocelyn told them with a chuckle.

"That's so sweet," Chloe said. "You did the right thing."

"Someday she'll be able to thank you," Lauryn said.

Jocelyn nodded. "I hope so."

"I'm glad you finally told us," Andrea said. "It helps me understand why you've had a hard time with boys."

Emma snorted. "Totally!" She was thoughtful for a moment. "So, what's happened to make you finally ready to tell us?"

"Well, I guess it's been my move to Milford Falls. Part of it was being forced out of my comfort zone and really having to be strong on my own, and partly because of Jack."

"How is Jack, by the way?" Chloe asked.

Jocelyn sighed. "I guess he's fine, but I'm not sure whether *we're* fine."

"Oh no! Why not?" Andrea slapped her hands on her knees.

"Long story," Jocelyn said. "Basically I think that it's because he found out about the baby and I guess it freaked him out."

"You're kidding!" Emma exclaimed. "Why should that matter to him?"

"I don't really know. We haven't talked about it since Wednesday, the night he found out," Jocelyn said.

"You need to talk to him," Lauryn said. "Find out what is going on."

"He's just confused," Andrea said. "Give him a chance to explain himself."

"I think she should dump him," Chloe said. "If he can't take five minutes and talk to her about it, then he doesn't deserve her."

"Good point." Emma gave a nod of agreement. "It's definitely his loss."

The other girls were quick to assure her they felt the same. Even though it wasn't enough to take away the pain she felt regarding Jack, it did help a little to have their support.

"I do owe him one thing, though," she said, putting the bracelet back in the box. "He helped me know that my heart does work, you know? That I could actually fall in love someday."

"Did you fall in love with him?" Chloe asked.

The question summoned emotions she'd been fighting, and she had to take a moment to put them back in check.

She swallowed and cleared her throat. She nodded. "Yeah, I did, at least a little."

"Oh, sweetie." Chloe leaned forward and gave her a hug. "I'm sorry.

"Me too," Lauryn said, giving her a hug.

The other girls took turns hugging her and expressing their love for her.

"So, enough about me," Jocelyn said brightly. She turned to Emma, "Tell us more about your wedding. I can't believe you're married! Please tell me you have pictures."

The room turned into a sudden surge of excitement. Emma showed off her two-and-a-half carat ring some more and some wedding pictures she had on her Blackberry. Nicholas looked very handsome and distinguished. All the same, Jocelyn didn't think the two were a match. At least, not with the Emma she knew, the Emma who was down-to-earth, warm, and wonderful. The Emma in the picture—with the skimpy dress, fake nails, and black, sculptured hairdo—was no one she even knew.

Jocelyn watched curiously as Emma told them about all the money her new husband had spent on his bride. She seemed determined to convince them that Nicholas was the most adoring, caring, and generous man on the planet.

"He literally showers me with gifts," Emma said. "I'm totally spoiled."

"Wow," Chloe said. "I could go for spoiled."

"Me too," Andrea said.

Emma beamed, but Jocelyn and Lauryn exchanged worried looks. Something didn't feel right.

Eventually the girls decided to order in pizza and watch a movie. Emma seemed to revert back to herself for a while, then she'd flip back into the "new Emma" whenever she got a text from Nicholas. By the time the pizza arrived, Jocelyn was nauseated at Emma's goofy, giddy, lovesick updates on what Nicholas was doing.

"He just went to the store and bought new bedding and linens."

"He said he misses me so much it hurts!"

"Oh, my gosh, listen to this! He said he's going over to his friend's house to sleep because he can't sleep in his house without me. How sweet is that!"

By the end of the night they were all so sick of hearing Emma's play-by-play they were about to drive her back to Las Vegas themselves.

* * *

Their attempts to find out about the investigation regarding Ava's death turned out to be fruitless. The detective covering the case had been called out of town on a family emergency and couldn't be reached. The officer they spoke with was sympathetic to their concerns and assured them that they were safe and had no reason to believe anyone was "coming after them." He promised he would have the detective contact them as soon as he was back in town to give them any updates.

As soon as they left the police station, Emma wasted no time loading up and heading back to Vegas.

More worried than sad to see her go, the other four went back to the hotel so Chloe could get her belongings together. The other women had flights on Monday, but Chloe needed to drive home later that night.

"I'm so glad Emma left early," Andrea confided. "I know that sounds rude, but she was really getting on my nerves."

"It didn't make sense to have her here if she was going to spend the entire time texting or talking to Nicholas on the phone," Chloe added.

"I didn't even feel like I knew her," Lauryn said. "She was different when we were together in June, but it was like the transformation was complete this time."

"She's become the person she swore she'd never be." Jocelyn didn't like the fact that they were talking about her behind her back, but it hadn't been possible to say anything while she was there. They loved Emma and didn't want to hurt her feelings, but something was seriously wrong.

"I just feel like we'd better be ready to pick her up when all of this comes crashing down around her." Chloe zipped her suitcase shut and stood it on its end on the floor.

"That's not being very optimistic," Andrea said. Then, with a crestfallen expression, she added, "But I think she's headed for a heartache too."

"I thought he was going to come and get her so everyone could meet him." Chloe plopped down on the bed.

"It almost seems like he's avoiding us. Emma doesn't even seem to notice that the situation is a little weird."

"Love is blind," Chloe said. "Believe me. Not only is it blind, it's stupid too."

"So, Andrea," Jocelyn said, trying to get them on a lighter subject, "When do you have to decide whether to do *Looking for Mrs. Right* or not?"

"End of next week."

"It would be so fun watching you on TV," Lauryn told her. "I think you'd be a fan favorite."

Andrea rolled her eyes. "I don't know about that. My agent thinks it would really boost my career."

"I hope you do it," Lauryn said.

"Me too," Jocelyn agreed.

* * *

As Jocelyn packed her bags Monday morning, she realized that as good as it felt to be back home in St. George with her friends, part of her was ready to go back to Milford Falls. She wanted to keep working on the house and start decorating her classroom. And, of course, there was the big raspberry planting at the end of the summer. Harry had explained that ideally the bushes should be planted in early spring, but since Jocelyn would be in school then, it would be fine for them to do it in late August. There was still a lot of preparation to be done to the back of the property in order to be ready in time.

The good-bye this time was bittersweet. With plenty of concerns between them, it was hard to have everyone go their separate ways.

With promises to keep in touch and a few tears, they bid farewell until next June when they'd meet for their regular Butterfly Girls reunion.

Even though Jocelyn was filled with worry about Chloe and Emma, she felt a measure of peace in her heart that she'd never felt before. Usually, after each reunion, she would berate herself for not being forthcoming about her secret. The anticipation and worry had caused her great angst for many years, and now it was over. She'd opened her soul up to the people she trusted the most, and they hadn't let her down. Maybe she could have confided in them earlier—certainly they would have been understanding and supportive—but she hadn't been ready then. She'd grown over the past month and had been given the strength and courage to face her past.

She returned to Milford Falls a more confident and secure woman. Still, she was saddened that she didn't have Jack there, waiting for her return. She couldn't control Jack or what he felt, but she told herself she didn't have to let it affect her. She could keep moving forward and look ahead rather than dwell on the past.

* * *

"He's home!" Marilyn exclaimed as she ran into Jocelyn's room at school. Jocelyn had been there the last two days organizing, arranging, and decorating the art room. She knew some people would think she did things out of order, decorating midsummer when she didn't even have all her lesson plans sorted out. But Jocelyn had always found she could work better in a beautiful environment.

When she'd moved to Milford Falls, she'd been shocked at the sheer quantity of art supplies and decorations she had from past years of teaching, but now she was so glad she still had her collections and treasures to use in her room. On the large interior wall of the room, she hung selections from her abundant poster collection of favorite works of art.

"I'm sorry?" Jocelyn said from up on the ladder, "Who's home?"

"Celeste's boyfriend, Nick. He's home!"

"Have they seen each other?" Jocelyn asked, climbing carefully down the ten-foot ladder.

"Just once, at his house, right after he got released. He had to go with his family over the weekend for a family reunion. He'll be back today. He wants to see her when he gets home tonight."

"I can't wait to meet him," Jocelyn said.

"You'll get to meet him at church Sunday. He's speaking."

"How's Celeste doing?" Jocelyn pulled the roll of tape off her wrist and took a drink from her water bottle.

"The girl's feet haven't touched the ground since she saw him." Marilyn stopped for a moment and looked around at the decorations. "Okay, whoa! This room looks amazing."

Jocelyn smiled and pulled her shoulders back with pride.

"I love the poster wall and all the color," Marilyn enthused. "The kids are going to love it."

"Thanks. I hope so."

"It suits you," Marilyn said. "You have such a warmth about you. Even more so lately. What's up? Where do I get some?"

Jocelyn laughed. "I have no idea what you're talking about."

"So, have you heard from him yet?" Marilyn asked, picking up an African bowl and examining it.

Jocelyn was unloading a box of art books to put on her desk. "From who?" she replied.

"Santa Claus," Marilyn said then quickly added, "Jack, silly. Any word? Have you seen him around town?"

Shaking her head, Jocelyn sorted and stacked books in piles. Some she could put on the shelf, but others she wanted for ready reference.

"I'm sorry things don't seem to be working out. I was positive you two were meant for each other," Marilyn said. "You still have no idea what went wrong?"

Jocelyn had her suspicions but didn't feel like sharing them with her.

"I suppose I ought to tell you before you find out from someone else. Jack was out with Lacey over the weekend," Marilyn said.

A pain zinged through her heart, but Jocelyn covered up the reaction with a fake cough. "Oh"—she coughed again—"really?" She didn't want to act like she cared, but she couldn't help it.

"I bumped into them at the diner, then Celeste saw them leave together. I think you're better off without him if he's dumb enough to even give that woman the time of day."

Jocelyn nodded, not trusting her voice. She didn't want to care about Jack; she didn't want to let even the mention of his name have this kind of reaction on her.

"Well, I'll let you get back to your room," Marilyn said. "Be careful up there on that ladder."

"I will. Thanks, Marilyn."

Marilyn gave her a sympathetic smile then left the room.

Jocelyn had to shut her eyes and breathe for a minute as she forced the image of Jack and Lacey together out of her mind. She wondered why in the world he would be with her? He couldn't stand that woman, or so she'd thought.

Shaking her head, she resigned herself to the fact that it didn't matter if she understood the rhyme or reason to his behavior; it wouldn't change it.

During the remainder of the week, she made certain that each time she went into town she kept her Jack radar on high alert. The last thing she wanted to do was run into him and Lacey together—or him at all, even though she missed him terribly. She missed his funny sense of humor, his kindness, his strong, calming nature, and she missed the closeness they'd shared. Being with him had felt so right, at least to her. Apparently not so much to him.

Saturday afternoon she went to MJ's hair salon, looking for a trim and her usual highlights. She wore her hair long, layered, and simple. MJ had other plans.

"I think you need to warm up the color of your hair," MJ said. "With your skin tone, you would look beautiful with a rich deep brown color. It would really play up your dark eyes."

Jocelyn had been highlighting her hair since high school because she'd always disliked its natural drab ash-brown color. She'd never considered going darker.

"I'd also like to take several inches off; it will really help your hair look thick and healthy. And if you're worried about the upkeep on the all-over color, you don't need to worry. I would go with a semipermanent that will last well but won't give you a harsh line as it grows out."

Jocelyn looked in the mirror trying to picture her hair in a dark chocolate color. Then, feeling somewhat brave and reckless enough to go along with it, she said, "You've convinced me. Let's do it!" Just like with what the Butterfly Box represented, she needed to embrace change and emerge stronger and better after overcoming a challenge. Her recent triumph in revealing her painful past had felt like breaking out of a cocoon. She felt like flying free. Why not try out a new hair color and cut?

MJ didn't want to let her see anything until she was completely finished. Jocelyn noticed a lot of long hair strands falling on the floor and felt a little nervous at what she was going to see when she looked in the mirror. She'd never been one to experiment with cuts and colors, much to Chloe's frustration.

After MJ finished her hair, she still wouldn't let her see it. Instead, she convinced her to let Robin, a makeup specialist, give Jocelyn a quick makeover.

"You have incredible eyes," Robin said. "You're very Audrey Hepburn looking."

Jocelyn burst out laughing. Her friends had been telling her that for years.

"It's true. Especially with your hair dark like this. Hasn't anyone ever told you that?"

"Well, yeah, but I mean, you're talking about Audrey Hepburn. I don't really see it."

"I guess you'll just have to judge for yourself," Robin said. She continued to apply color, explaining about each color and brush choice as she went. Within five minutes she was done.

"That was fast," Jocelyn said.

"You don't need a lot of makeup," Robin told her. "You just need to have the right colors and technique to really maximize your assets, like your eyes and lips."

"My turn," MJ said. "I just need to fix a couple of pieces of hair," she said, spraying, arranging, and teasing her hair to get the perfect look. "There. I think you're done."

Jocelyn felt excitement swell up inside of her.

"Ready?" MJ said, her eyes wide with excitement.

"I think so," Jocelyn answered, shutting her eyes.

"You're going to be surprised," Robin said, clapping her hands together.

Jocelyn kept her eyes shut while MJ turned the chair around.

"Okay, open," MJ said.

Jocelyn slowly opened her eyes, and then a smile grew on her face until she had to laugh with delight. "Oh, my gosh!" She laughed again, turning her head from side to side. She finger combed the sides of her hair to feel the movement and glossy softness of the strands. "How did you do that?"

Her reflection caught her off guard. Even though her hair had an up-to-date loose and softly curled style, the dark color, along with the way the makeup accentuated her eyes, really did give her that wide, doe-eyed Audrey Hepburn look.

"Wow," Jocelyn said again, leaning toward the mirror and studying the expertly placed eye shadow and liner. She had strong, full eyebrows that framed her eyes, along with full lips that had been stained a soft, coppery rose.

"You look just beautiful," MJ said.

"You're more than beautiful, you are stunning!" Robin said. "We should have taken before and after photos. You were already pretty, but now . . . you look like a celebrity."

Jocelyn felt heat rise to her cheeks, and she brushed their praise away with her hands. Still, she had to admit, it was a marked improvement.

Robin and MJ high-fived each other and nodded with approval.

Jocelyn left the salon with her head held high. She loved the feel of a sassy new look and an update to her old worn-out style.

She needed to get a few things at the grocery store, so she popped into Moose's market. Carrying a basket over her arm she strolled down the aisles grabbing a loaf of bread, some milk, and a dozen eggs. She couldn't resist a bag of peanut M&M's but couldn't help thinking of Lenny and Jack when she put them in her basket.

Moose's voice boomed, "May I help you, m—" He stopped midsentence. "Jocelyn?"

"Hi, Moose. How are you?"

"Just fine," he said. "You're looking especially nice this afternoon. Are you on your way somewhere special?"

She almost snorted with laughter. Did a date with a good book and a bubble bath count? "No, not really."

"Too bad," he said. "You should be on your way to the city for a night out on the town."

"Wouldn't that be fun," she said. "I'll have to do that sometime. I haven't spent a lot of time in Seattle."

Another customer walked through the door and took his attention. Jocelyn found the last few items she needed and took them to the counter.

A young man, probably in his late teens, was at the register.

"Hey," he said, ringing up her purchases without even looking at her.

She got out her debit card and swiped it through the machine.

He bagged her items and totaled the sale. "Is that debit or credit?" he asked with a bored sigh.

"Debit," she answered.

The machine clicked and whirred then spit out a receipt, which the employee tore off and handed to Jocelyn. He looked up at her and said, "Whoa." A big smile split his face.

"Thank you," she said, returning his smile.

"Thanks for coming in," he said. "Come in again."

His eager invitation brought another smile to her face. It was foreign to her to get attention like this. She wasn't sure how to handle it or what to think. Ten years ago the attention would have bothered her, but now . . . it wasn't so bad.

She left the grocery store feeling the boy's eyes on her. He wouldn't be smiling so much if he knew how old she was, she thought.

Avoiding Jack's fix-it shop, she turned the other direction.

"Jocelyn!" a man's voice called after her.

For a split second, she thought, *Jack!* then realized it wasn't his voice. Turning, she saw Warren Darvill coming after her.

"I found you a copy of *Don Quixote.* I was hoping I'd see you in town today." The man rushed up to her then stopped to pant. He wasn't terribly overweight, but the sudden burst of activity was probably more than he was used to.

He handed the book to her.

"You did. This is wonderful."

"Just come in and pay for it next time you come to town. You look like you've got your hands full," he said. "Do you need some help?"

"I'm fine, thank you. If you don't mind slipping it inside one of these bags, that would help." She lifted her left arm and displayed two filled plastic grocery bags.

He did as she asked then gave her a smile. "Making dinner for someone special?" he asked.

She shrugged and shook her head. "No. Why do you ask?"

"Oh, I just noticed the groceries. And, you look especially lovely today."

She definitely needed to get her hair and makeup done more often. Then she began to wonder, had she looked really so bad before that this was such a shocking difference?

"Well, thank you," she replied, "but I don't have any big plans. Now that you found this book, I've got a wonderful evening ahead of me."

His mouth turned to a frown. "A pretty girl like you should be out having fun, not sitting home with a book."

She didn't tell him she had better luck with books.

"I'm very excited to read the book," she said, choosing not to further the discussion. "Thank you for getting it for me."

He still didn't seem convinced.

She lifted her arm again. "Well, I'd better get going; these bags aren't getting any lighter."

With a promise to come and pay for the book soon, she headed for her car, relieved that she was going home. She wasn't up to running into anyone else.

Stowing the groceries in the back of the car, she got inside and started her car then quickly unrolled all the windows to let out the warm air from her car sitting in the sun. She slid on a pair of sunglasses and relaxed, waiting for the air conditioner to cool the interior.

A car pulled up to the curb two parking stalls down from her. Jocelyn didn't give it a second thought until two women stepped out of the car, yelling at each other. Jocelyn glanced over and then turned back, trying to disappear against her seat.

"I don't care," Lacey said. "I'm a grown woman, and you can't tell me who I can and can't date, Mother!"

"But what will people say?"

"I don't care what people say. I never have!" Lacey shot back.

"I don't know what you could possibly see in him," her mother remarked. "Sometimes I think you are just out to get the attention. You've always been that way."

"What? That doesn't make any sense. You're my mother; we're supposed to be on the same side."

Jocelyn hoped that they were so preoccupied with their argument they weren't paying attention to anything else. Still, she felt a little guilty for eavesdropping. She was fascinated that they were having an argument over Lacey dating Jack. Clearly her mother was dead set against it. Was Jack not sophisticated enough? Rich enough?

"Now, can we please stop talking about this," Lacey demanded.

Iris, her mother, clamped her mouth shut, and the two women walked toward the diner. Luckily they didn't see Jocelyn, or maybe they just didn't recognize her with her sunglasses and new look. Either way she was glad she didn't have to deal with Lacey, especially when she was clearly upset already.

As she drove away she thought about Jack and the connection she'd felt with him and wondered how it was that she'd felt something so strongly and he hadn't. Male-female relationships were complicated and confusing. Maybe she hadn't been missing out all these years after all.

* * *

Sunday morning, the first person Jocelyn saw when she got to the chapel was Marilyn, who was waving excitedly at Jocelyn to come and sit by them.

"Look at you!" Marilyn exclaimed, giving Jocelyn a big hug as she sat down. "Good grief, girl, you look hot!"

"Marilyn!" Jocelyn said, shielding her face with her hand with embarrassment.

"Celeste." Marilyn ignored Jocelyn's reaction and elbowed her daughter. "Look at Jocelyn. Isn't her new hair color gorgeous?"

"Hi, Jocelyn," Celeste said. "You do look incredible. I love your hair."

"So," Jocelyn said, trying to shift the attention away from herself, "is Nick here?"

Celeste looked around the chapel. "He was here a minute ago. He must've stepped into the foyer."

"How is everything going with you two?" Jocelyn asked.

"It's wonderful," Celeste said. "He's wonderful."

Marilyn piped in. "It's like they've picked up right where they left off. I'm telling you, I've never seen a couple so made for each other."

"I'm so happy for you, Celeste. You deserve someone wonderful," Jocelyn said.

Marilyn gave Jocelyn a squeeze. "And so do you. Someday your prince will come."

Jocelyn smiled but had to suppress her real emotions. She had avoided dating for years, had avoided getting close to a man. She had assumed that she would never meet someone or get married, and she had been okay with that. Then she met Jack. She'd had a glimmer of "happily ever after," and it was difficult to give up that dream.

The chapel began to fill up, and before Jocelyn got a chance to meet Nick, the meeting was about to start. She looked at the young returned missionary with his exuberant smile and glowing goodness and remembered feeling the Spirit and power that came with being a missionary. She missed that. As hard as she tried to keep the Spirit in her life, she never had it as intensely as she'd had it as a missionary.

A sudden chill caused goose bumps to cover her arms and tingle up the back of her neck. She turned to see Jack making his way down the aisle into one of the side pews.

She quickly looked away and took in several breaths to calm her pounding heart. Dang that man. Why did he have to have this effect on her? Why had he kissed her and spent so much time with her then just dropped all contact?

As the meeting began, she tried hard to focus on the announcements and words of the opening hymn. Through the prayer she finally relaxed, and the tension eased from her muscles.

During the sacrament she read in her scriptures, searching for help, strength, and answers. She came across a couple passages in Alma 7 that caught her attention:

"And now I would that ye should be humble, and be submissive and gentle; easy to be entreated; full of patience and long-suffering; being temperate in all things; being diligent in keeping the commandments of God at all times; asking for whatsoever things ye stand in need, both spiritual and temporal; always returning thanks unto God for whatsoever things ye do receive.

"And now, may the peace of God rest upon you . . ."

Peace. She needed peace even more than she needed to make sense of things or have answers. Just peace.

With her eyes shut, she prayed for the Spirit to be with her. She never felt lonely when she was close to the Spirit. She knew she was blessed, and she chastised herself for not focusing more on her blessings. She'd been asking Heavenly Father for a lot lately, but she hadn't been thanking Him nearly enough.

Last night she'd found herself falling into the trap that seemed to crop up all too frequently for her: feeling like the reason she didn't get every good blessing was that she wasn't worthy. Sometimes she started to criticize herself for the poor choices that she had repented of long ago, blaming each past infraction for her current woes. She knew that wasn't how it worked with the Lord, and she realized, as she thought about it now, how ungrateful that train of thought was—as if she refused to recognize the Lord's Atonement on her behalf.

Tears formed in her eyes, and she quickly dabbed at them with a tissue, trying not to draw attention to herself. Pulling in several cleansing breaths, she slowly raised her head . . . and caught Jack looking at her. Quickly, she looked back down, avoiding his gaze.

Had he noticed her crying? She felt so stupid yet mad at the same time. Why did she have to care so much about what he thought?

After the sacrament, the first speaker, a young girl, reported on girls camp and shared some stories of tipping over in canoes, snipe hunts, and even a bear sighting. Girls camp hadn't changed from when Jocelyn and her friends had gone.

After a musical number, Nick stood up. As Jocelyn listened to Nick talk about the people he'd taught on his mission and the powerful message of repentance, forgiveness, and the Atonement, she felt her tears bubble to the surface again. She had taught these truths on her mission; investigators had embraced them, received testimonies, and experienced miracles in their lives. She herself had felt the Atonement work in her life, lifting the burdens of her mistakes, freeing her from the chains of sin. But when she started to focus on her weaknesses and became more self-critical than humble, she stopped recognizing the hand of the Lord in her life—the blessings and even miracles. It was the adversary's greatest tool on her.

Sometimes she felt like she was having to prove over and over—to herself and others—that she was clean and worthy. When Lacey brought her past out in the open, she'd felt so exposed, like she needed to cover something up, explain it away. Lacey probably didn't know the whole story surrounding Jocelyn's pregnancy, and it was even less likely that Jack did. But Jocelyn wondered now whether that should even matter to them, at least to Jack, who had supposedly cared for her.

She was trying to face her past, recognize the strength it had given her, and move on with confidence. When would she ever be able to be free and have peace from something that happened almost half a lifetime ago?

The minute the final amen was said, Jocelyn shot out of the chapel like a rocket. Luckily Marilyn didn't notice because she was so busy with Celeste and Nick.

Jocelyn didn't want to run into anyone, especially with her red-rimmed eyes. She managed to get to her car and climb inside before the tears fell freely as she allowed her emotions to surface. Even after all she had done to move on from the rape, she still couldn't completely seem to do it. She didn't doubt that she'd received forgiveness from God for ignoring the prompting to not accept that ride that night. But in spite of all her growth, she realized she hadn't been willing to fully accept that forgiveness in her heart. She was still too preoccupied with gaining the acceptance of others.

With her face in her hands, she sobbed, wishing her grandmother was alive. She'd been the one person who had been there to soothe her and assure her and help her have strength when storms like these came around.

She felt so alone.

Tap, tap, tap.

Jocelyn froze. She was afraid to look but knew she had to. Pulling her hands from her face, she turned and looked up at her window.

Jack!

"Crud," she said under her breath.

After wiping her face as best she could with a wadded-up napkin she found stuffed in the armrest of her car, she rolled down the window.

"Hey," he said, "are you okay?" His voice was soft and kind.

She wanted to punch him.

Instead, she nodded then turned her head away. "Yeah, I'm fine."

"Can we talk?"

He was trying to kill her. That's all it could be. He literally wanted to just stomp all over her broken heart.

"What do we need to talk about?" she asked.

"I owe you an explanation."

"You don't owe me anything, Jack." Strength was returning to her backbone. She lifted her head a little higher.

"No, I think I do."

Inwardly she groaned. She didn't feel like talking to him, especially not about her past, not right now. It had been hard enough telling her friends. She wondered how many people here knew about it. Maybe she should just publish it in the newspaper so she could just get it over with already.

"Please, Jocelyn."

"Sure, okay." She couldn't see a way out without potentially running him over. He wasn't going away until they talked.

He went around and got in the passenger side of the car. "Why don't we go somewhere else?"

She agreed. The last thing she needed was ward gossip on top of everything else.

They drove to Lake Edmund and parked in the shade, rolling down the windows to let the summer breeze in.

"I need to tell you something about me, about my past," he said.

Startled, all she could say was, "What?"

"I need to apologize. I know you probably hate me now. I was a jerk. I just want to explain."

She shook her head, trying to make sense of what he was saying.

"That day, the Fourth of July, was wonderful with you. I haven't felt that comfortable with or close to a woman for many years. I've never allowed myself to get that close. And then, after we kissed . . ."

She knew what he was going to say next: they'd run into Lacey and he'd found out about her past. She'd been there. Why did they need to rehash it?

". . . My feelings totally caught me off guard. I guess I freaked out a little."

Caught him off guard? What in the world was he talking about?

"I knew I had feelings for you, but in that moment, the feelings . . . well . . . I didn't expect to feel that way ever again. I told myself that I would never hurt anyone ever again, and now that's exactly what I've done. I'm very, very sorry. Can you forgive me?"

She wasn't sure what they were even talking about. Wasn't this about her being pregnant at seventeen and giving away her baby?

He looked at her, waiting for her answer.

"Jack . . ." She paused, wishing his intentions would become clear to her. "I'm not even sure what you're talking about. I'm kind of confused."

"Sorry. I'm really making a mess of this." He clenched and unclenched his fists. "Maybe I need to start at the beginning."

Judging by his inability to relax, she realized that what he was about to say must be very hard for him. Her heart softened somewhat.

"There are only a few people in town who know what I'm about to tell you. Lenny knows, and each of the bishops I've had since I moved here know. But that's about all. It's not really something I want people to know about. But you need to know."

She was not sure what he could possibly say that would cause him so much discomfort.

"Okay," he said, with a big breath, "here goes. When I was in high school, I started a band. You know, like every other kid in high school who wants to be a rock star."

She smiled and nodded.

"Well, the weird thing was, we actually were good—good enough to get noticed by someone who knew a record executive. One day, out of the blue I got a call from a guy from Ibex Records telling me that he was interested in my music."

"Whoa! That's amazing."

"Yeah, well, if I knew then what I know now, I would have hung up the phone and gone to football practice. But I didn't. I got totally sucked into it and made my first mistake."

"What was that?"

"The guy, Randy Wolfe, said he was only interested in me as a solo artist. I should have told him I was with a group and would only allow this to happen if it could be with the group. But I was young and stupid and selfish and completely swept off my feet, so to speak. I thought that if I got signed, somehow I could get the guys involved, too—I mean, I'd still need all the instruments, right? But it didn't happen that way.

"So, anyway, I went to Hollywood to meet with Randy. My dad went with me, and I was able to play some of my stuff for Randy. We even cut a demo record of one of my songs."

"Jack, this is incredible. How exciting."

"Yeah, well, the story doesn't end there. Randy really liked my style and the grunge look I had going on and thought I was marketable as a solo artist, so long story short, he signed me and I made an album."

"You're kidding me," Jocelyn exclaimed. "I can't believe this." She thought for a moment. "I'm afraid I'm not familiar with your work. I don't remember an artist named Jack Emerson."

"That's because back then my name was JC Em."

Jocelyn gasped so fast she began to cough. "You're . . . JC . . . Em?"

He shut his eyes and nodded.

"Shut up!" She was still coughing. A major famous rock star was sitting in her car!

"It's true."

"But . . . JC Em! I loved you," she said, then she clapped her hand over her mouth. "I mean, your music was awesome. My friends and I were insane over your song "Don't Leave." That whole album was incredible. We were planning on going to your next concert, even if we had to drive to California. But then there wasn't a next concert. We heard it was because of . . . Oh." She suddenly remembered the press releases.

"Yeah, well, that's why I'm telling you this story," he said.

"Sorry. I'll let you talk."

"I'm not proud of my story. I messed up. Big time." His voice grew quiet. He took a deep breath. "You see, I didn't handle being famous very well. It all seemed to happen overnight. I lost track of everything that was important to me. My friends, my family, my roots. None of it mattered. I got in with a whole new set of friends and surrounded myself with people who were just using me. I began to party . . . hard. I got into alcohol and drug use pretty heavily. I thought I was invincible and that the world revolved around me. I really did."

She could tell he was ashamed of what he was telling her, and her heart went out to him.

"Man, I was stupid. My parents tried to get me to slow down and get a grip on what I was doing with my life and my career. By the time I turned twenty-one I basically wrote them off. If I wasn't touring, I was partying with friends. The one good thing in my life was Samantha. I met her at a party, and it was like love at first sight. She wasn't fazed at all by my celebrity. I loved that about her. She wasn't afraid to call me on stuff when I got out of line. She was really good for me. Everyone thought so."

Jocelyn noticed the faraway look in his eyes as he gazed out at the calm lake in front of them.

"I truly loved Samantha. She was everything to me. I toned down the partying, I focused on my music, and I began treating people better. She kept me in line, and that's what I needed.

"I can't tell you how excited I was when she got pregnant. We'd just gotten married, on the beach in Maui, and soon after, she told me the news. That next year I wrote the song 'My Baby Loves Me.'"

"Jack, I love that song. I used to play it over and over. I thought it was about a girlfriend or wife. But it was about your child?"

"Yeah. I mean, it was kind of for Samantha too, but we had a little girl named Sophia Grace. She was my inspiration." He stopped and swallowed hard. "She was the most beautiful thing I'd ever seen. She had her mother's incredibly blue eyes and this head of blond curls and the softest skin." He shut his eyes for a moment. "The way she smelled after her bath, all snuggly and warm . . ."

Jocelyn felt tears sting her eyes. She knew where the story was going. She remembered reading about it.

"The night I won the Grammy for song of the year was the most incredible night of my life. I had the most amazing wife and child, I'd just won the most important award of my career, and I was on top of the world.

"We'd been to a celebration party—even Samantha and Sophia were there because I wanted them with me. It was only important to me because of them, you know?"

Jocelyn nodded, even though he didn't look at her.

"I'd only had a few drinks. Nothing I couldn't handle but too much to be driving. I felt fine, though, so we headed home. Everything happened so fast I don't even know exactly what happened after that. All I remember is lights coming straight at us and trying to turn the steering wheel to get us out of the way."

He grew completely silent, his face contorted with the pain of remembering.

Jocelyn wanted to reach out and touch him, hold him, comfort him. She didn't know what to do.

"They both died at the scene of the accident, and I walked away with a few bumps and bruised ribs."

"Jack," Jocelyn whispered, reaching for his hand, "I am so sorry."

He gave her hand a squeeze but stayed looking straight ahead.

"I wanted to die. I hated being alive when they were dead. Dead because of me." Tears slipped onto his cheeks, but his voice remained steady. "The accident report came back and, according to it, the accident wasn't even my fault. The guy driving the other car had also been drinking and crossed the line into oncoming traffic. How ironic is that?" he said with a pained laugh.

"I can't imagine how hard this was for you."

"It destroyed me. It really did. I had no reason to live. I didn't care about anything. I didn't want to sing ever again. I didn't feel like I had anything to sing for. I didn't want anything to do with my career because I felt like it had taken away the most precious part of my life—if I hadn't gone to that stupid awards party . . .

"One day, I couldn't take it anymore. I got in my car and started to drive. Just outside of Milford Falls my car broke down. A guy happened to drive by and find me. He helped me get my car into town and even let me stay at his place."

"Lenny?" she guessed.

He nodded.

"One thing after another fell into place, and I found that I could fade into the shadows and start all over as a new person. So that's what I did. With different hair and a beard, I didn't even look like the same guy. Luckily, because my dad was a carpenter by trade, I'd learned enough to help me get started doing repairs and remodeling. One thing led to another, and I built a nice little business. I tried not to let anyone get too close, and it worked well for me. Of course, Lenny knew what had happened. He's an amazing friend. It's because of him I joined the Church. He talked to me about the Atonement and the plan of salvation, and it was the one thing that helped bring peace to my soul. It made sense, even though it's hard to wrap my brain around completely."

Jocelyn totally understood that.

"It took a few years but I got baptized. Best decision I'd ever made."

"No one has discovered you and your real identity?"

"Nope." He looked at her as if pleading for her to keep his secret.

"They won't hear it from me." She was still trying to absorb everything he was telling her when she had a question. "I guess I still don't understand what this has to do with me."

"Yeah, well, I was getting to that." He still held her hand and rubbed his thumb across her knuckles. "You see, even though I've dated a little here and there, I hadn't really ever found anyone that mattered to me . . . until you."

Jocelyn didn't know what to say.

"It was different with you because I felt like we had become friends, and then it grew into something more, for me at least. And that night, when we kissed, well"—he licked his lips and cleared his throat—"it was amazing."

She wanted to tell him that it had been amazing for her too, but it didn't feel right to speak. He was sharing his deepest feelings, and she didn't want to stop him from what he was saying.

"It also freaked me out and scared me to death."

"Why?"

"I hadn't felt that way since . . ."

She waited for him to continue, still not feeling like she should speak, but it hurt to see the pain inside of him evidenced so clearly on his face.

". . . since Sam."

She held onto his hand tightly.

"I blame myself for that accident, no matter what the report said. If I had called a taxi we wouldn't have been there at that moment. Or, if I had been completely sober, maybe I could've reacted more quickly. After everything that happened, I promised myself that I would never love again. I didn't want to ever hurt anyone or feel that kind of pain again." His voice trembled and he shut his eyes.

Jocelyn watched him wrestle with his emotions, her heart aching for him. "I think, in a way, I really believed that God wouldn't let me get close to someone else after I killed my wife and daughter, you know?"

This poor man's heart and soul were broken. Even though her pain was different, she empathized with the anguish and hopelessness he felt.

He released her hand and rubbed both hands on his eyes then ran them through his hair. "Oh, man, I can't believe I just laid all that on you. You are probably thinking I'm . . . I'm . . . I don't even know what you possibly could be thinking."

"I'm thinking," she found herself saying, "that you can't forgive yourself for something that you would give anything to have prevented from happening. I'm thinking you listen to talks in church about forgiveness and the Atonement and believe that it's true with all your heart—but for everyone else, not yourself. And I believe that you are blaming yourself for something that God isn't blaming you for."

His forehead wrinkled and he looked at her.

She shrugged.

"That's amazing," he said.

"What is?"

"What you just said. How did you know that was how I felt?"

Well, here goes nothing. "I feel the same way, for a different reason, but I know how it feels to not be able to forgive yourself."

He looked at her with understanding in his eyes.

"I mean, I believe that the Atonement is real. I know it is." She paused for a moment to pull in a few breaths. "I have felt its power in my life. But as I get older, I find myself getting discouraged and disillusioned about where my life is going, and I start doubting whether I'm worthy enough to deserve blessings, like maybe if I were a better person certain things would work out better. I think I need therapy," she said with a half laugh, trying to lighten the conversation.

"Actually, I think you're pretty wonderful the way you are," he said, taking her hand in his again.

Why was he acting like he was interested? She was beginning to think she'd dreamed the whole Lacey-divulging-her-secret-to-Jack thing. He hadn't said anything about it. Again, she was confused.

"Is something wrong?" he asked. "You're forehead's all squinched up."

"Squinched?" she said with a smile.

"Yeah, you know, bunched up and wrinkled. You look worried."

Could this man be more charming?

"Not worried, really. It's more like I'm confused about something."

"What's that?"

"I can't believe I'm about to do this," she said out loud but mostly to herself. "That night, on the Fourth of July, you remember running into Lacey, right?"

"Yeah, of course. She's like running head on into a bulldozer."

Jocelyn smiled briefly then became serious again. "She shared some very personal information about me with you. You haven't even said anything about it. I thought that was why you pulled away from me so suddenly. I thought it bothered you that much."

He let go of her hand and looked at her with complete shock. "Jocelyn, I am the last person to ever judge someone. I don't know what the circumstances were back when you had that baby, but I do know what a wonderful, amazing woman you are here, today. That's all that matters to me."

She looked at him in shock. This was not at all what she had expected.

"And when you're ready, I know you'll tell me what you'd like me to know about it. But Jocelyn, I know who you are. And whatever you've been through, good or bad, has made you who you are. And I'm glad for it all, because I wouldn't change anything about you."

Her bottom lip trembled as fresh tears stung her eyes. She couldn't help it. He'd said the most glorious thing she'd ever heard from anyone in her life.

"What's wrong? Did I say something that hurt your feelings?"

"No," she croaked. Her tears kept coming. She couldn't stop them.

"Hey, don't cry," he said.

"I'm sorry," she said, her voice soft and shaky.

"Jocelyn. C'mere." He pulled her hand and gathered her in his arms. "It's okay. Everything is okay."

Her tears flowed as he held her close. He stroked the back of her head and rocked her gently.

She didn't need to run away from her past. She could finally see that. Just as her friends had tried to tell her last weekend, her trials were, in fact, part of her, and they ultimately made her a stronger, better person. She wished she had understood that years ago but realized that she probably didn't have the strength then to spread her wings like she did now. It had been a long, hard process, but she was ready to embrace who she was and move forward. After her tears, she stayed in his arms, exhausted, but filled with peace and security.

"You okay?" he asked softly.

She nodded and sniffed her running nose. She needed a tissue.

Pulling away, she reached for her purse, but he came to the rescue with one from his pocket. "It's crumpled, but I promise it's not used."

She laughed as she wiped her eyes and nose. "Thank you."

He smiled, looking at her with complete focus. "You've been holding that in for a while, haven't you?"

With a nod, she wiped her nose again, hoping it would dry up soon.

"Are you okay?"

"Yes. I'm fine. Really." Another cleansing breath helped her settle down.

"I think I'm the cause for some of these tears, aren't I?" He looked at her, his strong gaze locking onto her, forcing her to look back at him.

"I figured that was why you cut me off."

"I am so sorry. I was a jerk for not explaining things."

"I understand now."

"Yeah, but I should have talked to you a lot sooner. I wanted to, but you left town. I figured that was your way of saying that you wanted me out of your life."

"No, not at all. But as long as we're clarifying things, I've got to ask you one more question: Did you and Lacey ever . . . date?"

"No." He actually looked a little sick at the thought. "I've tried to fellowship her, to be a good home teacher, but I've never been interested in her otherwise."

"Really?" Jocelyn knew it didn't really matter in the long run, but she couldn't help feeling pleased. She was quiet for a moment. "I guess I really misread that one."

"You thought . . . ? All this time? I'll just say it again: I've never been interested in her."

"It doesn't matter now," she said. When she looked up into his eyes, she saw that he did care about her. Her heart swelled inside her chest.

"I will try to never hurt you again," he said, leaning toward her.

She smiled as she leaned toward him.

"Why are you smiling?" he asked.

"Because you're going to kiss me."

"How do you know?"

"I just do."

"You're right."

* * *

"What are you doing?" Jack asked.

"I'm at the school trying to get some more organizing done." She shifted her phone to the other ear.

"When will you be done?"

"When do you want me done?" She tossed a handful of papers into the recycling bin.

"Now," he said.

"But you don't close till five. It's barely four thirty now." She should know—she watched the clock constantly, waiting until he was done with work so they could be together. For the last two weeks they'd been together every evening after he'd finished work, sometimes meeting for lunch, sometimes meeting for breakfast, sometimes meeting for all three meals.

Jocelyn didn't know why she bothered wearing shoes because her feet never touched the ground.

"I miss you," he said.

"I miss you, too," she said.

"I'm coming to get you."

"I'll be ready."

She hung up her phone and leaned back in her chair, clasping her hands behind her head and stretching her shoulders.

With all the talking they'd done, and all the sharing of their hearts and souls, Jocelyn had never grown so close to a person in such a short time as she had with Jack. They laughed at the same jokes, liked the same movies, and they both enjoyed being outdoors and taking long walks along the wooded paths in the hills around Milford Falls.

She couldn't explain it, but being with Jack felt right. It felt natural. The fit was as perfect as being in her own skin.

So far they'd managed to stay out of sight of most of the townspeople. Not that they were trying to hide; they just wanted to avoid all the talk and gossip that would spiral out of control when the news broke.

A scuffle outside her room caught Jocelyn's attention, and she looked up just as Marilyn exploded into her room.

"They have a date," she announced.

"Who? Celeste and Nick?"

"Yes!"

"But haven't they already been on a few dates since he's been home?" Jocelyn got up from her desk chair and stretched her neck from side to side. She was almost done getting her lessons and files sorted and arranged in order.

"Yes, but this time he asked her to bring the quilt he made for her years ago. He also had her take a pair of scissors and the puzzle pieces."

"Oh! This must be huge."

"I know." Marilyn grabbed both of Jocelyn's hands and did some sort of jig. "I am dying!"

"Where did they go?"

"I don't know, or I'd be tempted to go spy on them."

"Marilyn!"

"I know. But I can't help it." Marilyn dropped her hands and paced around the floor. "I hope she calls or texts me to tell me what's going on."

"It's so exciting," Jocelyn said. She didn't know Nick very well, but what she did know of him she liked a lot. Jocelyn didn't blame Marilyn for being so excited.

"I gotta get back to my desk," Marilyn said. "I'm leaving early so I can be home."

"Wait," Jocelyn said, causing Marilyn to skid to a halt. "You have to let me know what happens, okay?"

"I will. I promise," she said then was off in a dither.

Jocelyn began to hum as she worked, pleased to see her progress. Closing the flaps on the cardboard box and stacking it in the corner with the rest of her storage, she was glad she almost had everything ready for the start of school. She had to get it done early so she could have most of

August to spend planting raspberries. Harry had spent hours and hours plotting, planning, and ordering everything they needed for the farm. Jocelyn was excited to make her grandmother's dream come true because, in a way, Jocelyn felt her grandmother had helped make her dream come true.

Footsteps in the hallway stopped just outside the door to her room.

She looked up and saw a well-dressed man enter the room.

"Can I help—"

She felt her jaw drop and took a sharp breath.

Blinking to make sure she wasn't hallucinating, Jocelyn squinted, just to make sure.

"Say something," he said.

"Jack?"

He smiled. "Do I really look that different?"

She couldn't quit staring. Yes, he actually did look quite different. He had never been unkempt, but he certainly was not the suave type. She'd always found him ruggedly handsome, with his long hair and beard, but the man standing in front of her was drop-dead gorgeous.

His face had been shaven clean, and his hair had been cut short but just long enough that the natural curl of his hair hung in shaggy layers. His incredibly blue eyes seemed even more intense now.

"Oh, wow," she said under her breath. Her teenage crush on JC Em came flooding back to her. He looked a lot like he had in his youth, but age had softened his features and given him an incredibly inviting warmth. Irresistible.

"I probably should have warned you," he said walking toward her. "I hope you like it, because if you don't, well, I don't know. It's too late."

"I like it," she said, feeling like a giddy school girl. "A lot."

She reached up and felt the smoothness of his cheek then fingered the soft curls at his neck. He still had rock-star good looks.

"You're sure?"

"Um, yeah," she said, feeling starstruck and completely weak at the knees. "I'm sure."

"I was hoping you'd say that." He pulled her close.

"Jack"—she looked him straight in the eye—"it doesn't matter if your hair is long, short, or if you're bald. It's what's on the inside that counts. But for the record, you look amazing. Why did you do it?"

He took a step back and leaned on the edge of the desk. She stood in front of him.

"Because of you."

Alarm struck like a bolt of lightning. "Me! Jack, I never said anything about your hair and beard."

"Oh, no, I don't mean that," he said with a start.

She breathed a sigh of relief.

"I mean, that you gave me the strength to quit hiding behind that . . . mask, I guess you could call it."

"You feel ready for that?"

"Yeah, absolutely. Before, I wanted to bury the person I was. I never wanted to be him again, and I wanted everyone to forget about him completely. I just wanted to run and hide. But you've helped me see that it's okay to be myself, that the best way to leave the old me behind is to accept what was, to stop hiding, and to just move on. It's all because of you."

She knew what he was talking about. She'd run from her problems for years. Becoming strong enough to face them, own them, and then let them go had been the most liberating moment of her life. Finally, after all these years, she felt free.

"So tell me, what did I do?"

He took one of her hands in his. "You unlocked my heart."

Her cheeks hurt from the smile she could not contain. But she couldn't help it. She was going to explode because there was so much happiness inside her. This was what all the romance novels and movies were about: this feeling of being part of something bigger than yourself, of caring about someone else more than yourself, of knowing that you are better because of them and you aren't complete without this person in your life. It was love. She was in love. Big time!

He wrapped his arms around her. "You've made me want to live again." He looked into her eyes. "Jocelyn, you've made me want to *love* again."

Tears quickly filled her eyes. There was no room inside for her heart to expand any bigger. She felt like she was going to launch into orbit with all the emotion building inside of her.

"Say something," he said, wiping at her tears.

"I can't," she said. "I'm going to explode."

His forehead crinkled. "Is that good?"

"Yes, I don't want it to go away."

He nodded. "Me neither."

She blinked and sent more tears trailing down her cheeks.

"I love you, Jocelyn."

"I love you, Jack."

Their kiss was tender and sweet and filled with love.

* * *

"Are you home?" Marilyn asked.

"I am," Jocelyn said.

"We'll be right there." Marilyn hung up, not waiting for a response.

Jocelyn finished making her bed then tilted the blinds to block out the strong morning sun. It was a glorious day, and she felt like singing as she did her housework. Of course, that was probably due to the fact that she was in love!

She felt like a character in a Disney princess movie. Like she could open the window and have woodland creatures perch on the windowsill and sing happy songs and dance around with her.

She loved Jack and *he loved her!*

She looked at the Butterfly Box on her dresser. It had no magical powers, no guarantee of granting dreams to come true, but while it had been in her possession, she had been able to resolve issues she'd never been able to before. She'd also grown in ways she never thought possible. It wasn't the box, she knew that. The faith and prayers of herself and her friends had helped her put things in her life in order. It had taken a long time, too long probably, but it had been worth the wait, worth every ounce of effort it had taken.

Downstairs she opened curtains and plumped pillows, still feeling like twirling and dancing with joy. She loved her house and all the changes she'd made. Her grandmother's spirit would always be there, but it was now her home, the place where she'd invested time and energy, but mostly, the place where she'd invested her heart.

Passing her dining-room-turned-art-studio, she marveled at how much progress she'd been making on her newest oil painting. She hadn't messed around with oils for years, but recently she'd gotten the urge to start a new canvas. It felt wonderful to create something new.

Car doors slammed outside, and Jocelyn peeked out the window to see Marilyn and Celeste racing up the walk.

Jocelyn had the door open before they could break it down.

"What happ—"

"I'm engaged," Celeste announced. She held up her finger. "Nick proposed to me!"

Jocelyn screamed, Marilyn joined her, and Celeste laughed with glee. They all hugged at the same time.

"Let me see this ring," Jocelyn said, reaching for Celeste's left hand.

The diamond was brilliant and beautiful.

"Oh, Celeste, it's incredible!"

"I know," Celeste gushed. "I can't believe it. I didn't even pick it out, but it's exactly the kind of ring I wanted. Simple and elegant and not overly flashy but totally classy."

"I love it," Jocelyn said. "I'm so excited for you. How did he propose? What did he do?"

The women sat down together on the couch as Celeste recounted the story.

"Well, yesterday Nick called and said he was coming to pick me up and I was supposed to bring the quilt he'd given me for my sixteenth birthday, a pair of scissors, and all the puzzle pieces he'd given me through the years we've known each other.

"We drove up to Grover's Peak where we used to go hiking and have picnics and stuff. It's kind of a special place for us."

Marilyn was beside herself with excitement and kept bouncing up and down on the couch cushion. Celeste flashed her an annoyed look.

"Sorry, I can't help it," Marilyn said. "This is just so amazing."

"Anyway, we were talking about our relationship and saying things like how it felt like he hadn't even left and that we were picking up right where we left off and that our feelings were still there for each other but even stronger . . ."

"Yeah," Jocelyn said, urging her to continue. Marilyn tried not to bounce but couldn't restrain herself.

"So he reaches into his pocket and pulls out the last puzzle piece. He told me to put the puzzle together. Of course, he helped me a little and we put the puzzle together."

"Tell her what it said," Marilyn exclaimed.

"I will, Mom! Can you please calm down?" Celeste rolled her eyes. "She didn't even sleep last night she was so excited. I think she planned our entire wedding last night."

Jocelyn smiled, knowing now wasn't the time, but one day she would tell Celeste just how lucky she was to have a mother so involved and so happy for her.

"Okay, so the message on the puzzle instructed me to cut open the red patch that was on the bottom left-hand corner of the quilt and then

I would know just how much he loved me."

"Serious?" Jocelyn asked. "He gave this to you when you were sixteen? Like five years ago?"

"They'd only been dating a month when he gave it to her," Marilyn added. "Can you believe it!" She quickly clamped her mouth shut so her daughter could continue.

"So I cut the patch open, and inside was a little piece of the red cloth with the words *Will You Marry Me* sewn into it."

"What? You are kidding!" Jocelyn exclaimed. "That's unbelievable."

"Isn't it?" Marilyn agreed.

"You're telling me that he knew he wanted to propose a month after you started dating, five years ago?" Jocelyn asked.

"Yes!" Celeste answered.

Jocelyn collapsed into the back of the couch. "Amazing. That is simply amazing."

"I know. I wouldn't believe it myself if it hadn't happened to me."

"I assume you said yes," Jocelyn teased.

"I said heck yes!" Celeste answered. "We already set the date. What are you doing October fifteenth?"

"I'm going to your wedding," Jocelyn replied happily. All three of them erupted in excited squeals and hugs and happy dancing.

It was a wonderful way to start the day. Jocelyn glanced out the window to see if any woodland creatures had shown up because it truly felt like she was living in a fairy tale at that moment.

Chapter Twenty-one

"Did you like the movie?" Jack asked as they walked hand in hand toward the diner. Every Friday night the small auditorium at the town library showed classic movies for free. Since the town had no other movie theater, the showing at the library was usually huge. And tonight was no exception.

"How did I miss seeing *Butch Cassidy and the Sundance Kid* growing up? I loved it," she said. "It's probably wrong of me to wish they wouldn't have gotten killed at the end. I mean, I guess they deserved what they got, but they certainly were a pair of charming criminals."

"Yeah, well, of course we're talking Paul Newman and Robert Redford. I doubt anyone would care if they were robbed by either of them."

Jocelyn laughed.

"I actually met Redford at a charity event I did one time. He's an environmentalist and had some kind of fundraiser that I performed at. He was really cool."

"You have a whole other life you have to tell me about sometime. I mean, all the places you've been and people you've met. Your awards and stuff. And . . . wait, weren't you in a movie, too?" She thought for a moment. "You were. I remember. You had a small part in that scary movie . . . *Horror High*. Was that it? I don't like scary movies so I never saw it."

"Not many people did. It was 'horror' ible," he said.

They both laughed. Then she asked, "Do you ever miss it? Being famous and rich and being a celebrity?"

"There are things about it I miss. I mean, it was kind of cool getting all the free stuff and not having to wait in lines and having people bend over backward for you. Of course, I was a self-centered, arrogant jerk back then so I loved it. But now it would embarrass me to have someone treat me that way. And I do not miss all the crowds and paparazzi and headlines and gossip magazines. That's not me at all."

"It doesn't fit you, but I didn't know you back then."

"You probably wouldn't have liked me. I wasn't a very nice person."

"I'm glad I got to know *this* you and not *that* you," she said, nuzzling her shoulder next to his.

"Me too. I'm glad that guy is gone. I didn't like him very well either."

They stopped at the corner to cross and stole a couple of kisses while they waited, neither of them caring who saw them together. The secret was out, and together they managed to deal with all the tongue-wagging and wildfire of town news it had created.

Just as they were about to step off the curb and cross the street they both heard a woman giggling. A door opened in the small alleyway between the butcher shop and the shoe repair shop then closed with a squeak.

They looked at each other with amusement and smiled. "I wonder who that is," Jack said.

There was another giggle, this time followed by a loud, "Shhh."

"Oh, Bernie," the woman said. "You're so cute when you do that."

"Bernie," Jack mouthed the name to Jocelyn.

Jocelyn shrugged. The name meant nothing to her.

"Mayor Duncan," he whispered.

She stifled a laugh. "Who's he with?"

The voices carried their direction. Jack grabbed Jocelyn's hand, and they hid behind a large lilac bush in front of the butcher shop.

From around the corner walked Mayor Duncan, and draped over his arm was none other than Lacey.

Jocelyn gasped. She clapped her hand over her mouth and looked at Jack's amused expression.

Mayor Duncan immediately shook his arm free and straightened his tie. The two were obviously trying to be discreet.

Lacey walked a few steps away from the mayor then turned and gave the mayor a coy little wave and blew him a kiss.

Jack and Jocelyn nearly fell over, they were trying so hard not to laugh.

The mayor cleared his throat authoritatively then strode the opposite direction. It was almost dark, so it was possible they hadn't been seen by anyone else. Still, they were taking a risk. Jocelyn wondered if maybe they had been seeing each other enough that they were getting braver about being seen together in public.

All in all, she actually thought they were a pretty good match up. He was full of himself and would benefit from having a trophy wife, and she would thrive with the status and wealth being his wife would afford. And, Jocelyn thought, maybe they really cared about each other.

No wonder Lacey's mother was having such a fit that one day. It wasn't about Lacey seeing Jack, it was about her seeing the mayor. It made so much sense to her now.

Another perk to having Lacey with the mayor: it would keep Lacey out of her life, and Jack's!

* * *

Jocelyn checked her watch for the fifteenth time. Jack had told her he was stopping by because he had something for her. He just hadn't said an exact time, and she was dying of anticipation. He was up to something. She just didn't know what.

She looked around the room, feeling a sense of pride and accomplishment. She'd finished getting the room ready and had all her supplies ordered. With several weeks until school started, she was right on schedule. Her next project was planting the raspberries with Harry. Jack was going to help, Lenny had also volunteered, and MJ's boys were coming too. It was going to be quite the planting party.

Straightening one of the framed pieces of art, she looked at her watch again. What was he doing and where was he?

Voices in the hallway caught her attention.

She whirled toward the door just in time. Jack poked his head inside.

He gave her a heart-melting smile and said hi.

"What are you up to?" she said, walking toward him.

"Stop!"

She froze.

"Now shut your eyes."

"Jack—" she started.

"Just trust me. It's a surprise."

She couldn't imagine what it was. He'd talked about buying a Blu-Ray player, but she doubted he would bring that here, and it wouldn't be much of a surprise.

"Okay," she said. "They're shut."

"Great. Keep them shut," he said.

She heard the shuffling of feet and realized he wasn't alone. Someone had come into the room with him.

"Hang on," he said. "Just a few more seconds."

She squeezed her eyes tight and fought to not open them. She was dying with curiosity.

"Just one more second." Jack came close to her and put his arm around her. "I think we're ready. Okay, open your eyes."

She slowly opened her eyes and saw an elderly man standing in front of her holding what appeared to be a picture, though she could only see the back of it. She wasn't sure what to do next.

"Um, hello," she said to the man then looked questioningly at Jack, who was grinning.

"I met him at the gallery," he told her. "I believe you know him."

The man looked vaguely familiar.

"At least you know his name."

"I do?"

"Yes, this is Pablo Bocelli."

She rolled her eyes then started to laugh.

The man supposedly named Pablo Bocelli looked at Jack with a confused expression.

Jack shrugged and shook his head.

Her laughter started to die when she realized they weren't laughing with her.

"Jack, you aren't serious."

Jack nodded.

Pablo nodded.

"What? Oh, my gosh!" she exclaimed, feeling suddenly weak at the knees.

Jack held onto her.

"Really?" she asked.

Jack laughed. "Really."

She quickly arranged her hair then wiped her palms on the thighs of her jeans. She held her hand toward him. "Mr. Bocelli, it's wonderful to meet you. I am such a fan of your work. I've studied your philosophies and techniques for years."

His hands were full with the picture, so he placed it on the desk and stretched out his hand to shake hers.

"It's wonderful to meet you also, Jocelyn." He spoke with a charming accent, but his English was perfect. "Your boyfriend would like me to show you something." He picked up the frame and turned it around.

"No . . . way. I don't believe it. I don't believe it!" Jocelyn grabbed Jack in a hug then turned back to Mr. Bocelli. "As Jack probably told you, I really love this painting."

"Thank you. This is where I grew up," he explained, pointing to the painting. "Of course, I didn't live in a home like this. My family was very poor." He paused for a moment, as if remembering. "I saw the wonderful villas with their gardens and vineyards and dreamed of living there someday. This is where my desire to paint came from. It was my way of creating the world I wanted. Something like bringing my dreams to life, I guess you could say. Many of my paintings were inspired by the area around my home in Italy."

"I have always dreamed of visiting there someday," Jocelyn said.

"You must. And you must tell me when you come so I can show you the beauty of Tuscany."

Jocelyn pulled in a quick breath of air, laying her hand on her chest. What would it be like to have Pablo Bocelli show her the actual places in his paintings? Her gaze slipped to Jack, who was smiling with satisfaction at her delight in being in the presence of this great artist.

"I wouldn't want to intrude on your time," she said, "but that would be a dream come true. Someday."

"It would be my pleasure. My wife passed away several years ago, and we had no children. My work is all I have."

Her heart went out to him. How was it that someone so famous was all alone?

"This is why I have come to America," he said. "I love my home and my work, but I have nothing else to fill my days."

"What will you do while you're here?" she asked.

"Visit galleries, teach master classes—"

She gasped again. "You are? Where, when?"

"I will be in Seattle for the next three days. You wouldn't be interested in joining one of my classes, would you?"

His teasing and his charming accent made him every bit as delightful as she'd hoped he would be. She still couldn't believe she was standing in front of such a great legend.

"I would be honored," she said.

"Then I will expect you in class first thing in the morning," he said.

"Are you sure there is a spot for me?" she asked, positive that his classes had filled up long ago.

"I will make a spot for you, dear Jocelyn," he said.

"Thank you, Mr. Bocelli. This is a dream come true for me." She said it to him, but her eyes were on Jack. He'd made all of this possible.

"Please, call me Pablo."

"It's good to see the painting again," she said. "I have missed it."

"It's yours."

"I'm sorry?" She shook her head.

"I said, it is yours."

"It was mine, but I had to part with it," she explained.

"I know, and now it is yours again," he said.

"But how?" she said, telling herself not to cry. Lately she'd been an emotional dripping faucet.

"I wish I could say I was giving it to you, but it belonged to the gallery, not me," Pablo said. He turned to Jack. "This fine gentleman is the one to thank."

She looked at Jack, still fighting back tears. "You did this for me?"

"I knew how much it meant to you and how hard it was for you to part with it."

"But I can't let you spend that kind of money."

"I wanted to. It was important to me."

If she couldn't cry, then at least she could hug him.

"Ah, to be so in love," Pablo said, clutching his heart. "I would like to capture that emotion on canvas."

Jocelyn laughed, connecting with his use of emotion for art. All of her favorite works of art were a result of the emotion they stirred inside of her. Her best painting happened when she was emotionally driven.

Jack explained, "I called the gallery to see if they still had the painting, and they surprised me by telling me that not only was it available but that Pablo was going to be visiting. Well, I couldn't pass up such a great opportunity. And the gallery gave me an incredible deal on the painting, thanks to Pablo," Jack explained.

Jocelyn turned to the sweet man. "Thank you so much. You have been such an inspiration to me. I will never forget this. I would love to do something for you in return."

"Then promise me that you will pay a visit someday," he said.

"I promise," she said, giving him a hug. He wasn't large in stature, but his heart filled the entire room.

"Now, I believe part of the deal was one of your American hamburgers and some French fries?" Pablo said.

Jocelyn gave a surprised laugh and looked at Jack. "This is about fast food?"

"Actually, I was thinking about taking him to the diner. Can you come with us? I need to get him back to the gallery for a reception this evening."

"I would be honored if you would both be my guests," Pablo said.

Holding out her arm, Jocelyn said, "Pinch me. This can't be happening to me."

Instead, Jack took her hand and gave her knuckles a kiss. "No one deserves it more than you."

Jocelyn looked at Pablo, who said, "Go on. Kiss him. The man deserves a kiss."

She threw her arms around Jack's neck and did just as Pablo told her.

Her heart was full of joy and gratitude. Sure, there would be more challenges ahead—she wasn't naive enough to believe she was free from trials—but she did know that it was important to thoroughly enjoy and appreciate the good things that happened in her life. And right now, things were very, very good.

5

Epilogue

"I wish Emma were here," Jocelyn said as Chloe put the final touches of hairspray on her updo. "It's not the same without her."

"She could have put off her trip by one week," Andrea said, picking up Jocelyn's veil and straightening the soft, white tulle. "One week!"

"There's something so wrong about that whole thing," Lauryn said, picking up Jocelyn's bouquet and smelling the fragrant gerbera daisies and other colorful blooms. "I just feel it in my gut."

"I do too," Chloe said. "She would never, ever miss one of our weddings if she had a choice." She reached toward Andrea for the veil then carefully placed it on Jocelyn's head.

Jocelyn was grateful that the rest of her best friends were here to help her get ready for the open house in her backyard. The wedding that morning, in the Seattle Temple, had been like a perfect, happily-ever-after dream. All of her loved ones, except Emma, had been able to come. Even Andrea had been there, having gone through the temple several years ago.

"She said she'd call today," Jocelyn told them. "But I haven't talked to her. Have any of you?"

None of them had heard anything from Emma since she left the country.

"Don't let it ruin your day," Andrea said, holding the veil in place while Chloe bobby-pinned the daylights out of it.

"That's right," Lauryn said. "Today is just for you and Jack, who, by the way, is so incredibly gorgeous and amazing!"

"He is, isn't he," Jocelyn said. She glanced quickly at Chloe, not wanting to make her more uncomfortable than she probably already was. Chloe had informed them that she and Roger were getting divorced.

She'd been willing to work things out, to help him with his addiction, but he wasn't making the necessary changes in his life to bring them closer together. He was willing to lose his wife and kids over it. Chloe was doing her best to be strong for her daughters, but she was clearly in pain.

"The girls look like angels," Jocelyn said.

"They do, don't they?" Chloe said brightly. "I love the dresses you brought for them, Lauryn."

"I had so much fun designing their dresses. Cooper and I are seriously thinking about doing a girl's dress line," Lauryn told them.

"Where are the girls, anyway?" Jocelyn asked.

"With my mom," Lauryn said. "They wanted to visit your neighbor again."

"Harry?" Jocelyn said. "What are they doing over there?"

"Who knows? To be honest, I'm not so sure it's just the girls wanting to go over. I'm just sayin' . . ." Lauryn held up her hands in a helpless gesture.

"Your mom and Harry?" Jocelyn said with a delighted laugh. "Wouldn't that be something? I'm going to have to say it again: she's like a new woman. "

"Isn't it amazing? I mean, she knows her days are numbered, but once she got off the alcohol and started taking her medication, her health improved immediately," Lauryn explained. "She spends time with me at work, helping around the office, doing filing and answering phones."

"She sure looks good," Andrea said.

"She does, doesn't she," Lauryn said. "The one thing she misses about living in the city is not having a yard or a garden. I think that's why she and Harry hit it off like they did. They got talking about your raspberry farm."

"We'll find out next summer if it's going to be successful or not," Jocelyn said, "but so far everything seems to be going right on track."

"That must have been some project, putting in all those plants," Chloe said, glancing out the upstairs bedroom window at the hill behind Jocelyn's house.

"We couldn't have done it without all the people who came to help. I've made some really great friends here," Jocelyn said.

"Speaking of friends, I met Marilyn and her daughter, Celeste," Chloe said. "They sure love you. They told me Celeste just got married last month."

"I think I met her husband at the temple," Lauryn said. "Are they the ones who have that cool proposal story?"

"The one that's hard to believe?" Andrea said.

"Yep, that's them," Jocelyn said, "but these two are both really great. They deserve each other."

Andrea sighed. "I wish I deserved someone. Someone like Cooper. I can't believe he didn't come!"

"He wanted to," Lauryn told her. "He tried every way he could to rearrange this trip to China, but it wasn't possible. You just need to come to New York and visit."

"I'll have to come soon. We start shooting *Looking for Mrs. Right* in two months," Andrea said. "Hey, speaking of which, what about that Karl guy? He seems pretty nice."

"I'd hold out for Cooper if I were you," Jocelyn said, examining her veil in the mirror and feeling very pleased with the results. "Thank you, Chloe." She hugged her friend. "I don't know what I'd do without all of you." She hugged Andrea and Lauryn.

"You won't need us as much anymore," Andrea said. "You have Jack now."

Jocelyn looked at the fallen expression on her friend's face. "Hey, I will always need my girlfriends. I wouldn't have made it this far without each of you. I wouldn't have come here without your encouragement. I wouldn't have met Jack."

"Can I just say how totally amazing he is, by the way," Andrea said.

"Yes, you may," Jocelyn said with a smile.

"At the luncheon, when he sang that song he wrote for you," Chloe said, pretending to fan herself, "I swear, I nearly melted. That was so sweet of him to do that."

"I felt like a schoolgirl again," Lauryn said. "Even Jace said he'd been a fan of JC Em's, I mean, Jack's, music."

"Is he really never going to do music again?" Andrea asked.

"He says he won't. It was a huge step for him to sing to me today."

"Well, he's still got it, but I liked the new, softer sound," Chloe said. "He's really something, Joss. I'm glad you two found each other."

Jocelyn nodded. She felt so blessed. "Thanks, Chloe." She gave her friend a hug.

"Okay. Good." Chloe stepped back and wiped at her eyes. "Let's take a final look at you."

Jocelyn turned around, pulling the train of the heavily beaded French-lace wedding gown with her. It was by far the most exquisite dress any of them had ever seen. A pure masterpiece by Lauryn.

"How do I look?" she asked.

"Like a princess," Chloe said, sniffing into a tissue.

"You really do," Andrea said.

"Thanks to Lauryn," Jocelyn said.

"No," Lauryn replied, "it's you. I have never seen you so happy. It's like you have an aura of light around you."

It had to be the feeling of pure joy she felt inside. The day had been perfect, even more amazing than she could have ever dreamed it would be. She'd felt strongly that her grandmother was there with her, giving her a sense of love, support, and family that she'd needed. Then, to kneel across from Jack at the altar, looking into eternity together, feeling their hearts and souls become one, had felt like pure heaven.

The girls gathered for a group hug then left the room to give her a moment alone before joining the festivities outside. Through the window she saw the top of the tent, surrounded by white twinkle lights on the trees and white balloons tied to every possible branch in her yard. Marilyn and Celeste had worked tirelessly to help her plan the open house, even though they had just had a wedding of their own. MJ had also taken on a large share of responsibility and had treated this celebration as though she were planning it for her own daughter. She was the one who had come up with the crazy idea of having it in the yard and renting the freestanding patio heaters to take the chill off the November night air. Jocelyn's favorite part of the open house was that she and MJ had come up with ways to use raspberries in most of the refreshments: on tarts, on the cheesecake, in the crumbly bars, and in the drink.

Jocelyn had been having fun creating as many recipes as she could using raspberries. She decided she wanted to have a cookbook available at their raspberry stand when it opened. She just hoped Jack and Harry didn't get sick of all of her experiments. They were both her guinea pigs and had tasted as many of her failures as they had her successes.

Jocelyn felt so blessed to have been led to Milford Falls—that she'd had the sense to follow the prompting to do so and listened to Jack's encouragement to stay. It had changed her life, and she knew that the Lord had been there, ready to guide her along the way, as long as she had been willing to truly listen.

Her eyes misted over as she thought about the greatest blessing she'd received in coming to Milford Falls. Had she not come she never would have met Jack. He was her best friend, her sweetheart, her strength. His unconditional love and support had helped her come to terms with who she was and what she'd been through. She knew that together, side by side, they would meet life head-on with joy and faith.

A light tap on the door pulled her from her thoughts. She turned to see Jack walk into the room.

"Hey there," he said, walking toward her.

They kissed, embraced, then kissed again. He held her closely but gently so he didn't wrinkle or damage her hair and makeup.

"Everything okay?" he asked.

"Everything is absolutely perfect," she said. "Especially you."

He laughed. "I think you must have married the wrong man. I'm far from perfect."

"You're perfect for me," she said.

"Ah, well, when you put it that way . . ." He gave her another quick kiss. "The guests are starting to show up, and we still have some pictures to take. Are you ready?"

"Almost," she said. She kissed him again then held him for a moment, her hug filled with intensity. "Thank you."

"What for?"

"For being here when I came to town, and for being here with me now."

"It's been a long road for each of us," he said. "I'm glad we don't have to do it alone anymore."

"Me too."

He kissed the end of her nose.

"It's just the beginning of a lot of new adventures together," he said.

"Starting with our trip to Italy. You know you're spoiling me, don't you?"

"I'm completely aware of that fact. Thank you for noticing."

"I feel like I'm living in a fairy tale."

"Well, you know how fairy tales end," he said.

"Happily ever after?"

He nodded. "But ours will be forever after." He dazzled her with a smile. "Are you ready to begin your new journey, Mrs. Emerson?"

"I'm totally ready, Mr. Emerson."

He took her hand in his, and they walked out of the room together to join their family and friends in a celebration of life, love, forgiveness, and eternal happiness.

"Perfect Proposal" Contest Grand Prize Winner

A month before my sixteenth birthday, I started dating a boy whom I had met through mutual friends. We liked each other a lot, and we could both tell that our friendship was swiftly becoming something very special. On my birthday, he gave me two gifts: a patchwork quilt (that he had made by himself) and a custom puzzle piece that had a portion of some text on it that he had written. He told me to keep this piece and that I would receive more as we had more "special" days. From that point on, I would receive a puzzle piece on days like Valentine's Day, Easter, Christmas, even Canada Day.

We continued to date for three years. When he left on his mission to Ireland, we continued our relationship and wrote to each other frequently. On occasion, I would get a puzzle piece in the mail too.

About two weeks after he got home, he took me on a date up to the canyon. On the way out, he grabbed the quilt and told me to bring a pair of scissors and my puzzle pieces. After we arrived and as we were discussing our relationship, he reached into his pocket and brought out the last puzzle piece. He told me I could put the puzzle together. When I put the puzzle together, the message on the puzzle instructed me to cut open the red patch that was on the bottom left-hand corner of the Holly Hobbie patch and then I would know just how much he loves me. (Remember, it had been five years since he had given me the quilt!) I cut the patch open, and inside was a little piece of cloth with the sewn words, "Will you marry me?" I said yes!

We were married three months later.

—Jill Lott of Forest Hills, New York

About the Author

In the fourth grade, Michele Ashman Bell was considered a daydreamer by her teacher and was told on her report card that "she has a vivid imagination and would probably do well with creative writing." Her imagination, combined with a passion for reading, has enabled Michele to live up to her teacher's prediction. She loves writing books, especially those that inspire and edify while entertaining.

Michele grew up in St. George, Utah, where she met her husband at Dixie College before they both served missions—his to Pennsylvania and hers to Frankfurt, Germany, and San Jose, California. Seven months after they returned they were married, and are now the proud parents of four children: Weston, Kendyl, Andrea, and Rachel.

A favorite pastime of Michele's is supporting her children in all of their activities, traveling both in and outside the United States with her husband and family, and doing research for her books. She also recently became scuba certified. Aside from being a busy wife and mother, Michele is an aerobics instructor at the Life Centre Athletic Club near her home, and she currently teaches in the Relief Society and is the activity day leader.

Michele is the best-selling author of several books and a Christmas booklet and has also written children's stories for the Friend magazine.

If you would like to be updated on Michele's newest releases or correspond with her, please send an e-mail to info@covenant-lds.com. You may also write to her in care of Covenant Communications, P.O. Box 416, American Fork, UT 84003-0416.